Greek Playboys: Unbending Demands

LYNNE GRAHAM

SHARON KENDRICK

PIPPA ROSCOE

MILLS & BOON

First Published in Great Britain 2022
By Mills & Boon, an imprint of HarperCollins*Publishers,* Ltd
1 London Bridge Street, London, SE1 9GF

www.harpercollins.co.uk

HarperCollins*Publishers*
1st Floor, Watermarque Building,
Ringsend Road, Dublin 4, Ireland

GREEK PLAYBOYS: UNBENDING DEMANDS © 2022 Harlequin Books S.A.

The Secret Valtinos Baby © 2018 Lynne Graham
The Pregnant Kavakos Bride © 2017 Sharon Kendrick
Claimed for the Greek's Child © 2019 Pippa Roscoe

ISBN: 978-0-263-30443-5

MIX
Paper from
responsible sources
FSC™ C007454

This book is produced from independently certified FSC™ paper
to ensure responsible forest management.

For more information visit: www.harpercollins.co.uk/green

Printed and Bound in Spain using 100% Renewable electricity at
CPI Black Print, Barcelona

Greek Playboys

About the Authors

Lynne Graham lives in Northern Ireland and has been a keen romance reader since her teens. Happily married, Lynne has five children. Her eldest is her only natural child. Her other children, who are every bit as dear to her heart, are adopted. The family has a variety of pets, and Lynne loves gardening, cooking, collecting allsorts and is crazy about every aspect of Christmas.

Sharon Kendrick started story-telling at the age of eleven and has never stopped. She likes to write fast-paced, feel-good romances with heroes who are so sexy they'll make your toes curl! She lives in the beautiful city of Winchester – where she can see the cathedral from her window (when standing on tip-toe!). She has two children, Celia and Patrick and her passions include music, books, cooking and eating – and drifting into daydreams while working out new plots.

Pippa Roscoe lives in Norfolk, near her family, and makes daily promises to herself that this is the day she'll leave the computer to take a long walk in the countryside. She can't remember a time when she wasn't dreaming about handsome heroes and innocent heroines. Totally her mother's fault, of course – she gave Pippa her first romance to read at the age of seven! She is inconceivably happy that she gets to share those daydreams with you. Follow her on Twitter @PippaRoscoe.

THE SECRET
VALTINOS BABY

LYNNE GRAHAM

CHAPTER ONE

THE GREEK BILLIONAIRE, Angel Valtinos, strode into his father's office suite to find both his brothers waiting in Reception and he stopped dead, ebony brows skating up. 'What is this? A family reunion?'

'Or Papa is planning to carpet us for something,' his Italian half-brother, Prince Vitale Castiglione, commented with perceptible amusement because they were all beyond the age where parental disapproval was a normal source of concern.

'Does he make a habit of that?' Zac Da Rocha demanded with a frown.

Angel met Vitale's eyes and his jawline squared, neither passing comment. Zac, their illegitimate Brazilian sibling, was pretty much a wild card. As he was a new and rather mysterious addition to the family circle his brothers had yet to fully accept him. And trust came no more easily to the suspicious Angel than it did to Vitale.

Vitale grinned. 'You're the eldest,' he reminded Angel. 'You get top billing and first appearance.'

'Not sure I want it on this occasion,' Angel conceded, but he swiftly shrugged off the faint and comically unfamiliar sense of unease assailing his innately rock-solid confidence.

After all, Charles Russell had *never* played the heavy father in his sons' lives, but even without exercising that authority he had still been a remarkably decent father, Angel conceded reflectively. Charles had not stayed married to either his or Vitale's mother for very long but he had taken a keen interest post-divorce in fostering and maintaining a close relationship with his sons. Angel had often had cause to be grateful for his father's stable approach to life and the shrewd business brain he suspected he had inherited from him. His mother was a thoroughly flighty and frivolous Greek heiress, whose attitude to childcare and education would have been careless without his father's stipulations on his son's behalf.

Charles Russell crossed his office to greet his eldest son. 'You're late,' he told him without heat.

'My board meeting ran over,' Angel told him smoothly. 'What's this all about? When I saw Zac and Vitale in Reception I wondered if there was a family emergency.'

'It depends what you call an emergency,' Charles deflected, studying his very tall thirty-three-year-old eldest son, who topped him in height by several inches.

A son to be proud of, Charles had believed until very recently when the startling discovery of certain disquieting information had punctured his paternal pride. To be fair, Angel also carried the genes of a fabulously wealthy and pedigreed Greek family, more known for their self-destructiveness than their achievements. Even so, Charles had prided himself on Angel's hugely successful reputation in the business world. Angel was the first Valtinos in two generations to make more money than he spent. A very astute high-achiever and a loyal and loving son, he was the very last child Charles had expected to disappoint him. Nonetheless, Angel had let him down by revealing a ruthless streak of Valtinos self-interest and irresponsibility.

'Tell me what this is about,' Angel urged with characteristic cool.

Charles rested back against his tidy desk, a still handsome man with greying hair in his early fifties. His well-built frame was tense. 'When do you plan to grow up?' he murmured wryly.

Angel blinked in bewilderment. 'Is that a joke?' he whispered.

'Sadly not,' his father confirmed. 'A week ago, I learned from a source I will not share that I am a *grandfather*...'

Angel froze, his lean, extravagantly handsome features suddenly wiped clean of all animation, while his shrewd dark eyes hardened and veiled. In less than a split second, though, he had lifted his aggressive chin in grim acknowledgement of the unwelcome shock he had been dealt: an issue he had hoped to keep buried had been unexpectedly and most unhappily disinterred by the only man in the world whose good opinion he valued.

'And, moreover, the grandfather of a child whom I will never meet if you have anything to do with it,' Charles completed in a tone of regret.

Angel frowned and suddenly extended his arms in a very expansive Greek gesture of dismissal. 'I thought to protect you—'

'No, your sole motivation was to protect *you*,' Charles contradicted without hesitation. 'From the demands and responsibility of a child.'

'It was an accident. Am I expected to turn my life upside down when struck by such a misfortune?' Angel demanded in a tone of raw self-defence.

His father dealt him a troubled appraisal. 'I did not consider *you* to be a misfortune.'

'Your relationship with my mother was on rather a different footing,' Angel declared with all the pride of his wealthy, privileged forebears.

A deep frown darkened the older man's face. 'Angel… I've never told you the whole truth about my marriage to your mother because I did not want to give you cause to respect her less,' he admitted reluctantly. 'But the fact is that Angelina deliberately conceived you once she realised that I wanted to end our relationship. I married her because she was pregnant, *not* because I loved her.'

Angel was startled by that revelation but not shocked, for he had always been aware that his mother was spoilt and selfish and that she could not handle rejection. His luxuriant black lashes lifted on challenging and cynical dark golden eyes. 'And marrying her didn't work for you, did it? So, you can hardly be suggesting that I marry the mother of *my* child!' he derided.

'No, marrying Angelina Valtinos didn't work for me,' Charles agreed mildly. 'But it worked beautifully for *you*. It gave you a father with the right to interfere and with your best interests always at heart.'

That retaliation was a stunner and shockingly true and Angel gritted his even white teeth at the comeback. 'Then I should thank you for your sacrifice,' he said hoarsely.

'No thanks required. The wonderful little boy grew up into a man I respect—'

'With the obvious exception of this issue,' Angel interjected tersely.

'You have handled it all wrong. You called in the lawyers, those Valtinos vulture lawyers, whose sole motivation is to protect you and the Valtinos name and fortune—'

'Exactly,' Angel slotted in softly. 'They protect me.'

'But don't you *want* to know your own child?' Charles demanded in growing frustration.

Angel compressed his wide, sensual mouth, his hard bone structure thrown into prominence, angry shame engulfing him at that question. 'Of course, I do, but getting past her mother is proving difficult.'

'Is that how you see it? Is that who you are blaming for this mess?' the older man countered with scorn. 'Your lawyers forced her to sign a non-disclosure agreement in return for financial support and you made no attempt at that point to show enough interest to arrange access to your child.'

Angel went rigid, battling his anger, determined not to surrender to the frustrating rage scorching through him. He was damned if he was about to let the maddening baby business, as he thought of it, come between him and the father he loved. 'The child hadn't been born at that stage. I had no idea how I would feel once she was.'

'Your lawyers naturally concentrated on protecting your privacy and your wealth. Your role was to concentrate on the *family* aspect,' Charles asserted with emphasis. 'Instead you have made an enemy of your child's mother.'

'That was not my intention. Using the Valtinos legal team was intended to remove any damaging personal reactions from our dealings.'

'And how has the impersonal approach worked for you?' Charles enquired very drily indeed.

Angel very nearly groaned out loud in exasperation. In truth, he had played an own goal, getting what he'd believed he wanted and then discovering too late that it wasn't what he wanted at all. 'She doesn't want me to visit.'

'And whose fault is that?'

'Mine,' Angel acknowledged fiercely. 'But she is currently raising my child in unsuitable conditions.'

'Yes, working as a kennel maid while raising the next Valtinos heiress isn't to be recommended,' his father remarked wryly. 'Well, at least the woman's not a gold-digger. A gold-digger would have stayed in London and lived the high life on the income you provided, not stranded herself in rural Suffolk with a middle-aged aunt while working for a living.'

'My daughter's mother is *crazy!*' Angel bit out, betraying his first real emotion on the subject. 'She's trying to make me feel bad!'

Charles raised a dubious brow. 'You think so? Seems to be a lot of sweat and effort to go to for a man she refuses to see.'

'She had the neck to tell my lawyer that she couldn't allow me to visit without risking breaching the non-disclosure agreement!' Angel growled.

'There could be grounds for that concern,' his father remarked thoughtfully. 'The paparazzi do follow you around and you visiting her *would* put a spotlight on her and the child.'

Angel drew himself up to his full six feet four inches and squared his wide shoulders. 'I would be discreet.'

'Sadly, it's a little late in the day to be fighting over parental access. You should have considered that first and foremost in your dealings because unmarried fathers have few, if any, rights under British law—'

'Are you suggesting that I marry her?' Angel demanded with incredulity.

'No.' Charles shook his greying head to emphasise that negative. 'That sort of gesture has to come from the heart.'

'Or the brain,' Angel qualified. 'I could marry her, take her out to Greece and then fight her there for custody, where I would have an advantage. That option *was* suggested at one point by my legal team.'

Charles regarded his unapologetically ruthless son with concealed apprehension because it had never been his intention to exacerbate the situation between his son and the mother of his child. 'I would hope that you would not even consider sinking to that level of deceit. Surely a more enlightened arrangement is still possible?'

But *was* it? Angel was not convinced even while he assured his concerned father that he would sort the situation out without descending to the level of dirty tricks. But was an access agreement even achievable?

After all, how could he be sure of anything in that line? Merry Armstrong had foiled him, blocked him and denied him while subjecting him to a raft of outrageous arguments rather than simply giving him what he wanted. Angel was wholly unaccustomed to such disrespectful treatment. Every time she knocked him back he was stunned by the unfamiliarity of the experience.

All his life he had pretty much got what he wanted from a woman whenever he wanted it. Women, usually, adored him. Women from his mother to his aunts to his cousins and those in his bed worshipped him like a god. Women lived to please Angel, flatter him, satisfy him: it had always been that way in Angel's gilded world of comfort and pleasure. And Angel had taken that enjoyable reality entirely for granted until the very dark day he had chosen to tangle with Merry Armstrong...

He had noticed her immediately, the long glossy

mane of dark mahogany hair clipped in a ponytail that reached almost to her waist, the pale crystalline blue eyes and the pink voluptuous mouth that sang of sin to a sexually imaginative male. Throw in the lean, leggy lines of a greyhound and proximity and their collision course had been inevitable from day one in spite of the fact that he had never before slept with one of his employees and had always sworn *not* to do so.

Merry's fingers closed shakily over the letter that the postman had just delivered. A tatty sausage-shaped Yorkshire terrier gambolled noisily round her feet, still overexcited by the sound of the doorbell and another voice.

'Quiet, Tiger,' Merry murmured firmly, mindful that fostering the little dog was aimed at making him a suitable adoptee for a new owner. But even as she thought that, she knew she had broken her aunt Sybil's strict rules with Tiger by getting attached and by letting him sneak onto her sofa and up onto her lap. Sybil adored dogs but she didn't believe in humanising or coddling them. It crossed Merry's mind that perhaps she was as emotionally damaged as Tiger had been by abuse. Tiger craved food as comfort; Merry craved the cosiness of a doggy cuddle. Or was she kidding herself in equating the humiliation she had suffered at Angel's hands with abuse? Making a mountain out of a molehill, as Sybil had once briskly told her?

Sadly the proof of that pudding was in the eating

as she flipped over the envelope and read the London postmark with a stomach that divebombed in sick dismay. It was another legal letter and she couldn't face it. With a shudder of revulsion laced with fear she cravenly thrust the envelope in the drawer of the battered hall table, where it could stay until she felt able to deal with it...*calmly*.

And a calm state of mind had become a challenge for Merry ever since she had first heard from the Valtinoses' lawyers and dealt with the stress, the appointments and the complaints. Legally she seemed mired in a never-ending battle where everything she did was an excuse for criticism or another unwelcome and intimidating demand. She could feel the rage building in her at the prospect of having to open yet another politely menacing letter, a rage that she would not have recognised a mere year earlier, a rage that threatened to consume her and sometimes scared her because there had been nothing of the virago in her nature until her path crossed that of Angel Valtinos. He had taught her nothing but bitterness, hatred and resentment, all of which she could have done without.

But he had also, although admittedly *very* reluctantly, given her Elyssa...

Keen to send her thoughts in a less sour direction, Merry glanced from the kitchen into the tiny sitting room of the cottage where she lived, and studied her daughter where she sat on the hearth rug happily engaged with her toys. Her black hair was an explosion of curls round her cherubic olive-toned face, highlighting striking ice-blue eyes and a pouty little mouth. She had her father's curls and her mother's eyes and mouth and was an extremely pretty baby in Merry's opinion, although she was prepared to admit that she was very biased when it came to her daughter.

In many ways after a very fraught and unhappy pregnancy Elyssa's actual birth had restored Merry to startling life and vigour. Before that day, it had not once occurred to her that her daughter's arrival would transform her outlook and fill her to overflowing with an unconditional love unlike anything she had ever felt before. Nowadays she recognised the truth: there was nothing she would not do for Elyssa.

A light knock sounded on the back door, announcing Sybil's casual entrance into the kitchen at the rear of the cottage. 'I'll put on the kettle…time for a brew,' she said cheerfully, a tall, rangy blonde nearing sixty but still defiantly beautiful, as befitted a woman who had been an international supermodel in the eighties.

Sybil had been Merry's role model from an early age. Her mother, Natalie, had married when Merry was sixteen and emigrated to Australia with her husband, leaving her teenaged daughter in her sister's care. Sybil and Merry were much closer than Merry had ever been with her birth mother but Sybil remained very attached to her once feckless kid sister. The sanctuary had been built by her aunt on the proceeds of the modelling career she had abandoned as soon as she had made enough money to devote her days to looking after homeless dogs.

In the later stages of her pregnancy, Merry had worked at the centre doing whatever was required and had lived with her aunt in her trendy barn conversion, but at the same time Merry had been carefully making plans for a more independent future. A qualified accountant, she had started up a small home business doing accounts for local traders and she had a good enough income now to run a car, while also insisting on paying a viable rent to Sybil for her use of the cottage at the gates of the rescue centre. The cottage was small and old-fashioned but it had two bedrooms and a little garden and perfectly matched Merry and Elyssa's current needs.

In fact, Sybil Armstrong was a rock of unchanging affection and security in Merry's life. Merry's mother, Natalie, had fallen pregnant with her during an affair with her married employer. Only nineteen at the time, Natalie had quickly proved ill-suited to the trials of single parenthood. Right from the start, Sybil had regularly swooped in as a weekend babysitter, wafting Merry back to her country home to leave her kid sister free to go out clubbing.

Natalie's bedroom door had revolved around a long succession of unsuitable men. There had been violent men, drunk men, men who took drugs and men who stole Natalie's money and refused to earn their own. By the time she was five years old, Merry had assumed all mothers brought different men home every week. In such an unstable household where fights and substance abuse were endemic she had missed a lot of school, and when social workers had threatened to take Merry into care, once again her aunt had stepped in to take charge.

For nine glorious years, Merry had lived solely with Sybil, catching up with her schoolwork, learning to be a child again, no longer expected to cook and clean for her unreliable mother, no longer required to hide in her bedroom while the adults downstairs screamed so loudly at each other that the neighbours called the police. Almost inevitably that phase of security with Sybil had ended when Natalie had made yet another fresh start and demanded the return of her daughter.

It hadn't worked, of course it hadn't, because Natalie had grown too accustomed to her freedom by then, and instead of finding in Merry the convenient little best friend she had expected she had been met with a daughter with whom she had nothing in common. By the time Keith, who was younger than Natalie, had entered her life, the writing had been on the wall. Keen to return to Australia and take Natalie with him, he had been frank about his reluctance to take on a paternal role while still in his twenties. Merry had moved back in with Sybil and had not seen her mother since her departure.

'Did I see the postman?' Sybil asked casually.

Merry stiffened and flushed, thinking guiltily of that envelope stuffed in the hall table. 'I bought something for Elyssa online,' she fibbed in shame, but there was just no way she could admit to a woman as gutsy as Sybil that a letter could frighten and distress her.

'No further communication from He Who Must Not Be Named?' Sybil fished, disconcerting her niece with that leading question, for lately her aunt had been very quiet on that topic.

'Evidently we're having a bit of a break from the drama right now, which is really nice,' Merry mumbled, shamefacedly tucking teabags into the mugs while Sybil lifted her great-niece off the rug and cuddled her before sitting down again with the baby cradled on her lap.

'Don't even think about him.'

'I don't,' Merry lied yet again, a current of self-loathing assailing her because only a complete fool would waste time thinking about a man who had mistreated her. But then, really, what would Sybil understand about that? As a staggeringly beautiful and famous young woman, Sybil had had to beat adoring men off with sticks but had simply never met one she wanted to settle down with. Merry doubted that any man had ever disrespected Sybil and lived to tell the tale.

'He'll get his comeuppance some day,' Sybil forecast. 'Everyone does. What goes around comes around.'

'But it bothers me that I hate him so much,' Merry confided in a rush half under her breath. 'I've never been a hater before.'

'You're still hurting. Now that you're starting to

date again, those bad memories will soon sink into
the past.'

An unexpected smile lit Merry's heart-shaped
face at the prospect of the afternoon out she was
having the following day. As a veterinary surgeon,
Fergus Wickham made regular visits to the rescue
centre. He had first met Merry when she was off-
puttingly pregnant, only evidently it had not put him
off, it had merely made him bide his time until her
daughter was born and she was more likely to be re-
ceptive to an approach.

She *liked* Fergus, she enjoyed his company, she
reminded herself doggedly. He didn't give her but-
terflies in her tummy, though, or make her long for
his mouth, she conceded guiltily, but then how important were such physical feelings in the overall
scheme of things? Angel's sexual allure had been
the health equivalent of a lethal snakebite, pulling
her in only to poison her. Beautiful but deadly. Dear
heaven, she hated him, she acknowledged, rigid with
the seething trapped emotion that sent her memory
flying inexorably back sixteen months…

CHAPTER TWO

MERRY WAS FULL of enthusiasm when she started her first job even though it wasn't her dream job by any stretch of the imagination. Having left university with a first-class honours degree in accountancy and business, she had no intention of settling permanently into being a front-desk receptionist at Valtinos Enterprises.

Even so, she had badly needed paid employment and the long recruitment process involved in graduate job applications had ensured that she was forced to depend on Sybil's generosity for more months than she cared to count. Sybil had already supported Merry through her years as a student, helping her out with handy vacation jobs at the rescue centre while always providing her with a comfortable home to come back to for weekends and holidays.

Her job at Valtinos Enterprises was Merry's first step towards true independence. The work paid well and gave her the breathing space in which to look for a more suitable position, while also enabling her to base herself in London without relying on her aunt's financial help. She had moved into a room in a grotty apartment and started work at VE with such high hopes.

And on her first day Angel strode out of the lift and her breath shorted out in her chest as though she had been punched. He had luxuriant black curls that always looked messy and that lean, darkly beautiful face of his had been crafted by a creative genius with exotic high cheekbones, a narrow, straight nose and eyes the colour of liquid honey. Eyes that she had only very much later discovered could turn as hard and cutting as black diamonds.

'You're new,' he commented, treating her to the kind of lingering appraisal that made her feel hot all over.

'This is my first day, Mr Valtinos,' she confided.

'Don't waste your smiles there,' her co-worker on the desk whispered snidely as Angel walked into his office. 'He doesn't flirt with employees. In fact the word is that he's fired a couple of his PAs for getting too personal with him.'

'I'm not interested,' Merry countered with amusement, and indeed when it came to men she rarely was.

Growing up watching her mother continually search for the man of her dreams while ignoring everything else life had to offer had scared Merry. Having survived her unsettled childhood, she set a high value on security and she was keen to establish her own accountancy firm. She didn't take risks...

ever. In fact she was the most risk-averse person she had ever met.

That innate caution had kept her working so hard at university that she had taken little part in the social whirl. There had been occasional boyfriends but none she had cared to invite into her bed. Not only had she never felt passion, but she had also never suffered from her mother's blazing infatuations. Watching relationships around her take off and then fail in an invariably nasty ending that smashed friendships and caused pain and resentment had turned Merry off even more. She liked a calm, tidy life, a *quiet* life, which in no way explained how she could ever have become intimate with a male as volatile as Angel, she acknowledged with lingering bewilderment.

But it was the truth, the absolute truth, that on paper she and Angel were a horrendous match. Angel was off-the-charts volatile with a volcanic hot temper that erupted every time someone did or said something he considered stupid. He wasn't tolerant or easy to deal with. In the first weeks of her employment she regularly saw members of his personal staff race out of his office as though they had wings on their feet, their pale faces stamped with stress and trepidation. He was very impatient and equally demanding. He might resemble a supermodel in his fabulously sophisticated designer suits, but he had the temperament of a tyrant and an overachiever's appetite for work and success. The only thing she admired about him in those initial weeks was his cleverness.

Serving coffee in the boardroom, she heard him

dissect entire arguments with a handful of well-chosen words. She noticed that people listened when he spoke and admired his intellect while competing to please and impress him. Occasionally beautiful shapely blondes would drift in to meet him for lunch, women of a definite type, the artificial socialite type, seemingly chosen only for their enviable faces and figures and their ability to look at him with stunned appreciation. Those who arrived without an invite didn't even get across the threshold of his office. He treated women like casual amusements and discarded them as soon as he got bored, and the procession of constantly changing faces made it obvious that he got bored very quickly and easily.

In short, nothing about Angel Valtinos *should* have attracted Merry. He shamelessly flaunted almost every flaw she disliked in a man. He was a selfish, hubristic, oversexed workaholic, spoiled by a life of luxury and the target of more admiration and attention than was good for him.

But even after six weeks in his radius, dredging her eyes off Angel when he was within view had proved impossible. He commanded a room simply by walking into it. Even his voice was dark, deep and smoulderingly charismatic. Once a woman heard that slumberous accented drawl she just had to turn her head and look. His dynamic personality suffused his London headquarters like an energy bolt while his mercurial moods kept his employees on edge and eager to please. Valtinos Enterprises felt dead and flat when he was abroad.

When one of Angel's personal assistants left and the position was offered internally, Merry applied, keen to climb the ladder. Angel summoned her to his office to study her with frowning dark golden eyes. 'Why is a candidate with your skills working on Reception?' he demanded impatiently.

'It was the first job I was offered,' Merry admitted, brushing her damp palms down over her skirt. 'I was planning to move on.'

Rising to his feet, making her uneasily aware of his height, he extended a slim file. 'Find somewhere quiet to work. You're off Reception for the morning. Check out this business and provide me with an accurate assessment of its financial history and current performance. If you do it well, I'll interview you this afternoon.'

That afternoon, he settled the file back on the desk and surveyed her, his wide, sensual mouth compressing. 'You did very well but you're a little too cautious in your forecasts. I *enjoy* risk,' he imparted, watching with amusement as she frowned in surprise at that admission. 'You've got the job. I hope you can take the heat. Not everyone can.'

'If you shout at me, I'll probably shout back,' Merry warned him warily.

And an appreciative grin slashed his shapely lips, making him so powerfully attractive that for a split second she simply stared, unable to look away. 'You may just work out very well.'

So began the most exciting phase of Merry's working life. Merry was the most junior member of Angel's personal staff but the one he always entrusted with figures. Sybil was thrilled by the promotion her niece had won but would have been horrified by the long hours Merry worked and the amount of responsibility she carried.

'The boss has got the hots for you,' one of her male co-workers told her with amusement when she had been two months in the job. 'Obviously you have something all those long tall blondes he parades through here don't, because he's always watching you.'

'I haven't noticed anything,' she said firmly, reluctant to let that kind of comment go unchallenged.

But even as she spoke she knew she was very carefully impersonal and unobtrusive in Angel's vicinity because she was conscious of him in a way she had not been conscious of a man before. If she was foolish enough to risk a head-on collision with his spectacular liquid honey eyes, her tummy somersaulted, her mouth dried and she couldn't catch her breath. Feeling like that mortified her. She knew it was attraction and she didn't like it, not only because he was her boss, but also because it made her feel out of control.

And then fate took a hand when Merry firmly believed that neither of them would ever have made any sort of a move. A highly contagious flu virus had decimated the staff and as his employees fell by the wayside Merry found herself increasingly exposed to working alone with Angel. At the office late one evening, he offered her a drink and a ride home. She said no thanks to the drink, deeming it unwise, and yes to the ride because it would get her home faster.

In the lift on the way down to the underground car park, Angel studied her with smouldering dark golden eyes. She felt dizzy and hot, as if her clothes were shrink-wrapped to her skin, preventing her from normal breathing. He lifted a long-fingered brown hand and traced his fingertips along the full curve of her lower lip in a caress that left her trembling, and then, as though some invisible line of restraint had snapped inside him, he crushed her back against the mirrored wall and kissed her, hungrily, feverishly, wildly with the kind of passion she was defenceless against.

'Come home with me,' he urged in a raw undertone as she struggled to pull herself back together while the lift doors stood open beside them.

Her flushed face froze. 'Absolutely not. We made a mistake. Let's forget about it.'

'That's not always possible,' Angel breathed thickly. 'I've been trying to forget about the way you make me feel for weeks.'

Disconcerted by that blunt admission as he stepped out of the lift, Merry muttered dismissively, 'That's just sex. Ignore it.'

Angel stared back at her in wonderment. '*Ignore* it?'

As the lift doors began to close with her still inside it, he reached in and held them open. 'Come on.'

'I'll get the Tube as usual.'

'Don't be childish,' Angel ground out. 'I am fully in control.'

Merry wasn't convinced, remembering that mad, exciting grab and the slam of her body back against the lift wall, but that instant of hesitation was her undoing because without hesitation Angel closed a hand over hers and pulled her out of the lift. 'I'll drop you home.'

'There are boundaries that shouldn't be crossed,' she told him with precision on the way to his car.

'Don't preach at me,' Angel sliced back in a driven undertone. 'I don't have a history of making moves on my staff. You are a one-off.'

'And it won't happen again now that we're both on our guard so let's forget about it,' Merry counselled, sliding breathlessly into a long silver low-slung bullet of a vehicle that she suspected was worth many times more than her annual salary. 'I prevented you from making a mistake.'

'You're preaching again,' Angel derided. 'If I hadn't stopped kissing you we'd still be in the lift!'

'No. I would've pushed you away,' she insisted with cool assurance.

She gave him her address, although he didn't seem to need it, and the journey through heavy traffic was silent, tense and unnerving. He pulled up at the kerb outside the ugly building where she lived. 'You could afford to live in a better area than this,' he censured.

'I have a healthy savings account,' she told him with pride, releasing her seat belt at the same time as he reached for her again.

His wide sensual mouth crushed hers with burning hunger and no small amount of frustration. Her whole body leapt as though he had punched a button detonating something deep down inside her, releasing a hot surge of tingling awareness in her pelvis that made her hips squirm and her nipples pinch painfully tight.

Angel lifted his tousled dark head. 'I'm still waiting on you pushing me away. You're all talk and no action,' he condemned.

'I don't think you'd appreciate a slap,' Merry framed frigidly, her face burning with mortification.

'If it meant that you ditched the icy control I'd be begging for it,' Angel husked suggestively, soft and low, the growl of his accent shaking her up.

Merry launched out of his sports car as though jet-propelled, uncharacteristically flustered and shaken that she had failed to live up to her own very high principles on acceptable behaviour. She should've pushed him away, slapped him, thumped him if necessary to drive her message home. Nothing less would cool his heels. He was a highly competitive, aggressive male, who viewed defeat as an ongoing challenge.

His car stayed at the kerb until she stalked into the building and only then did she breathe again, filling her compressed lungs and shivering as though she had stepped out of a freezing snowstorm. She felt all shaken up, shaken up and *stirred* in a way she didn't appreciate and almost hated him for.

The feel of his mouth on hers, the *taste* of it, the

explosive charge of heat hurtling at breakneck speed down into her belly and spreading to other, more intimate places she never ever thought about. How dared he do that to her? She would lodge a complaint of sexual harassment! Didn't he know what he was risking? But being Angel, he wouldn't care, wouldn't even stop to consider that he was playing with fire. Indeed, the knowledge would only energise and stimulate him because he loved to push the limits.

She curled up tight in her bed that night, overwhelmed by her first real experience of sexual temptation. When he kissed her she couldn't think, couldn't breathe. A kiss had never had that effect on her before and she was unnerved by the discovery that a kiss could be that influential. She toyed with the idea of complaining about sexual harassment, pictured Angel laughing fearlessly in the face of such a threat and finally decided that she didn't want the embarrassment of that on her employment record. Particularly when such a claim would fail because she hadn't pushed him away, hadn't given him an immediate rejection.

The next day she was very nervous going into work, but Angel didn't do or say anything that was different and she was strangely irritated by that reality: that he could act as though he had never offered to take her home to bed for the night and, afterwards, simply treat her like everyone else. But those same moments of intimacy had carried a higher price for *her*. It was as though he had stripped away her tough outer layer and chipped her out of her cautious shell to ensure that she began feeling physical and emotional responses she had comfortably held at bay until she'd met him.

During the week that followed she was feverishly aware of Angel to a degree that sent her temperature rocketing. When he looked at her, it was as if a blast of concentrated heat lit her up inside and her bra would feel scratchy against her tender nipples and a dull ache would stir between her thighs, her every tiny reaction in his presence like a slap in the face that shamed her. It was a terrible destructive wanting that wouldn't go away. He had lit the spark and she seemed stuck with the spread of the fire licking away at her nerves and her fierce pride.

At the end of that week, Angel asked her to stay behind after everyone else had left to go for drinks.

'Next on the agenda…*us*,' Angel murmured sibilantly.

Merry shot him a withering appraisal. 'There is no us.'

'Exactly,' Angel pronounced with satisfaction. 'Scratch the itch and it goes away and dies, ignore it and it festers.'

'Your seduction vocabulary needs attention,' Merry quipped, standing straight in front of him, grudging amusement dancing in her crystalline eyes.

Angel grimaced. 'I don't do seduction.'

'I don't do one-night stands.'

'So if I make it dinner and sex I'm in with a chance?' A sardonic ebony brow elevated.

'No chance whatsoever,' Merry contradicted with

pleasure. 'I'm a virgin and I'm not trading that for some sleazy night with my boss.'

'A virgin?' Angel was aghast. *'Seriously?'*

'Seriously,' Merry traded without embarrassment, reflecting on how her mother had fallen pregnant with her and determined to make every choice that took her in the opposite direction. 'Sex should mean something more than scratching an itch.'

Angel sprang upright behind his desk, all supple, graceful motion, the fine, expensive fabric of his suit pulling taut over powerful thigh muscles and definable biceps. Her mouth ran dry, her eyes involuntarily clinging to his every movement. 'It's never been anything more for me,' he admitted drily. 'But I take offence at the word "sleazy". I am never sleazy and... I don't do virgins.'

'Good to know,' Merry breathed tightly, watching his shirt ripple ever so slightly over his muscular chest as he exhaled while cursing her intense physical awareness of him. 'May I go home now?'

'I'll drop you back.'

'That's not necessary,' she told him coolly.

'I decide what's necessary around here,' Angel pronounced, throwing the door wide and heading for the lift. 'You realise you're as rare as a unicorn in my world? Are you holding out for marriage?'

Involuntarily amused by his curiosity, Merry laughed. 'Of course not. I'm just waiting for something *real*. I'm not a fan of casual or meaningless.'

Angel lounged back fluidly against the wall of the lift, all naked predator and jungle grace. 'I'm casual but I'm very real,' he told her huskily, his deep dark drawl roughening and trickling down her taut spine like a spectral caress.

'Oh, switch it off,' Merry groaned. 'We're like salt and pepper except you can't mix us.'

'Because you've got too many rules, too many barriers. Why is that?'

'Like you are actually interested?' Merry jibed.

'I *am* interested,' Angel growled, dark golden eyes flashing as the lift doors sprang back. 'I want you.'

'Only because you can't have me,' Merry interposed drily, her skin coming up in gooseflesh as he flashed her a ferocious appraisal capable of flaying her skin from her bones. 'That's how basic you are.'

'You're becoming rude.'

'Your persistence is making me rude,' Merry told him.

'I want to see your hair loose,' Angel bit out impatiently. 'It's unusually long.'

'My mother kept on cutting it short when I was little because it was easier to look after. Now I grow it because I can,' she said truthfully, her stomach flipping as he shot a sudden charismatic smile at her, his lean, darkly beautiful face vibrant with amusement.

'You're a control freak,' he breathed lazily. 'Takes one to know one, *glikia mou.*'

'That's why we don't get on,' Merry pointed out.

'We don't get on because you have a very annoying sort of pious vibe going,' Angel contradicted. 'You're smug.'

'No, I'm not,' she argued instantly as they crossed the half-empty car park.

'You think you're superior to me because you're not at the mercy of your hormones…but you *were* when I touched you,' Angel breathed, caging her in against the passenger door of his car, the heat of his lean, powerful body perceptible even through the inches separating them and the rich, evocative scent of husky male and exotic cologne filling her nostrils. His hands braced either side of her, not actually touching her quivering length, and her knees turned weak at the thought that he *might* touch her. 'You can hardly breathe when I'm this close to you. I *see* that, I *know* that…every time I try to step back, it sucks me back in.'

He was like an impenetrable force field surrounding her. She knew she could push him away, she knew he wouldn't fight, she knew he wouldn't do anything she didn't want him to do and a weird sense of unexpected power engulfed her. He was still coming back at her because he couldn't resist the pull between them and she couldn't resist it either. It was a weakness deep down inside her that she couldn't suppress. Nobody had ever made her feel the way he was making her feel and that was a thrill on its own, a shot of adrenalin in her veins to match the feverish pound of her heartbeat. She wanted him. The knowledge ploughed through her like a battering ram, casting everything she had thought she knew about herself into a broken jumble of messy pieces.

'You're not my type,' she whispered in dry-mouthed protest.

'You're not my type either,' Angel admitted thickly. 'But I'd still have sex in a car park with you any time you cared to ask.'

'Not about to ask,' Merry confided shakily. 'Take me home…back off.'

'You're making a major production of this again,' Angel accused, flashing his key fob to open the car. 'Stop doing that. It's…it's bizarrely unnerving.'

She climbed into his car in a daze, the throb between her legs angry and unsettling, the sensual smoulder in the air almost unbearable, every nerve ending painfully aware of it. She didn't know how he did that using only words and looks. It was terrifying. He had wiped her mind clean, made her feel stuff she didn't want to feel, rocked the foundations of her security.

'I don't like you,' she admitted.

'*Thee mou*…you don't have to like me, you only have to want me…and you do.'

And it was agonisingly true, she registered in dismay. Her brain didn't seem to have anything to do with the equation. She thoroughly disapproved of everything he was and yet the chemistry between them was wild and dominant.

'We have one night together and sate the craving. Then we put it away and bury it,' Angel intoned in a driven undertone.

'I thought you didn't do virgins.'

'Evidently you were born to be my single exception.'

'Is this an actual negotiation?' Merry enquired incredulously.

'We have to sort this out. You're taking my mind off work,' Angel complained. 'I can't handle watching you all day and fantasising about you all night. It's bad for business.'

'What's in it for me?' Merry whispered unevenly.

'I'm superlative at sex.'

'Oh…' Her lashes fluttered, her tummy somersaulting again as she wondered if she really was about to do what he wanted her to do, what *she* herself wanted to do. And that was the answer there and then when she was least expecting to see or understand it.

He would make a great introduction to sex for her, she thought dizzily. It would end the insane craving he had awakened inside her and maybe then she could return to her normal tranquil self. That prospect had huge appeal for her. The need would be satisfied, the intolerable longing ended. All right, it wasn't the big romance with hearts and flowers that she had dimly envisioned, but then possibly that had never been a very practical aspiration. What he was offering was basic and honest even if it was casual and uncommitted and everything she had once sworn she would never participate in. It was not as though she had been saving herself for a wedding ring. She had been saving herself for love, but love hadn't happened.

'So, you're suggesting that I just use you,' Merry remarked grittily as he pulled into another underground car park.

'We use each other,' Angel exhaled in a rush and, killing the engine, stretched out a long powerful arm to enclose her in almost the same moment.

His mouth crashed down on hers with a hunger that blew her away. Somehow he made it that she didn't remember getting out of the car, didn't remember getting into a lift or emerging from it. There was only that insane, greedy melding of their mouths and the frantic impatient activity of their hands in a dimly lit hall. Her coat fell off or maybe he helped it. His jacket disappeared at similar speed. She kicked off her shoes. He wrenched off his tie and cannoned into a door as he lifted her off her feet.

'We have to slow down,' he told her roughly, dark golden eyes shimmering like gold ingots, his sexual excitement patent. 'Or I'll screw this up for you.'

He laid her down on a wide, comfortable mattress and stood over her, stripping without inhibition. All she wanted was his mouth on hers again, that magical escape from the limits of her own body that sent her flying higher than she had ever known she could fly. He shed his trousers and her attention locked warily on the very obvious bulge in his boxers while she struggled to accept that she could, even briefly, be with a man who was chronically untidy and dropped clothes in a heap on the floor. Not her type, not her type; she rhymed it like a mantra inside her head, her bulwark against getting attached in any way. It was sex and she didn't want to regard it as anything else.

He unzipped her dress and flipped her over to

remove it with deft precision and release her bra, before pausing to carefully unsnap the clasp in her hair and let his skilled mouth roam across her pale shoulders. He tugged her round and up to him then, long fingers lifting to feather her curtain of dark coffee-coloured hair round her shoulders, thready shimmers of lighter caramel appearing in the light filtering in from the hall.

'You have amazing hair,' he muttered intently, gazing down into blue eyes as pale as an Arctic sky.

'Is that a fetish of yours?'

'Not that I've noticed, but that prissy little smile of yours turns me on no end,' Angel confided, disconcerting her.

'I do *not* have a prissy smile.'

'Talking too much,' Angel growled, crushing her ripe mouth beneath his again, running his hands down the sides of her narrow ribcage to dispose of her bra and let his hands rise to cup the small delicate mounds of her breasts.

As his thumbs grazed her sensitive nipples a gasp parted Merry's lips, and when his hungry mouth followed there she fell back against the pillows and dug her fingers into his thick tangle of curls. Heat arrowed in stormy flashes right to her core, leaving her insanely conscious of how excited she was becoming. Her thighs pressed together, her hips dug into the mattress as she struggled to get a grip on herself, but it was as if her body were streaking ahead of her and no matter how hard she tried to catch it, she couldn't.

He shifted position, ran his tongue down over her

straining midriff to her navel, parted her from her knickers without her noticing, traced her inner thighs with a devil's expertise until she was splayed out like a sacrifice. And then the flood of crazy pleasure came at her in breathless, jolting stabs that shocked and roused her to a level that was almost unbearable. She was shaken by what she was allowing him to do and how much her body craved it and how very little she could control her own reactions. She twisted and turned, hauled him back to her at one point and kissed him breathless, wanting, needing, trembling on the edge of something she didn't understand.

The tight bands in her pelvis strained to hold in the wild searing shots of pleasure gripping her and then her control broke and she writhed in a wild frenzy of release. The sound of her own gasping cry startled her, her eyes flying wide, and Angel grinned shamelessly down at her like a very sexy pirate, a dark shadow of stubble merely accentuating his fantastic bone structure.

'You're staying the whole night,' he told her thickly.

'No,' Merry muttered, head rolling back on the pillows as he crawled up her body like the predator he truly was. 'Once it's done, it's over.'

'You are so stubborn,' Angel groaned in frustration, nipping up her slender throat to find her swollen lips again, teasing and tasting and letting his tongue plunge and twin with hers until she was beyond thought and argument again. He donned protection.

He eased into her slowly, very slowly, and impatience assailed her. She didn't want or need to be treated like fine china that might shatter or like that rare unicorn he had mentioned. Her body was slick and eager again, the pulse at the heart of her racing with anticipation. She tilted under him, angling up her hips, and the invitation was too much for his control and he jerked over her and plunged deep. A brief burning sting of pain made her stiffen and gasp.

'That's your own fault,' Angel growled in exasperation. 'If you would just lie still.'

'I'm not a blow-up doll.'

'I was trying not to hurt you.'

'I'm not breakable either,' Merry argued, every skin cell on red alert as she felt her body slowly stretch to enclose his, tiny little shimmers of exquisite sensation flying through her as he began to move, hinting that the best was yet to come. 'Don't stop.'

And he didn't. He sank deep into her with a shuddering groan of pleasure and the pace picked up, jolting her with waves of glorious excitement. She arched her body up, suddenly needy again, hungry again, marvelling at the limitless capacity of her body to feel more and yet more. But this time the climb to pleasure was slower and she writhed, blue eyes lighting up with impatience and a need she had never expressed before. Her heart raced, her pulses pounded and that sweet, seductive throb of delight grew and grew inside her until she could contain it no longer. Every barrier dropped as her body exploded into an ecstatic climax that left her limp and stunned.

Angel released her from his weight but made a move to pull her under his arm and retain a hold on her. Quick as a flash Merry evaded him, her whole being bent on immediate escape. They had had sex but she didn't want to hang around for the aftermath. Dignity, she told herself staunchly, dictated an immediate departure. She slid out of the other side of the bed, bending down to scoop up her discarded clothes.

'I asked you to stay,' Angel reminded her.

'I'm going home,' she said as he vaulted out of bed and headed into what she presumed was a bathroom, his lean, powerful body emanating impatience and annoyance in perceptible waves.

She would have liked a shower but she was determined not to linger. With a grimace, she pulled her clothes back on and was out in the hall cramming her feet back into her shoes and hurriedly calling a taxi when Angel reappeared, bronzed and still unashamedly naked in the bedroom doorway. 'I don't want you to leave.'

'I've already ordered a taxi.' Merry tilted her chin, her long hair streaming untidily round her flushed heart-shaped face. 'We agreed and it's better like this.'

'I asked for one night—'

'You can't have everything your way,' Merry declared flatly. 'I enjoyed myself but all good things come to an end.'

Angel swore in Greek. 'You drive me insane.'

'What's your problem? According to your forecast, we're done and dusted now,' she pointed out helplessly.

Yet for all her proud nonchalance in front of him, Merry travelled home in a daze of mounting panic. Back at her apartment she had to wait until the shower was free. She felt shell-shocked by what she had done. Her body ached but her brain ached almost as much, trying to rationalise the fleeting madness that had overtaken her. She tried to examine it from Angel's unemotional point of view, but that didn't work for her when her own emotions were throwing tantrums and storming about inside her as much as if she had killed someone. *Done and dusted, forget about it now,* she reminded herself doggedly. He had much more experience in such encounters than she had, had to know what he was talking about. The curiosity and that unnatural hunger had been satisfied and now it would all die a natural death and become an embarrassing memory that she'd never ever share with anyone, she told herself with determination.

Only in the days that followed Merry slowly came to appreciate that, for all his evident experience, Angel Valtinos had got it badly wrong. Feed a cold, starve a fever was a saying she had grown up with, and before very long had passed she knew that it had been a serious mistake to *feed* the fever. She saw it in the way Angel's stunning dark eyes locked on her like magnets, heard it in the terseness of his instructions to her and she felt the pull of him inside herself as if he had attached a secret chain to her. Excitement crashed over her when he was close by, her temperature climbing, her heart thumping. Slowly, painfully, she came to appreciate that she was infatuated with him and very nearly as giddy and mindless as a silly schoolgirl in his vicinity. The suspicion that she was more her mother's daughter than she had ever dreamt she could be appalled her.

Was that the real explanation of why she had slept with Angel Valtinos? She had asked herself again and again why she had done that, why she had made such an impulsive decision that went against everything she believed, and now she was being faced with an answer that she loathed. At some point in their relationship she had begun getting attached to him, possibly around the time she had started admiring his intellect and shrewd business instincts. That attachment was pitiful, she decided with angry self-loathing, and in haste she began to look for another job, desperate to leave Angel and Valtinos Enterprises behind her.

Two weeks after their first encounter, Angel showed up at her apartment one evening without the smallest warning. The same angry frustration that powered him was running through her.

'What are you doing here?' she demanded, far from pleased to be surprised in her cotton pyjamas, fresh from the shower and bare of make-up.

Angel grimaced, his lean, darkly handsome features taut and troubled as he leant back against her bedroom door to close it. 'My car brought me here.'

'What on earth—?' she began, disconcerted by his sudden appearance in a place where she had never imagined seeing him.

Angel settled volatile dark golden eyes on her angrily. 'I *can't* stay away,' he grated rawly, his beautiful mouth compressing.

'B-but…we agreed,' she stammered.

'Massive fail,' Angel framed darkly. 'Biggest bloody mistake of my life!'

Merry almost laughed and fortunately killed the urge. It was simply that Angel's innate love of drama not only amused her, but somehow touched her somewhere down deep inside, somewhere where she was soft and emotional and vulnerable even though she didn't want to be. He had come to her even though he didn't want to. He resented his desire for her, had tried to stamp it out and failed. She grasped immediately that that weakness for her infuriated him.

'I want to be with you tonight.'

'Angel—'

He came down on the bed beside her and framed her face with long, cool brown fingers. 'Say my name again,' he demanded.

'No,' she said stubbornly. 'I don't do what you tell me to do outside working hours.'

'*Thee mou*…stop challenging me,' he groaned, tilting her head back to follow the long, elegant column of her throat down to the slope of her shoulder, nipping and kissing a tantalising path across her sensitised skin while she quivered. 'This isn't me. This isn't what I'm about.'

'Then why are you here?' she whispered weakly.

'Can't stay away.' He carried her hand down to where he was hot and hard and wanting and groaned without inhibition as she stroked him through the fine, crisp fabric of his well-cut trousers.

Heat coursed through her in molten waves, the hunger unleashed afresh. Simply touching him inflamed her. She tried to fight it, she tried to fasten it down and ground herself, but Angel smashed any hope of control by welding dark golden eyes to hers and kissing her with barely contained ferocity. Not a single thought passed her mind beyond the thrillingly obvious reality that he needed her and couldn't stay away. That knowledge vanquished every other consideration. She kissed him back with the same uncontrollable, desperate passion.

'I intended to take you out to dinner,' Angel admitted breathlessly as he fought with her pyjamas, his sleek, deft skills with feminine clothing deserting him.

'You hungry?' she gasped, almost strangling him with his own tie in her struggle to loosen it.

'Only for you,' he growled fiercely against her swollen mouth. 'Watching you round the office all day, being unable to touch, even to look.'

And then they were naked in her bed, naked and frantic and so tormentingly hungry for each other that she writhed and squirmed and he fought to hold her still. He produced a condom, tore it from the wrapper with his teeth. 'We don't want an accident,' he said unevenly.

'No, no accidents,' she agreed helplessly, lying there, shocked by what she was doing but participating all the same, quite unable to deny him. Their clothes lay festooned all around them and she didn't care. Angel had come to her and she was happy about that, there in her pin-neat room made messy by his presence.

He drove into her yielding flesh with a heartfelt sound of satisfaction and she wrapped her legs round him, arching up and gasping at every fluid stroke. The excitement heightened exponentially, the pulsing pound of intolerable desire driving them off the edge fast into a hot, sweaty tangle of limbs and shuddering fulfilment.

Angel pressed his sensual mouth against her brow and eased back, only to grate out a curse in Greek. 'I broke the condom!' he growled in harried explanation as she stared up at him, recognising the stress and anxiety in his expressive gaze.

As if a simultaneous alarm bell had sounded, Angel flipped back from her and slid fluidly out of bed while Merry hurriedly hid her fast-cooling body under the duvet they had lain on. Her eyes were wide with consternation.

'This has never happened to me before,' Angel assured her, hastily getting back into his clothes.

Merry pondered the idea of mentioning that dinner invite and discarded it again. She had nothing comforting to say to him, nothing likely to improve his mood. She wasn't on the pill, wasn't taking any contraceptive precautions, a reality that now made her feel very foolish. Why hadn't she rethought her outlook the minute she'd ended up in bed with Angel Valtinos? Wasn't a woman supposed to look after herself?

'I'm not on anything,' she admitted reluctantly.

Angel dug out his wallet and flipped out a card. 'Come in late tomorrow. See this doctor first. He's a friend of mine. He'll check you out,' he told her, setting the card down by the bed.

And within a minute he was gone. *Wham-bam— no, thank you, ma'am,* she acknowledged with a sinking heart and a strong need for a shower.

If only she could shower the thoughts out of her head and the feelings in her heart as easily, she concluded wretchedly. She felt sick, humiliated and rejected. She also hated herself. A contraceptive accident had sent Angel into a nosedive, his horror unconcealed. Did she hold that against him when trepidation had seized her by the throat as well?

But luckily, that night she had no grasp at all of the nightmare that was waiting to unfold and the many months of unhappiness that would follow as punishment for her irresponsibility. In effect, she was still a complete innocent then. She was hopelessly infatuated with a man who only lusted after her and with a lust that died the instant a condom failed. That was why she had held herself back from casual sex, seeking the feelings and the certain amount of safety that came with them…

Her first wake-up call to what she was truly dealing with came early the next morning. She went, as instructed, to see the suave private doctor, who ran a battery of tests on her and then casually offered her the morning-after pill. She didn't want it, hadn't ever even thought about whether or not she approved of that option, but when it was suggested to her, it grated on her, and even though she could see the doctor's surprise at her refusal she saw no reason to explain her attitude. Had such a possibility been available to her mother, she reckoned that she herself would never have been born and that was a sobering acknowledgement. Had Angel sent her to that doctor quite deliberately to ensure that she was offered that option? She planned to have that out with him the instant she got a moment alone with him.

Unfortunately what she didn't know then was that it would be many, many weeks before she had the opportunity of a moment alone with Angel again and even then she only finally achieved that meeting by stalking him to one of his regular retreats.

When she finally arrived at work after seeing the doctor she was sent straight into one of the meeting rooms where a senior HR person and a company lawyer awaited her. There she was presented with a compromise agreement by which, in return for substantial compensation, she would immediately cease working for Valtinos Enterprises and leave without disclosing her reasons for doing so to anyone.

The shock and humiliation of that meeting marked Merry long after the event. As soon as she realised that Angel wanted her out of the building and away from him, no matter what it cost him, she felt sick

inside. Had he assumed that she would make a nui-
sance of herself in some way? His ruthless rejection
and instant dismissal of what they had briefly shared
shook her rigid and taught her a hard lesson. Angel
always put himself first and evidently her continued
presence at the office would make him uncomfortable. That she did not deserve such harsh treatment
didn't come into it for him.

In disgust and mortification Merry took the
money she was offered because she felt she had no
better alternative and she had to live until she found
another job. But that was the day the first seed of
her hatred had been sown…

CHAPTER THREE

'FERGUS ASKED ME where he should take you tomorrow,' Sybil volunteered, shooting Merry straight back into the present with that surprising announcement. 'I thought that was a bit wet of him. I mean, doesn't he have any ideas of his own? But obviously he wants you to enjoy yourself.'

A bit wet sounded all right to Merry, who was still reeling from the consequences of Angel's me-me-me approach to life. A macho, self-assured man was hugely impressive and sexy only until he turned against you and became an enemy, armed to the teeth with legal sharks.

'I suggested a trip to the seaside for you and Elyssa. I know you love the beach,' Sybil mused. 'Fergus does like children.'

'Yes,' Merry agreed quietly, scooping Elyssa off the older woman's lap to feed her while wondering what it would have been like to have a father for her daughter. Would he have helped out with their child? Taken a real interest? She suppressed the thought, knowing it probably came from the reality that *she* had had to grow up without a father. She had, however, visited her father once, but his enraged betrayed wife had been present as well and the visit had been a disaster. Her father had only asked to see her on that one occasion and then never again.

The next morning, Merry finished drying her hair and took the time to apply a little make-up because Elyssa was having her morning nap. Pulling on skinny jeans and a vibrant cerise tee, she dug her feet into comfy shoes. She was heading downstairs again with Elyssa anchored on her hip when the phone rang. Breathless, she tucked it under her chin while she lowered her daughter to the hearth rug.

'Yes?'

'I'm in the office,' her aunt told her curtly. 'Elyssa's father is here demanding to see her. I'll keep him here with me until you come.'

Shock and disbelief engulfed Merry in a dizzy tide. She snatched Elyssa back off the rug and wondered frantically what to do with her daughter while she dealt with Angel, because she didn't want him to see her. Her mind was a chaotic blur because she couldn't imagine Angel travelling down to Suffolk just to see the child he had once done everything possible to avoid and deny. It was true that since he had been informed of Elyssa's birth he had made repeated requests to meet his daughter, but Merry had seen no good reason to cater to his natural human curiosity and she herself wanted nothing more to do with him.

After all, as soon as Angel had learned that she was pregnant he had brought his lawyers in to handle everything. They had drawn up a legal agreement by which Merry was paid a ridiculous amount of money every month but only for as long as she kept quiet about her daughter's parentage. Merry currently paid the money into a trust she had set up for Elyssa's future, reckoning that that was the best she could do for her daughter.

She left the cottage with Elyssa tucked into her well-padded pushchair, her toy bunny clutched between her fingers. Walking into the rescue centre, she saw a long black limousine sitting parked and she swallowed hard at the sight of it. Angel didn't flaunt the Valtinos wealth but even at the office she had seen occasional glimpses of a world and lifestyle far different from her own. He wore diamond cufflinks and his shirts had monograms embroidered on the pockets. Every garment he wore was tailored by hand at great expense and he thought nothing of it because from birth he had never known anything else.

She pushed the buggy into the barn, where the kennel staff hung out when they took a break. 'Will you watch Elyssa for me for ten minutes?' she asked anxiously of the three young women, chattering over mugs of coffee.

'Can we take her out of the pram and play with her?' one of them pressed hopefully.

A smile softened Merry's troubled face. 'Of course…' she agreed, hastening out again to head for the rescue centre office.

What on earth was Angel doing here? And how could she face him when the very idea of facing him again made her feel queasy with bad memories? They had last met the day she'd tracked him down to tell him that she was pregnant. Those liquid-honey eyes had turned black-diamond hard, his shock and distaste stark as a banner.

'Do you want it?' he had asked doubtingly, earning her hatred with every syllable of that leading question. 'Scratch that. It was politically incorrect. Naturally I will support you in whatever choice you make.'

How could she come back from that punishing recollection and act normally? She thought of Elyssa's innocent sweetness and the reality that her father didn't want her, had *never* wanted her, and the knowledge hurt Merry, making her wonder if her own father had felt the same about her. Even worse, she was convinced that allowing any kind of contact between father and daughter would only result in Elyssa getting hurt at some later stage. In her opinion, Angel was too selfish and too spoiled to be a caring or committed parent.

As she rounded the corner of the tiny office building a startling scene met her eyes. Poised outside the door, Sybil had her shotgun aimed at Angel, who was predictably lounging back against the wall of the kennels opposite as though he had not a care in the world.

'Will you call this madwoman off me?' Angel demanded with derisive sibilance when he heard her footsteps and without turning his arrogant dark head. 'She won't let me move.'

'It's all right, Sybil,' Merry said tautly. 'Elyssa is in the barn.'

Angel's arrogant dark head flipped, the long, predatory power of his lean, strong body suddenly rippling with bristling tension. 'What's my daughter doing in a barn? And who's looking after her?' he demanded in a driven growl.

Sybil lowered her shotgun and broke it open to safely extract the cartridges. 'I'll take her back home with me,' she declared, entirely ignoring Angel.

'Come into the office and we'll talk,' Merry framed coldly as his dark eyes locked on her tense face.

'I'm not very good at talking,' Angel acknowledged without embarrassment as he straightened. 'That's why I use lawyers.'

In an angry defensive movement, Merry thrust wide the door of the little office before spinning back round to say, 'What the hell are you doing here?'

'I warned you that I intended to visit,' Angel bit out impatiently.

Merry thought about the letter she had bottled out of opening and uneasily looked at him for the first time in months. The sheer power of his volatile presence made her tummy turn hollow and her legs wobble. He was still so wickedly beautiful that he made her teeth clench with fierce resentment. It wasn't fair that he should look so untouched by all that had passed between them, that he should stand there perfectly at his ease and glossily well groomed, sheathed in his elegant charcoal-grey designer suit. It was especially unfair that he should still have the nerve to voice a demand for a right he had surrendered entirely of his own volition before their daughter was even born. 'And I've already told your lawyers that I won't accept *any* kind of visit from you!'

'I won't accept that, not even if I have to spend the rest of my life and yours fighting you.' Angel mapped those boundaries for her, wanting her to know that there would be no escape from his demands until he got what he wanted. He would not accept defeat, regardless of what it cost him. He had lost his father's respect and he was determined to retrieve it and get to know his child.

Frowning, black brows lowering, he studied Merry, incredulous at her continuing defiance while marvelling at the quiet inner strength he sensed in her, which he had never noticed in a woman before. She had cut her hair, which now fell in glossy abundance to just below her shoulders. He was ridiculously disappointed by that fashion update. There had been something ultra-feminine about that unusually long hair that he had liked. She was also thinner than she had been and there had not been much of her to begin with, he conceded reflectively. She looked like a teenager with her long, coltish legs outlined by distressed denim and with her rounded little breasts pushing at the cotton of her top so that he could see the prominent points of her lush nipples. He went hard and gritted his teeth, furious with himself for that weakness but... *Thee mou*, shorn of her conservative office apparel, she looked ridiculously sexy.

'Why can't you simply move on from this and forget we exist?' Merry demanded in fierce frustration. 'A year ago, that's what you wanted and I gave it to you. I signed everything your legal team put in front of me. You didn't want to be a father. You didn't want to know anything about her and you didn't want her associated with your precious name. What suddenly changed?'

Angel's lean, hard jaw line took on an aggressive slant. 'Maybe I've changed,' he admitted, sharply disconcerting her.

Merry's tense face stiffened with suspicion. 'That's doubtful. You are what you are.'

'Everyone is capable of change and sometimes change simply happens whether you want it to or not,' Angel traded, his lean, dark features taut. 'When you first told me that you were pregnant a year ago, I didn't think through what I was doing. Gut instinct urged me to protect my way of life. I listened to my lawyers, took their advice and now we've got…now we've got an intolerable mess.'

Merry forced herself to breathe in deep and slow and stay calm. He sounded sincere but she didn't trust him. 'It's the way you made it and now you have to live with it.'

Angel threw back his broad shoulders and lifted his arrogant dark head high, effortlessly dominating the small cluttered room. Even though Merry was a comfortable five feet eight inches tall, he was well over six feet in height and stood the tallest in most gatherings. 'I can't live with it,' he told her with flat finality. 'I *will* continue to fight for access to my daughter.'

The breath fluttered in Merry's drying throat,

consternation and fury punching up through her, bringing a flood of emotion with it. 'I *hate* you, Angel! If you make any more threats, if you bombard me with more legal letters, I will hate you even more! When is enough *enough*?' she hurled at him with bitter emphasis.

'When I can finally establish a normal relationship with my daughter,' Angel responded, his lean, strong face set with stubborn resolve. 'It is my duty to establish that relationship and I won't shirk it.'

'The way you shirked everything else that went with fatherhood?' Merry scorned. 'The responsibility? The commitment? The caring? I was just a pregnant problem you threw money at!'

'I won't apologise for that. I was raised to solve problems that way,' Angel admitted grittily. 'I was taught to put my faith in lawyers and to protect myself first.'

'Angel…you are strong enough to protect yourself in a cage full of lions!' Merry shot back at him wrathfully. 'You didn't *need* the lawyers when I wasn't making any demands!'

A ton of hurt and turbulent emotion was sucking Merry down but she fought it valiantly. She was trying so hard not to throw pointless recriminations at him. In an effort to put a physical barrier between them she flopped down in the chair behind the desk. 'Did you ever…even once…think about *feelings*?' she prompted involuntarily.

Angel frowned at her, wondering what she truly wanted from him, wondering how much he would be willing to give in return for access to his daughter. It wasn't a calculation he wanted to do at that moment, not when she was sitting there, shoulders rigid, heart-shaped face stiff and pale as death. 'Feelings?' he repeated blankly.

'My feelings,' Merry specified helplessly. 'How it would feel for me to sleep with a man one night and go into work the next day and realise that he couldn't even stand to have me stay in the same building to do my job?'

Angel froze as if she had fired an ice gun at him, colour receding beneath his bronzed skin, his gorgeous dark eyes suddenly screened by his ridiculously luxuriant black lashes. 'No, I can't say I did. I didn't view it in that light,' he admitted curtly. 'I thought separation was the best thing for both of us because our relationship had crossed too many boundaries and got out of hand. I also ensured that your career prospects were not damaged in any way.'

Merry closed her eyes tight, refusing to look at him any longer. He had once told her that he didn't do virgins and it seemed that he didn't do feelings either. He was incapable of putting himself in her shoes and imagining how she had felt. 'I felt…absolutely mortified that day, completely humiliated, *hurt*,' she spelt out defiantly. 'The money didn't soften the blow and I only took it because I didn't know how long it would take for me to find another job.'

Angel saw pain in her pale blue eyes and heard the emotion in her roughened voice. Her honesty unnerved him, flayed off a whole layer of protective skin, and he didn't like how it made him feel. 'I had no desire to hurt you, there *was* no such intent,' he countered tautly. 'I realised that our situation had become untenable and in that line I was guiltier than you because I made all the running.'

It was an acknowledgement of fault that would once have softened her. He had created that untenable situation and brutally ditched her when he had had enough of it but his admission didn't come anywhere near soothing the tight ball of hurt in her belly. 'You could have talked to me personally,' she pointed out, refusing to drop the subject.

'I've never talked about stuff like that. I wouldn't know where to begin,' Angel confessed grimly.

'Well, how could you possibly forge a worthwhile bond with a daughter, then?' Merry pressed. 'The minute she annoys you or offends you will you turn your back on her the way you turned your back on me?'

Angel flashed her a seethingly angry appraisal. 'Not for one minute have you and that baby been out of my mind since the day you told me you were pregnant! I did not turn my back on you. I made proper provision for both of you.'

'Yeah, you threw money at us to keep us at a safe distance, yet now here you are breaking your own rules,' Merry whispered shakily.

'What is the point of us wrangling like this?' Angel questioned with rank impatience. 'This is no longer about you and I. This involves a third person with rights of her own even if she is still only a baby. Will you allow me to meet my daughter this afternoon?'

'Apart from everything else—like it being immaterial to you that I hate and distrust you,' Merry framed with thin restraint, 'today's out of the question. I've got a date this afternoon and we're going out.'

Angel tensed, long, powerful muscles pulling taut. He could not explain why he was shocked by the idea of her having a date. Maybe he had been guilty of assuming that she was too busy being a mother at present to worry about enjoying a social life. But the concept of her enjoying herself with another man inexplicably outraged and infuriated him and the vision of her bedding another man when he had been the first, the *only*, made him want to smash something.

His lean brown hands clenched into fists. 'A date?' he queried as jaggedly as if he had a piece of glass in his throat.

Merry stood up behind the desk and squared her slim shoulders. 'Yes, he's taking us to the beach. You have a problem with that as well?'

Us? The realisation that another man, some random, unknown stranger, had access to his daughter when he did not heaped coals of fire on Angel's proud head. He snatched in a stark breath, fighting with all his might to cage his hot temper and his bitterness. 'Yes, I do. Can't you leave her with your aunt and grant me even ten minutes with my own child?' he demanded rawly.

'I'm afraid there isn't time today.' Merry swallowed

the lump in her throat, that reminder that Elyssa had
rights of her own still filtering back through her like
a storm warning, making her appreciate that every
decision she made now would have to be explained
and defended to satisfy her daughter's questions some
years down the road. And just how mean could she
afford to be to Angel before her daughter would question her attitude? Question whether her mother had
given her daughter's personal needs sufficient weight
and importance? Her tummy dive-bombed, her former conviction that she was totally in the right taking a massive dent.

Nobody was ever totally in the right, she reminded
herself reluctantly. There were always two sides to
every story, every conflict. She was letting herself
be influenced by her own feelings, not looking towards the future when Elyssa would demand answers
to certain tough questions relating to her father. And
did she really want to put herself in the position of
having refused to allow her daughter's flesh and
blood to even *see* her? Dully it dawned on her that
that could well be a step too far in hostilities. Angel
had hurt *her*, but that was not indisputable proof that
he would hurt his daughter.

'Pick another day this week,' she invited him
stiffly, watching surprise and comprehension leap
like golden flames into his vivid eyes. 'But you make
your arrangements with me, not through your lawyers. You visit for an hour. Let's not raise the bar too
high, let's keep it simple. I won't let you take her out

anywhere without me and I don't want you arriving with some fancy nanny in tow.'

His dramatic dark eyes shone bright, a tiny muscle jerking taut at the corner of his wide, sensual mouth. He swung away, momentarily turning his back on her before swinging back and nodding sombrely in agreement with her strictures. But in those revealing few seconds she had recognised the stormy flare of anticipation in his stunning gaze, finally registering that he *had* been serious in his approach and that he did genuinely want to meet his infant daughter.

'Tomorrow morning, then,' Angel pronounced decisively. 'We'll take it from there.'

Take what from where? she almost questioned but she ducked it, worn out by the sheer stress of dealing with him. Inside herself she was trembling with the strain of standing straight and unafraid and hiding her fearful anxiety from him because she knew that Angel would pounce on weakness like a shark catching the scent of blood. 'About ten,' she suggested carefully. 'I have someone to see at half eleven.'

Angel gritted his even white teeth, wanting to ask if she was seeing the boyfriend again, but he had no intention of being foolish enough to ask questions he had no right to demand answers to. She had been under covert surveillance for weeks and he would soon identify the boyfriend from the records he had yet to examine. His mouth quirked because he knew she would be outraged if she knew he was paying a private firm to watch her every move.

But, when it came to protecting a member of the

Valtinos family, Angel had no inhibitions. Hired security was as much a part of his life as it was for his mother. Safety came first and his daughter would be at risk of kidnapping were anyone to work out who had fathered her. It was his duty to safeguard his child and he would not apologise for the necessity.

Merry opened the office door to urge him out and followed him to where the limousine sat parked. 'I live in the cottage at the front gate,' she informed him.

'I thought you lived with your aunt,' Angel admitted with a frown.

'When I became a mother I thought it was time for us to get our own space. Sybil practically raised me. I didn't want her to feel that she had to do the same for my daughter,' Merry confided ruefully.

In the summer sunlight she studied Angel's lean, strong face, marvelling at the sleek symmetry of the hard cheekbones and hollows that enhanced his very masculine features. He was a literal work of art. It was little wonder that she had overreacted to his interest and refused to accept how shallow that interest was, she told herself squarely, struggling to calm the stabs of worry that erupted at the prospect of having any further dealings with him.

She would cope. She *had* to cope. So far she had contrived to cope with everything Angel Valtinos had thrown at her, she reminded herself with pride. As long as she remembered who and what he was, she would be fine...wouldn't she?

CHAPTER FOUR

'LETTING ELYSSA'S FATHER visit is the right way to go,' Fergus opined, scrutinising her troubled face with concern before turning to gaze out to sea. 'He treated you badly but that doesn't automatically mean he'll be a bad father. Only time will answer that.'

Merry went pink. As Fergus had combined picking her up with an examination of the latest arrival at the rescue centre, he had heard about the fuss created by Angel's visit earlier in the day and had naturally asked her about it. She looked up at Fergus, drawn by his calm and acceptance of her situation, wondering if it was possible to feel anything or even trust a man again. Fergus stood about an inch under six feet. He had cropped brown hair and cheerful blue eyes and she had never heard him so much as raise his voice while she had already witnessed his compassion and regret when he was treating abused animals.

'Are you over him?' Fergus asked her bluntly.

Merry vented a shaken laugh. 'I certainly hope so.'

And then he kissed her, wrapping her close in the

sea breeze, and she froze only momentarily in surprise. Suddenly she found herself wanting to feel more than she actually felt because he was a good guy, ostensibly straightforward and as different from Angel as day was to night. Angel was all twists and turns, dark corners and unpredictability and she had never had any genuine hope of a future with him. Furthermore, Angel had never been her type. He wasn't steady or open or even ready to settle down with conventional expectations. Feelings were foreign and threatening to Angel yet he bristled with untamed emotion. As Fergus freed her mouth and kept an arm anchored to her spine she realised in horror-stricken dismay that she'd spent their entire kiss thinking about Angel and her face burned in shame and discomfiture.

Angel sat in his limo and perused the photo that had been sent to his phone while he angrily wondered if he was a masochist or, indeed, developing sad stalker tendencies. But no, he had to deal with the situation as it was, not as he would've preferred it to be. Even worse, Merry had just upped the stakes, ensuring that Angel had now to raise his game. He wanted to stalk down to that beach and beat the hell out of the opposition. Because that was what Fergus Wickham was: opposition, *serious* opposition.

And naturally, Angel was confident that he was not jealous. After all, with only one exception, he had never experienced jealousy. He had, however, once cherished a singularly pathetic desire for his mother to take as much of an interest in him as she took in her toy boys. He *had* only been about seven years old at the time, he reminded himself forgivingly, and a distinctly naïve child, fondly expecting that, his having spent all term at boarding school, his mother would make him the centre of her loving attention when he finally came home.

Well, he wasn't that naïve now, Angel acknowledged grimly. From his earliest years he had witnessed how fleeting love was for a Valtinos. A Valtinos *bought* love, paid well for its upkeep, got bored in exactly that order. His mother ran through young men as a lawnmower ran through grass. By the time Angel was in his twenties he was dealing with blackmail attempts, compromising photos and sordid scandals all on his mother's behalf. His mother had tremendous charm but she remained as immature and irresponsible as a teenager. Even so, she was the only mother he would ever have and at heart he was fond of her.

But he didn't get jealous or possessive of lovers because he didn't ever get attached to them or develop expectations of them. Expectations *always* led to disappointment. Merry, however, was in a different category because she was the mother of his daughter and Angel didn't want her to have another man in her life. That was a matter of simple good sense. Another man would divide her loyalties, take her focus off her child and invite unflattering comparisons…

'You heard the pitter patter of tiny feet and literally ran for the hills,' his brother Vitale had summed up a week earlier. 'Not a very promising beginning.'

No, it wasn't, Angel conceded wrathfully while endlessly scrutinising that photo in which his daughter appeared only as a small indistinct blob anchored in a pram. He had screwed up but he was a terrific strategist and unstoppable once he had a goal. He didn't even need an angle because his daughter was all the ammunition he required. Was Merry sleeping with that guy yet? Angel smouldered and scowled, beginning for the first time to scroll through the records he had studiously ignored to respect Merry's privacy. To hell with that scruple, he thought angrily. He had to fight to protect what was *his*.

'So, how are you planning to play it with Elyssa's father tomorrow?' Sybil asked that evening, having tried and failed to get much out of her niece concerning the date with Fergus.

Merry shrugged. 'Cool, calm...'

'He's impossibly headstrong and obstinate,' her aunt pronounced with disapproval. 'I only cocked the gun because I didn't want him landing on your doorstep unannounced but he wouldn't take no for an answer.'

'He isn't familiar with the word no,' Merry mused ruefully. 'I do wish I'd treated him to it last year.'

'Do you really wish you didn't have Elyssa?'

Merry flushed and, thinking about that, shook her head in dismissal. 'I thought I would when I was pregnant but once she was here, everything changed.'

'Maybe it changed for Angel as well. Maybe he wasn't lying about that. He does value family ties,' Sybil remarked.

Merry frowned. 'How do you know that?'

Sybil reddened, her eyes evasive. 'Well, you told me he meets up with his father twice a month and never cancels...and naturally I've read about his mother, Angelina's exploits in the newspapers. She's a real nut-job—rich, stupid, fickle. If he's still close to her, he has a high tolerance threshold for embarrassment. She's not far off my age and the men in her bed are getting younger by the year.'

Merry's eyes widened. 'I had no idea.'

'Shallow sexual relationships are all he saw growing up, all he's ever had as an example to follow. It's hardly surprising that he is the way he is. I won't excuse him for the way he treated you but I do see that he doesn't know any better,' Sybil completed, recognising Merry's surprise. 'But you could teach him different.'

'I don't think you can domesticate a wild animal.'

Sybil rolled her eyes. 'Elyssa has enough charisma to stop a charging rhinoceros.'

Merry tossed and turned in her bed, despising herself for her nervous tension. Angel had cast a long shadow over her afternoon with Fergus, depriving her of relaxation and appreciation. She had made hateful, unforgivable comparisons. On some secret, thoroughly inexcusable level, she still craved the buzz of excitement that Angel had filled her with and that unsettled and shamed her. After all, once the excitement had gone she had been left pregnant and alone and now her memory trailed back fifteen months…

Discovering that she was pregnant had proved a real shock for Merry because she had not seriously considered that that single accident was likely to result in conception and had hoped for the best. She had barely settled into a new and very challenging job, and falling pregnant had seemed like the worst possible news. She had suffered from severe morning sickness and at one stage had even feared she was on the brink of having a miscarriage. She had waited until she was over three months along before she'd even tried to contact Angel to tell him that she was carrying his child. She had never had his personal mobile number and had never got to speak to him when she'd phoned the office, suspecting that calls from her were on some discreet forbidden list. The prospect of sending a letter or an email that would probably be opened and read by a former colleague had made her cringe. In the end she had used her working knowledge of Angel's diary and had headed to the hotel where he met his father for lunch twice a month.

That unwise but desperate move had put in motion the most humiliating, wounding encounter of Merry's life. Angel had had a very tall and beautiful blonde with him when he entered the bar, a blonde with bare breasts on display under a gauzy see-through dress. She had looked like the sort of woman who didn't ever wear underwear and every man in the place had stared lustfully at her, while she'd clung to Angel's arm and giggled and touched him with easy confidence. Just looking at her, Merry had felt sick and ugly and plain and boring because pregnancy had not been kind to her. Her body had already been swelling and thickening, her eyes had been shadowed because she couldn't sleep and the smell of most foods had made her nauseous. She had stayed concealed in the bar behind a book and round a corner while Angel, his companion and eventually his father had sat down to lunch on an outside terrace.

If Angel had not reappeared at the bar alone, she would probably simply have gone back to work without even trying to achieve her goal. But when she'd seen him she had forced herself up out of her seat and forward.

'I have to speak to you in private,' she had said. 'It's very important. It will only take five minutes.'

He had spun back from the bar to appraise her with cool, guarded eyes. 'I'm listening.'

'Could we go out into the foyer?' she had pressed, very conscious of the number of people around them. 'It would be more private.'

He had acquiesced with unconcealed reluctance. 'What is this about?' he had demanded as soon as they'd got there.

And then she had made her announcement and those expressive beautiful eyes of his had glittered like cold black diamonds, his consternation and annoyance obvious.

'Do you want it?' he had asked doubtingly, earning her hatred with every syllable of that leading question. 'Scratch that. It was politically incorrect. Of course, I will support you in whatever choice you make.' He had drawn out a business card and thrust it into her unwilling hand. 'I will inform my lawyers. Please provide them with contact details and I will make provision for you.'

And that had been Angel's knee-jerk response to unexpected fatherhood: brief and brutal and wholly unemotional and objective. *Go away and I'll give you cash to keep you quiet and at a distance.*

Remembering that encounter, Merry shuddered and tears stung her eyes afresh. That was the final moment when she had faced the reality that she had given her body to a ruthlessly detached man without a heart. How could she let such a man come within ten feet of her precious, loving daughter? That question kept her awake until dawn. Suddenly keeping the peace and giving Angel another chance seemed the stuff of stupidity.

Having done his baby research diligently before his visit, Angel believed he was prepared for all eventualities. His second cousin had six-month-old twins and a toddler and lived in London. It was hard to say who had been most startled by his interest: his cousin at the shock of his curiosity or Angel at finding himself festooned in wriggling babies, who cried, pooped and threw up while poking and pulling at him. There were loads of babies in his extended family circle but Angel had always given them a very wide berth.

He put on his oldest jeans for the occasion and, after consulting his cousin, he purchased only one modest gift. Merry wouldn't be impressed by a toyshop splurge. She was already saving every penny he was giving her into a trust for their daughter. Merry and her endless rainy-day fund, he thought incredulously, deeming her joyless, fearful attitude to spending money depressing. She was a natural-born hoarder of cash. If only his mother suffered from the same insecurity, he conceded wryly.

From upstairs, Merry watched the sleek, expensive car pull into the driveway. She had dressed smartly that morning. After all she had a potential new client coming at half eleven and she needed to look professional, so her hair was freshly washed, her make-up was on and she wore a summer dress that clung to her slender curves. What she wore had nothing whatsoever to do with Angel's visit, except in so far as looking smart lifted her confidence, she told herself soothingly.

Angel sprang fluidly out of his car, his lean, powerful body clad in black jeans and a green sweater that was undoubtedly cashmere. He found English summers cold. She carried Elyssa downstairs. Her daughter wore one of the fashionable baby outfits that Sybil often bought her, a pretty blue floral tunic and leggings that reflected her eyes. The door knocker rapped twice and she hastily settled Elyssa down on the rug before rushing breathlessly back to the door, scolding herself for the unmistakeable sense of anticipation gripping her.

Angel stepped in and his stunning dark golden gaze locked to her with the most electrifying immediacy. Tension leapt through Merry along with a growing unease about the decision she had made. He looked amazing. He *always* looked amazing, she reminded herself mockingly, striving not to react in any way. But it was impossible. Her breath shortened in her tightening throat and her breasts tingled and a sensual warmth made her thighs press together.

Angel's scrutiny roamed from the glossy bell of her dark hair, down to the modest neckline of the dress that clung to the delectably full swell of her breasts, before skimming down over her waist to define the feminine swell of her hips. He didn't let himself look at her legs because she had fantastic legs and the heat pooling in his groin didn't need that added encouragement. He didn't know how she had contrived to get skinnier and at the same time more interestingly curvy but he especially didn't like the feeling of being sexually drawn against his will.

'Elyssa's in here,' she framed stiffly.

'That's a Greek name.'

'Yes, she's entitled to a Greek name,' Merry proclaimed defensively.

'I wasn't…criticising.' Angel registered the white-knuckled grip she had on the edge of the door and recognised that he would be treading on eggshells every time he spoke. He gritted his teeth on the awareness but as Merry pushed the door fully open he finally saw his daughter and for several timeless moments stayed rigid in the doorway drinking in the sight of her.

'She's got my hair,' he almost whispered, moving forward and then dropping down onto the rug a couple of feet from his daughter. 'But curls look cute on her…'

Merry watched him closely, registering that he had enough sense not to try to get too familiar too fast with a baby that didn't know him. No, Angel was far too clever to make an obvious wrong move, she reflected bitterly, before catching herself up on that suspicious but hardly charitable thought and crossing the room to go into the kitchen. 'Coffee?'

'If it's not too much trouble.'

'Don't go all polite on me,' she said drily.

'What do you expect?' Angel shot her a sardonic glance of rebuke. 'I know you don't want me here.'

Merry paled at that blunt statement. 'I'm trying not to feel like that.'

She put on the kettle and watched him remove a toy from his pocket, a brightly coloured teething toy, which he set on the rug at his feet. It was a strategic move and Elyssa quickly fulfilled his expectations by extending the toy she held to him in the hope of gaining access to the new and more interesting one. Angel accepted it and handed over his gift. Elyssa chortled with satisfaction and bestowed a huge smile on him before sticking the new toy into her mouth and chewing happily on it.

'She has your eyes,' Angel remarked. 'She's incredibly pretty.'

In spite of her desire to remain unmoved, Merry flushed with pride. 'I think so too.'

'She's also unmistakeably mine,' Angel intoned with unashamed approval.

'Well, you already knew that,' Merry could not resist reminding him. 'She was DNA tested after she was born.'

Angel winced. 'I never once doubted that the child you were carrying was mine but in view of inheritance rights...and us not being married...it was best to have it legally confirmed.' He hesitated before turning his classic bronzed profile to study her levelly. 'But I let the lawyers take over and run the whole show and that was a mistake. I see that now.'

Merry jerked her chin in acknowledgement, not trusting herself to speak.

'I didn't know any other way to handle it,' Angel admitted grimly. 'I took the easy way out... unfortunately the easy way turned out to be the wrong way.'

Taken aback by that admission, Merry dragged in a ragged breath and turned away to make the coffee. A fat burst of chuckles from her daughter made her flip back and she saw Elyssa bouncing on the rug, held steady by Angel's hands and revelling in both the exercise and the attention.

When Elyssa tired of that, Angel turned out her

toy box for her. Tiger slunk out from under the chair where he had been hiding since Angel's arrival and moved hesitantly closer to investigate.

'Diavolos!' Angel exclaimed in surprise. 'Where did the dog come from?'

Startled by Angel's deep voice, Tiger shot back under the chair.

'He's been here all along. His name's Tiger.'

'Kind of nervous for a dog called Tiger and hardly a stream-lined predator.'

'OK. He's fat, you can say it. He's addicted to food and he wasn't socialised properly when he was young. He came from a puppy farm that was closed down,' Merry volunteered, extending a cup of black coffee to Angel as he vaulted lithely upright, suddenly dominating the small room with his height and the breadth of his shoulders.

'I didn't know you were keen on dogs.'

'I practically grew up helping in the rescue centre.' Merry could hear herself gabbling because her heart was pounding wildly in her chest as Angel moved towards her and even breathing was a challenge beneath the onslaught of his gleaming dark golden eyes. 'I—'

'Tell it like it is,' Angel urged sibilantly.

Her smooth brow furrowed. 'What are you talking about?'

'You still want me as much as I want you,' he breathed huskily, sipping his coffee as if he were merely making casual conversation.

'I don't want to have that sort of discussion with

you,' Merry told him curtly, colour burnishing her cheeks as she wondered if he really could tell that easily that she was still vulnerable around him. Not that she would do anything about it or let *him* do anything about it, she reasoned with pride. Attraction was nothing more than a hormonal trick and, in her case, a very dangerous misdirection.

'Avoid? Deny?' Angel derided, his beautiful wilful mouth curling, his smouldering gaze enhanced by unfairly long black lashes welded to her fast-reddening face. 'What's the point?'

'If you continue this I'm going to ask you to leave,' Merry warned thinly.

And genuine amusement engulfed Angel and laughter lit up his lean, dark features. 'I'm not about to pounce on you with our daughter watching! Believe me, while she's around, you're safe,' he assured her smoothly.

Inexplicably that little exchange made Merry feel foolish and rather as though she had ended up with egg on her face, which was burning like a furnace. Even now, many months after the event, she couldn't laugh about what had happened between them. Looking back, it was as if blinding sunlight overlaid and blurred the explosive passion she couldn't begin to explain and never wanted to experience again. Unfortunately for her, her body had a different ambition. One glimpse of Angel's darkly handsome face and long, sleek, muscular frame and she was as tense as a bowstring, caught between forbidden pleasure at his sheer physical beauty and angry self-loathing at her susceptibility to it.

'I brought lunch with me,' Angel revealed, startling her.

Her eyes widened. 'But I have a client due.'

'I'll return in an hour. You know we need to talk about Elyssa and how we move on from here,' Angel pointed out as if it were the most reasonable and natural thing in the world when in truth they had never ever talked about anything.

'Yes…yes, of course,' she muttered uneasily, because she could see that a talk made sense and it was surely better to get it all over in one go and in one day, she told herself soothingly. 'I should be free in an hour, but—'

'I'll make it an hour and a half,' Angel cut in decisively as he moved towards the door.

Merry skimmed his arm with an uncertain finger to attract his attention. 'I'm afraid Elyssa has… er…stained your sweater,' she told him awkwardly.

His amused grin flashed perfect white teeth and enhanced the sculpted fullness of his wide, sensual mouth. 'It's not a problem. I brought a change of clothes with me.'

'My goodness, you were organised,' she mumbled in surprise as he strode down the path and leant down into his car, straightening to peel off the offending sweater and expose the flexing muscles of his bronzed and powerful torso. Her mouth ran dry and she stared, watching him pull on another sweater, black this time, before she closed the door.

She ignored her reeling senses to concentrate on what was truly important. Angel was unpredictable, she reminded herself worriedly, devious to a fault and dangerously volatile. What did he truly want from her? Why was he putting himself to so much trouble? *Lunch?* All of a sudden he was bringing her lunch? Merry was stunned by the concept and the planning that must have gone into that. Did Angel really want access to his daughter *that* badly? Did he have sufficient interest and staying power to want a long-term relationship with his daughter? And where did that leave her when she really didn't want Angel to feature *anywhere* in her life?

You should've thought of that before you let him visit, Merry told herself in exasperation. Possibly Angel was only trying to smooth over the hostilities between them. And possibly she was a suspicious little shrew, still bitter and battered from her previous encounters with him. At the very least she ought to acknowledge that she would never ever second-guess Angel Valtinos and that he would always take her by surprise. After all, that was how he did business and how he thrived in a cut-throat world.

CHAPTER FIVE

MERRY SHOOK HANDS with her new client, who had
got into a mess with his tax returns, and promised to
update him on the situation within the week. Soon
she would have to try to fit in a refresher course to
update her knowledge of recent legislative changes,
she reflected thoughtfully, incredibly keen to think
of anything other than the awareness that Angel was
sliding supple as a dancer out of his car as her visitor departed.

Sybil had swooped in to take enthusiastic charge
of Elyssa soon after Angel's earlier departure. Hearing of the lunch plan, she had laughed and drily observed, 'He's treating you to a charm offensive. Well,
if you must have a serious talk with him, it'll be
easier not to have Elyssa grizzling for her lunch and
her nap in the midst of it. Phone me when you want
to steal her back.'

And once again, Merry had reflected how very,
very lucky she had always been to have Sybil in her
life, standing by her when life was tough, advising
and supporting her, in short being the only caring

mother figure that she had ever known. Sybil had cured the hurts inflicted by her kid sister's lack of interest in and impatience with her child and, although Merry knew her aunt had been disappointed when she became pregnant without being in a serious relationship, she had kept her disappointment to herself and had instead focused her attention on how best to help her expectant niece.

'Lunch,' Angel told her carelessly, carting a large luxurious hamper in one hand.

'I've got a terrace out the back. Since it's sunny, we might as well eat there,' Merry suggested, preferring the idea of that casual setting in which she thought Angel would be less intimidating.

'This is unexpectedly pleasant,' Angel remarked, sprawling down with innate grace on a wrought-iron chair and taking in the pleasant view of fields and wooded hills visible beyond the hedge.

'This was Sybil's Christmas surprise for us,' Merry explained. 'Her last tenant was elderly and the garden was overgrown. Sybil hired someone to fix it up and now Elyssa will have somewhere safe to play when she's more mobile.'

'You're very close to your aunt,' Angel commented warily. 'She doesn't like me.'

Crystalline blue eyes collided with his in challenge. 'What did you expect?' she traded.

Angel had not been prepared to meet with a condemnation that bold and unapologetic and his teeth clenched, squaring his aggressive jaw, the faint dark shadow of stubble already roughening his bronzed skin accentuating the hard slant of his shapely mouth.

'Yes, you ensured I had enough money to survive but that was that,' Merry stated before he could remind her of the reality.

Angel sidestepped that deeply controversial issue by ignoring it. Instead he opened the hamper and stacked utensils and dishes on the table and asked where his daughter was. After all, what could he say about his treatment of Merry? The facts were the facts and he couldn't change them. He knew he had done everything wrong and he had acknowledged that. Didn't his honesty and his regret lighten the scales even a little? Was she expecting him to grovel on hands and knees?

'Wow…this is some spread,' Merry remarked uneasily as she set out the food and he uncorked the bottle of wine and filled the glasses with rich red liquid. 'Where did it come from?'

'From one of my hotels,' Angel responded with the nonchalance that was the sole preserve of the very rich.

Merry placed a modest selection of savoury bites on her plate and said tensely, 'What did you want to discuss?'

'Our future,' Angel delivered succinctly while Tiger sat at his feet with little round pleading eyes pinned to the meat on his fork.

'Nobody can foretell the future,' Merry objected.

'I can where we're concerned,' Angel assured her, every liquid syllable cool as ice. 'Either we spend at least the next ten years fighting it out over Elyssa in court *or*…we get married and *share* her.'

Merry studied him over the top of her wine glass with steadily widening pale blue eyes, and then gulped in more wine than she intended and coughed and spluttered in the most embarrassing manner as she struggled to get a grip on her wildly fluctuating emotions. First he had frightened the life out of her by mentioning a court battle over her beloved daughter, and then he'd sent her spinning with a suggestion she had never dreamt that she would hear from his lips.

'Married?' she emphasised with a curled lip. 'Are you crazy or just trying to unnerve me?'

Having forced himself to pull the pin on the marriage grenade straight away, Angel coiled back in his chair and savoured his wine. 'It's an unnerving idea for me as well. Apart from my mother, who wanders in and out of my properties, I've never lived with a woman before,' he admitted curtly. 'But we do need to think creatively to solve our current problems.'

'I don't have any problems right now. I also can't believe that you want Elyssa so much after one little meeting that you would sink to what is virtually blackmail,' Merry framed coldly, eyes glinting like chipped ice in the sunlight.

'Oh, I would sink a lot lower than that and I think you know it,' Angel traded without shame, unyielding dark golden eyes steady with stubborn resolve. 'I will do whatever I have to do to get what I want…

or in this case to ensure that my daughter benefits from a suitable home.'

'But Elyssa already *has* a suitable home,' Merry pointed out, working hard to stay calm and appear untouched by his threat of legal intervention. 'We're happy here. I have work that I can do at home and we have a decent life.'

'Only not by my standards. Elyssa is my heir and will one day be a very wealthy woman. When you're so prejudiced against spending my money, how do you expect her to adapt to my world when she becomes independent?' he demanded with lethal cool.

Merry compressed her sultry mouth and lifted angrily out of her seat. 'I'm not prejudiced!' she protested. 'I didn't want to *depend* on your money. I simply prefer to stand on my own feet.'

Angel dealt her a perceptive appraisal that made her skin tighten uneasily over her bones. 'Like me, you have trust issues and you're very proud.'

'Don't you tell me that I have trust issues when you know absolutely nothing about me!' Merry practically spat back at him in her fury. 'Newsflash, Angel…we had two sexual encounters, *not* a relationship!'

Angel ran lingering hooded dark eyes over her slender figure and her aggressive stance, remembering that fire in bed, how it had stoked his own and resulted in a conflagration more passionate than anything he had ever known. As a rule, she kept that fire hidden, suppressed beneath her tranquil, prissy little surface, but around him she couldn't manage that feat and he cherished that truth. Anger was much more promising than indifference.

Merry planted her hands on her curvy hips and flung him a fierce look of censure. 'And don't you *dare* look at me like that!' she warned him, helplessly conscious of that smouldering sexual assessment. 'It's rude and inappropriate.'

Angel shifted lithely in his chair, murderously aware of his roaring arousal and the tightness of his jeans and marvelling at the reality that he could actually be enjoying himself in her company, difficult though she was. A slow-burning smile slashed his lean, strong face. 'The burn is still there, *glyka mou*,' he told her. 'But let's concentrate our energies on my solution for our future.'

'That wasn't a solution, that was fanciful nonsense!' Merry hissed back at him. 'You don't want to marry me. You don't want to marry anybody!'

'But I'll do it for Elyssa's benefit because I believe that she needs a father as much as she needs a mother,' Angel asserted levelly. 'A father is not expendable. My father was very important in my life, even though he wasn't able to be there for me as much as he would have liked.'

Unprepared for that level of honesty and gravity from a man as naturally secretive and aloof as Angel, Merry was bemused. 'I never said you were expendable, for goodness' sake,' she argued less angrily. 'That's why I let you finally visit and meet her.'

'How much of a relationship did you have with your own father?' Angel enquired lethally.

Merry's face froze. 'I didn't have one. My mother, Natalie, fell pregnant by her boss and he was married. I met him once but his wife couldn't stand the sight of me, probably because I was the proof of his infidelity,' she conceded uncomfortably. 'He never asked to see me again. When it came to making a choice between me and his wife, naturally he chose his wife.'

'I'm sorry.' Angel disconcerted her with a look of sympathy that hurt her pride as much as a slap would have done.

'Well, I'm not. I got by fine without him,' Merry declared, lifting her chin.

'Maybe you did.' Angel trailed out the word, letting her know he wasn't convinced by her face-saving claim. 'But others don't do so well without paternal guidance. My own mother grew up indulged in every financial way, but essentially without parents who cared enough about her to discipline her. She's well past fifty now, although she doesn't look it, but she's still a rebellious teenager in her own head. I want my daughter to have stability. I don't want her to go wild when she becomes an adult with the world at her feet along with every temptation.'

Involuntarily impressed by that argument, Merry shook her head. 'That's a long way off and if I don't stand in the way of her having a relationship with you now, you'll still be around.'

Angel lounged back in his chair and crossed an ankle over one knee, long, powerful thigh muscles flexing below tight, faded denim. He looked outrageously relaxed, as if he were posing for a publicity shot, and drop-dead gorgeous from the spill of glossy black curls to the golden caramel brilliance of his eyes. Merry dragged her guilty gaze from his thighs and his crotch, sudden heat rising inside her and burning her cheeks. His hard-boned, thoroughly raunchy masculine beauty broke through her defences every time she looked at him and it made her feel like a breathless fan girl.

'But the bottom line is that unless we marry I won't be around *enough*,' Angel intoned with grim emphasis. 'I spend at least fifty per cent of the year abroad. I want her to meet my relatives and learn what it means to be a Valtinos…'

He could have said nothing more calculated to cool Merry's fevered response to him. Dismay filled her because she understood the message he was giving her. As soon as Elyssa was old enough, Angel would be spiriting her out to Greece, taking her away from her mother, leaving Merry behind, shorn of control of what happened in her child's life. It was a sobering prospect.

'Did you mean it…what you said about fighting me in court?' Merry prompted angrily.

'For once in my life I was playing it straight,' Angel declared.

'But where the heck did all this suddenly come from?' Merry demanded in heated denial. 'You didn't want anything to do with us last winter!'

'It took time for me to come to terms with how I felt about fatherhood. At first I thought the most important objective was to conserve my world as it was. I thought I could turn my back on you and my child but I found that I couldn't,' Angel breathed in a roughened undertone as though the words were being extracted forcibly from him. 'I couldn't stop thinking about her...or you.'

'*Me?*' Merry gasped in sharp disbelief. 'Why would you have been thinking about me?'

Angel lifted and dropped a broad shoulder in questioning doubt. 'So, I'm human. Learning that a woman is carrying your child is an unexpectedly powerful discovery—'

'Angel,' Merry cut in without hesitation, 'let's come back down to earth here. Learning that I was pregnant sent you into retreat so fast you left a smoke trail in your wake!'

'And all I learned was that there was no place to run from reality,' Angel countered with sardonic bite. 'I fought my curiosity for a long time before I finally gave way to it and asked to see her. You said no repeatedly but here we are now, supposedly acting like adults. I'm *trying* to be honest... I'm *trying* not to threaten you but I've come to see marriage as the best option for all three of us.'

'You threatened me quite deliberately!' Merry slung at him furiously.

'You need to know that I'm serious and that this is not some whim that will go away if you wait for long enough. I'm here to stay in your lives,' Angel intoned harshly.

'Well, that's going to be rather awkward when it's

not what I want and I will fight you every step of the way!' Merry flung back at him. 'You wanted me out of your life and I got out. You can't force me back.'

'If it means my daughter gets the future she deserves, I will force you,' Angel bit out in a raw, wrathful undertone as he plunged upright, casting a long dark shadow over the table. 'You need to accept that this is not just about you and me any more, it's about *her*!'

Merry paled. 'I do accept that.'

'No, you don't. You're still set on punishing me for the selfish decisions I made and that approach isn't going to get us anywhere. I don't *want* to go to court and fight but I *will* if I have no alternative!' Angel shot at her furiously, dark golden eyes scorching, his Greek accent edging every vowel with piercing sibilance in the afternoon stillness. 'When I asked you to marry me I was trying to show respect!'

'You wouldn't know respect if it bit you on the arse!' Merry flamed back at him with helpless vulgarity. 'And I am so sorry I didn't grovel with gratitude at the offer of a wedding ring the way you obviously expected.'

'No, you're not sorry!' Angel roared back at her equally loudly. 'You enjoyed dragging me over the coals, questioning my motivation and commitment, and not for one minute did you seriously consider what I was offering…'

'Stop shouting at me!' Merry warned him, reeling in shock from that sudden volatile surge of anger from him, not having appreciated that that rage could lie so close to his seemingly cool surface.

'I've said sorry every damn way I know how but you're after revenge, not a way forward, and there's nothing I can do to change that!' Angel growled, throwing open the back door to go back into the house and leave.

There was sufficient truth in that stormy welter of accusations to draw Merry up short and make her question her attitude. 'I'm not after revenge…that's ridiculous!' she protested weakly, closing a staying hand over his arm as he shot her yet another murderous smouldering glance before turning back to the door.

Sorry every damn way I know how rang afresh in her ears and tightened her grip on his muscular forearm. 'Angel, please…let's calm down.'

'For what good reason would I calm down?' Angel raked down at her. 'This was a pointless attempt on my part to change things between us.'

Her teeth were chattering with nerves. 'Yes, I can see that but you storming off in a rage is only going to make things worse,' she muttered ruefully. 'Maybe I haven't been fair to you, maybe I haven't given you a decent hearing, but you came at me with this like a rocket out of nowhere and I don't adapt quickly to new ideas the way you do!'

'You adapted fast enough to me in bed!' Angel husked with sizzling clarity.

'That's your massive ego talking!' Merry launched back at him irately.

'No, it's not,' Angel growled, yanking her up against him, shifting his lithe hips, ensuring she recognised how turned-on he was. 'You make me want you.'

'It's *my* fault?' Merry carolled in disbelief even as her whole body tilted into his, as magnetised by his arousal as a thirsty plant suddenly placed within reach of water. Little tremors were running through her as she struggled to get a grip on the prickling tightness of her nipples and the heat building between her thighs. An unbearable ache followed that she positively shrank from reliving in his vicinity. She wanted to slap herself, she wanted to slap him, she wanted to freeze the moment and replay it *her* way, in which she would draw back from him in withering disgust and say something terribly clever and wounding that would hold him at bay.

'You just can't bring yourself to admit that you're the same,' Angel gritted, bending his arrogant dark head, one hand meshing into the tumble of her hair to drag her head back and expose her throat. His mouth found that slender corded column and nipped and tasted up to her ear, awakening a shower of tingling sensation, and she was electrified and dizzy with longing, wanting what she knew she shouldn't, wanting with a hunger suppressed and denied for too many months, craving the release he could give.

And then he kissed her, crushing her ripe mouth, his tongue plunging and retreating, and she saw stars and whirling multicoloured planets behind her lowered lids while her body fizzed like a firework display, leaving her weak with hunger. She kissed him back, hands rising to delve into the crisp luxuriance of his hair, framing, holding, *needing*. It was frantic, out of control, the way it always was for them.

Angel wrenched her back from him, long brown fingers biting into her slim shoulders to keep her upright and gazing up into his blazing liquid-honey eyes. 'No, I'm not a one-trick pony or a cheap one-night stand. You'll have to marry me to get any more of that,' he told her with derision as he slapped a business card down on the table. 'My phone number…should you think better of your attitude today.'

When he was gone, Merry paced back and forth in her small sitting room, facing certain realities. She hadn't seriously considered Angel's supposed solution. But then that was more his fault than her own. Warning her that he intended to trail her into court and fight for access to their daughter had scarcely acted as a good introduction to his alternative offer. She was angry and bitter and she wasn't about to apologise for the fact, but possibly she should have listened and asked more and lost her temper less.

In addition, Angel's visit had worsened rather than improved their relations because now she knew he was prepared to drag her through the courts in an effort to win greater access to Elyssa. And what if his ambitions did not stop there? What if he intended to try and gain sole custody of their daughter and take Elyssa away from her? Paling and breathing rapidly, Merry decided to visit her aunt and discuss her mounting concern and sense of being under threat with her.

Sybil, however, was nowhere to be found in the comfortable open-plan ground floor of her home and it was only when Merry heard her daughter that she realised her aunt and her daughter were upstairs. She was disconcerted to walk into Sybil's bedroom where Elyssa was playing on the floor and find her aunt trailing clothes out of the wardrobes to pile into the two suitcases sitting open on the bed.

'My goodness, where are you going?' Merry demanded in surprise.

Sybil dealt her a shamefaced glance. 'I meant to phone you but I had so many other calls to make that I didn't get a chance. Your mother's in trouble and I'm flying out to Perth to be with her,' she told her.

Merry blinked in astonishment. 'Trouble?' she queried.

Sybil grimaced. 'Keith's been having an affair and he's walked out on your mother. She's suicidal, poor lamb.'

'Oh, dear,' Merry framed, sinking down on the edge of the bed to lift her daughter onto her lap. She was sad to hear that news, but her troubled relationship with her dysfunctional parent prevented her from feeling truly sympathetic and that fact always filled her with remorse. Not for the first time she marvelled that Sybil could be so forgiving of her kid sister's frailties. Time and time again she had watched her aunt wade into Natalie's emotional dramas and rush to sort them out with infinite supportive compassion. Sometimes, too, Merry wondered why it was that she, Natalie's daughter, could not be so forgiving, so tolerant, so willing to offer another fresh chance. Possibly that could be because Merry remembered Natalie's resentment of her as a child too strongly, she told herself guiltily. Natalie hadn't wanted to be anyone's Mummy and her constant rejections had deeply wounded Merry.

'Oh, dear, indeed,' her aunt sighed worriedly. 'Natalie was distraught when she phoned me and you *know* she does stupid things when she's upset! She really shouldn't be alone right now.'

'Doesn't she have any friends out there?' Merry prompted.

Sybil frowned, clearly finding Merry's response unfeeling. 'Family's family and you and her don't get on well enough for you to go. Nor would it be right to subject Elyssa to that journey. Natalie wouldn't want a baby around either,' she conceded ruefully.

'She really can't be bothered with young children,' Merry agreed wryly. 'Do you *have* to go?'

Sybil looked pained by that question. 'Merry, she's got nobody else!' she proclaimed, sharply defensive in both speech and manner. 'Of course, that means I'm landing you with looking after things here…will you be able to manage the centre? Nicky is free to take over for you from next week. I've already spoken to her about it. Between minding Elyssa and running your own business, you're not able to drop everything for me right now.'

'But I would've managed,' Merry assured the

older woman, resisting the urge to protest her aunt's decision to call on the help of an old friend, rather than her niece. Seeing the lines of tension and anxiety already indenting Sybil's face, Merry decided to keep what had happened with Angel to herself. Right now, her aunt had enough on her plate and didn't need any additional stress from Merry's corner.

That evening, once Elyssa was bathed and tucked into her cot, Merry opened a bottle of wine. Sybil had already departed for the first flight she had been able to book and Merry was feeling more than a little lonely. She lifted her laptop and put Angel's name into a search engine. It was something she had never allowed herself to do before, deeming any such information-gathering online to be unhealthy and potentially obsessional. Now drinking her wine, she didn't care any more because her spirits were low and in need of distraction.

A cascade of photos lined up and in a driven mood of defiance she clicked on them one after another. Unsurprisingly, Angel looked shockingly good in pictures. Her lip curled and she refilled her glass, sipping it while she browsed, only to freeze when she saw the most recent photo of Angel with the same blonde he had brought to lunch with his father the day Merry had told him that she was pregnant. That photo had been taken only the night before at some charitable benefit: Angel, the ultimate in the socialite stakes in a designer dinner jacket, smooth and sleek and gorgeous, and his blonde companion,

Roula Paulides, ravishing in a tight glittering dress that exposed an astonishing amount of her chest.

She was Greek too, a woman Angel would presumably have much more in common with. Merry fiercely battled the urge to do an online search on Roula as well. What was she? A stalker?

She finished her glass of wine and grabbed the bottle up in a defiant move to fill the glass again. Well, she was glad she had looked, wasn't she? The very night before he proposed marriage to Merry, Angel had been in another woman's company and had probably spent the night in her bed. Even worse the sexy blonde was clearly an unusual woman, being one who was an enduring interest in Angel's life and not one of the more normal options, who swanned briefly on scene and then was never seen again with him.

Merry fought the turbulent swell of emotion tightening her chest, denying that it hurt, denying that it bothered her in the slightest to discover that Angel was still seeing that same blonde all these many months later. But denial didn't work in the mood she was in as she sat sipping her wine and staring into the middle distance, angry bitterness threatening to consume her.

How *dared* he propose to her only hours after being in another woman's company? How *dared* he condemn her for not taking him seriously? And how dared he come on to her as he had out on the terrace before he'd left? Didn't he have any morals at all?

Any conscience? And how could she even begin to be jealous over such a brazen, incurable playboy?

And yet she *was* jealous, Merry acknowledged wretchedly, stupidly, pointlessly jealous of a thoroughly fickle, unreliable man. Rage flared inside her afresh as she recalled that careless suggestion that they marry. Oh, he had played that marriage proposal down, all right, shoving it on the table without ceremony or even a hint of romance. Was it any wonder that she had not taken that suggestion seriously?

In a sudden movement Merry flew out of her seat and stalked out to the kitchen to lift the business card Angel had left with her. She was texting him before she had even thought through what she wanted to say…

Do you realise that if you married me you would have to give up other women?

Angel studied the screen of his phone in disbelief. He was dining with his brother Vitale and the sudden text from an unfamiliar number that belonged to Merry took him aback. He breathed in deep, his wide, sensual mouth compressing with exasperation.

Are you finally taking me seriously? If I married you there would be NO OTHER WOMEN.

Merry had texted him in shouty capitals.
'Problems?' Vitale hazarded.
Angel shook his dark head and grinned while won-

dering if Merry was drunk. He just could not imagine her being that blunt otherwise. Merry of all women drunk-dialling him, Merry who was always so careful, so restrained. A sudden and quite shocking degree of wondering satisfaction gripped Angel, washing away his edgy tension, his conviction that he had made a fatal misstep with her and a hash of their meeting.

And no other men for you either.

He pointed this out with pleasure in his reply.

That wasn't a problem for Merry, who was stunned that he was replying to her so quickly. In truth, she had never ever wanted anyone as much as she wanted Angel Valtinos. All thoughts of kindly and dependable Fergus flew from her mind. She didn't like the fact and certainly wasn't proud of it. Indeed, she wouldn't have admitted it even if Angel slow-roasted her over an open fire but it was, indisputably, the secret reality she lived with.

'Who are you texting?' his brother demanded.

'My daughter's mother.' Angel shot his sibling a triumphant glance. 'I believe that you will be standing up at my wedding for me as soon as I can get it arranged.'

Vitale frowned. 'I thought you crashed and burned?'

'Obviously not,' Angel savoured, still texting, keener yet to get a clear response.

Exclusivity approved. Are you agreeing to marry me?

* * *

Merry froze, suddenly shocked back to real life and questioning what she was doing. What *was* she doing? Raging, burning jealousy had almost eaten her alive when she saw that blonde with him again.

We'd have to talk about that.

I'm a doer, not a talker. You have to give me a chance.

But he'd had his chance with her and wrecked it, Merry reminded herself feverishly. He didn't do feelings or proper relationships outside his own family circle. Yet there was something curiously and temptingly seductive about proud, arrogant Angel asking *her* to give *him* another chance.

She decided to give him a warning.

One LAST chance.

YES! WE HAVE A DEAL!

Angel texted back with amusement and an intense sense of achievement.

He had won. He had gained his daughter, the precious chance to bring Elyssa into his life instead of losing her. In addition, he would be gaining a wife, a very unusual wife, who didn't want his money. Another man would have celebrated that reality but, when it came to women, Angel was always suspicious, always looking out for hidden motives and secret objectives. Women were complicated, which was why he never got involved and never dipped below the shallow surface with his lovers...and Merry was infinitely *more* complicated than the kind of women he was familiar with.

Could such a marriage work?

Only time would tell, he reflected with uncharacteristic gravity. No other women, he pondered abstractedly. Well, he hadn't been prepared for that demand, he acknowledged ruefully, having proposed marriage while intending the union as more of a convenient parental partnership than anything more personal. After all, he knew several couples who contrived to lead separate lives below the same roof while remaining safely married. They stayed together for the sake of their children or to protect their wealth from the damage of divorce, but nothing more emotional was involved.

In reality, Angel had never seen anything positive about the marital state. The official Valtinos outlook on marriage was that it was generally disastrous and extremely expensive. His own mother's infidelity had ensured that his parents had parted by the time he was four years old. His grandparents had enjoyed an equally calamitous union while shunning divorce in favour of living in separate wings of the same house. Nor was Angel's attitude softened by the number of cheating spouses he had met over the years. In his early twenties, Angel had automatically assumed that he would never marry.

But, self-evidently, Merry had a very different take on marriage and parenthood, a much more conventional take than a cynical and distrustful Valtinos. Here she was demanding fidelity upfront as though it was the very bedrock of stability. And maybe it *was*, Angel conceded dimly, reflecting on the constant turmoil caused by his mother's rampant promiscuity. He thought equally hard about the little scene of apparent domestic contentment he had glimpsed at his cousin's house, where a husband rushed into his home to greet a wife and children whom he obviously valued and missed. That glimpse had provided Angel with a disturbing vision of another world that had never been visible to him before, a much more personalised and intimate version of marriage.

And Merry, it seemed, had chosen to view his suggestion of marriage as being personal, *very* personal, rather than practical as he had envisioned. Beneath his brother's exasperated gaze, Angel lounged back in his dining chair, his meal untouched, and for the first time in his life smiled with slashing brilliance at the prospect of acquiring a wife and a wedding ring...

CHAPTER SIX

'YOU SHOULD'VE WARNED Angelina,' Charles Russell censured his son while they waited at the church. 'Your mother isn't ready to be a grandmother.'

'Tough,' Angel dismissed with sardonic bite. 'I'm thirty-three, not a teenager. It shouldn't be that much of a surprise.'

Always more sympathetic to other people's vulnerabilities, Charles sighed. 'She can't help being vain. She is what she is. By not telling her in advance, you're risking her causing a scene.'

On her way to the church that same morning, Merry was lost in the weird daze that had engulfed her from the moment she had agreed by text to marry Angel. She was stunned by what she had done in the hold of more wine and jealousy than sense but, in the two weeks that had passed, any urge to renege on the deal Angel had named it had slowly faded away. She wasn't willing to walk away from Angel Valtinos and face a court battle for custody of her daughter. She was also fully aware that he had blackmailed her into marriage and was quite unsurprised by his ruthlessness, having seen how he operated on the business front.

Angel would undoubtedly hurt her but when push came to shove she had decided that she would infinitely rather have him as a husband than not have him at all. He would be hers with a ring on his finger and she would have to settle for that level of commitment, was certainly not building any little fantasies in which Angel, the unfeeling, would start doing feelings. She was trying to be realistic, trying to be practical about their prospects and she would have been happier on her wedding day had she not somehow contrived to have a massively upsetting row with Sybil about her plans.

Quite how that dreadful schism had opened, Merry had no very clear idea. Her aunt had been understandably shocked and astonished when Merry had phoned her in Australia to announce that she was getting married. Sybil had urged her to wait until she got home and could discuss that major step with her. But Merry, fearful of losing her nerve to marry a man who did not love her, had refused to wait and Sybil had taken that refusal to wait for her counsel badly. The more Sybil had criticised Angel and his reputation as a womaniser, the stiffer and more stubborn Merry had become. She was very well acquainted with Angel's flaws but had not enjoyed having them rammed down her throat in very blunt words by her protective aunt. It was all very well, she had realised, for *her* to criticise Angel, but inexplicably something else entirely for anyone else to do it.

And throughout the past tumultuous and busy two weeks, Angel had been terrific in trying to organise everything to ensure that Merry could cope with the gigantic life change he was inflicting on her. Unfortunately, it was also true that between their various commitments they had barely seen each other. Handing Tiger over to the new owner Sybil had approved had been upsetting because she had become very fond of the little dog and only hoped that his quirks would not irritate in his new home.

Angel had had so much business to take care of while Merry had been engaged in closing down her own business and packing. Even so, Angel had managed to meet with her twice in London to see Elyssa and in his unfamiliar restraint she had recognised the same desire not to rock the boat that beat like an unnerving storm warning through her every fibre. He had been very detached but playful and surprisingly hands-on with Elyssa. It was clear to her that Angel didn't want to risk doing anything that could potentially disrupt their marital plans and deprive him of shared custody of their daughter.

Of course it would take time for Angel to adapt to the idea of marriage and a family of his own and Merry appreciated that reality. He wasn't going to be perfect from the word go, but the imperfect that warned her that he was trying hard was enough to satisfy her…admittedly somewhat low…expectations. She couldn't set the bar too high for him at the start, she told herself urgently. She had to compromise and concentrate on what was truly important.

And what could be more important than Elyssa and seizing the opportunity to provide her daughter with a father? Merry knew what it was like to live with a yawning space in her paternal background. She had never known her father and, unpleasant though it was to acknowledge, her father hadn't cared enough to seek her out to get to know her. But Angel *was* making that effort, right down to having interviewed nannies with Merry to find the one he thought would be most suitable. Entirely raised by nannies before boarding school, Angel had contrived to ask questions that wouldn't even have occurred to Merry and she had been impressed by his concern on their daughter's behalf and his determination to choose the most caring candidate.

So what if his input on the actual wedding and their future relationship had been virtually non-existent? He had hired a wedding organiser to take care of the arrangements and hadn't seemed to care in the slightest about the details that had unexpectedly consumed Merry. Was that just Angel being a man or a dangerous sign that he couldn't care less about the woman he was about to marry? Merry stifled a shiver, rammed down the fear that had flared and contemplated her manicured fingernails with rampant nervous tension. She had made her choice and she had to live with it when the alternative was so much worse and so much emptier. Surely it was better to give marriage a chance?

It had been embarrassing to tell Fergus that she was marrying Angel but he had taken the news in good part, possibly having already worked out that she was still far from indifferent to her daughter's father.

The first shock of Merry's wedding day was the unexpected sight of Sybil waiting on the church steps, a tall, slender figure attired in a very elegant blue dress and brimmed hat. Eyes wide with astonishment, Merry emerged from the limousine that had ferried her to the church from the hotel where she had stayed the night before and exclaimed in shaken disbelief, 'Sybil?'

'Obviously I couldn't miss your big day, darling. I got back in the early hours,' Sybil breathed with a revealing shimmer in her eyes as she reached for Merry's hand. 'I'm so sorry about the things I said. I overstepped, interfered—'

'No, I was too touchy!' Merry slotted in, stretching up on tiptoe to press a forgiving kiss to the older woman's cheek. 'You were shocked, of course you were.'

'Yes, especially as you're contriving to do what I never managed…you're getting married,' Sybil murmured fondly. 'And you didn't do too badly at all picking that dress without my advice. It's a stunner.'

Her heartache subsiding in the balm of her aunt's reassuring presence, Merry grinned. 'Your voice was in my head when I was choosing. Tailored, structured,' she teased, stepping into the church porch. 'Where's Angel's father? He offered to walk me down the aisle, which I thought was very kind of him.'

'Yes, quite the charmer, that man,' Sybil pronounced a shade tartly, evidently having already met

Charles Russell. 'But I told him he could sit back down because I'm here now and I'll do the long walk.'

'I think you'd rather take a long walk off a plank,' Merry warned the older woman gently.

Sybil squeezed the hand she was gripping and smiled warmly down at the young woman who had been more her daughter than her niece, only to stiffen nervously at the prospect of the confession that she knew she *had* to make some time soon. Natalie had asked her to tell Merry the truth and Sybil was now duty-bound to reveal that family secret. Sadly, telling that same truth had shattered her relationship with Natalie when Natalie was eighteen years old and she could only hope that it would not have the same devastating effect on her bond with Merry and her child.

Gloriously ignorant of that approaching emotional storm, Merry smoothed down her dress, which effortlessly delineated the high curve of her breasts and her neat waist before falling softly to her feet, lending her a shapely silhouette. Straightening her slight shoulders, she lifted her head high, her short flirty veil dancing round her flushed face, accentuating the light blue of her eyes.

Even before she went down the aisle, she heard Elyssa chuckling. Her daughter was in the care of her new nanny, a lovely down-to-earth young woman from Yorkshire called Sally, who had impressed both Merry and Angel with her genuine warmth and interest in children. Merry's eyes skimmed from her daughter's curly head and waving arms as she danced on Sally's knee and settled on Angel, poised at the

altar with an equally tall dark male, Vitale, whose
resemblance to Angel echoed his obvious family relationship to his brother. But Angel had the edge in
Merry's biased opinion, the lean, beautiful precision
of his bronzed features highlighting the shimmering
brilliance of his dark eyes and his undeniable hold
on her attention.

Her breath caught in her dry throat and butter-
flies ran amok in her tummy, her chest stretched so
tightly that her lungs felt compressed. Her hand slid
off Sybil's arm, suddenly nerveless as she reached
the altar to be greeted by the Greek Orthodox priest.
Angel gripped her cold fingers, startling her, and she
glanced up at him, noticing the tension stamped in
his strong cheekbones and the compressed line of
his wide, sensual mouth. Yes, getting wed had to be
a sheer endurance test for a wayward playboy like
Angel Valtinos, Merry reflected with rueful amusement, but it was an unfortunate thought because she
started wondering then whether he would find the
tedious domestic aspects of family life and the unchanging nature of a wife a trial and a bore. The service marched on regardless of her teeming anxiety.
The vows were exchanged, an ornately plaited gold
wedding ring that she savoured for its distinctive-
ness and his selection of it slid onto her finger and
then a matching one onto his.

And then, jolting her out of the powerful spell
that Angel cast, Charles Russell surged up to her to
kiss her warmly on both cheeks, closely followed
by Sybil, who strove to conceal her shotgun attitude

to Angel with bright, determined positivity. Elyssa, seated in a nearby pew on Sally's lap, held out her arms and wailed pathetically for her mother.

'That little chancer knows how to pick her moment,' Sybil remarked wryly as Merry bent to accept her daughter and hoisted her up, only to be intercepted by Angel, who snagged his daughter mid-manoeuvre, saying that the bride could scarcely cart a child down the aisle.

'Says who?' Merry teased, watching Elyssa pluck at his curls and his tie with nosy little hands, watching Angel suddenly slant a grin at his lack of control over the situation. Once again she found herself suppressing her surprise at his flexibility when at the mercy of a wilful baby.

Angel maintained a grip on his daughter for the handful of photos taken on the church steps. Merry watched paparazzi wield cameras behind a barrier warded by security guards, their interest visibly sharpened by her daughter's first public appearance. Her eyes widened in dismay when she finally recognised how much her life and Elyssa's were about to change. For years, Angel's every move had been fodder for the tabloid press. He had his own jet, his own yacht and the glitzy lifestyle of great wealth and privilege. His very marked degree of good looks and predilection for scantily dressed blonde beauties only added to his media appeal. Naturally his sudden marriage and the apparent existence of a young child were worthy of even closer scrutiny. Merry wondered gloomily if she would be denounced as a fertile scheming former Valtinos employee.

As they were moving towards the limousine to depart for the hotel another limo drew up ahead of them and a tiny brunette on skyrocketing heels leapt out in a flurry of colourful draperies and a feathered hat. She was as exquisite as a highly sophisticated and perfectly groomed doll. 'Oh, Charles, have I missed it?' she exclaimed very loudly while all around her cameras began to flash.

Angel murmured something very terse in Greek while his father moved off to perform the welcome that his son clearly wasn't in the mood to offer to the late-arriving guest. Angel relocated Elyssa with Sally and swept Merry into their vehicle without further ado.

'Who was that?' Merry demanded, filled with curiosity, glancing out of the window to note that the brunette was actually lodged at the security barriers exchanging comments with the paparazzi while posing like a professional. 'Is she a model or something?'

'Or something,' Angel breathed with withering impatience. 'That's Angelina.'

'Your *mother*?' Merry gasped in disbelief. 'She *can't* be! She doesn't look old enough.'

'And it's typical of her to miss the ceremony. She hates weddings,' Angel divulged. 'At a wedding the bride is the centre of attention and Angelina Valtinos cannot bear to be one of the crowd.'

Merry frowned. 'Oh, I'm sure she's not as bad as that,' she muttered, chiding him.

'No doubt you'll make your own mind up on that score,' Angel responded wryly, visibly reluctant to say any more on the topic of his mother.

'Is she likely to be the interfering mother-in-law type?' Merry prompted apprehensively.

'*Thee mou*, you have to be kidding!' Angel emitted a sharp cynical laugh. 'She couldn't care less that I've got married or who I've married but she'll be furious that I've made her a grandmother because she will see that as aging.'

Merry could not comprehend the idea of such an attitude. Sybil had approached maturity with grace, freely admitting that she found it more relaxing not to always be fretting about her appearance.

'I love the dress.' Swiftly changing the unwelcome subject, Angel enveloped Merry in a smouldering appraisal that somehow contrived to encompass the ripe swell of her breasts below the fitted bodice. 'You have a spectacular figure.'

Heat surged into Merry's cheeks at that unexpected and fairly basic compliment. His fierce appraisal emanated raw male appreciation. Her stomach performed a sudden somersault, a shard of hunger piercing her vulnerable body with the stabbing accuracy of a knife that couldn't be avoided. He could do that to her simply with a look, a tone, a smile. It always, *always* unnerved her, making her feel out of control.

The reception was being held at a five-star exclusive city hotel. Merry met her mother-in-law for the first time over the pre-dinner drinks. By then Angelina Valtinos had a young and very handsome Italian man on her arm, whom she airily introduced as Primo. She said very little, asked nothing and virtually ignored her son, as though she blamed him for the necessity of her having to attend his wedding.

'She's even worse in person than I expected,' Sybil hissed in a tone most unlike her.

'Shush...time will tell,' Merry said with a shrug.

'I wish that wretched man would take a hint,' Sybil complained as Charles Russell hurried forward with a keen smile to escort her aunt to their seats at the top table.

Merry tried not to laugh, having quickly grasped that Angel's father had one of those drivingly energetic and assured natures that steamrollered across Sybil's polite lack of interest without even noticing it. But then she had equally quickly realised that she liked her father-in-law for his unquestioning acceptance of their sudden marriage. His enthusiastic response to Elyssa had also spelled out the message that he was one of those men who absolutely adored children. He exuded all the warmth and welcome that his ex-wife, Angelina, conspicuously lacked.

Angel's brother, Prince Vitale, drifted over to exchange a few words. He was very smooth, very sophisticated and civil, but Merry was utterly intimidated by him. From the moment Angel had explained that his half-brother was of royal birth and the heir to the throne of a small, fabulously rich European country, Merry had been nervous of meeting him.

A slender blonde grasped Merry's hand and, look-

ing up at the taller woman, Merry froze in consternation. Recognition was instant: it was the *same* blonde
she had twice seen in Angel's company, a slender,
leggy young woman in her early thirties with sparkling brown eyes and an easy, confident smile.

'Merry…allow me to introduce Roula Paulides,
one of my oldest friends,' Angel proffered warmly.

With difficulty, Merry flashed a smile onto her
stiff lips, her colour rising because she was mortified by her instant stiffening defensiveness with the
other woman. An old friend, she should've thought
of that possibility, she scolded herself. That more
than anything else explained Angel's enduring relationship with the beautiful blonde. Unfortunately,
Roula Paulides was stunning and very much Angel's
type. Even worse and mortifyingly, she was the same
woman who had been lunching with Angel on the
dreadful dark day when Merry had had to tell him
that she was pregnant.

It was only when Sally retrieved Elyssa to whisk
her upstairs for a nap that Angel's mother finally approached Merry. A thin smile on her face, she said,
'Angel really should have warned me that his bride
already had a child.'

'He should've done,' Merry agreed mildly.

'Your daughter is very young. Who is her father?'
Angelina demanded with a ringing clarity that encouraged several heads to turn in their direction. 'I
hope you are aware that she cannot make use of the
Valtinos name.'

'I think you'll find you're wrong about that,' Sybil

declared as she strolled over to join her niece with
a protective gleam in her gaze. 'Elyssa is a Valtinos too.'

Angel's mother stiffened, her eyes widening, her
rosebud mouth tightening with disbelief. 'My son
has a child with you?' she gasped, stricken. 'That
can't be true!'

'It is,' Merry cut in hurriedly, keen to bring the
fraught conversation to an end.

'He should've married Roula... I always thought
that if he married anyone, it would be Roula,' Angelina Valtinos volunteered in a tone of bitter complaint.

'Well, tact isn't one of her skills,' Sybil remarked
ruefully when they were alone again. 'Who's Roula?
Or don't you know?'

Merry felt humiliated by the tense little scene and
her mother-in-law's closing comment about Roula
Paulides. Roula, evidently, was something more than
a harmless old friend, she gathered unhappily.

Meanwhile, shaken by what she had learned and
very flushed, Angelina stalked to the end of the table
to approach her son, who was talking to Vitale. A
clearly hostile and brief dialogue took place between
mother and son before the older woman careened angrily away again to snatch a glass of champagne off
a passing waiter's tray and drop down into her chair.

Sybil's eyes met Merry's but neither of them commented.

'Your mother's all worked up about Elyssa,' Merry
acknowledged when Angel sank fluidly down into
his seat by her side. 'Why?'

'The horror of being old enough to be a grandparent,' Angel proffered wryly.

'Are you serious?'

'There's nothing we can do about it. She'll have to learn to deal.'

'Do you see much of your mother?' Merry probed uneasily.

'More than I sometimes wish. She makes use of all my properties,' Angel admitted flatly. 'But if she wants that arrangement to continue she will have to tone herself down.'

As the afternoon wore on Merry watched Angel's mother drink like a fish and then put on a sparkling display on the dance floor with Primo. She did not behave like a woman likely to tone her extrovert nature down. Merry also saw Angelina seek out Roula Paulides and sit with the blonde for a long time while enjoying an animated conversation. So, she was unlikely to be flavour of the month with her mother-in-law any time soon, Merry told herself wryly. Well, she could live with that, she decided, secure in the circle of Angel's arms as they moved round the dance floor. His lean, powerful body against hers sparked all sorts of disconcerting responses. The prickly awareness of proximity and touch rippled through her in stormy, ever-rolling waves. She rested her head down on his shoulder, drinking in the raw, evocative scent of him like a drug she could not live without and only just resisting the urge to lick the strong brown column of his masculine throat.

Early evening, the newly married couple flew out

to Greece and the Valtinos home on the island of Palos where Angel had been born. Merry was madly curious about the small island and the darkness that screened her view of it frustrated her. Serried lines of light ascending a hillside illuminated a small white village above the bay as the helicopter came in to land. A pair of SUVs picked them up, ferrying them up a steep road lined with cypress trees to the ultramodern house hugging the promontory. Like a giant cruise ship, the entire house seemed to be lit up.

They stepped out into the warmth of a dusky evening and mounted the steps into the house. Staff greeted them in an octagonal marble hall ornamented by contemporary pieces of sculpture.

'Sally will take Elyssa straight to bed,' Angel decreed, closing his hand over Merry's before she could dart off in the wake of her daughter. 'She's so tired she'll sleep. This is *our* night.'

Merry coloured, suddenly insanely conscious of the ridiculous fact that she had barely acknowledged that it was their wedding night. She was tempted to argue that she had to take care of Elyssa, but was too well aware of their nanny's calm efficiency to tilt at windmills. Even so, because she was accustomed to being a full-time mother, she found it difficult to step back from the role and accept that someone else could do the job almost as well. Her slender fingers scrabbled indecisively in the grip of Angel's large masculine hand until she finally followed his lead and the staff already moving ahead of them with their bags.

'Supper has been prepared for us. We'll eat in our room,' Angel told her lazily. 'I'm glad to be home. You'll love it here. Midsummer it can be unbearably hot but in June Palos is lush with growth and the air is fresh.'

'I didn't realise that you were so attached to your home,' Merry confided, running her attention over the display of impressive paintings in the corridor.

'Palos has been the Valtinos base for generations,' Angel told her. 'The original house was demolished and rebuilt by my grandfather. He fancied himself as something of an architect but his design ambitions were thwarted when he and my grandmother split up and she refused to move out. His house plan was then divided in two, one half for him, the other half for her and it's still like that. Some day I hope to turn it back into one house.'

Merry was frowning. 'Your grandparents divorced?'

'No, neither of them wanted a divorce, but after my mother's birth they separated. He was an incorrigible Romeo and she couldn't live with him,' Angel admitted as carved wooden doors were spread back at the end of the corridor. 'I never knew either of them. My grandfather didn't marry until he was almost sixty and my grandmother was in her forties when my mother was born. They died before my parents married.'

On the threshold, Merry paused to admire the magnificent bedroom. An opulent seating area took up one corner of the vast room. Various doors led

off to bathroom facilities and a large and beautifully fitted dressing room where staff were already
engaged in unpacking their cases. A table sat beside
patio doors that led out onto a terrace overlooking
a fabulous infinity swimming pool lit with under-
water lights. In the centre of the room a giant bed
fit for Cleopatra and draped in spicy Mediterranean
colours sat on elaborate gilded feet. Her expressive
face warmed, her pulses humming beneath her calm
surface because she ached for him, and that awareness of her own hunger embarrassed her as nothing
else could because she was mortifyingly conscious
that she had no control around Angel.

'Let's eat,' Angel suggested lazily.

A slender figure clad in loose linen trousers and
an emerald-green top with ties, Merry took a seat.
She had dressed comfortably for the flight and had
marvelled that, even in designer jeans and a black
shirt, Angel could still look far more sleek and sophisticated than she did. No matter what he wore, he
had that knack, if there was such a thing, of always
looking classy and exclusive.

Wine was poured, the first course delivered. It
was all food calculated to tempt the appetite, nothing
heavy or over spiced and, because she hadn't eaten
much at the wedding, Merry ate hungrily. During
the main course, she heard splashing from the direction of the pool and then a sudden bout of high-
pitched giggling. She began awkwardly to twist her
head around to look outside.

'Diavole!' Angel swore with a sudden frown, flying upright to thrust open the doors onto the terrace.

Merry rose to her feet more slowly and followed him to see what had jerked him out of his seat as though rudely yanked up by invisible steel wires. She was very much taken aback to discover that the source of the noise was her mother-in-law and her boyfriend, both of whom appeared to be cavorting naked in the pool. She blinked in disbelief while Angel addressed the pair in angry Greek. Primo reacted first, hauling himself hurriedly out of the water and yanking a towel off a lounger to wind it round his waist. Angelina hissed back at her son in furious Greek before leaving the pool by the steps, stark naked and evidently quite unconcerned by that reality. Her companion strode forward to toss her a robe, his discomfiture at the interruption unhidden. Angel's mother, however, took her time about covering up, her tempestuous fury at Angel's intrusion fuelling a wealth of outraged objections.

Merry swallowed hard on her growing embarrassment while Angel stood his ground, his dark deep voice sardonic and clipped with derision as he switched to English. 'You will not use this pool while I, my wife or my daughter are in residence.'

'This is my home!' Angelina proclaimed. 'You have no right to make a demand like that!'

'This house belongs to me and there are now rules to be observed,' Angel sliced back harshly. 'If you cannot respect those rules, find somewhere else to stay on the island.'

And with that final ringing threat, Angel swung back and pressed a hand to Merry's shoulder to guide her firmly back indoors. His mother ranted back at him in Greek and he ignored the fact, ramming shut the doors again and returning to their interrupted meal.

Unnerved by what she had witnessed, Merry dropped heavily back into her chair, her face hot with unease. 'I think your mother's had too much to drink.'

Angel shot her a grim glance. 'Don't make excuses for her. I should have told her that she was no longer welcome here *before* we married. Her conduct is inappropriate and I refuse to have you or Elyssa subjected to her behaviour in what is now your home.'

Merry sipped at her wine, stunned by the display she had witnessed and wondering helplessly what it had been like for him to grow up with so avant-garde a mother. Angelina seemed to have no boundaries, no concept of what was acceptable. It must have been a nightmare to grow up in the care of so self-indulgent a woman. For the first time she understood why Angel was so close to his father: he only had one parent, he had only *ever* had one parent. Parenting had been something that Angelina Valtinos had probably never done and she understood why Angel had been placed in a boarding school at a very young age.

As silence reclaimed the pool beyond the terrace, Angel audibly expelled his breath, the fierce tension in his lean, darkly handsome features and the set of his wide shoulders fading. He was determined that Merry would not be embarrassed by his mother's attention-grabbing tactics. Merry was too prim to comfortably cope with the scenes his mother liked to throw. In any case, his wife was entitled to the older woman's respect. Angelina could dislike her all she wished but, ultimately, she had to accept that her son's wife was the new mistress of the house and had the right to expect certain standards of behaviour.

'How is it that the family home belongs to you and not to your mother?' Merry asked curiously.

'My grandmother survived my grandfather by several months. She was never able to control her daughter and once she realised that Angelina was pregnant, she left this house to my mother's descendants rather than to her,' he advanced.

Merry frowned. 'That's kind of sad.'

'Don't feel sorry for Angelina. My grandfather adored her and endowed her with a massive trust fund. All her life she has done exactly what she wanted to do, regardless of how it harms or affects others. At some stage, there's got to be a price to pay for that,' Angel declared with dry finality. 'I have long wished that my mother would buy her own property where she could do as she likes without involving me.'

'Why doesn't she do that?' Merry asked with genuine curiosity.

'The ownership of property involves other responsibilities. Hiring staff, maintenance, running costs…all the adult stuff,' he pointed out with a sardonic twist of his wide, sensual mouth. 'My mother avoids responsibility of any kind. May we drop this subject?'

'Of course,' Merry conceded, a little breathless while she collided with smouldering dark eyes and sipped at her wine. Her mind, however, remained awash with conjecture about her mother-in-law and her disconnected and antagonistic relationship with her son. At the same time she wasn't worried about Angelina causing trouble between them because she could see that Angel had few illusions about his parent and intended to protect her from any fallout. And that made her a little sad, made her wonder what it must have been like for him to be saddled with a spoilt heiress of a mother, a party girl, who flatly refused to accept responsibility and grow up. A mother who, from what she could see, had never behaved like a normal mother. Surely that truth must've lessened his respect for women and his ability to trust her sex, she reasoned helplessly.

'Let's concentrate on us,' Angel suggested with emphatic cool.

She felt overheated and her mouth ran dry. Her entire body tensed, tiny little tremors shimmying through her pelvis, tremors of awareness, arousal and anticipation. She was embarrassed by the level of her sheer susceptibility, shaken by the power he had over her, suddenly wondering if he too knew the full extent of it…

CHAPTER SEVEN

ANGEL GRASPED HER HAND and eased her up out of her seat. 'I have a special request,' he admitted almost harshly.

Enthralled by the golden glimmer of his intense appraisal, Merry moistened her dry lips with the tip of her tongue. 'And what would that be?'

Long fingers flicked the silken bell of hair that fell to just below her shoulders. 'You cut your hair. I loved it the way it was. Will you grow it again for me?' he asked levelly.

Surprise darted through Merry, who had wondered if he had even noticed that she had shortened her hair. 'I suppose that could be arranged,' she breathed shakily.

'Why did you cut it?' he demanded. 'It was really beautiful.'

Even more taken aback by that blunt question and the compliment, Merry coloured. She couldn't tell him the truth, couldn't afford to dwell on unfortunate memories at this stage of their marriage or mention truths that he might think were aimed at reproaching him. But when she had been pregnant and struggling against an unending tide of exhaustion and sickness to get through every day, the amount of care demanded by very long hair had simply felt like an unnecessary burden.

'It was too much work to look after when I was pregnant,' she muttered awkwardly.

'Fortunately, you no longer have to look after your own hair,' Angel informed her lazily. 'Add a stylist to your staff—'

Merry opened pale blue eyes very wide. 'I'm to have my own staff?' she gasped.

'Of course. You'll need a social secretary to take care of your calendar, someone to shop for you… unless you want to do it yourself,' Angel volunteered doubtfully. 'I've started you off with a new wardrobe—'

'Have you indeed?' Merry cut in jerkily.

'It's a wedding present. I wasn't sure you'd want to be bothered,' Angel volunteered, a fingertip tracing the quivering fullness of her lower lip, sending a shiver through her taut, slender body. 'You've never struck me as being that interested in clothes or appearances.'

'I'm not,' she agreed almost guiltily. 'Sybil was always trying to persuade me that shopping was enjoyable.'

'I don't want you having to do things you don't want to do,' Angel told her huskily. 'I don't want you to change who you are to fit into my world, so it's easier to have someone else take care of the less welcome aspects for you.'

Her heartbeat was thumping hard and fast inside her tightening chest. 'You like me the way I am?'

'Very much,' Angel asserted. 'You're unusual and I value that.'

A smile slowly tilted and softened the tense line of her mouth. 'And you have a fetish for very long hair?'

A wolfish grin slashed his expressive mouth, cutting his dark male beauty into high-cheekboned perfection and interesting hollows while his intense gaze held hers fast. 'Only from the first moment I saw you.'

Warmth flushed through Merry, leaving her breathless. 'That must be the most romantic thing you've ever said to me.'

'I don't do romantic, *koukla mou*,' Angel told her uneasily, a frown line building between his fine ebony brows as he stared down at her in frustration. 'For me, it was a sexual charge and instantaneous...'

And if she was honest, Merry reflected ruefully, it had been the same for her that first day, a powerful instant physical reaction that had only deepened with repeated exposure.

Lean brown hands dropped to the sash at her waist and jerked it loose so that her breath hitched in her throat. She could feel her breasts swelling inside her bra, her nipples prickling into feverish prominence, the sense of melting at her feminine core. She was trembling, awake on every level even be-

fore he picked her up against him and crushed her
ripe mouth hungrily under his.

'*Thee mou*... I want you even more now than I
wanted you then,' Angel intoned rawly. 'And that's
saying something. But then I've never had to be pa-
tient before.'

'You don't have any patience,' she whispered
through reddened lips. 'You want everything yesterday.'

'Once I got you back I didn't want to be too demanding in case it made you change your mind. Before the wedding, I felt like I was in a straitjacket
around you, forced to be on my best behaviour,' he
complained.

Merry laughed, riveted to appreciate that she
had read his uncharacteristic restraint correctly.
She knew him better than she had believed, she
thought victoriously, and his admission thrilled her.
He hadn't wanted to risk driving her away and losing
her. Losing *them*, she corrected with a sudden inner
flinch of dismayed acceptance, the thrilled sensation swiftly dying again. He had practised patience
with Elyssa's mother for Elyssa's benefit, fearful of
losing access through their marriage to his daughter, which put a very different slant on his attitude.

'Unhappily for me, I am a naturally demanding man,' Angel admitted thickly, long, deft fingers
twitching the buttons loose on her top, parting the
edges, pushing them off her slim, taut shoulders until
the garment dropped to the tiled floor. 'No good at
waiting, no fan of deferred gratification either...'

Her ribcage tensed as she snatched in a sustaining breath, ridiculously self-conscious standing there in her simple white lace bra. Although they had been intimate twice before, on the first occasion they had been in semi-darkness and on the second they had both been so frantic that she hadn't had the time or space to feel remotely shy. But now, her face burned as Angel released the catch on her bra and her breasts tumbled free, plump and swollen and heavy.

'I have died and gone to heaven,' Angel intoned, scooping her up and carrying her across to the bed. 'I love your curves.'

'I'm pretty much stuck with them,' Merry pointed out, resisting a very strong urge to cup her hands over the swells that pregnancy had increased in size.

Angel cupped the burgeoning creamy swells, gently moulded and stroked them before leaning back to peel his shirt off over his head. Tangled black curls, glossy below the discreet lights, tumbled over his brow, his lean, strong face taut with hunger, dark golden eyes glittering like polished ingots. A thumb teased a quivering pink nipple until it hardened into a tight bud and throbbed, her breath escaping from her parted lips in an audible hiss of quaking response.

'You *should* tremble… I want to eat you alive,' Angel warned her, settling his hands to her waist to extract her from her linen trousers, yanking them off with scant ceremony and trailing off her last garment with brazen satisfaction. 'But we've never taken the time to do this properly. We were always in a ridiculous hurry to reach the finishing line. It won't be like that tonight.'

Merry felt the dampness between her thighs and reddened fiercely, wildly aware that her body was even now ready for him, surging impatiently ahead without shame to that finishing line he had mentioned. He made her single-minded and greedy and shameless, she thought helplessly. He turned everything she thought she knew about herself on its head and he had done that from the outset.

Watching her, Angel sprang upright again to strip off what remained of his clothes. He was, oh, so beautiful that she stared, taking in the long, bronzed flexing torso lightly sprinkled with black curling hair, the superb muscle definition, the long, powerful, hair-roughened thighs and the bold, eager thrust of his erection. Her belly fluttered, her mouth ran dry, her body flexed with sinful eagerness.

He returned to her again, all smouldering sexual assurance and with eyes that ravished her as she lay there. His hands found her curvy hips, his mouth locked to a rosy crest, and she simply gasped while he played with the puckered buds until they throbbed almost unbearably. A finger trailed through her slick folds and her spine arched, another sound, a plea for more that she couldn't help, dragged from her. He spread her thighs to invade her body with skilful fingers and slid down her pale body to explore her most tender flesh.

Merry was already so aroused that she could barely contain herself. He toyed with her, brought his mouth to her and licked and teased until she writhed helplessly beneath his ministrations, her body alight like a forest fire, hot and twitchy and excited beyond bearing. It was as though every nerve ending had reached saturation point, thrusting her higher and higher with every passing second until her body shattered in an ecstatic climax without her volition. A high keening cry fell from her, her body jerking and gasping with the intensity of her relief as the long, convulsive waves of pleasure rippled through her again.

'You really needed that,' Angel husked knowingly, his brilliant gaze locked to her hectically flushed and softened face. 'So did I. I needed to see you come for me again. I need to know I'm the only man to see you like this.'

'Why?' she asked baldly, taken aback by that admission.

Angel shrugged a broad shoulder. 'I don't know,' he admitted, quite unconcerned by his own ignorance of what motivated him. 'But when I saw you kissing that vet guy I wanted to wipe him off the face of the earth.'

Merry sat up with a start and hugged her knees in consternation. 'How did you see that?'

'You and Elyssa have had a security detail discreetly watching over you for months. It's standard in this family and not negotiable,' Angel told her without apology. 'I needed to know you were both safe. I was sent a photo of you kissing him. I didn't need to see that. I didn't ask for it. I hated it.'

Merry sat there frozen, shock and resentment momentarily holding her fast. 'Standard?' she queried.

'It's my job to keep you both safe,' he delivered flatly. 'But sometimes you don't want the details. Did you have sex with him?'

'None of your business!' Merry framed jaggedly, swinging her legs off the bed and standing up. 'How many women have you been with since the night Elyssa was conceived?'

The silence simmered like a kettle suddenly pushed close to noisy boiling point.

Merry swung back to him, too angry to even care that she was naked. 'I thought that would shut you up!'

'After our little contraceptive mishap it was months before I was with anyone again. I couldn't get you or that accident out of my head. I still wanted you but I *had* to stay away from you,' Angel ground out with suppressed savagery, his lean, dark features rigid with remembered frustration and resentment. 'Every other woman turned me off. You destroyed my sex drive until I got very, very drunk one night and finally broke the dry spell.'

Well, that was blunt and very Angel brutal, Merry acknowledged, stalking into the bathroom with hot stinging tears brimming in her eyes. And she still wanted to kill him, rake jealous fingernails down over his beautiful face and draw blood in punishment. Jealousy and hatred ate her alive, threatening to rip her asunder because she had no defence against such honesty. Of course, she had guessed there would be other women, other flings and sexual dalliances while they were apart, but guessing and *knowing* were two very different things.

Inside the bathroom, Angel closed two strong arms round her to hold her fast. 'It was the worst sex I've ever had.'

'Good!' she bit out with raw sincerity.

'It wasn't like you and me. It wasn't what I really wanted but I couldn't *have* what I wanted and celibacy made me feel like a weakling,' he groaned against the damp nape of her neck. 'The sexual hold you had over me unnerved me right from the beginning. It felt toxic, dangerous...'

'Thanks... I think,' Merry framed weakly as he wrapped his strong arms even more tightly round her, imprisoning her in the hard, damp heat of his lean, powerful body.

'It was the same for you. You fought it as well,' he reminded her.

And that was true, she conceded grudgingly. That overpowering hunger had scared her, overwhelmed her, made her all too aware of her vulnerability. Could it really have been the same for him?

'Even if the condom hadn't broken that night, I'd have run like a hare,' Angel admitted in a driven undertone. 'I felt out of control. I couldn't live like that.'

'Neither could I,' she confessed unevenly.

'But now that I've got that ring on your finger, everything feels different,' Angel stated, his breath fanning her shoulder, his hands smoothing up her body in innate celebration of the possessiveness roaring through him. 'You're mine now, *all* mine.'

'Am I?' she dared.

An appreciative laugh vibrated through him and his hands swept up over her breasts, moulding the ripe swells, tugging at the still-distended peaks, sending a piercing arrow of sweet shuddering sensation right down to the moist heart of her. 'If you don't know that yet, I'm doing something very wrong,' he growled, lifting her off her feet to carry her back into the bedroom.

'You have a one-track mind, Mr Valtinos,' Merry condemned helplessly as he spread her on the bed and hovered over her body, brazenly eager for more action.

'No, I have a wife to claim,' Angel declared urgently, sliding between her slender thighs, gathering them up and plunging into her with ravenous sexual dominance. 'And tonight nothing will keep me from you. Not my mistakes, not my clumsy efforts to make amends, not your disappointment in me, not my inability to live up to your impossibly high ideals. We are married and we will do the best we can with that challenge.'

His sudden intrusion into her honeyed depths stretched her tight and then sent a current of melting excitement surging through Merry. She closed her eyes as he moved, her head falling back, her body an erotic instrument in his charge, glorious sensation spilling through her, washing away the hurt and the disillusionment. Oh, later she would take out the hurt again and brood on it and hate herself, but just then she couldn't hold onto that pain, not when a delicious flood of exquisite feeling clenched her core with his every sensual movement. He felt like hers for the first time, and as an explosive orgasm lit her up from inside out and he groaned with passionate pleasure into her hair she was soothed, quieted and gratified to be the source of that uninhibited satisfaction.

CHAPTER EIGHT

MERRY AND ANGEL lay side by side in the orange grove above the private beach. Day after day had melted into the next with a curiously timeless quality that had gradually teased all the tension from Merry's bones and taught her how to relax. She could hardly credit that they had already spent an entire month on the island. Her body ached from his demands, not that she wasn't willing, but she was still in shock at the extent of Angel's ravenous hunger for her.

It was sex, only sex, she told herself regularly, and then in the dark of the night when Angel wasn't his sardonic know-all self she snuggled up to him, revelling in the intimacy that now bonded them. Maintaining a controlled distance wasn't possible with a man as unashamedly physical as the one she had married. Angel had no limits. He would go and work for a couple of hours in his home office and then sweep down on her wherever she was and cart her off to bed again as if he had been parted from her for at least a month.

'I missed you,' he would say, replete with satisfaction while her pulses still pounded and her body hummed in the aftermath.

'I could work *with* you,' she would say.

'You're my wife, the mother of my child, no longer an employee.'

'I could be a junior partner,' she had proffered pathetically.

'We can't live in each other's pockets twenty-four-seven,' Angel had pointed out drily. 'It would be unhealthy.'

No, what Merry sometimes thought was unhealthy was the sheer weight of love that Angel now inspired in her. That was a truth she had evaded as long as possible: she *loved* him.

Only because she loved him and her daughter had she been willing to give Angel one last chance, she acknowledged ruefully. There were still a thousand things she wanted to punish him for, but she knew that vengeful, bitter thoughts were unproductive and would ultimately damage any hope of their having a stable relationship. In that line, she was sensible, very sensible, she acknowledged ruefully. Unfortunately, she only became stupid when it came to Angel himself.

Sometimes she had to work uncomfortably hard to hide her love. She would see him laughing over Elyssa's antics in the bath, amusement lightening and softening his lean, darkly handsome features, and she wouldn't be able to drag her eyes from him. He had taken her down to the village *taverna* above the harbour and dined with her there, introducing her to the locals, more relaxed than she had ever seen him in company, his usually razor-edged cynicism absent. He had tipped her out of bed to climb the highest hill on the island to see in the dawn and told her off for moaning about how tired she was even though he had drained her energy at the summit with *al fresco* sex. But of course she was tired, making love half the night and half the day, physically active in all the hours between as she strove to match his high-voltage energy levels.

Ironically, complete peace had engulfed the Valtinos house the day after the wedding once Angel had revealed that his mother and her boyfriend had departed at dawn for an unknown destination, leaving the other half of the house in a fine mess for the staff to deal with. Merry had felt relieved and then guilty at feeling relieved because, like it or not, Angel's challenging and difficult mother was family and had to somehow be integrated into their lives or become a continuing problem.

They had gone sailing on the yacht, visiting other islands, shopping, picnicking. They had thrown a giant party at the house attended by all Angel's relatives, near and distant. She had met his second cousin who lived in London and had heard all about Angel's visit to her home before he first met Elyssa, and Merry had laughed like a drain when she'd recognised how wily he had been to find out a little more about babies before he'd served himself up as a new father to one.

'What's your favourite colour?' she asked drowsily.

'I'm not a girl. I don't have a favourite,' Angel parried with amusement.

'Birth sign?'

'Look at your marriage certificate, lazy-bones,' he advised. 'I'm a Scorpio, but I don't believe in that sh—'

'Language,' she reminded him, resting a finger against his parted lips.

'Prim, proper, prissy,' Angel labelled without hesitation.

'Your first lover? What age were you?' she pressed, defying that censure while wondering how on earth he could still think of her that way after the time they had spent together.

'Too young. You don't want to know,' Angel traded.

'I *do* want to know,' Merry argued, stretching indolently in the drenching heat, only vaguely wondering what time it was. They had spent the morning swimming and entertaining Elyssa on the beach and then Sally had come down to collect their daughter and take her back up to the house for lunch and a nap. Now the surf was whispering onto the shore a hundred yards below them while the cane forest that sheltered the orange grove from the coastal breezes concealed them entirely from view.

'I was fourteen. She was one of my mother's friends,' Angel admitted grimly.

Frowning, Merry flipped over to stare at him. *'Seriously?'*

'You're still so naïve,' Angel groaned, lifting up on his elbows to study her, hard muscles flexing on his bare bronzed torso, the vee at his hipbones prominent above the low-slung shorts as he leant back. Just looking at that display of stark masculine beauty made her mouth run dry and her heart give a sudden warning thud, awareness thundering through her at storm-force potency.

'What do you think it was like here when I was an adolescent with Angelina in charge?' he chided. 'I came home for the summer from school and there were no rules whatsoever. Back then it was all wild, decadent parties and the house was awash with people. Believe it or not, my mother was even less inhibited in those days and, being an oversexed teenager, I naturally thought the freedom to do anything I liked was amazing and I never let my father know how debauched it was.'

'So, your first experience was with an older woman,' Merry gathered, determined to move on past that sordid revelation and not judge, because when he had been that young and innocent she believed he had been more sinned against than he had been a sinner.

'And the experience was disappointing,' Angel admitted with derisive bite. 'It felt sleazy, not empowering. I felt used. When the parties here got too much I used to go down and camp out with Roula's family for a few days.'

'She lived here on the island back then?' Merry said in surprise.

'Still does. Roula was born and bred on Palos, like me. This is her home base too. She runs a chain of beauty salons, comes back here for a break. Unlike me, she had a regular family with parents who were still married and their home was a little oasis of peace and normality... I loved escaping there,' he confided. 'Rules and regular meal times have more appeal than you would appreciate.'

'I can understand that,' Merry conceded ruefully. 'My mother was very disorganised. She'd want to eat and there'd be nothing in the fridge. She'd want to go out and she wouldn't have a babysitter arranged. Sometimes she just left me in bed and went out anyway. I never told Sybil that. But when I was with Sybil, everything was structured.'

'*Thee mou*... I forgot!' Angel exclaimed abruptly. 'Your aunt phoned to ask me if there was any chance we'd be back in the UK in the next couple of weeks because your mother's coming over to stay with her for a while and she wants to see you. I said I'd try to organise it.'

Merry frowned, reluctant to get on board with yet another reconciliation scene with her estranged mother. Natalie enjoyed emotional scenes, enjoyed asking her daughter why she couldn't act more like a normal daughter and love and appreciate her, not seeming to realise that the time for laying the foundation for such bonds lay far behind them. They had missed that boat and Merry had learned to get by without a mother by replacing her with the more dependable Sybil.

'You're not keen,' Angel gathered, shrewd dark golden eyes scanning her expressive troubled face. 'Sybil made it sound like it was really important that you show up at some stage. I think she's hoping you'll mend fences with her sister.'

Merry shrugged jerkily. 'I've tried before and it never worked. Sybil's a peacemaker and wants everyone to be happy but I always annoy Natalie by saying or doing the wrong thing.'

'Try giving her another chance,' Angel urged, surprising her. 'I don't get on with my mother either, but then she doesn't make any effort to get on with me. At least yours is willing to make the effort.'

'And when it goes pear-shaped, she blames me every time,' Merry said bitterly.

'You can be an unforgiving little soul when people fail your high expectations,' Angel murmured softly. 'I know you haven't forgiven me yet for running out on you.'

Her face froze. 'What makes you think that?'

'Be honest. I'm still on probation. You're always waiting for me to do something dreadful and show my true colours,' Angel told her impatiently. 'You hold back. You watch everything you say and do and always give me the carefully sanitised version.'

Merry clashed in shock with hot dark golden eyes and recognised his exasperation. Guilty dismay pierced her and she was even more taken aback by how very clearly he saw through her pretences to her fearful desire to keep the peace. He lifted a hand and traced the full, soft curve of her lower lip as she caught it between her teeth.

'I don't mean to be like that,' she admitted uncomfortably.

'I'll have to work that pessimistic streak out of you. By all means, set the bar high because I do rise to a challenge,' Angel assured her. 'But don't drown me before I can even begin in low expectations.'

'I *don't* have low expectations,' Merry protested breathlessly, flipping over to face him, her colour high.

Angel grasped her hand and spread her fingers low on his belly with a glittering smile of disagreement. 'Go on, tell me you're too tired or just not in the mood for once,' he urged.

Her small fingers flexed against his sun-warmed skin and then pulled defiantly free to trace the furrow of silky hair that ran down from his navel to vanish beneath the waistband of his shorts. Heat uncoiled and spread low in her belly. 'You don't get it, do you?' she whispered, flicking loose the first metal stud separating her from him. 'No matter how tired, I can't help always being in the mood for you,' she confided unsteadily. 'It's not fake, it's not me trying to please.'

She heard the startled catch of his expelled breath as she attacked the remaining studs, felt too the hardness of the arousal he couldn't possibly hide from her and she thrilled at his unashamed need for her. She had assumed that initial enthusiasm would die a death once she was no longer a novelty in his bed but he hadn't flagged in the slightest. She jerked the shorts down and reached for him.

Angel watched her in fascination. Here she was again taking him by surprise, defying his own expectations with a bold counter-attack, despite her inexperience. And he treasured her ability to disconcert him, revelling in the reality that she appeared to have more interest in his body than she had in the new wardrobe he had bought for her. She was quite unlike any other woman he had ever been with, gloriously unimpressed by his wealth and what he could buy her. Her shy fingers found him, stroked him and the sweet swell of shattering pleasure washed over him. His breath hissed out between his even white teeth. He lay back, giving her control without hesitation.

Merry licked the long, strong column of him, swiping with her tongue, eager to return the favour of his attention even if it meant she delivered a less than polished performance. The muscles on his abdomen rippled, his tension building, his hips rising as a sexy sound of reaction escaped his parted lips and she smiled, loving his responsiveness, his unexpected willingness to let her take charge for a change. She closed him between her lips and he groaned out loud, long fingers knotting into her hair, urging her on, controlling the rhythm.

'Enough!' Angel bit out abruptly, pulling her back and slotting her deftly under him, rearranging her for what he really wanted and needed.

Splayed beneath him starfish-mode, Merry cried out as he plunged straight into her, all ferocious urgency and unleashed passion, his lean hips rising and falling between her slender thighs to send jolt after jolt of hot, sweet pleasure surging in waves through her. Her excitement climbed exponentially and when he flipped her over onto her knees and slammed into her again and again while the ball of his thumb stroked against her, he sent her flying into an explosive orgasm that left her sobbing for breath and control in the aftermath.

'No, that definitely wasn't fake or you trying to please me,' Angel murmured with roughened satisfaction in her ear as he gently tugged her hair back from her hot face and planted a lingering kiss there.

At some stage of the night, Angel shook her awake and her eyes flew open to focus on him in drowsy surprise. He was already fully dressed, sheathed in a sleek business suit, freshly shaven. He sank down on the side of the bed. 'I'm heading back to London. There's a stock-market crisis and I prefer to handle it on the spot with my staff around me. I've made arrangements for you to fly back first thing tomorrow morning…you need your sleep right now,' he said, stroking her cheekbone with unexpected tenderness. 'Once you've seen your aunt and your mother you can come and join me.'

Angel stared down at his wife, more than a little unnerved by the guilt sweeping him when he noticed the shadows below her eyes and the weary droop of her eyelids. He had been too demanding. He couldn't get enough of her in or out of bed and she was so busy being the perfect wife and perfect mother that she wasn't taking time out for her own needs. He was selfish, had always been selfish, was trying in fits and starts to be less selfish, but when he wanted her with him it was a challenge to defy his own need. Leaving her to sleep the night through was a sacrifice when he would sooner have had her by his side.

'It drives me mad when you make decisions for me!' Merry groaned in frustration. 'I could have flown back with you.'

'It wouldn't be fair to take Elyssa out of bed in the middle of the night and you're already tired out. I suggest that you leave her here with Sally unless you're planning to stay with your family for a few days,' Angel opined with an ebony brow rising in question on that score.

Merry sighed, unenthusiastic about the prospect of seeing her mother again. 'Not very likely. After a couple of hours catching up I'll probably be glad to escape,' she forecast ruefully.

Angel sprang upright again, all lithe, sexy elegance and energy, holding her gaze like a live flame burning in the darkness. 'And I'll be glad to have you back,' he declared with a flashing smile that tilted her heart inside her and made her senses hum.

Merry recalled that brief snatch of dialogue over coffee on the terrace the following morning. It was Sally's day off and Elyssa had just gone upstairs for her nap, leaving her mother free to relax in the sunshine. She smoothed a hand down over the bright red sundress she wore, preventing it from creeping any further up her slender thighs because she didn't want to flash the gardener engaged in trimming the edges of the lawn.

Angel had bought her a new wardrobe and it had very much his stamp on it. She thought the hemlines were too short, the necklines too revealing or snug in fit and the colour choices too bold, but then she wasn't used to showing off her figure or seeking attention. Maybe that had been Angel's nefarious plan all along, she reflected with wry amusement; maybe he hoped to drive her out shopping by landing her with a selection of garments she considered too daring. She certainly wouldn't put such scheming past him. The lingerie, however, was a superb fit and very much to her taste, plain and comfortable rather than provocative or elaborate.

One of the maids walked onto the terrace to announce a visitor and a moment later Roula Paulides strolled out to join Merry, a wide smile of greeting pinned to her beautiful face. 'I heard Angel's helicopter taking off during the night and thought this would be a good opportunity for us to get better acquainted,' she admitted.

Determined to look welcoming, Merry smiled and ordered fresh coffee. Roula was one of Angel's most long-standing friends yet Merry was also conscious of the possessive vibe that flared through her whenever she relived how she had once felt seeing her husband in the glamorous blonde's company.

Roula took a seat, very self-assured in her designer casuals, her blonde hair secured in a stylish twist, her brown eyes bright as she smiled again. And something about that second smile warned Merry that her visitor wasn't half as relaxed as she was trying to appear.

'I want to make it clear that I won't make a habit of visiting like this,' Roula assured her smoothly as she lifted her coffee cup. 'We're both entitled to our privacy. We'll only occasionally meet when Angel holds a big party because that is the only time he invites me to his home.'

'You're welcome to visit any time you like,' Merry responded easily, wondering if, in a roundabout, devious way, she was being accused of being a jealous, possessive wife likely to resent and distrust any female friend of her husband's.

'Oh, that wouldn't do. Angel wouldn't allow that,' Roula declared. 'He wouldn't consider that appropriate in the circumstances. I thought he would've mentioned our arrangement by now but, although he never justifies his lifestyle, he's like most men: keen to avoid conflict.'

Merry's eyes had steadily widened throughout that speech as she struggled to work out what the other woman was talking about. 'What arrangement?' she heard herself ask baldly. 'I'm afraid I don't know what you're referring to.'

Roula Paulides settled cynically amused brown eyes on her. 'I'm Angel's mistress. I have been for years.'

For a split second, Merry didn't believe that she had heard that announcement because it struck her like a blow, freezing her brain into incredulous inactivity, leaving her staring back at her companion in blank disbelief.

Roula lifted and dropped a thin shoulder in acknowledgement. 'It's how he lives and I have never been able to refuse Angel anything. If you and I can reach an accommodation that we can both live with, all our lives will run much more smoothly. I'm not the jealous type and I hope you aren't either.'

Merry sucked in a shuddering breath. 'Let me get this straight. You came here today to tell me that you're sleeping with my husband?'

'Oh, not recently. Angel has no need of me right now with a new wife in his bed,' the Greek woman declared drily. 'But in time, when you are no longer a novelty, he will return to me. Other women have always come and gone in his life. I accept that. I've *always* accepted that and if you are wise and wish to remain his wife you will accept it too. You can't own him, you can't cage him.'

Merry looked beyond Roula, unnerved by the sudden throbbing intensity of her low-pitched voice and the brash, hard confidence with which she spoke, the suggestion that *she* knew Angel better than anyone else. On the hill above the village sat the Paulides home, a rather boxy modern white villa, which Angel had casually identified as being where Roula lived. Shock was winging through Merry in giddy waves of increasingly desperate denial, her fingers curling into defensive claws on her lap. It couldn't be true, it couldn't possibly be true that Angel had some permanent, non-exclusive sexual arrangement with the other woman that he had remained silent about.

'You seem shocked, but why? We were childhood friends and have always been very close. We understand each other very well,' Roula told her calmly. 'In the same way I accepted that after your child was born, Angel would inevitably end up marrying you. He doesn't love you any more than he loves me but he will do his duty by his daughter. I'm here now only to assure you that I will never try to interfere in your marriage in any way and that I hope you will not be spiteful and try to prevent Angel from seeing me.'

Merry swallowed hard at that unlikely hope. 'What's in this weird arrangement for you?' she asked bluntly.

Roula vented a laugh and tossed her head. 'I have a share of him. I'm willing to settle for that. I've loved him since I was a girl. He rescued my father from bankruptcy and financed the set-up of my beauty salons. When I was younger I hoped that he would eventually see me as a possible wife, but of course that hasn't happened. Marrying the mistress isn't in the Valtinos genes.'

Nausea stirred in Merry's tummy. Swallowing her coffee without choking on it was a challenge. Roula managed to make it all sound so normal, so inevitable. She loved Angel, unashamedly did what it took to hold onto her small stake in his life while accepting that there would be other women and eventually a wife she would have to share him with.

But such acceptance was nowhere within Merry's grasp. She was an all-or-nothing person. She had told Angel before she agreed to marry him that he could have no other women in his life and that she expected complete fidelity. He had agreed to that boundary. Had he lied? Had he expected her to change her mind? Or had he been planning to be so discreet that she never found out that he sometimes slept with Roula Paulides?

Shock banging through her blitzed brain, Merry struggled to relocate her reasoning powers. Did she simply accept that the blonde was telling her the truth? Why would Roula lie about such a relationship? Could she simply be trying to cause trouble in Merry's marriage? But what would be the point of that unless she was already engaged in an affair with Angel with something to gain from his marriage breaking down?

And then, according to Roula, Angel had not been *with* her recently? Or simply since his marriage? Merry's head was spinning. She wanted to pack her bags, gather up her daughter and run back to the UK to establish a sane and normal life where a blonde beauty did not calmly stroll into her home one morning to announce that she was in love with Merry's husband and keen to continue having hassle-free sex with him.

Stark pain sliced through Merry, cutting through the numbness of shock. She had been happy, she registered wretchedly, hopelessly, helplessly happy with Angel and their marriage as it was. She had seen nothing to question, nothing to rouse her suspicions. She had believed his promise of fidelity, believed that they had a future, but if she believed Roula her future with Angel could only be a deceitful and fragile farce because she would never ever accept him betraying her with another woman. Nor would she ever share him.

'Well, you've said your piece. Now I think you should leave,' Merry told Roula quietly, her self-discipline absolute because wild horses could not have dredged a more vulnerable reaction from her.

'I do hope I haven't upset you,' the Greek woman said unconvincingly. 'I suspected you didn't know and that wasn't right.'

As far as Merry was concerned there was nothing right about Roula's attitude to either Angel or his marriage or even his wife. Roula had developed her own convictions based on what she wanted. Roula, it seemed, lived to please Angel. Merry loved Angel but she had never been blind to his flaws. Had he discounted his intimate relationship with Roula in the same way as he had once ignored the reality that his pregnant former employee might need more than financial support from him?

It would have been uncomfortable for Angel to overcome his own feelings back then and offer Merry his support, and he had been unable to force himself to go that extra mile for her benefit. In the same way being honest about his relationship with Roula would have put paid to any hope of Merry marrying him and sharing their daughter. Was that why he had kept quiet? Or was it possible that he believed the relationship with Roula was at an end? But then wouldn't Roula know that? Had Angel lied to Merry to get her to the altar? Was he that ruthless?

Oh, yes, a little voice chimed inside her head.

CHAPTER NINE

'MRS VALTINOS INSISTED that she had to make an immediate departure from the airport,' Angel's driver repeated uneasily. 'I did tell her that you were expecting her to join you for lunch before she left London but she said—'

'That she didn't have time,' Angel slotted in flatly.

'I took her to Foxcote Hall at two and then an hour later dropped her off at her aunt's house. She said she'd call when she needed to be picked up again,' the older man completed.

Angel breathed in slow and deep. Something was wrong. His wife had flown back to London with their daughter and mounds of luggage even though she had only been expecting to remain in the UK for forty-eight hours at most. She had blown him off for lunch. She wasn't answering his calls or his texts. Such behaviour was unlike her. Merry wasn't moody or facetious and she didn't play games. If something had annoyed her, she was more likely to speak up straight away. His growing bewilderment was starting to give way to righteous anger and an

amount of unfamiliar apprehension that only enraged him more.

What could possibly have happened between
his departure and her arrival in London? Why the
mounds of luggage? Wasn't she planning to return
to Greece? Was it possible that she was leaving him
and taking their daughter with her? But why would
she do that? He had checked with the staff on Palos.
Merry had had only one visitor and that was Roula,
and when he had phoned Roula she had insisted that
Merry had been perfectly friendly and relaxed with
her. His lean brown hands knotting into fists, his
tension pronounced, Angel resolved to be waiting
at Foxcote when Merry got back.

Merry emerged from the rambling country house
that she had not until that day known that Angel
owned and climbed into the waiting limousine. She
had left Elyssa with Sally, deeming it unlikely that
her mother was likely to be champing at the bit to
meet her first grandchild because Natalie had never
had much time for babies. Furthermore, if Natalie
was likely to be chastising her daughter and creating one of her emotionally exhausting scenes it was
better to keep Elyssa well away from the display
because Merry always lost patience with the older
woman. What did it matter after all these years anyway? Natalie hadn't even made the effort to attend
her daughter's wedding. But then she hadn't made
the effort to attend Merry's graduation or, indeed,

any of the significant events that had marked her daughter's life.

Obsessed with the recollection of Roula's sleazy allegations, Merry was simply not in the mood to deal with her mother. Landing in London to discover that Angel had arranged to meet her for lunch had been unsettling. Merry was determined to confront him but only in her own time and only when she had decided exactly what she intended to say to him. Not yet at that point, she had ducked lunch and ignored his calls and texts. Let him fester for a while as she had had to fester while she'd run over Roula's claims until her head had ached and her stomach had been queasy and she had wept herself empty of tears.

Angel hadn't asked her to love him, she reminded herself as the limo drew up outside Sybil's house. But he had asked her to trust him and she had. Now that trust was broken and she was so wounded she felt as though she had been torn apart. She had trailed all her belongings and her daughter's back from Greece but she still didn't know what she would be doing next or even where she would be living. While she had been getting married, life had moved on. The cottage now had another tenant and she didn't want to move in with her aunt again. Nor did she want to feel like a sad, silly failure with Angel again.

'So glad you made the time to come,' Sybil gabbled almost nervously as Merry walked through the front door into the open-plan lounge where her mother rose stiffly upright to face her. Natalie bore little resemblance to her daughter, being small, blonde and rather plump, but she looked remarkably young for her forty odd years.

'Natalie,' Merry acknowledged, forcing herself forward to press an awkward kiss to her mother's cheek. 'How are you?'

'Oh, don't be all polite and nice as if we're strangers. That just makes me feel worse,' her mother immediately complained. 'Sybil has something to tell you. You had better sit down. It's going to come as a shock.'

Her brow furrowing in receipt of that warning, Merry sank down into an armchair and focused on her aunt. Sybil remained standing and she was very pale.

'We have a big secret in this family, which we have always covered up,' Sybil stated agitatedly. 'I didn't see much point in telling you about it so long after the event.'

'No, you never did like to tell anything that could make you look bad,' Natalie sniped. 'But you *promised* me that you would tell her.'

Sybil compressed her lips. 'When I was fifteen I got pregnant by a boy I was at school with. My parents were horrified. They sent me to live with a cousin up north and then they adopted my baby. It was all hushed up. I had to promise my mother that I would never tell my daughter the truth.'

Merry was bemused. 'I—'

'I was that adopted baby,' Natalie interposed thinly. 'I'm not Sybil's younger sister, I'm her *daughter* but I didn't find that out until I was eighteen.'

Losing colour, Merry flinched and focused on Sybil in disbelief. 'Your *daughter*?'

'Yes. Then my mother died and I felt that Natalie had the right to know who I really was. She was already talking about trying to trace her birth mother, so it seemed sensible to speak up before she tried doing that,' Sybil explained hesitantly.

'And overnight, when that truth came out, Sybil went from being my very exciting famous big sister, who gave me wonderful gifts, to being a liar, who had deceived me all my life,' Merry's mother condemned with a bitterness that shook Merry.

'So, you're actually my grandmother, not my aunt,' Merry registered shakily as she studied Sybil and struggled to disentangle the family relationships she had innocently taken for granted.

'It wasn't my secret to share after the adoption. I gave up my rights but when I came clean about who I really was, it sent your mother off the rails.'

'Lies…the gift that keeps on giving,' Natalie breathed tersely. 'That's part of the reason I fell pregnant with you, Merry. When I had that stupid affair with your father, I was all over the place emotionally. I had lost my adoptive mother and then discovered that the sister I loved and admired was in fact my mother…and I didn't like her very much.'

'Natalie couldn't forgive me for putting my career first but it enabled me to give my parents enough money to live a very comfortable life while they raised my daughter,' Sybil argued in her own defence. 'I was grateful for their care of her. I wasn't ready to be a mother.'

'At least, not until *you* were born, Merry,' Natalie slotted in with perceptible scorn. 'Then Sybil interfered and stole you away from me.'

'It wasn't like that!' Sybil protested. 'You *needed* help.'

Merry's mother settled strained eyes on Merry's troubled face and said starkly, 'What do you think it was like for me to see *my* birth mother lavishing all the love and care she had denied me on my daughter instead?'

Merry breathed in deep and slow, struggling to put her thoughts in order. In reality she was still too upset about Roula's allegations to fully concentrate her brain on what the two women were telling her. Sybil was her grandmother, *not* her aunt and Merry had never been told that Natalie was an adopted child. She abhorred the fact that she had not been given the full truth about her background sooner.

'The way Sybil treated you, the fuss she made of you, made me *resent* you,' Merry's mother confessed guiltily. 'It wrecked our relationship. She came between us.'

'That was never my intention,' Sybil declared loftily.

'But that's how it was…' Natalie complained stonily.

Merry lowered her head, recognising that she saw points on both sides of the argument. Sybil had only been fifteen when she gave Natalie up to her parents for adoption and she had been barred from admitting that she was Natalie's birth mum. Merry refused to condemn Sybil for that choice but she also saw how devastating that pretence and the lies must've been for her own mother and how finding out that truth years afterwards had distressed her.

'You *say* you want a closer relationship with me and yet you still had no interest in coming to my wedding or in meeting my daughter,' Merry heard herself fire back at her mother.

'I couldn't afford the plane fare!' Natalie snapped defensively. 'Who do you think paid for this visit?'

'How do you feel about this?' Sybil pressed anxiously.

'Confused,' Merry admitted tightly. 'Hurt that the two of you didn't tell me the truth years ago. And I hate lies, Sybil, and now I discover that you've pretty much been lying to me my whole life.'

In actuality, Merry felt as if the solid floor under her feet had fallen away, leaving her to stage a difficult balancing act. Her grandmother and her mother were both regarding her expectantly and she didn't know what she was supposed to say to satisfy either of them. The sad reality was that she had always had more in common with Sybil than with Natalie and that, no matter how hard she tried, she would probably never be able to replicate that close relationship with her mother.

'All I ever wanted to do was try to help you still have a life as a single parent,' Sybil told her daughter unhappily. 'You were so young. I never wanted to come between you and Merry.'

'I'd like to meet Elyssa,' Natalie declared. 'Sybil's shown me photos. She is very cute.'

And Merry realised then that she had been guilty of holding her own unstable childhood against her mother right into adulthood instead of accepting that Natalie might have changed and matured. 'I will bring her over for a visit,' she promised stiffly. 'How long are you staying for?'

'Two weeks,' Natalie told her. 'But now that Keith's gone and we've split up, I'm thinking of moving back to the UK again. I'd like to meet your husband while I'm here as well.'

Tears suddenly stinging her hot eyes, Merry nodded jerkily, not trusting herself to speak. She understood why her mother had wanted the story told but wasn't at all sure that she could give the older woman the warmer relationship she was clearly hoping for. But then too many of her emotions were bound up in the bombshell that had blown her marriage apart, she conceded guiltily. Roula's confession had devastated her and at that moment having to turn her back on the man she loved and her marriage was still all she could really think about. It was the thought, the terrifying awareness, of what she might have to do next that left room for nothing else and paralysed her.

She shared photos of the wedding and Elyssa with both women, glossed over Sybil's comment that she seemed very pale and quiet and returned to Foxcote

Hall as soon as she decently could, having promised
to bring Elyssa back for a visit within a few days.
The limo travelled at a stately pace back up to the
elegant country house that had the stunning architec-
ture of an oversized Georgian dolls' house. Informal
gardens shaded by clusters of mature trees spread
out from the house and slowly changed into a land-
scape of green fields and lush stretches of woodland.
Foxcote was a magnificent estate and yet Angel had
not even mentioned that he owned a property near
her aunt's home.

She had originally planned to go to a hotel from
the airport, but when she had yet even to see and
speak to Angel such a statement of separation had
seemed a tad premature. Walking into the airy hall
with its tall windows and tiled floor, she heard Elyssa chuckling and stringing together strings of nonsense words and she followed the sounds.

Several steps into the drawing room, she stopped
dead because Angel was down on the floor with Elyssa, letting his daughter clamber over him and finally
wrap her chubby arms round his neck and plant a triumphant noisy kiss on his face. He grinned, delight-
ing in the baby's easy trusting affection, but his smile
fell away the instant he glimpsed Merry. Suddenly
his lean, darkly handsome features were sober and
unsmiling, his beautiful dark eyes wary and intent.

'You never mentioned that you owned a house
near Sybil's,' Merry remarked in a brittle voice as
he vaulted lithely upright with Elyssa clasped to
his chest.

'My father bought the estate when he was going through a hunting, shooting, fishing phase but he soon got bored. Angelina used it for a while when she was socialising with the heir to a local dukedom. It should really be sold now,' Angel contended, crossing the room to lift the phone and summon their nanny to take charge of their daughter.

A current of pained resentment bit into Merry when Elyssa complained bitterly about being separated from her father. That connection, that bond had formed much sooner than she had expected. Elyssa had taken to Angel like a duck to water, revelling in his more physical play and more boisterous personality. If her father was to disappear from her daily life, their daughter would miss him and be hurt by his absence. But then whose fault would that be? Merry asked herself angrily. It certainly wouldn't be *her* fault, she told herself piously. She had played by the rules. If their marriage broke down, it would be entirely Angel's responsibility.

'So, what's going on?' Angel enquired, taking up a faintly combative stance as Sally closed the door in her wake, his long powerful legs braced, shoulders thrown back, aggressive jaw line at an angle. 'You blew me off at lunch and all day you've been ignoring my calls and texts...*why*?'

Merry sucked in a steadying breath. 'I'm leaving you...well, in the process of it,' she qualified stiffly, her face pale and set.

'Why would you suddenly decide to leave me?' Angel demanded, striding forward, all brooding intimidation, dark eyes glittering like fireworks in the night sky. 'That makes no sense.'

Anger laced the atmosphere, tensing every defensive muscle in her body, and she cursed the reality that she was not mentally prepared for the confrontation about to take place.

'Roula told me everything.'

Angel looked bemused. 'Everything about... *what*?' he demanded with curt emphasis.

'That she's been your mistress for years, that you always go back to her eventually.'

'I don't have a mistress. I've never had one. Before you, I've never wanted repeat encounters with the same woman,' Angel told her almost conversationally, dark golden eyes locked to her strained face. 'You must've misunderstood something Roula said. There's no way that she told you that we were lovers.'

'There was no misunderstanding,' Merry framed stiffly. 'She was very frank about your relationship and about the fact that she expected it to continue even though you were married.'

'But it's not true. I don't know what she's playing at but her claims are nonsense,' Angel declared with harsh emphasis. 'Is this all we've got, Merry? Some woman only has to say I sleep with her and you swallow the story whole?'

Merry clasped her trembling hands together and tilted her chin, her spine rigid. 'She was very convincing. I believed her.'

'*Diavolos!* You just judge me out of hand? You believe her rather than *me*?' Angel raked at her in a burst of incredulous anger, black curls tumbling across his brow as he shook his head in evident disbelief. 'You take her word over mine?'

'She's your friend. Why would she lie about such a thing?'

'How the hell am I supposed to know?' Angel shot back at her. 'But she *is* lying!'

'She said you'd been lovers for years but that you've always had other women,' Merry recounted flatly. 'I will not accept you being with other women!'

Angel settled volatile eyes on her and she backed away a step at the sheer heat she met there.

'Then try not to *drive* me into being with them!' he slammed back. 'I have not been unfaithful to you.'

'She did say that you hadn't been with her since you got married but that eventually you would return to her because apparently you always do.'

'You are the only woman I have *ever* returned to!' Angel proclaimed rawly. 'I can't believe we're even having this stupid conversation—'

'It's not a conversation, it's an argument,' she interrupted.

'I promised you that there would be no other women,' Angel reminded her darkly. 'Didn't you listen? Obviously, you didn't believe—'

'Your reputation goes before you,' Merry flung back at him bitterly.

'I will not apologise for my past. I openly acknowledge it but I have never cheated on any woman I have been with!' Angel intoned in a driven undertone. 'I grew up with a mother who cheated on all her lovers and I lived with the consequences of that kind of behaviour. I know better. I'm honest and I move on when I get bored.'

'Well, maybe I don't want to hang around waiting for you to get bored with me and move on!' Merry fired back with ringing scorn. 'Maybe I think I'm worth more than that and deserve more respect. That's why I'm calling time on us now before things get messy!'

'You're not calling time on us. That's not your decision to make,' Angel delivered with lethal derision. 'We got married to make a home for our daughter and if we have to work at achieving that happy outcome, then we *work* at it.'

A cold, forlorn hollow spread like poison inside Merry's tight chest as she recognised how foolish and naïve she had been to dream that Angel could eventually come to care for her. He had only married her for Elyssa's sake. She would never be important to him in her own right, never be that one special woman in his eyes, never be anything other than second best to him. He could have had any woman, and a woman like Roula Paulides, who shared his background and nationality as well as a long friendship with him, would have had infinitely more to offer him. He wouldn't have had to talk about having to *work* at being married to anyone else. In fact her mind boggled at the concept of Angel being prepared to do anything as dully conventional and sensible as *work* at a relationship.

'I don't want to work at it,' she heard herself say, and it was truthfully what she felt at that moment because her pride could not bear the idea of him having to suppress his natural instincts before he could accept being married to her and staying faithful.

'You don't get a choice,' Angel spelled out grimly. 'We'll fly back to Palos in the morning—'

'No!' she interrupted. 'I'm not returning to Greece with you!'

'You're my wife and you're not leaving me,' Angel asserted harshly. 'That isn't negotiable.'

Merry tossed her head, dark hair rippling back from her flushed cheeks, pale blue eyes icy with fury. 'I'm not even trying to negotiate with you… I already know what a slippery slope that can be. Our marriage is over and I'm staying in the UK,' she declared fiercely. 'I'll move out of here as soon as I decide where I'm going to be living.'

Angel stared back at her, his hard bone structure prominent below his bronzed skin, his eyes very dark and hard. 'You would just throw everything we've got away?' he breathed in a tone of suppressed savagery that made her flinch. 'And what about our daughter?'

Merry swallowed with difficulty, sickly envisioning the likely battle ahead and cringing from the prospect. 'I'll fight you for custody of our daughter here in the UK,' she told him squarely, shocked at what she was saying but needing to convince him that she would not be softened or sidelined by threats.

Angel froze almost as if she had struck him, black

lashes lifting on grim dark eyes without the smallest shade of gold, his lean, strong face rigid with tension. 'You would separate us? That I will not forgive you for,' he told her with fierce finality.

Ten seconds later, Merry was alone in the room, listening numbly to the roar of a helicopter taking off somewhere nearby and presumably ferrying Angel back to London. And she was in shock, her head threatening to explode with the sheer unbearable pressure that had built up inside it, her stomach churning sickly. Tears surged in a hot stinging tide into her eyes and she blinked furiously but the tears kept on coming, dripping down her face.

Their marriage was over. Hadn't she always feared that their marriage wouldn't last? Why was she so shocked? Yes, he had denied that Roula Paulides was his mistress but she hadn't believed him, had she? When she had packed her bags on the island she had known she wasn't coming back and certainly not to a marriage with a husband who had to *work* at being married to her!

CHAPTER TEN

MISERY AND GUILT kept Merry awake for half the night. She had threatened Angel just as he had once threatened her and now it lay like a big rock of shame on her conscience because she had witnessed the depth of his attachment to Elyssa, had watched it develop, had even noticed how surprised Angel was at the amount of enjoyment he received from being a parent. He did not love his wife but he definitely *did* love his daughter.

All her emotions in free fall after the sensitive family issues that had been explored at Sybil's house, she had been in no fit state to deal with Angel. She had drawn up battle lines for a war she didn't actually want to wage, she acknowledged wretchedly. A divorce or separation didn't have to be bitter and nasty and she hadn't the smallest desire for them to fight like cat and dog over their daughter. Angel was a good father, a *very* good father and she would never try to deprive him of contact with his child. Just because she couldn't trust him with the Roulas of the world didn't mean she was blind to his skills as a parent or that she wasn't aware that Elyssa benefitted as much as Angel did from their relationship. She wasn't that selfish, that prejudiced against him, *was* she?

Anguish screamed through her as she sniffed and blew her nose over her breakfast in the dining room. She was a garish match for her elegantly furnished surroundings, clad as she was in comfy old pyjamas and a silky, boldly patterned kimono robe that had seen better days. She had left her fancy new wardrobe behind on Palos as a statement of rejection that she wanted Angel to notice. She had wanted him to appreciate that she didn't need him or his money or those stupid designer clothes, even if that was a lie.

Her real problem, however, was that pain and hurt magnified everything and distorted logic. She had told Angel that she was leaving him because pride had demanded she act as though she were strong and decisive rather than betray the reality that she was broken up and confused and horribly hurt.

The thwack-thwack of a helicopter coming into land made her head ache even more and she gulped down more tea, desperate to soothe her ragged nerves. She heard the slam of the front door and she stiffened, her head jerking up as the dining-room door opened without warning and framed Angel's tall, powerful form. She could not have been more appalled had he surprised her naked because she knew she looked like hell. Her eyes and nose were red, her hair was tangled.

'Will you come into the drawing room?' Angel asked grimly. 'There's someone here to see you.'

'I'm not dressed,' she protested stiltedly, her head lowering to hide her face as she stumbled upright, desperate to make a quick escape from his astute gaze.

'You'll do fine,' Angel told her callously, dark eyes cold and treacherous as black ice.

'I can't see anyone looking like this,' Merry argued vehemently, striving to leave the room and flee upstairs by sidestepping him, but she found him as immoveable in the doorway as a rock.

'You'll be in very good company. I swear she's cried all the way from Greece,' Angel informed her incomprehensibly, gripping her elbow with a firm hand and practically thrusting her into the room next door.

Merry's feet froze to the floor when she saw the woman standing by the window. It was Roula, looking something less than her usually sophisticated and stylish self. Her ashen complexion only emphasised her swollen eyes and pink nose and she was convulsively shredding a tissue between her restive fingers.

'I'm so…*so* sorry!' she gasped, facing Merry. 'I lied to you.'

Angel shot something at the other woman in irate Greek and she groaned and snapped something back, and then the door closed behind Merry and when she turned her head again, Angel was gone, leaving them alone.

'You *lied* to me?' Merry prompted in astonishment.

'I was trying to frighten you off. I thought if you left him he might finally turn to me,' Roula framed shakily, her voice hoarse with embarrassment and misery.

'Oh,' Merry mumbled rather blankly. 'You're not his mistress, then?'

'No, that was nonsense,' Roula framed hoarsely. 'We've never had sex either. Angel's never been interested in me that way, but because we were such good friends I thought if you broke up with him he would confide in me and maybe start seeing me in a different light. But it's not going to happen. He said the idea of me and him ever being intimate was disgusting, *incestuous*. I wish I'd worked out that that's how he saw me years ago. I'd have saved myself a lot of heartache.'

Merry experienced a very strong desire to pat the blonde's shoulder to comfort her and had to fight the weird prompting off. She could see that the other woman felt humiliated and guilty and very sad. 'Did Angel force you to come here and tell me this?'

'Well, it wasn't my idea, but he said I owed him and he was right. From the moment he told me that he was marrying you I was so *jealous* of you!' Roula confessed with a sudden wrenching sob, clamping her hand to her mouth and getting herself back under control again before continuing, 'Why you? I asked myself. Why *not* me? You worked for him and he never ever sleeps with his employees and yet he slept with *you*…and you've got a great figure and you're very pretty but you're not exactly supermodel material…and then you totally freak him out by having a baby and yet somehow he's now crazy about the baby as well!'

'Have you always been in love with him?' Merry mumbled uncomfortably, grasping that, by Roula's reckoning, Angel deciding to marry her qualified as an unbelievable and quite undeserved miracle.

'When I was a teenager it was just a crush. He was my best friend. I knew all the rotten things Angelina has ever done to him and it broke my heart. I learned how to handle her to keep her out of his hair, to try and help him cope with her. That's why she likes me, that's why she decided that he should marry me if he ever married anyone. I've had other relationships, of course,' Roula told her wryly. 'But every time one broke down, I told myself it would've been different with Angel. He was my ideal, my Mr Right…at least he was until he dragged me onto that plane and shouted at me half the night!'

'His temper's rough,' Merry conceded while frantically trying to work out how she had so badly misjudged the man whom she had married. It was obvious that Roula was now telling her the truth. Bitter jealousy had driven the blonde into an attempt to destroy Angel's marriage.

'And he's like the elephant who never forgets when you cross him. He'll never forgive me for causing all this trouble,' Roula muttered with weary regret.

'He'll get over it,' Molly said woodenly, wondering if he would ever forgive her either.

'I'm sorry. I'm truly sorry,' the blonde framed guiltily. 'I know that's not much consolation in the circumstances but I deeply regret lying to you. I didn't think it through. I told myself you'd probably got deliberately pregnant and planned the whole thing to trap him. I could see he was happy on your wedding day but I wouldn't admit that to myself and if anyone merits being happy, it's Angel.'

'I think we can forget about this now,' Merry commented uncomfortably. 'I can't put my hand on my heart and say that I forgive you, but I am grateful you explained why you did it and I do understand.'

'Fair enough,' Roula sighed as she opened the door to leave.

Merry tensed when she saw Angel poised across the hall, straightening to his full predatory height, shrewd dark eyes scanning her like a radiation counter.

'I told the truth,' Roula told him flatly. 'Can I leave now?'

'You're satisfied?' Angel demanded of Merry.

She nodded in embarrassed confirmation.

'I'll have you returned to the airport,' Angel informed Roula curtly.

Merry took advantage of his momentary inattention to head for the stairs at a very fast rate of knots. She wanted to splash her face, clean her teeth, brush her hair and ditch the pyjamas with the pink bunny rabbits on them. Then she would work out what she had to say to him to redress the damage she had done with her lack of faith. Possibly a spot of grovelling would be appropriate, obviously a heartfelt apology...

She was caught unprepared and halfway into a pair of jeans when Angel strode into the bedroom. He thrust the door shut, leant his long, lean frame sinuously back against it and studied her with brooding dark eyes.

'I'm sorry... I'm really sorry,' she muttered, yanking up the jeans. 'But she was very convincing and I don't think she's a bad person. I think she was just jealous and she got a bit carried away.'

'I don't give a damn about Roula or why she did what she did,' Angel declared impatiently. 'I care that even after being married to me for weeks you were still willing to threaten me with the loss of my daughter.'

Merry lost colour, her eyes guiltily lowering from the hard challenge of his. 'That was wrong,' she acknowledged ruefully. 'But you used the same threat to persuade me into marrying you...or have you forgotten that?'

'My intentions were good. I wanted to persuade you to give us a chance to be a proper family. But your intentions were bad and destructive,' Angel countered without hesitation. 'You wanted to use Elyssa like a weapon to punish me. That would have damaged her as much as me.'

'No, I honestly wasn't thinking like that,' Merry argued, turning her back to him to flip off the despised pyjama top and reaching for a tee shirt, having decided for the sake of speed and dignity to forgo donning a bra. 'Even when I was mad at you I accepted that you are a great father, but I assumed you would make any divorce a bitter, nasty battle.'

'What made you assume that?' Angel asked drily. 'I didn't even ask you to sign a pre-nuptial agreement before the wedding. That omission sent the family lawyers into a tailspin but it was a deliberate move on my part. It was an act of faith formed on my foolish assumption that you would respect our marriage as much as I did.'

Merry reddened with more guilt. He really knew what buttons to push, she reflected wretchedly. It hadn't occurred to her that he hadn't asked her to sign a pre-nup before the ceremony, but in retrospect she could see that that had been a glaring omission, indeed a very positive statement, in a marriage involving a very wealthy man and a reasonably poor woman. His continuing coldness was beginning to unnerve her. He had never used that tone with her before. He sounded detached and negative and he was still icily angry. She glanced up, scanning his lean, strong features for another, more encouraging reading of his mood, and instead noted the forbidding line of his wide, sensual mouth, the harsh angle of his firm jaw and the level darkness of his accusing gaze.

'But the instant we hit the first rough patch in our marriage you were ready to throw it all away,' Angel condemned.

'A long-term mistress is more than a rough patch,' Merry protested helplessly. 'I believed Roula because you introduced me to her as a friend that you trusted.'

'She's the sister I never had,' Angel asserted with sardonic bite. 'The thought of anything of a sexual nature between us is…repellent.'

And the last piece of the puzzle fell into place for Merry, who, while believing Roula, had not quite been able to grasp why Angel had never been tempted into having a more intimate relationship with her. After all, Roula was a beauty and had to share a lot with him. But if he saw the blonde in the same light as a sibling, his indifference to her as a woman was instantly understandable and highly unlikely to ever change.

'I've seen a lot of divorces,' Angel admitted. 'In my own family, amongst friends. Nobody comes out unscathed but the children suffer the most. I don't want my daughter to ever suffer that damage, but neither do I want a wife who runs like a rabbit at the first sign of trouble.'

'I did *not* run like a rabbit!' Merry argued, hotfaced. 'Maybe you're thinking of what you did after I told you I was pregnant!'

'I took responsibility. I ensured your financial needs were covered.'

'But you weren't there when I was throwing up every morning and trying to drag myself into work to keep my job.'

'You didn't need to keep on working. Your allowance would have covered your living costs.' Angel hesitated before asking with a frown, 'Were you sick that often?'

'Every day for about four months, often more than

once a day. And then one evening I started bleeding and I assumed I was having a miscarriage. After that, I resigned from my job and went home to stay with Sybil.'

Angel levered his long, lean frame lithely off the door, moving with that innate grace of his towards her, his lean, dark face troubled. 'You almost lost Elyssa?'

'Well, I *thought* I was losing her and I panicked and went to the hospital, but it was just one of those pregnancy mishaps that seem more serious than they are. It was very frightening, though, and very upsetting.'

'And I wasn't there when I should've been,' Angel registered for himself, studying her grimly. 'Can't turn the clock back and be there for you either, so that can't be changed. Do you think you will always hold my absence during those months against me?'

'I try not to dwell on it. If you didn't want a relationship with me at the time there would've been no point in you coming back into my life,' she conceded simply. 'It would've been too awkward for both of us.'

Angel winced. 'I didn't even realise that I *did* want to be in a relationship with you back then. I would have to admit that I was completely blind to my own hang-ups. Growing up I only saw shallow, chaotic relationships, which is why when I was an adult I avoided anything that could have been construed as a relationship. I had sex and that was that, end of…only then I met you and my blueprint for a relaxed and unemotional life went up in flames.'

'How could you have an unemotional life when you're so full of emotion?' Merry asked him incredulously.

'I keep that side of me under control…at least I did until you and Elyssa sneaked through my defences,' Angel reasoned wryly. 'You know, you may not have been a happy camper while you were pregnant but I wasn't any happier. You shook me up. You made me want more and that scared me because I had no experience of a normal relationship.'

'You don't do relationships,' she reminded him drily.

'What have I been doing with you for the past month?' Angel shot back at her. 'There's nothing casual about our connection. Do you really think it's normal for me to be content to spend so much time with one woman?'

'I didn't ask you to do that.'

'I'm a selfish bastard. I did it only because I wanted to.'

'For your daughter's sake, you *worked* at being married to me,' Merry paraphrased with pained dismissiveness.

Angel shook his arrogant dark head in wonderment. 'I've got to admit that right now I'm having to *work* at being married to you because you are so stubbornly determined to think the worst of me.'

'That's not true.'

'You don't trust me. You're always waiting for the roof to fall in! I used to think that was cute but now I'm beginning to wonder if you'll ever recognise that, even though I've made a hell of a lot of mistakes along the way, I do love you,' he completed almost defiantly.

Merry stared at him in astonishment. 'You don't.'

'Even when you're wearing the bunny pyjamas you were wearing the night I got you pregnant,' Angel assured her with confidence. 'I didn't recognise it as love until after we were married. Even though I'm always worrying about you, I'm incredibly happy being with you. I wake up in the morning and everything feels good because you're there beside me. When you're not there, everything feels *off* and I feel weirdly lonely...'

Merry's lower lip parted company with her upper and she stared at him in wide-eyed consternation.

'And the most extraordinary thing of all is that I thought you loved me too until you walked out and accused me of cheating on you,' Angel admitted ruefully. 'I thought that for the first time in my life I was loved for who I was, not for what I can do or buy or provide. You know I'm flawed and you accept it. You know I'm still finding my way in this family set-up.'

'You're not the only one. Yesterday I discovered that Sybil is not my aunt but my grandmother,' Merry told him in a sudden surge. 'That's another reason why I was so upset and over the top with you yesterday. I was already all shaken up. My mother was adopted by Sybil's parents and only learned the truth when she was eighteen. Oh, never mind, I'll explain it all to you later, but finding out that Sybil and Natalie had been keeping all that from me all my life made me feel deceived…and you're right, I *do* love you,' she completed almost apologetically. 'I have almost from the start. Don't know why, don't know how, just got attached regardless of common sense.'

Angel rested his hands down on her taut shoulders. 'We had an electric connection from the first day. Somehow, we match. I just wish I hadn't wasted so much time staying away from you when I wanted to be with you. I was existing in a sort of fog of denial that everything had changed and that I wanted the sort of relationship that I had never trusted or experienced with a woman.'

'And I let you down,' she whispered guiltily. 'I did think the worst at the first sign of trouble. I wasn't strong and sensible the way I should have been.'

'It's sort of comforting that your common sense leaves you when you're upset. When I arrived and saw you'd been crying, obviously upset, it gave me hope that you did care.'

'I'll always care,' she muttered softly, turning her cheek into the caress of his long fingers.

'I've never trusted love. I know my father cares about me but my mother lost interest the minute I grew beyond the cute baby stage,' he confided. 'What you said about Sybil and your mother? Take it back to basics, *agape mou*. You may not have known the whole story but you were *always* loved. That's a blessing. It's much harder to love without that experience and the confidence it gives you.'

Merry stretched up to him and buried her face in his shoulder, drinking in the musky familiar aroma of his skin like a restorative drug. He caught her chin in his fingers and tipped up her mouth to taste her with hungry urgency.

'You taste so good,' he ground out, walking her back towards the bed with single-minded intent. 'Tell me you love me again… I like hearing it.'

'How did you guess how I felt?' Merry pressed. 'I thought I was hiding it.'

'You put up with all my unreasonable demands and still smiled at me. I didn't deserve it so there had to be some other reason why you were being so tolerant and sometimes I couldn't help testing you to see if you'd crack.'

'I don't crack. I'm loyal and loving…as long as you don't take on a mistress.'

'Where would I get the energy?' Angel growled, his attention elsewhere as he slid his hand below the tee shirt to mould it to a plump breast with satisfaction, and then wrenched her out of its concealment with unashamed impatience. '*Thee mou*, I want you so much it hurts… I thought I was losing you.'

'And then I disappointed you.'

'You're not supposed to walk away, you're supposed to stand and fight for me,' Angel told her. 'I fought for you.'

'I was hiding behind my pride.'

'I don't have any where you're concerned and I have even fewer scruples. I was willing to drug and kidnap you to get you back to Greece. You don't want to know the things that ran through my mind when

I thought I was losing you,' he assured her. 'A large helping of crazy, if I'm honest.'

'That's because you love me,' Merry told him happily. 'You're allowed to think crazy things if you want to fight to keep me…'

And their clothes fell away in a messy heap as Angel moved to make her his again and satisfy the last lurking stab of insecurity inside him. Merry was his again and all was right with his world, well, almost all. He shifted lithely against her, holding her close.

'When you feel up to the challenge, we'll have another baby and I will share the whole experience with you,' Angel promised, jolting her out of her drowsy sensual daydream.

'*Another*…baby?' Merry gasped in disbelief. 'You've got to be kidding! Elyssa's only seven months old!'

'You could consider it…eventually, hopefully,' Angel qualified. 'Although I'll settle for Elyssa if you don't want another child. It's not a deal breaker.'

'Are you sure the threat of that extra responsibility won't make you run for the hills again?' Merry asked snidely.

'No, set me the challenge of getting you pregnant and I assure you that I will happily meet every demand, no matter how strenuous or time consuming it becomes.' Dark golden eyes alive with tender amusement, Angel gazed down with a wide, relaxed smile. 'In fact I find the concept quite exciting.'

Merry punched a bare brown shoulder in reproach. 'Anything to do with sex excites you!'

Angel looked reflective and a sudden wicked grin lit his darkly handsome features. 'I'm sure if we had about six children, six very *noisy* and *lively* children, I could persuade my mother to find her own accommodation. You see, expansion could be a complete game changer in the happy-family stakes...'

'I do hope that was a joke,' Merry sighed, warm and contented and so happy she felt floaty. He loved her and it shone out of him. How had she not seen that? How had she tormented herself for so long when what she desperately wanted was right there in front of her, waiting to be claimed?

And now Angel was hers, finally all hers, and equally suddenly she was discovering that she was feeling much more tolerant and forgiving of other people's frailties. Her mother was trying to show her that she cared and perhaps it was past time she made more of an effort in that quarter. And then there was Roula, unhappy and humiliated—possibly she could afford to be more forgiving there as well. Happiness could spread happiness, she decided cheerfully, running a seeking hand down over a long, sleek male flank, keen to increase his happiness factor too...

'Well, I have to confess that I never saw this coming,' Natalie admitted, studying her mother, Sybil, and Angel's father, Charles, as they stood across the room graciously receiving the guests at the wedding reception being held at Angel and Merry's home on the island of Palos. 'I thought it would fizzle out long before they got this far.'

'He's daft about her and she has made him wait six years to put that ring on her finger,' Merry reminded the small blonde woman by her side. 'I think she's just finally ready to settle down.'

'Well, she took her time about it,' Natalie pronounced wryly. 'Angel's mother isn't here, is she?'

'Hardly, considering that she was Charles' first wife,' Merry remarked.

'Not much chance of *her* settling down.'

'No,' Merry agreed quietly, reflecting that they saw remarkably little of Angelina these days. Angelina had bought a Manhattan penthouse where she now spent most of her time. Occasional scandalous headlines and gossip pieces floated back to Angel and Merry, but Angel was no longer forced to be involved in his mother's life and now found it easier to remain detached.

Elyssa rushed up, an adorable vision in a pink flower girl's dress that already had a stain on it. 'Keep this for me,' she urged, stuffing the little wicker basket she had carried down the aisle into her mother's hand. 'Cos and I are going to play hide and seek.'

Merry bent down. 'No, you're not. This is a very special party for grown-ups and children aren't allowed to run about.'

Her son, Cosmas, four years old to his big sister's almost six years, rushed up, wrenching impatiently at the sash tied round his waist. 'Take this off.'

'Not until Sybil says you can,' Merry warned. 'There are still photos to be taken.'

'Where's the rest of the horde?' Natalie enquired curiously.

Their two-year-old twins, Nilo and Leksi, were chasing Tiger through the hall. Merry hurtled in that direction to interrupt the chase before it got out of hand. Tiger was a mere shadow of the fat and inactive little dog he had once been. Living in a household with five children had slimmed him down. His first rehoming hadn't worked out and when he had been returned to Sybil soon afterwards, after shaming himself and stealing food, Merry had scooped him up for a rapturous reunion and brought him back to Greece. As she hovered Angel appeared, a baby clutched securely below one arm, and spoke sternly to his youngest sons. Atlanta beamed gummily across the hall at her mother and opened her arms.

'I don't know where you get the energy,' Natalie confessed, watching Merry reclaim her eight-month-old daughter. 'Either of you. You produce like rabbits. Please tell me the family's complete now.'

Colour warmed Merry's cheeks because their sixth child was already on the way, even if they had not yet announced the fact, and Angel grinned down at his tongue-tied wife with wicked amusement. 'We haven't decided yet,' he said lightly.

Atlanta tugged on her mother's long hair as Merry walked out onto the terrace to take a break from the festivities. It had taken weeks of careful planning to organise the wedding and accommodation for all the guests. She had wanted everything to be perfect for Sybil and Charles, both of whom were frequent visitors to their home. After all the years of feeling short-changed in the family stakes, Merry had come full circle and now she was surrounded by a loving family.

She was even happier to have achieved a more normal relationship with her mother, who had returned to the UK and started up a very successful yoga studio. These days she regularly saw Natalie when she went over to London with Angel. Her mother had mellowed and Merry had put the past behind her in every way.

A year earlier she had acted as Roula's matron of honour when the other woman had married the island doctor in a three-day-long bout of very Greek celebration. Roula was still a friend of the family, and sometimes Merry suspected that the trouble the other woman had caused with the mistress lie and the truths that had then come out had actually helped Roula to move on and meet someone capable of loving her back.

But then Merry was willing to admit that she had learned from the same experience as well. Discovering that she was married to a man who loved her so much that he was willing to do virtually anything it took to hang onto her and their marriage had banished her insecurity for ever. She liked being a mother and Angel revelled in being a father. The rapid expansion of their family had been exhausting but also uniquely satisfying.

Lean brown hands scooped the slumbering baby from Merry's lap and passed her to Jill, Sally's co-nanny, for attention. Angel then scooped his wife out of her chair and sank back down with her cradled in his arms.

'You are very tired,' he scolded. 'We've talked about this. You agreed to take afternoon naps.'

'After the meal,' she murmured, small fingers flirting with his silk tie as she gazed up at him, loving and appreciating every line of his lean, startlingly handsome features and thinking back lazily to the poor beginning they had shared that had miraculously transformed over the years into a glorious partnership.

'Thee mou,' Angel intoned huskily. 'Sometimes I look at the life you have created for all of us and I love you so much it hurts, *agape mou*. My wife, my family, is my anchor.'

Happy as a teenager in his public display of affection where once she would have wrenched herself free, Merry giggled. 'You mean we drag you down?'

And Angel gave up the battle and kissed her, hungrily, deeply, tenderly while somewhere in the background his mother-in-law snorted and said in a pained voice, 'You see…like rabbits.'

* * * * *

THE PREGNANT
KAVAKOS BRIDE

SHARON KENDRICK

For the ever-amusing Amelia Tuttiett, who is a
brilliant ceramicist and an inspirational teacher.

CHAPTER ONE

SHE WAS EVERYTHING he hated about a woman and she was talking to his brother. Ariston Kavakos grew very still as he stared at her. At curves guaranteed to make a man desire her whether he wanted to or not. And he most definitely did not. Yet his body was stubbornly refusing to obey the dictates of his mind and a powerful shaft of lust arrowed straight to his groin.

Who the hell had invited Keeley Turner?

She was standing close to Pavlos, her blonde hair rippling beneath the overhead lights of the swish London art gallery. She lifted her hand as if to emphasise a point and Ariston found his gaze drawn to the most amazing breasts he had ever seen. He swallowed as he remembered her in a dripping wet bikini with rivulets of water trickling down over her belly as she emerged from the foamy blue waters of the Aegean. She was memory and fantasy all mixed up in one. Something started and never finished. Eight years on and Keeley Turner made him want to look at her and only her, despite the stunning photographs of his private Greek island which dominated the walls of the London gallery.

Was his brother similarly smitten? He hoped not, although it was hard to tell because their body language excluded the rest of the world as they stood deep in conversation. Ariston began to walk across the gallery but if they noticed him approach they chose not to acknowledge it. He felt a flicker of rage, which he quickly cast aside because rage could be counterproductive. He knew that now. Icy calm was far more effective in dealing with difficult situations and it had been the key to his success. The means by which he had dragged his family's ailing company out of the dust and built it anew and gained a reputation of being the man with the Midas touch. The dissolute reign of his father was over and his elder son was now firmly in charge. These days the Kavakos shipping business was the most profitable on the planet and he intended to keep it that way.

His mouth hardened. Which meant more than just dealing with shipbrokers and being up to speed with the state of world politics. It meant keeping an eye on the more gullible members of the family. Because there was a lot of money sloshing around the Kavakos empire and he knew how women acted around money. An early lesson in feminine greed had changed his life for ever and that was why he never took his eye off the ball. His attitude meant that some people considered him controlling, but Ariston preferred to think of himself as a guiding influence—like a captain steering a ship. And in a way, life *was* like being at sea. You steered clear of icebergs for obvious reasons and women were like icebergs. You only ever saw ten per cent of what they were *really* like—the rest was buried deep beneath the self-serving and grasping surface.

His eyes didn't leave the blonde as he walked towards them, knowing that if she was going to be a problem in his brother's life he would deal with it—and quickly. His lips curved into the briefest of smiles. He would have her dispatched before she even realised what was happening.

'Why, Pavlos,' Ariston said softly as he reached them and he noticed that the woman had instantly grown tense. 'This *is* a surprise. I wasn't expecting to see you here so soon after the opening night. Have you developed a late-onset love of photography or are you just homesick for the island on which you were born?'

Pavlos didn't look too happy to be interrupted—but Ariston didn't care. Right then he couldn't think about anything except what was happening inside him. Because, infuriatingly, he seemed to have developed no immunity against the green-eyed temptress he'd last seen when she was eighteen, when she'd thrown herself at him with a hunger which had blown his mind. Her submission had been instant and would have been total if he hadn't put a stop to it. Displaying the sexist double standards for which he had occasionally been accused, he had despised her availability at the same time as he'd been bewitched by it. It had taken all his legendary self-control to push her away and to adjust his clothing but he had done it, though it had left him hard and aching for what had seemed like months afterwards. His mouth tightened because she was nothing but a tramp. A cheap and grasping little tramp.

Like mother, like daughter, he thought grimly—and the last type of woman he wanted his brother getting mixed up with.

'Oh, hi, Ariston,' said Pavlos with the easy manner which made most people surprised when they learned they were brothers. 'That's right, here I am again. I decided to pay a second visit and meet up with an old friend at the same time. You remember Keeley, don't you?'

There was a moment of silence while a pair of bright green eyes were lifted to his and Ariston felt the loud hammer of his heart.

'Of course I remember Keeley,' he said roughly, aware of the irony of his words. Because for him most women *were* forgettable and nothing more than a means to an end. Oh, sometimes he might recall a pair of spectacular breasts or a pert bottom—or if a woman was especially talented with her lips or hands, she might occasionally merit a nostalgic smile. But Keeley Turner had been in a class of her own and he'd never been able to shift her from the corners of his mind. Because she'd been off-limits and forbidden? Or because she had given him a taste of unbelievable sweetness before he'd forced himself to reject her? Ariston didn't know. It was as inexplicable as it was powerful and he found himself studying her with the same intensity as the nearby people peering at the photos which adorned the gallery walls.

Petite yet impossibly curvy, her thick hair hung down her back in a curtain of pale and rippling waves. Her jeans were ordinary and her thin sweater unremarkable yet somehow that didn't seem to matter. With a body like hers she could have worn a piece of sackcloth and still looked like dynamite. The cheap, man-made fabric strained over the lushness of her breasts and the blue denim caressed the curves of her bottom. Her mouth was bare of lipstick and her eyes wore only a lick of mascara as they studied him warily. Hers was not a modern look—yet there was something about Keeley Turner... An indefinable something which touched a sensual core deep inside him and made him want to peel her clothes from her body and ride her until she was screaming his name. But he wanted her gone more than he wanted to bed her—and maybe he should set about accomplishing that right now.

Deliberately excluding her from the conversation, Ariston turned to his brother and summoned up a bland smile. 'I wasn't aware you two were friends.'

'We haven't actually seen each other for years,' said Pavlos. 'Not since that holiday.'

'I suspect that holiday is an event which none of us particularly care to revisit,' said Ariston smoothly, enjoying the sudden rush of colour which had made her cheeks turn a deep shade of pink. 'Yet you've stayed in touch with each other all this time?'

'We're friends on social media,' Pavlos elaborated, with a shrug. 'You know how it is.'

'Actually, I don't. You know my views on social media and none of them are positive.' Ariston made no attempt to hide his frosty disapproval. 'I need to talk to you, Pavlos. Alone,' he added.

Pavlos frowned. 'When?'

'Now.'

'But I've only just met up with Keeley. Can't it wait?'

'I'm afraid it can't.' He saw Pavlos shoot her an apologetic glance as if to apologise for his brother's bullish behaviour but social niceties didn't bother him. He'd worked hard for most of his life to ensure that Pavlos was kept away from the kind of scandals which had once engulfed their family. He'd been determined he wouldn't go the same sorry way as their father. He'd made sure that he'd attended a good boarding school in England and a university in Switzerland, and he had carefully influenced his choice of friends—and girlfriends. And this pretty little tramp in her cheap dress and come-to-bed eyes was about to learn that his baby brother was strictly off-limits. 'It's business,' he added firmly.

'Not more trouble in the Gulf?'

'Something like that,' Ariston agreed, irritated at his brother's attitude and wondering why he'd forgotten you didn't talk family business in front of strangers. 'We can use one of the offices here at the gallery—they're very accommodating,' he added smoothly. 'The owner is a friend of mine.'

'But Keeley—'

'Oh, don't worry about Keeley. I'm sure she has the imagination to take care of herself. There's plenty for her to look at.' Ariston turned to give her a hard version of a smile, noticing that her knuckles had suddenly whitened as she clutched her thin shawl. For the first time he spoke directly to her, dropping his voice to a silken murmur which his business rivals would have recognised as being a tone you didn't mess with. 'And plenty of men hanging around who would be all too happy to take my brother's place. In fact, I can see a couple watching you right now. I'm sure you could have a lot of fun with them, Keeley. You really mustn't let us keep you any longer.'

Keeley felt her face freeze as Ariston spoke to her, wishing she could come up with a suitably crushing response to throw at the powerful Greek who was looking at her as if she was a stain on the pale floorboards and talking to her as if she was some kind of hooker. But the truth was that she didn't *trust* herself to speak—afraid that her words would come out as meaningless babble. Because that was the effect he had on her. The effect he had on all women. Even when he was talking to them—or should she say *at* them?—with utter contempt in his eyes, he could reduce them to a level of longing which wasn't like the stuff you felt around most men. He could make you have fantasies about him, even though he exuded nothing but darkness.

She'd seen the way her own mother had looked at him. She could see the other women in the gallery watching him now—their gazes hungry but wary—as if they were observing a different type of species and weren't sure how to handle him. As if they realised they should stay well away but were itching to touch him all the same. And she could hardly judge them for that, could she? Because hadn't *she* flung herself at him? Pressed her body hard against his and longed for him to take away the aching deep inside her. Behaved like a cheap little fool by misinterpreting a simple gesture on his part and managing to make a bad situation even worse.

The last time she'd seen him her life had pretty much imploded and eight years later she was still dealing with the fallout. Keeley's mouth tightened. Because she'd come through far too much to let the arrogant billionaire make her feel bad about herself. She suspected that the mocking challenge sparking from his blue eyes was intended to make her excuse herself and disappear, but she wasn't going to do that. A quiet rebellion began to build inside her. Did he really think he had the power to kick her out of this public gallery, as once he had kicked her off his private island?

'I wasn't planning on going anywhere,' she said, seeing his eyes darken with anger. 'I'm quite happy looking at photographs of Lasia. I'd forgotten just what a beautiful island it was and I can certainly keep myself occupied until you get back.' She smiled. 'I'll wait here for you, Pavlos. Take as long as you like.'

It clearly wasn't the response Ariston wanted and she saw the irritation which hardened his beautiful features.

'As you wish,' he said tightly. 'Though I cannot guarantee how long we'll be.'

She met his cold blue stare with a careless smile. 'Don't worry about it. I'm not in any hurry.'

He shrugged. 'Very well. Come, Pavlos.'

He began to walk away with his brother by his side and, although she told herself to look away, Keeley could do nothing but stand and stare, just like everyone else in the gallery.

She'd forgotten how tall and rugged he was because she had *forced* herself to forget—to purge her memory of a sensuality which had affected her like no other. But now it was all coming back. The olive skin and tendrils of hair which brushed so blackly against his shirt collar. Yet she thought he seemed uncomfortable in the exquisite grey suit he wore. His muscular body looked constrained—as if he was more at home wearing the sawn-off denims he'd worn on Lasia. The ones which had emphasised his powerful thighs as he'd dived deep into the sapphire waters surrounding his island home. And it suddenly occurred to her that it didn't matter what he wore or what he said because nothing had changed. Not really. You saw him and you wanted him, it was as simple as that. She thought how cruel life could be—as if she needed any reminding—that the only man she'd ever desired was someone who made no secret about despising her.

With an effort, she tore her gaze away and forced herself to focus on a photograph which showed the island which had been in the Kavakos family for generations. Lasia was known as the paradise of the Cyclades with good reason and Keeley had felt as if she'd tumbled into paradise the moment she'd first set foot on its silvery sands. She had explored its surprisingly lush interior with delight until her mother's startling fall from grace had led to their visit being cut brutally short. She would never forget the hordes of press and the flash of cameras in their faces as they'd alighted from the boat which had taken them back to Piraeus. Or the screaming headlines when they'd arrived back in England—

and the cringe-making interviews her mother had given afterwards, which had only made matters worse. Keeley had been tainted by the scandal—an unwilling victim of circumstances beyond her control—and the knock-on effect had continued to this day.

Wasn't it that which had made her come here this afternoon—to meet up with Pavlos and remind herself of the beauty of the place? As if by doing that she could draw a line under the past and have some kind of closure? She'd hoped she might be able to eradicate some of the awful memories and replace them with better ones. She'd seen a picture of Ariston in the paper, attending the opening night, with some gorgeous redhead clinging like a vine to his arm. She certainly hadn't expected him to show up here today. Would she have come if she had known?

Of course she wouldn't. She wouldn't have set foot within a million miles of the place.

'Keeley?'

She turned around to find that Pavlos was back—with Ariston standing slightly behind him, not bothering to disguise the triumph curving his lips as his gaze clashed with hers.

'Hi,' she said, aware that the blue burn of his eyes was making her skin grow hot. 'You weren't long.'

A look of regret passed over Pavlos's face and somehow Keeley knew what was coming.

'No. I know I wasn't. Look, I'm afraid I'm going to have to bail out, Keeley,' he said. 'And take a rain check. Ariston needs me to fly out to the Middle East and take care of a ship.'

'What, now?' questioned Keeley, before she could stop herself.

'This very second,' put in Ariston silkily before adding, 'Should he have checked with you first?'

Pavlos bent to brush a brief kiss over each of her cheeks before giving her a quick smile. 'I'll message you later. Okay?'

'Sure.' She stood and watched him leave, aware that Ariston was still standing behind her but not trusting herself even to look at him. Instead, she tried very hard to concentrate on the photo she'd been studying—a sheltered bay where you could just make out shapes of giant turtles swimming in the crystal-clear waters. Perhaps he might just take the hint and go away. Leave her alone so that she could get to work on forgetting him all over again.

'I can't quite work out whether you are completely oblivious to my presence,' he said, in his dark, accented voice, 'or whether you just get a kick out of ignoring me.'

He had moved closer to stand beside her and Keeley lifted her gaze to find herself caught in that piercing sapphire stare and the resulting rush of blood went straight to her head. And her breasts. She could feel them become heavy and aching as the slow beat of her blood engorged them. Her mouth dried. How did he *do* that? Her fingers had grown numb and she was feeling almost dizzy but somehow she managed to compose a cool sentence. 'Why, do women always notice you whenever you walk into a room?'

'What do you think?'

And it was then that Keeley realised that she didn't have to play this game. Or *any* game. He was nothing to her. Nothing. *So stop acting like he's got some kind of power over you.* Yes, she'd once made a stupid mistake—but so what? It was a long time ago. She'd been young and stupid and she'd paid her dues—not to him, but to the universe—and *she didn't owe him anything.* Not even politeness.

'Honestly?' She gave a short laugh. 'I think you're unbelievably rude and arrogant, as well as having the most over-inflated ego of any man I've ever met.'

He raised his brows. 'And I imagine you must have met quite a few in your time.'

'Nowhere near the amount of women *you* must have notched up, if the papers are to be believed.'

'I don't deny it—but if you try to play the numbers game I'm afraid you'll never win.' His eyes glittered. 'Didn't anyone ever tell you that the rules for men and the rules for women are very different, *koukla mou*?'

'Only in the outdated universe you seem to occupy.'

He gave a careless shrug. 'It may not be fair but I'm afraid it's a fact of life. And men are allowed to behave in a way which would be disapproved of in a woman.'

His voice had dipped into a velvety caress and it was having precisely the wrong effect on her. Keeley could feel a hot flush of colour flooding into her cheeks as she made to move away.

'Let me pass, please,' she said, trying to keep her voice steady. 'I don't have to stand here and listen to this kind of Neanderthal…*rubbish.*'

'No, you're right. You don't.' He placed a restraining hand on her forearm. 'But before you go, maybe this is the ideal opportunity to get a few things straight between us.'

'What kind of things?'

'I think you know what I'm talking about, Keeley.'

'I'm afraid you've lost me.' She shrugged. 'Mind-reading was never one of my talents.'

His gaze hardened. 'Then let me give it to you in words of one syllable, just so there can be no misunderstanding.' There was a pause. 'Just stay away from my brother, okay?'

She stared at him in disbelief. 'Excuse me?'

'You heard. Leave him alone. Find someone else to dig your beautiful claws into—I'm sure there must be plenty of takers.'

His hand was still on her arm and to the outside world it must have looked like an affectionate gesture between two people who'd just bumped into one another, but to Keeley it felt nothing like that. She could feel the imprint of his fingers through her sweater and it was almost as if he were branding her with his touch—as if he were setting her skin on fire. Angrily, she shook herself free. 'I can't believe you have the nerve to come out and say something like that.'

'Why not? I have his best interests at heart.'

'You mean you regularly go around warning off Pavlos's friends?'

'Up until now I haven't felt the need to do more than keep a watchful eye on them but today I do. Funny that.' He gave a mirthless smile. 'I have no idea of your success rate with men, though I imagine it must be high.

But I feel I'd better crush any burgeoning hopes you may have by telling you that Pavlos already has a girlfriend. A beautiful, decent woman he cares for very much and wedding bells are in the air.' His eyes glittered. 'So I wouldn't bother wasting any more time on him if I were you.'

It struck Keeley again how *controlling* he was. Even now. As if all he had to do was to snap his fingers and everyone would just jump to attention. 'And does he have any say in the matter?' she demanded. 'Have you already chosen the engagement ring? Decided where the wedding is going to be and how many bridesmaids?'

'Just stay away from him, Keeley,' he snapped. 'Understand?'

The irony was that Keeley had absolutely no romantic leanings towards Pavlos Kavakos and never had done. They'd once been close, yes—but in a purely platonic way and she hadn't seen him in years. Their current friendship, if you could call it that, extended no further than her pressing the occasional 'like' button or smiley face whenever he posted a photo of himself with a crowd of beautiful young things revelling in the sunshine. Meeting him today had been comforting because she realised he didn't care what had happened in the past, but she was aware that they moved in completely different worlds which never collided. He was rich and she was not. She didn't know or care that he had a girlfriend, but hearing Ariston's imperious order was like a red rag to a bull.

'Nobody tells me what to do,' she said quietly. 'Not you. Not anyone. You can't move people around like pawns. I'll see who I want to see—and you can't do a thing to stop me. If Pavlos wants to get in touch, I'm not going to turn him away just because *you* say so. Understand?'

She saw the disbelief on his face which was quickly followed by anger, as if nobody ever dared defy him so openly, and she tried to ignore the sudden sense of foreboding which made her body grow even more tense. But she'd said her piece and now she needed to get away. Get away quickly before she started thinking about how it had felt to have him touch her.

She turned away and walked straight out of the gallery, not noticing that her cream shawl had slipped from her nerveless fingers. All she was aware of was the burn of Ariston's eyes on her back, which made each step feel like a slow walk to the gallows. The glass elevator arrived almost immediately but Keeley was shaking as it zoomed her down to ground level and her forehead was wet with sweat as she stepped out onto the busy London pavement.

CHAPTER TWO

THE JOURNEY BACK to her home in New Malden passed in a blur as Keeley kept remembering the way Ariston had spoken to her—with a contempt he'd made no attempt to disguise. But that hadn't stopped her breasts from tightening beneath his arrogant scrutiny, had it? Nor that stupid yearning from whispering over her skin every time she'd looked into the blue blaze of his eyes. And now she was going to have to start forgetting him all over again.

A sudden spring shower emptied itself on her head as she emerged from the train station. The April weather was notoriously unpredictable but she was ill-prepared for the rain and hadn't packed an umbrella. By the time she let herself into her tiny bedsit she was dripping wet and cold and her fingers were trembling as she shut the door. But instead of doing the sensible thing of stripping off her clothes and boiling the kettle to make tea, she sank into the nearest chair, not caring that her clothes were damp and getting all crumpled. She stared out of the window but the rods of rain spattering onto the rooftops barely registered. Suddenly she was no longer sitting shivering in a small and unremarkable corner of London. Her mind was playing tricks on her and all she could see was a wide silver beach with beautiful mountains rising up in the distance. A paradise of a place. Lasia.

Keeley swallowed, unprepared for the sudden rush of memory which made the past seem so vivid. She remembered her surprise at finding herself on Lasia—a private island owned by the powerful Kavakos family, with whom she'd had no connection. She'd been staying on nearby Andros with her mother who had spent the holiday complaining about her recent divorce from Keeley's father and washing her woes away with too many glasses of *retsina*.

But Ariston's own father had been one of those men who were dazzled by celebrity—even B-list celebrity—and when he'd heard that the actress and her teenage daughter were so close, had insisted they join him on his exclusive island home to continue their holiday. Keeley had been reluctant to gatecrash someone else's house party but her mother had been overjoyed at the free upgrade, her social antennae quivering in the presence of so many rich and powerful men. She had layered on extra layers of 'war paint' and crammed her body into a bikini which was much too brief for a woman her age.

But Keeley had wanted none of the party scene because it bored her. Despite her relatively tender years, she'd had her fill of the decadent parties her mother had dragged her to since she'd been old enough to walk. At eighteen, she just tried to stay in the background because that was where she felt safest. Over the years her

mother's sustained girlishness had contributed to her becoming an out and out tomboy, despite her very bother-
some and very feminine curves. She remembered being
overjoyed to meet the sporty Pavlos, with whom she'd
hit it off immediately. The Greek teenager had taught
her how to snorkel in the crystal bays and taken her
hiking in the blue-green mountains. Physical attraction
hadn't come into it because, like many children brought
up by a licentious parent, Keeley had been something
of a prude. She'd never felt a single whisper of desire
and the thought of sex had been mildly disgusting. She
and Pavlos had been like brother and sister—growing
brown as berries as they explored the island paradise
which had felt like their own miniature kingdom.

But then one morning his older brother Ariston had
arrived in a silvery-white boat, looking like some kind
of god at its helm, with his tousled black hair, tawny
skin and eyes which matched the colour of the dark sea.
Keeley remembered watching him from the beach, her
heart crashing in an unfamiliar way. She remembered
her mouth growing dry as he jumped onto the sand, the
fine silver grains spraying up around his bronzed calves
like Christmas glitter. Later, she'd been introduced to
him but had remained so self-conscious in his presence that she'd barely been able to look him in the eye.
Not so all the other women at the house party. She'd
cringed at the way her mother had flirted with him—
even asking him to rub suncream into her shoulders.
Keeley remembered his barely perceptible shudder as
he delegated the task to a female member of staff, and
her mother's pout when he did so.

And then had come the night of the party—the impressive party to which the Greek Defence Minister had been invited. Keeley remembered the febrile atmosphere and Ariston's disapproving face as people started getting more and more drunk. Remembered wondering where her mother had disappeared to—only to discover that she'd been caught making out with the minister's driver, her blonde head bobbing up and down on the back seat of the official car as she administered oral sex to a man half her age. Someone had even filmed them doing it. And that was when all hell had broken loose.

Keeley had fled down to the beach, too choked with shame to be able to face anyone, too scared to read the disgust in their expressions and wanting nothing but to be left alone. But Ariston had come after her and had found her crying. His words had been surprisingly soft. Almost gentle. He'd put his arms around her, and it had felt like heaven. Was it because her mother never showed physical affection and her father had been too old to pick her up when she was little which had caused Keeley to misconstrue what was happening, so she mistook comfort for something else? Was that why the desire which had been absent from her life now shot through her like a flame, making her behave in a way she'd never behaved before?

It had been so powerful, that feeling. Like a primitive hunger which *had* to be fed. Pressing her body against Ariston's, she'd risen up on tiptoe as her trembling mouth sought his. After a moment he had responded and that response had been everything she could have dreamed of. For a few minutes the feeling had intensified as his lips had pressed down urgently against hers. She'd felt his tongue nudging against her mouth and she'd opened her mouth in silent invitation. And then his fingers had been on her quivering breasts, impatiently fingering her nipples into peaking points before guiding her hand towards his trousers. There had been no shyness on her part, just a glorious realisation of the power of her own sexuality—and his. She remembered the ragged groan he'd made as she'd touched him there. The way she'd marvelled at the hard ridge pushing against his trousers as, greedily, she had run her fingertips over it. Passion had swamped shyness and she'd been so consumed by it that she suspected she would have let him do whatever he wanted, right there and then on the silvery sand—until suddenly he had thrust her away from him with a look on his shadowed face which she would remember as long as she lived.

'You little…*tramp*,' he'd said, his voice shaking with rage and disgust. 'Like mother, like daughter. Two filthy little tramps.'

She'd never realised until that moment how badly rejection could hurt. Just like she hadn't realised how someone could make you feel so *cheap*. She remembered the shame which flooded through her as she vowed never to put herself in that position again. She would never allow herself to be rejected again. But her own pain had been quickly superseded by what had happened when they'd returned to England and her mother's lifestyle had finally caught up with her—and in one way and another they'd been paying the price ever since.

She pushed the bitter memories away because her

hair was still damp and she had now started to shiver so Keeley forced herself to get up and to go into the cramped bathroom, where the miserable jet of tepid water trickling from the shower did little to warm her chilled skin. But the brisk rub of a rough towel helped and so did the big mug of tea she made herself afterwards. She'd just put on her uniform when there was a knock on the door and she frowned. Her social circle was tiny because of the hours she worked, but even so she didn't often invite people here. She didn't want people coming in and judging her. Wondering how the only daughter of a wealthy man and an actress whose face had graced cinema screens in a series of low-budget vampire movies should have ended up living in such drastically reduced circumstances.

A louder knock sounded and she pulled open the door, her curiosity dying on her lips when she saw who was standing there. Her heart pounded in her chest as she looked into the blaze of Ariston's eyes and she gripped the door handle, hard. His black hair was wet and plastered to his head and his coat was spattered with raindrops. She knew she should tell him to get lost before slamming the door shut in his face but the powerful impact of his presence made her hesitate just as the siren tug of her body betrayed her yet again. Because he was just so damned *gorgeous*…with his muscular physique and that classical Greek face with the tiny bump midway down his nose.

'What are you doing here?' she said coldly. 'Did you think of a few more insults you'd forgotten to ram home?'

His lips curved into an odd kind of smile. 'I think you left…this.'

She stared down at the cream shawl he was holding, her heart automatically contracting. It was an old wrap which had belonged to her mother—a soft, cashmere drift of a thing embroidered with tiny pink flowers and green leaves. These days it was faded and worn, but it reminded her of the woman her mother used to be and a lump rose in her throat as she lifted her gaze to his.

'How did you find out where I live?' she questioned gruffly.

'It wasn't difficult. You signed the visitors' book at the gallery, remember?'

'But you didn't have to bring it yourself. Couldn't you have asked one of your minions to do it?'

'I could. But there are some things I prefer not to delegate.' He met her eyes. 'And besides, I don't think we've quite finished our conversation, do you?'

She supposed they hadn't and that somehow there seemed to be a lot which had been left unsaid. And maybe it was better that way. Yet something was stopping her from closing the door on him. She told herself he had gone out of his way to bring her mum's shawl back to her and he *was* very wet. Did he sense her hesitation? Was that why he took a step forward?

'So aren't you going to ask me inside?' he persisted softly.

'Suit yourself,' she said carelessly, but her heart was thumping like a crazy thing as she walked back into the little bedsit and heard him shut the door to follow her. And when she turned round and saw him standing there—so powerful and masculine—her breasts grew hot and heavy with desire. Why him? she thought despairingly. Why should Ariston Kavakos be the only man who should make her feel so insanely *alive*? Her smile was tight. 'Though if you're going to try to justify your ridiculously controlling behaviour, I wouldn't bother.'

'And what's that supposed to mean?' he questioned silkily.

'It means that you turn up and suddenly send your brother away to sea—just to get him away from me. Isn't that a little desperate?'

His lips hardened. 'Like I told you. He already has a girlfriend. A young woman of Greek origin who has just qualified as a doctor and is light years away from someone like you. And if you must know, the business in the Gulf is both urgent and legitimate—you flatter yourself if you think I'd manufacture some kind of catastrophe just to remove him from your company. But I'm not going to lie. I can't deny I'm happy he's gone.'

She felt the sting of his words yet she could almost understand his concern—even though it was misplaced—because the contrast between her and Pavlos's girlfriend couldn't have been greater. She could imagine how Ariston must see it, in that simplistic and chauvinistic way of his. The qualified professional doctor versus someone with barely an exam to her name. If he'd gone about it differently—if he'd asked her nicely—then Keeley might have done what he wanted her to do. She might have given him her word that she'd never see Pavlos again—which was probably true in any case. But he wasn't asking, was he? He was *telling*. And it wasn't so much the contempt in his eyes which was making her angry—it was the total lack of respect. As if she meant nothing. As if her feelings counted for nothing. As if she was to spend the rest of her life paying for one youthful mistake. She tilted her chin upwards. 'If you think you can tell me what to do, then you're wrong,' she said. 'Very, very wrong.'

Ariston stiffened because her defiance was turning him on and that was the last thing he wanted. He'd come here ostensibly to return the shawl she'd left behind and yet part of him had *wanted* to see her again, even though he'd convinced himself he was only looking out for his brother's welfare. In the car he had briefly buried his nose in the soft cashmere and smelt Keeley's faint and flowery perfume. He'd wondered whether she had deliberately left it behind to get his brother to come running after her when he arrived back in England. Had that been her not so subtle plan? Did she sense a softness in his younger sibling and a susceptibility to her blonde sexiness which could override what seemed to be a perfect relationship with his long-term girlfriend?

He remembered how close she and Pavlos had been on that holiday, how they used to run around together all the time. People said the past had powerful and sentimental tentacles and she'd known his brother when he was young and impressionable. Long before he'd reached the age of twenty-five and come into the massive trust fund which had changed people's attitude towards him, because wealth always did. Mightn't Pavlos read more into his date with the sexy blonde than there really was and forget the safe and settled future which was carefully laid out for him? What if Keeley Turner realised that a fortune was there for the taking if she just went about it the right way?

He glanced around her home, more surprised by her environment than he could remember being surprised by anything in a long time. Because this wasn't just a low standard of living—this was *breadline* living. He'd imagined peacock feathers and glittery necklaces draped over mirrors. Walls dripping with old photos depicting her mother's rather tawdry fame, but there was nothing other than neatness and an almost bland utilitarianism. The most overriding feature was one of *cleanliness*. His mouth hardened. Was that simply a clever ploy to illustrate what a good little homemaker she could be, if only some big and powerful man would take her away from all this and give her the opportunity?

He'd been doing his best not to stare at her because staring only increased his desire and a man could think more clearly when his blood wasn't heated by lust. But now he looked at her dispassionately and for the first time he registered that she was wearing some kind of *uniform*. He frowned. Surely she wasn't a nurse? He took in a shapeless navy dress edged by a paler blue piping and then noticed a small badge depicting a bright, cartoon sun and what looked like a chicken drumstick underneath the words 'Super Save'. No. His mouth twisted. Definitely not a nurse.

'You work in a shop?' he demanded.

He could see the indecision which fretworked her

brow, before she gave him another defiant tilt of her chin which made her lips look utterly kissable.

'Yes, I work in a shop,' she said.

'Why?'

'Why not?' she questioned angrily. 'Somebody has to. How else do you think all the shelves get stacked with new produce? Or, let me guess—you never actually *do* your own shopping?'

'You're a shelf-stacker?' he asked incredulously.

Keeley drew in a deep breath. If it had been anyone else she might have blurted out the truth about her mother and all the other dark stuff which had led her to having to leave so many jobs that, in the end, Super Save supermarket had been her unlikely saviour. She might have explained that she was doing her best to make up for all those lost, gypsy-like years by studying hard whenever she had a spare moment and was doing an online course in bookkeeping and business studies. She might even have plunged the very depths of her own despair and conveyed the sense of hopelessness she felt when she visited her mother every week. When she saw how the once vibrant features had become an unmoving mask while those china-blue eyes stared unseeingly into the distance. When, no matter how many times she prayed for a different outcome, her mother failed to recognise the young woman she had given birth to.

Briefly Keeley closed her eyes as she remembered the awkward conversation she'd had last week with the care-home manager. How she'd been informed that costs were spiralling and they were going to have to put the fees up and that there was only so much that the welfare state could do. And when she'd tried to protest about her mum being moved to that horrible great cavern of a place which was not only cheaper but miles away, she had been met with a shrugging response and been told that nobody could argue with economics.

But why imagine that Ariston Kavakos would have anything other than a cold and unfeeling heart? As if he would even *care* about her problems. The controlling billionaire clearly wanted to think the worst about her and she doubted whether coming out with her own particular sob story would change his mind. Suddenly she felt sorry for Pavlos. How awful to have a brother who was so determined to orchestrate your life that you weren't allowed the personal freedom to make your own friends. Why, the sexy Greek billionaire standing in front of her was nothing more than a raging megalomaniac!

'Yes, I'm a shelf-stacker,' she said quietly. 'Do you have a problem with that?'

Ariston wanted to say that the only problem he had was with *her*. With her inherent sensuality, which managed to transcend even the ugly outfit she was wearing. Or maybe it was because he'd seen her in a swimsuit, with the sopping wet fabric clinging to every feminine curve. Maybe it was because he knew what a killer body lay beneath the oversized uniform which was making him aroused. Yet it was a shock to discover just how humble her circumstances were. As a gold-digger she clearly wasn't as effective as her mother had been or she wouldn't have ended up in a crummy apartment, working unsociable hours in a supermarket.

In his mind he began to do rapid calculations. She was obviously broke and therefore easy to manipulate, but he also sensed that she presented an unknown kind of danger. If it hadn't been for Pavlos he would have fought the infuriating desire to kiss her and just walked away, consigning her to history. He would have phoned the sizzling supermodel he'd taken to the photographic exhibition and demanded she drop everything. Especially her panties. He swallowed, because the equally infuriating reality was that the model seemed instantly forgettable when he compared her to Keeley Turner in her unflattering uniform. Was it the fire spitting from her green eyes and the indignant tremble of those lips which made him want to dominate and subdue her? Or because he wanted to protect his brother from someone like her? He'd sent Pavlos off to sea to deal with a crew in revolt—but as soon as the situation was resolved he would return. And who was to say what the two of them might get up to if his back was turned? He couldn't keep them apart—no matter how powerful he was. Mightn't her ethereal blonde beauty tempt his brother into straying, despite the lovely young woman waiting for him in Melbourne?

Suddenly his thoughts took on a completely different direction as a solution came out of nowhere. A solution of such satisfying simplicity that it almost took his breath away. Because weren't men territorial above all else—especially Kavakos men? He and Pavlos hadn't been brought up to share—not their toys, nor their thoughts, and certainly not their women. The age difference between them had guaranteed that just as much as the bleak and unsettled circumstances of their childhood. So what if *he* seduced her before his brother got a chance? Pavlos certainly wouldn't be interested in one of *his* cast-offs—so wouldn't that effectively remove her from his brother's life for good?

Ariston swallowed. And sex might succeed in eradicating her from *his* mind, once and for all. Because hadn't she been like a low-grade fever all these years—a fever which still flared up from time to time? She was the only woman he'd ever kissed and not had sex with and perhaps it was his need for perfection and completion which demanded he remedy that aching omission.

He looked around her shabby home. At the thin curtains at the window which looked out over a rainy street and the threadbare rug on the floor. And suddenly he realised it could be easy. It always was with women, when you brought up the subject of cash. His mouth hardened with bitter recall as he remembered the monetary transaction which had defined and condemned him when he had been nothing more than a boy. 'Do you need money?' he questioned softly. 'I rather think you do, *koukla mou.*'

'You're offering me money to stay away from your brother? Seriously?' She stared at him. 'Isn't that what's known as blackmail?'

'Actually, I'm offering you money to come and work for me. More money than you could have ever dreamed of.'

'You mean you have your own supermarket?' she questioned sarcastically. 'And need your very own shelf-stacker?'

He very nearly smiled but forced himself to clamp his lips together before returning her gaze. 'I haven't been tempted into retail as of yet,' he said drily. 'But I have my own island, on which I occasionally entertain. In fact, I'm flying back there tomorrow to prepare for a house party.'

'How nice for you. But I don't see what that has to do with me. Am I supposed to congratulate you on having so many friends—even though it's difficult to believe you actually have *any*?'

A pulse began to beat insistently at his temple because Ariston wasn't used to such a feisty and insolent reaction—and never from a woman. Yet it made him want to pull her into his arms and crush his lips down hard against hers. It made him want to push her up against the wall and have her moaning with pleasure as he slid his fingers inside her panties. He swallowed. 'I'm telling you because during busy times on the island, there is always work available for the right person.'

'And you think I'm the right person?'

'Well, let's not push credibility too far.' His lips twisted as he looked around. 'But you're clearly short of money.'

'I'm sure most people are compared to you.'

'We're talking about your circumstances, Keeley, not mine. And this apartment of yours is surprisingly *humble*.'

Keeley didn't deny it. How could she? 'And?'

'And I'm curious. How did that happen? How did you get from being flown around Europe on private jets to… this? Your mother must have made a stack of money from her various *liaisons* with wealthy men and her habit of giving tell-all interviews to the press. Doesn't she help fund her daughter's lifestyle?'

Keeley stared him out, thinking how very wrong he'd got it but she wasn't going to tell him. Why should she? Some things were just too painful to recount, especially to a cold and uncaring man like him. 'That's none of your business,' she snapped.

A calculating look entered his eyes. 'Well, whatever it is you're doing—it clearly isn't working. So how about earning yourself a bonus?' he continued softly. 'A big, fat bonus which could catapult you out of the poverty trap?'

She looked at him suspiciously, trying to dampen down the automatic spring of hope in her heart. 'Doing what?'

He shrugged. 'Your home is surprisingly clean and tidy, so I assume you're capable of doing housework. Just as I assume you're able to follow simple instructions and help around the kitchen.'

'And you trust me enough to employ me?'

'I don't know. Can I?' His gaze seared into her. 'I imagine the reason for your relative poverty is probably because you're unreliable and easily bored by the mundane—and that maybe things didn't fall into your lap as effortlessly as you thought they might. Am I right, Keeley? Did you discover that you weren't as successful a freeloader as your mother?'

'Go to hell,' she snapped.

'But I suspect that if the price was right you would be prepared to knuckle down,' he added thoughtfully.

'So how about if I offered you a month as a temporary domestic on my Greek estate—and the opportunity to earn yourself the kind of money which could transform your life?'

Her heart was beating very hard. 'And why would you do that?' she croaked.

'You know why.' His voice grew harsh. 'I don't want you in London when Pavlos returns. He's due to fly to Melbourne in two weeks' time, hopefully with a diamond ring tucked inside his pocket—and after that, I don't care what you do. Let's just call it an insurance policy, shall we? I'm prepared to pay a big premium to keep you out of my brother's life.'

His disapproval washed over her like dirty water and Keeley wanted to tell him exactly what he could do with his offer, yet she couldn't ignore the nagging voice in her head which was urging her to be realistic. Could she really afford to turn down the kind of opportunity which would probably never come her way again, just because she loathed the man who was making it?

'Tempted?' he questioned softly.

Oh, she was tempted, all right. Tempted to tell him that she'd never met anyone so charmless and insulting. Keeley felt her skin grow hot as she realised he was offering her a job as some kind of *skivvy*. Someone to get her hands dirty by tidying up after him and his fancy guests. To chop vegetables and change his bed while he cavorted on the silvery beach with whoever his current squeeze was—probably the stunning redhead he'd taken to the gallery opening with him. He was looking down his proud and patrician nose at her and she opened her mouth to say she'd rather starve than accept his offer until she reminded herself of the significant fact she'd been in danger of forgetting. Because it wasn't just herself she had to consider, was it?

She stared down at one of the holes in the carpet as she thought of her mother and the little treats which added to her life, even though she was completely oblivious to them. The weekly manicure and occasional hairdo to primp those thinning curls into some sort of shape, so that in some ways she resembled the woman she had once been. Vivienne Turner didn't *know* that these things were being done for her, but Keeley did. Sometimes she shuddered to imagine what her mother's reaction would have been if she'd been able to look into a crystal ball and see the life she'd been condemned to live. But nobody had a crystal ball, thank goodness. Nobody could see what lay ahead. And when occasionally other patients' relatives or members of staff recognised the shell of the woman who had once been Vivienne Turner, Keeley was proud that her mother looked as good as she possibly could. Because that would have mattered. To her.

So test him, she thought. See what the mighty Ariston Kavakos is putting on the table. See if it's big enough to enable you to endure his company for longer than a minute. 'How much,' she said baldly, 'are you offering me?'

Ariston swallowed down his distaste as he heard the shrewd note which had entered her voice and he realised that Keeley's greed was as transparent as her mother's. His mouth twisted. How he despised her and everything she stood for. Yet his natural revulsion was not enough to destroy his desire for her and his mouth grew dry as he thought about having sex with Keeley Turner. Because it was inconceivable that she would return to Lasia and *not* sleep with him. It would bring about satisfaction and closure—for both of them. The fever in his blood would be removed and afterwards she could be quietly airbrushed from all their lives. She would be rewarded with enough money to satisfy her. She would disappear into the sunset. Most important of all—Pavlos would never see her again.

He smiled as he mentioned a sum of money, expecting her simpering gratitude and instant acceptance, but instead he was met with a look from her green eyes which was almost glacial.

'Double it,' she said coolly.

Ariston's smile died but he could feel the insistent beat of lust intensifying because her attitude made his callous plan a whole lot easier to execute. Every woman could be bought, he remembered bitterly. You just had to negotiate the right price.

'You have a deal,' he said softly.

CHAPTER THREE

LASIA WAS AS beautiful as Keeley remembered it. No. Maybe even more so. Because when you were eighteen you thought that sunny days would never end and beauty would last for ever. You never imagined that life could turn out so different from how you'd imagined. She'd thought the money would last. She'd thought...

No. She gazed out of the car window at the cloudless blue sky. She wasn't going to do that thing. She wasn't going to *look back*. She was here, on this stunning private island, to work for Ariston Kavakos and earn herself a nest egg for her poor, broken mother. Fixing her gaze on the dark blue line of the horizon, she reminded herself to start looking for the positives, not the negatives.

A fancy car had been waiting for her on Lasia's only airstrip—its air-conditioned interior deliciously welcoming because, even though it was still only springtime, the midday sun was intense. During the flight over she'd wondered if any of Ariston's staff might remember her and she was dreading any such recognition. But thankfully the driver was new—well, new to her—and his name was Stelios.

He seemed content to remain silent and Keeley said nothing as the powerful car snaked its way through the mountain roads towards the Kavakos complex on the other side of the island. But although outwardly calm, inside she was quaking for all kinds of reasons. For a start, she'd lost her job at the supermarket. Her manager had reacted with incredulity when she'd asked for a month's unpaid holiday, telling her that she must have taken leave of her senses if she expected *those* kinds of perks. He'd added rather triumphantly that she was in the wrong job, but deep down Keeley had already known that. Because no matter how hard she'd tried, she'd never fitted in. Not there. Not anywhere if she stopped to think about it—and certainly not here, on this private paradise which exuded untold wealth and privilege. Where costly yachts bobbed on the azure sea as carelessly as a baby floated toys in the bathtub. She leaned forward to get a better look as the car rounded the bend and made its slow descent towards the complex she'd last seen when she was eighteen, blinking her eyes in surprise because everything looked so different.

Oh, not Assimenos Bay—that hadn't changed. The natural cove with its silvery sand was as stunning as ever, but the vast house which had once dominated it had gone. The beachside mansion was no more and in its place stood an imposing building which seemed composed mainly of glass. Modern and magnificent, the transparent walls and curved windows reflected back the different hues of sea and sky so that Keeley's first impression was that everything looked so *blue*. As blue as Ariston's eyes, she found herself thinking, before reminding herself furiously that she wasn't here to fantasise about him.

And then, as if she had conjured him up from her restless imagination, she saw the Greek tycoon standing at one of the vast windows on the first floor of the house. Standing watching her—his stance as unmoving as a statue. A ripple of unwilling awareness ran through her body as she stared up at him because even at a distance he dominated everything. Even though she was surrounded by so much natural beauty and the kind of scenery she hadn't seen in a long time it still took a huge effort to drag her gaze away from him. And she mustn't be seen ogling him like some helpless fan-girl. Hadn't she made that mistake once before? And look where that had got her. This was her chance to redeem herself and the only way she could achieve that was by remaining immune to him and his effortless charisma. To show him she no longer wanted him—that ship had sailed—because she wasn't into cruel billionaires who treated you with zero respect.

The car stopped and Stelios opened the door and Keeley could smell lemons and pine and the salty tang of the nearby sea as she stepped onto the sun-baked courtyard.

'Here's Demetra,' said Stelios as a middle-aged woman in a crisp white uniform began walking through the shimmering heat towards them. 'She's the cook— but basically she's in charge! Even Ariston listens when Demetra speaks. She'll show you to your accommodation. You're pretty lucky to be staying here,' he observed. 'All the other staff live in the village.'

'Thank you.' Keeley turned to him in surprise. 'You speak perfect English!'

'Pretty much. I lived in London for a while. Used to drive taxis for a living.' Stelios gave an inscrutable smile. 'Though the boss doesn't like me to publicise it too much.'

No, she'd bet he didn't. A silent but understanding driver would be an asset for a control freak like Ariston, thought Keeley wryly. Someone able to eavesdrop on the conversation of his English-speaking guests should the need arise. Yet she heard the obvious affection in the driver's voice as he referred to his boss and wondered what the autocratic ship-owner had ever done to deserve it, apart from be born with a silver spoon in his mouth. But everyone liked you when you had money, she reminded herself. The world was full of hangers-on who were mesmerised by the lure of wealth. The same hangers-on who would drop you like a hot potato when all that wealth had gone.

She smiled as the cook approached, reminding herself it was important to be accepted by the people she was going to be working with and to show them she wasn't afraid of hard work.

'*Kalispera*, Demetra,' she said, holding out her hand. 'I'm Keeley. Keeley Turner.'

'*Kalispera*,' said the cook, looking pleased. 'You speak Greek?'

'Not really. Only a couple of phrases.' Keeley pulled a face. 'But I'd love to learn more. Do you speak English?'

'*Neh*. Kyrios Kavakos likes all his staff to speak English.' She smiled. 'We help each other. Come. I show you your house.'

Keeley followed the cook down a narrow sandy path leading directly to the beach, until they reached a small whitewashed cottage. She could hear the waves lapping against the shore and could see the moving glimmer of sunlight on the water, but, although she was surrounded by so much beauty, all she could remember was the uproar and the chaos. Because wasn't it over there beside that crop of rocks that Ariston pulled her into his arms for that tantalisingly sweet taste of pleasure, before thrusting her away again? She closed her eyes as goosebumps shivered over her bare arms, despite the heat of the day. How could the memory of something which had happened so long ago still be so vivid?

'You like it?' questioned Demetra, obviously misinterpreting her silence.

'Oh, gosh, yes. It's…beautiful,' said Keeley quickly.

Demetra smiled. '*Oreos*. All Lasia is *oreos*. Come to the house when you are ready and I show you everything.'

After Demetra had gone, Keeley went inside the cottage—leaving the door open so she could hear the waves as she set about exploring her temporary home. It didn't take long to get her bearings because, although it was small and compact, it was still bigger than her home in London. There was a sitting room and a small kitchen, while upstairs was a bedroom with space for little more than a large bed. The bathroom was surprisingly sophisticated and the whole place was simple and clean, with walls painted white and completely bare of decoration. But the light which flooded into every room was incredible—bright and clear and shot with the dancing reflection of the waves. Who needed pictures on the walls when you had that?

Keeley unpacked, showered and changed into shorts and a T-shirt—and was just making her way downstairs when she saw Ariston walking towards her cottage. And try as she might, she could do nothing to prevent the powerful squeeze of her heart and the molten tug deep inside her.

She wanted to turn away. To close her eyes and shut him out…yet she wanted to watch him like the rerun of a favourite TV show. The powerful thrust of his thighs as he walked. The broadness of his shoulders and the bunched muscle of his arms. The way his white T-shirt contrasted with the darkness of his olive skin. Her mouth dried as she noticed the narrow band of skin showing above the low-slung waistband of his faded jeans. Because this was Ariston as she remembered him—not wearing a sophisticated suit which seemed to constrain him, but looking as if he could have just finished work on one of the fishing boats.

He was the most alpha male she'd ever seen but it was vital he didn't guess she thought that way. She was going to have to respond to him indifferently— betraying none of her uneasy emotions whenever he came close. She needed to pretend he was just like any other man—even though he wasn't. Because no other man had ever made her feel this way. She sucked in an unsteady breath as he approached, because the most important thing she needed to remember was that she didn't actually *like* him.

'So. Here you are,' he observed, his blue eyes moving over her with their strange, cold fire.

'Here I am.' Feeling curiously insubstantial, she tugged at the hem of her T-shirt. 'You sound surprised.'

'Maybe I am. Part of me wondered whether you might change your mind at the last minute and not bother coming.'

'Should I have done?' She fixed him with a questioning gaze. 'Would it have been wiser to have dismissed your generous job offer and carried on with my life the way it was, Kyrios Kavakos?'

As she stared at him so fearlessly, her bright green eyes so cat-like and entrancing, Ariston thought about the answers he *could* have given her. If she was someone he cared about he would have told her that, yes, she should have stayed well away from his island and the doomed orbit of a man like him. But the point was that he didn't care. She was a commodity. A woman he intended to seduce and finish what she had started all those years ago. Why warn her to be on her guard against something which was going to bring them both a great deal of pleasure?

And closure, he reminded himself grimly. Because wasn't closure equally important?

He stared at the thick pale hair which hung in a twisted rope over one shoulder, wondering why he found it so difficult to tear his eyes away from her. He'd known women more beautiful. He'd certainly known women more *suitable* than some washed-up ex-party-girl with dollar signs in her eyes. Yet knowing that did nothing to diminish her impact on him. Her lush breasts were pushing against a T-shirt the colour of the lemons which grew in the hills behind the house and a pair of cotton shorts skimmed her shapely hips and legs. She'd slipped her bare feet into a pair of sparkly flip-flops so that she looked unexpectedly carefree—and young—as if she hadn't made the slightest effort to impress him with her appearance and the unexpectedness of this made desire spiral up inside him even more.

'No, I think you're in exactly the right place,' he said evenly. 'So let's go into the house and I'll show you around. I think you'll find things have changed quite a lot since last time you were here.'

'No, honestly. You don't have to do that,' she said. 'Demetra has already offered.'

'But I'm offering now.'

She tilted her head to one side. 'Surely it would be more appropriate if another member of staff took me round? You must have plenty of other things you'd rather be doing—a busy man like you, with a great empire to control.'

'I don't care whether or not it's *appropriate*, Keeley. I happen to be a very hands-on employer.'

'And what you say goes, right?'

'Exactly. So why don't you just accept that, and do what I say?'

He was so ridiculously *masterful*, Keeley thought resentfully. Didn't he realise how out of touch and *out-dated* he sounded when he spoke like that? But even though she objected to his overbearing attitude, she couldn't deny its effect on her. It was as if her body had been programmed to respond to his masculine dominance and there was nothing she could do to stop it. Her face was hot as she shut the cottage door and followed him across the beach towards his home, her flip-flops sinking into the soft sand as she scurried to match his pace.

'Any questions you want to ask?' he said, glancing down at her.

There were a million. She wanted to know why— at thirty-five and surely one of the world's most eligible bachelors—he still wasn't married. She wanted to know what made him so hard and cold and proud. She wanted to know if he ever laughed and if so, what made those sensual lips curve with humour. But she bit all those questions back because she had no right to ask them. 'Yes,' she said. 'What made you knock the old house down?'

Ariston felt a pulse flicker at his temple as he lessened his stride so she could keep up with him. How ironic that she should choose a subject which still had the power to make him feel uncomfortable. He remembered the disbelief he'd faced when he'd proposed demolition of the old house, which had been rich in history. How people had thought he was acting out of a sense of misplaced grief after the death of his father. But it had been nothing to do with that. For him it had been a necessary rebirth. Should he tell her that he'd wanted to raze away the past along with those impressive walls? As if believing that those dark memories could be reduced to rubble, just like the bricks. That he'd wanted to forget the house where his mother had played with him until the day she'd walked away—leaving him and Pavlos in the care of their father. Just as he wanted to forget the parties and sickly-sweet stench of marijuana and the women flown in from destinations all over Europe—their given brief to 'entertain' his father and his jaded friends. Why would he tell Keeley Turner something like that—when she and her mother had been exactly those kind of women?

'New broom, new era,' he said, with a hard smile. 'When my father died I decided I needed to make a few changes. To put my own stamp on the place.'

She was staring up at the wide glass structure. 'Well, you've certainly done that.'

Her cooing words sounded speculative—the instinctive reaction of an avaricious woman confronted by affluence—but that didn't quite cancel out the pleasure Ariston got from her praise. Or stop him thinking how much he'd like to hear that soft English voice whispering some very different things in his ear. Was she one of those women who talked during sex? he wondered. Or did she keep quiet until she started to come, gasping out her joyful pleasure into the man's ear? His lips curved into a speculative smile. He couldn't wait to find out.

He gestured for her to precede him though her wiggling bottom made it difficult for him to concentrate on the tour. He showed her the tennis court, the gym, his office and two of the smaller reception rooms—but decided against taking her upstairs to each of the seven en-suite bedrooms or, indeed, his own master suite. His throat tightened. Demetra could do that later.

At last he led her into the main sitting room, which was the focal point of the house, carefully watching her reaction as she was confronted by the sea view which dominated three of the massive glass walls. For a moment she stood there motionless—not appearing to notice the priceless Fabergé eggs which lay on one of the low tables, nor the rare Lysippos statue which he'd bought from under the noses of international dealers in an auction house in New York and which had sealed his reputation as a connoisseur of fine art.

'Wow,' she said indistinctly. 'Who came up with this?'

'I asked the architect to design me something to maximise the views and for each room to flow into the next,' he said. 'I wanted light and space everywhere—so that when I'm working it doesn't seem like being in the office.'

'I can't imagine any office looking like this. It looks…well, it's the most stunning place I've ever seen.' She turned to face him. 'The family business must be doing well.'

'Reassuringly well,' he said blandly.

'You're still building ships?'

He raised his eyebrows. 'My brother didn't tell you?'

'No, Ariston. He didn't tell me. We barely had time to reacquaint ourselves before you dragged him away.'

'Yes, we're still building ships,' he affirmed. 'But we're also making wines and olive oil on the other side of the island, which have become a surprising hit in all kinds of places. These days people seem to value organic goods and Kavakos products are on the shopping list of most of the world's big chefs.' He raised his eyebrows. 'Anything else you want to know?'

She brushed the palms of her hands down over her shorts. 'In England you said you were expecting guests this weekend.'

'That's right. Two of my lawyers are flying in from Athens for lunch tomorrow and there are five people arriving at the weekend for a house party.'

'And are they Greek?'

'International,' he drawled. 'You want to know who they are?'

'Isn't it always polite to know people's names in advance?'

'And handy when you're trying to research how much each is worth?' he offered drily. 'There's Santino Di Piero, the Italian property tycoon who is coming with his English girlfriend, Rachel. There's also a friend of mine from way back—Xenon Diakos who for some reason has decided to bring his secretary. I think her name is Megan.'

'That's four,' she said, determined not to rise to the nasty digs he was making.

'So it is. And Bailey Saunders is the other guest,' he said, as if he'd only just remembered.

'Her name seems familiar.' She hesitated. 'She's the woman you took to the opening night of the photographic exhibition, isn't she?'

'Is that relevant, Keeley?' he questioned silkily. 'Or, indeed, any of your business?'

She shook her head, not knowing why she'd mentioned it, and now she felt stupid—and vulnerable.

Embarrassed by her own curiosity and angry at the unwanted jealousy which was making her skin grow heated, Keeley walked over to the window and stared out unseeingly. Was she going to have to spend days witnessing Ariston making out with a beautiful woman? See them frolicking together in that amazing infinity pool or kissing on the beach in the moonlight? Would she have to change their bedsheets in the morning and see for herself the evidence of their shared passion? A shiver of revulsion shot through her and she prayed it didn't show. Because even if she had to contend with those things—so what? Ariston was nothing to her and she was nothing to him and unless she remembered that, she was going to have a very difficult month ahead of her.

'Of course it's none of my business,' she said stiffly. 'I didn't mean to—'

'Didn't mean to what?' He had walked across the room to stand beside her at the window and she found herself inhaling his subtle citrusy scent. 'Check out whether or not I had a girlfriend? Find out whether or not I was available? Don't worry, Keeley—I'm used to women doing that.'

She struggled to say something conventional. To make some witty remark which might dissolve the sudden tension which had suddenly sprung up between them. To act as if she didn't care or take him to task for his spectacular arrogance. But he was standing so close that she couldn't think of a single word, and even if she could she didn't think she'd be capable of saying it with any degree of conviction. Just like she didn't seem capable of preventing the way he was making her feel—as if her body were no longer her own. As if it was silently responding to things she'd only ever dreamed of.

She looked up into his face to discover that his eyes had become smoky and it was as if he'd read her thoughts because suddenly he lifted his hand to frame her face with his fingers, and he smiled. It wasn't a particularly nice smile and it didn't even reach his eyes but the sensation of his touch sent Keeley's already heightened senses into overdrive. His thumb stroked its way over her bottom lip so that it began to tremble uncontrollably. That was the only thing he was doing and yet it was making her want to melt. He was making her more aroused by the second and surely that must show. Her nipples had hardened into two painful little points and somewhere low in her belly she could feel a distracting and molten ache.

Did he realise that? Was that why his hold on her changed so that instead of cupping her face with his fingers, he was pulling her towards him? Pulling her into his arms as if it were his right to do so. His eyes were blazing as they stared into hers and she could feel the softness of her body moulding perfectly into the hardness of his, as he brought his mouth down on hers.

And Keeley shuddered because this was like no other kiss. It was like every fantasy she'd ever had— and wasn't the truth of it that those fantasies had always involved *him*? He kissed her slow and then he kissed her hard. He kissed her until she was squirming, until she thought she would cry out with pleasure. She could feel the rush of heat and the clamour of frustration and all she wanted was to give into that feeling. To wrap her arms around his neck and let desire take over. Whisper in his ear to have him do whatever he wanted. What she wanted. Have him ease this terrible ache inside her as she suspected only he could.

And then what? Let him take you to his bed even though you know how much he despises you? Even though Bailey Saunders is arriving in a couple of days? Because that was how these people operated. She'd seen for herself the world in which he lived. Easy come, easy go.

It didn't mean anything. *She* didn't mean anything— hadn't he already made that abundantly clear? And for someone with an already shaky sense of self-worth, such an action would be completely insane.

'No!' Keeley jerked away from him, taking a couple of steps back and trying to ignore the silent protest of her body. 'What the *hell* do you think you're doing, Ariston?' she demanded. 'Jumping on me like that!'

His short laugh was tinged with frustration. 'Oh, please,' he drawled. 'Please don't insult my intelligence, *koukla mou*—or your own for that matter. You were— *are*—hot and horny. You wanted me to kiss you and I was more than happy to oblige.'

'I did *not*,' she snapped back.

'Oh, Keeley—why deny the truth? Not the best start, in the circumstances—not when I consider honesty an invaluable asset for all my employees.'

'And surely crossing physical boundaries with your staff is unacceptable behaviour for any employer—have you stopped to consider *that*?'

'Maybe if you stopped looking at me with such blatant invitation,' he said silkily, 'then I might be able to stop responding to you as a man, rather than as a boss.'

'I was not!' she said indignantly.

'Weren't you? Ask yourself that question again, only this time don't lie to yourself.'

Keeley bit her lip. *Had* she been looking at him in invitation? Her heart pounded. Of course she had. And if she was being brutally honest, hadn't she wanted him to kiss her since she'd seen him standing at the windows of his glass mansion, his powerful physique dominating everything around him? Maybe even before that—when he'd come striding across the London gallery towards her and Pavlos with a face like thunder and a body which was tensed and powerful. And she mustn't let herself feel that way. She was here to earn money to help care for her stricken mother—not tangle with a self-confessed chauvinist like Ariston and get her heart broken in the process.

Drawing in a deep breath, she willed herself to at least *look* as if she were in control of her own emotions. 'I can't deny that there's an attraction between us,' she said. 'But that doesn't mean we're going to act on it. Not just because you're my boss and it's inappropriate, but because we don't even like each other.'

'What does liking have to do with it?'

'Are you serious?'

'Totally serious.' He shrugged. 'In my experience, a little hostility always adds a touch of spice. Surely your mama taught you that, Keeley?'

The implied slur piled on yet another layer of hurt

and Keeley wanted to hurl herself at him. To slam her fists angrily against that powerful chest and tell him to keep his opinions to himself because he didn't know what he was talking about. But she didn't trust herself to go near him because to touch him was to want him and she couldn't afford to put herself in that position again. He had asked for honesty, hadn't he? So why not just give it to him, even if it meant swallowing her pride in the process? Why pretend there was no elephant in the room when a whole herd of them were threatening to trample over her?

'I have no intention of getting close to you, Ariston, mainly because you're not the kind of man I like,' she said slowly. 'I came here to earn good money and that's what I intend to do. Actually, it's *all* I intend to do. I am going to work hard and to stay away from you as much as possible. I don't intend putting myself in a position of vulnerability again.' She forced a smile, injecting the requisite note of subservience into her voice, reminding herself to behave like the humble employee she was supposed to be. 'So if you'll excuse me—I'd better go and find out if there's anything Demetra wants me to do in the kitchen.'

CHAPTER FOUR

SHE WAS DRIVING him crazy.

Crazy.

Sucking in a lungful of air, Ariston dived beneath the inky waters of a sea just starting to be gilded by the sun coming up over the horizon. It was early. Too early for anyone else to be around. Not even the staff were awake yet and the shutters remained tightly closed in the bedroom windows of Keeley's cottage. And that was a pretty accurate metaphor for the current state of affairs between them, he thought grimly. For a man so utterly confident about his sexual power over women—and with good reason—things with Keeley Turner hadn't quite gone according to plan.

For a while he swam strongly beneath the shadowed surface of the water, trying to rid his body of some of the restless energy which had been building up inside him, but that was easier said than done. He had been sleeping badly, with images of Keeley in various imagined stages of undress haunting his erotic and frustrating dreams. Because she'd meant what she'd said, he was discovering with growing incredulity—and despite the sexual chemistry which sizzled so powerfully between them, she had stubbornly kept him at arm's length. He'd thought at first that her behaviour had been part of some contrived act intended to keep him on his toes. But there had been no relaxing of her attitude towards him. No sudden softening which might have indicated she was weakening. All interaction between them had followed a formal yet highly unsatisfactory path.

She politely enquired whether he would like coffee or bread, or water. She kept her eyes demurely lowered whenever their paths crossed. And no matter how many times he told her it was perfectly acceptable for her to use his Christian name in public, it fell on deaf ears. She was a conundrum, he thought. Was she really immune to the admiring glances she had attracted from his Athens-based lawyers when they had arrived on Lasia for lunch—or was she simply a very clever actress who knew the power of her own beauty? She acted as if she were made of marble, when he knew for a fact that beneath that cool and curvy exterior beat the heart of a passionate woman.

Had he thought that she would have succumbed to him by now? That the memory of the kiss they'd shared on her first day would have her sneaking in his arms to finish off what they'd started?

Of course he had.

That brief kiss had been the most erotic thing to happen to him in a long time but it had led precisely nowhere and although he wasn't a man used to being denied what he really wanted—he was now being forced to experience exactly that. So he'd been a little *distant* with her, intending to indicate his disapproval of women who teased, thinking his impatience would make her realise his patience was wearing thin. He'd anticipated her finding him alone in some quiet moment. He'd imagined her sliding down the zipper of his trousers and touching him where he ached to be touched. He swallowed. Any other woman would have done—and Keeley certainly had history on that score. If things had gone according to plan, by now he should have bedded her and enjoyed several sessions of mind-blowing sex. In fact, by now he probably would have been growing bored with her inevitable adoration and his only dilemma would be working out the best way to tell her it was over.

But it hadn't turned out like that.

She had thrown herself into her work with an enthusiasm which had taken him by surprise. Had she stacked supermarket shelves with such passion? he wondered wryly. Demetra had informed him that the Englishwoman was a joy to have around the kitchen and around the house. A joy? he wondered grimly. He had seen little evidence of it so far.

Was her frosty attitude intended to stoke up his sexual appetite? Because if that was the case then it was working. His blood pressure soared every time she walked onto the terrace in her crisp white uniform. The white cotton dress gave her a look of purity and her blonde hair was scraped neatly back into a no-nonsense chignon, which made her appear the perfect servant. Yet the glitter of fire in her green eyes whenever she was forced to meet his gaze was unmistakable—as if she was daring him to come near her again.

He resurfaced into the bright, golden morning, shaking droplets of water from his head before beginning to swim powerfully towards the shore. It was time to face the day ahead and to play at being host. Four of his guests had arrived but Bailey Saunders was no longer on the guest list. He'd phoned her a couple of days ago and asked for a rain check, and she had agreed. Of course she had. Women always did. He felt a beat of anticipation as he walked across the sand.

Maybe it was time for Keeley Turner to realise that it was pointless resisting the inevitable.

'Will you take the coffee out, Keeley?' Demetra pointed to the loaded tray.

'Of course.' Keeley smoothed down her white uniform dress. 'Shall I put some of those little lemon biscuits on a plate?'

'Efharisto.'

'Parakalo.' Automatically checking that she had everything she needed, Keeley carried it out onto the terrace with a heavy heart. Another trip to the table which had been set up next to the infinity pool, where Ariston was finishing a long lunch with his glamorous guests, and she was dreading it. Dreading seeing his rugged face watching her, his expression hidden behind his dark glasses as she tried to walk along the edge of the pool without appearing too self-conscious, but it was difficult. Just as it was difficult to forget that kiss they'd shared, when he'd made her usually non-responsive body spring to life—and left her in a state of frustrated arousal ever since. It was as if he'd lit the touchpaper of her repressed sexuality and set it on fire.

And she had only herself to blame.

Why hadn't she stopped him from pulling her into his arms like that? Because she'd been powerless to stop him. She had wanted him to do it. She still wanted him to do it.

She bit her lip. She'd done her best to push him to the back of her mind—avoiding him whenever possible and concentrating on her work, determined to do a job she could be proud of. She wanted to wipe out his negative impressions of her and show him she could be honest and hard-working and *decent*. Just like she was determined not to raise the suspicions of the people she worked with. She *liked* Demetra and Stelios, just as she liked the extra staff who'd been drafted in from the nearby village to help with the house party. She didn't want them to think she had some kind of *thing* with the boss. All she wanted was to be seen as the helpful Englishwoman who was eager to take on her fair share.

The sun was warm on her head as she took the coffee outside to where the five of them were sitting around the remains of the meal she'd served them—Xenon, Megan, Santino, Rachel and Ariston. She'd been introduced to them yesterday and they all seemed the jet-setting type of people she no longer associated with. She'd forgotten that life where women changed their outfits four times a day and spent more on a straw hat than Keeley spent on her entire summer wardrobe. She'd been as polite and as friendly as her position required but she was also aware that as a member of staff she was mostly invisible. Only the friendly Rachel had treated her as if she was a real person—and always made a point of chatting whenever she saw her.

Rachel's long, bronzed legs were stretched out in front of her and she brightened when she saw Keeley approaching with the silver coffee pot glinting in the sunshine.

'Oh, yum. I love this Greek coffee!' she said. 'It's so thick and sweet.'

'I won't make the obvious comparison,' commented Santino drily, easily catching the hastily balled napkin which his girlfriend hurled at him in mock rage.

Rachel took a small cup from the tray. 'Thanks, Keeley. Is it possible to have some more sparkling water? It's so hot today. You must be baking in that uniform,' she observed, with a frown. 'Does Ariston allow you to cool off in the pool or does he constantly keep your nose to the grindstone?'

'Oh, Keeley knows she has the run of the place when she isn't working,' murmured Ariston. 'She just chooses not to take advantage of it, don't you, Keeley?'

They were all looking at her and Keeley was acutely aware of the fact that Rachel and Megan were both wearing gauzy kaftans over tiny bikinis, while she was wearing a uniform which made her feel completely overdressed as well as overheated. All Ariston's staff wore uniforms—but somehow on her it looked all wrong. It was the right size and everything but it did unwanted things to her figure. It was the one thing she'd inherited from her mother which she could do nothing about. Because no matter how much she tried to disguise her shape with loose-fitting clothes, her bust always seemed too big and the curve of her hips that fraction too wide, so everything clung precisely where she didn't want it to cling.

'I have a great big ocean on my doorstep if ever I feel the need to swim, but when I'm not working I mostly spend time doing stuff on my computer,' she said and then, because they were still looking at her questioningly, she felt obliged to offer some kind of explanation. 'I'm studying for a diploma in business studies,' she added.

'Well, that's all very admirable but you need to take time off occasionally. What's it they say about all work and no play?' questioned Rachel, raking her fingers back through her dark hair and shooting Ariston a quizzical glance. 'Didn't you say that Bailey has bailed this weekend, if you'll excuse the pun?'

'Bailey is no longer coming, no,' Ariston said smoothly.

'So we'll be a woman short at dinner?' persisted Rachel.

'Oh, I'm sure you'll be able to cope with that,' said Santino. 'Since when did you ever worry about odd numbers, *cara*? You always seem to have enough conversation to compensate for any absent guests.'

'That much is true.' Rachel smiled. 'But why doesn't Keeley join us instead, to make the numbers up?'

Ariston removed his dark glasses and glimmered Keeley an unfathomable look. 'Yes,' he said, his velvety accent seeming to whisper like velvet across her skin. 'Why don't you join us for dinner later?'

She shook her head. 'No, honestly. I can't.'

'Why not? I'm giving you permission to take the evening off. In fact, look on it as an order.' His smile was hard and determined. 'I'm sure we have enough staff for you not to be missed waiting at table.'

'It's very…kind of you, but…' Keeley put the last of the coffee cups down with trembling fingers before straightening up. 'I don't have anything suitable to wear.'

It was the wrong thing to say. Why hadn't she just come out with an emphatic *no*?

'No worries. You're about the same size and height as me,' said Megan, looking her up and down. 'You can borrow something from me. Say yes, Keeley. You've been working so hard that you deserve a little downtime. And it would be my pleasure to lend you something.'

The two female guests were clearly on a mission to get her to change her mind and inwardly Keeley began to fume. She knew they were just trying to be kind, but she didn't want their kindness. It made her feel patronised but, even worse, it made her feel vulnerable. They thought they were giving her a treat but in reality they were pushing her closer to Ariston and that was a place she didn't want to be. But she could hardly give them the reason for her resistance, could she? She couldn't really tell them she was worried she would end up in bed with her boss! And in the end, opposition was pointless because it was five against one and there was no way she could get out of it.

You're having dinner with them, that's all, she reminded herself as she stood beneath the cool jets of the shower later that afternoon. All she had to do was put on a borrowed dress and try to be pleasant. She could leave whenever she wanted. *She didn't have to do anything she didn't want to do.*

Which was how she found herself walking towards the starlit terrace that evening, wearing the only dress of Megan's which fitted her and which was the last type of outfit she would normally have worn. It was too delicate. Too feminine. Too...*revealing.* In soft, blush pink, the low-cut bodice showcased her breasts and the silky fabric clung to her hips in precisely the way she didn't want it to. And she wasn't blind. Or stupid. She saw the way Ariston looked at her when she walked out onto the candlelit terrace. Saw the instinctive narrowing of his eyes, which set off an answering tightening in her breasts.

Her throat was so dry that she knocked back half a glass of champagne too quickly and it went straight to her head. It soothed her frazzled nerves but it also had the unwanted side effect of softening her reaction to her Greek boss, because naturally she found herself seated next to him. She told herself she wasn't going to be affected by him. That he was a callous manipulator who had no regard for her feelings. But somehow her thoughts weren't making it to her body. Her body didn't seem to be behaving itself at all.

She could feel it in the heavy rush of blood to her breasts and in her restlessness whenever Ariston subjected her to that cool stare, which he seemed to do far more than was necessary. And if that weren't bad

enough, she was having difficulty adjusting to this unexpected social outing. She hadn't been to a dinner
party this fancy for a long time and she'd never really
done so on her own terms before. She'd only ever been
invited because of her mother, and this was different.
She was no longer watching out of the corner of her eye
in case her mum did something outrageous, anxiously
wondering if she could get her home without making a
fool of herself. This time people seemed to be interested
in *her* and she didn't want them to be. What could she
say about herself—other than that she'd done a series
of menial jobs, because they were the only ones she
could get after a fractured education which had led to
zero qualifications?

She spent the evening blocking questions—something she'd learnt to do over the years—so that whenever she was asked something personal, she turned it
around and moved the subject swiftly onto something
else. She had become highly accomplished in the art
of evasion but tonight it seemed to be having entirely
the wrong effect. Was her elusiveness the reason why
Santino began to monopolise her for the second part
of the evening, while Rachel's pinched face seemed to
indicate she was regretting her impetuous decision to
have her join them? Keeley felt like standing up and announcing that she wasn't remotely interested in the Italian businessman—that there was only one man around
the table who had her attention and she was having to
fight very hard not to be mesmerised by him. Because
tonight Ariston looked amazing—very traditional and
heart-stoppingly masculine. His white shirt was unbut-

toned at the neck revealing a silky triangle of olive skin, and his tapered dark trousers emphasised his long legs and the powerful shafts of his thighs.

And all the while he was watching her, his blue gaze burning into her so intently that the breath caught in her throat and she was barely able to eat. Course after course of delicious food was placed in front of her, but Keeley could do little more than push it around her plate. Were the other guests amused by her lack of appetite—not realising the cause of it—especially as she seemed almost to be bursting out of Megan's dress? Did they think she was one of those women who never ate in public but enjoyed secret binges with the biscuit packet whenever she was alone?

'Enjoying yourself, Keeley?' asked Ariston softly.

'Very much,' she said, not caring if he heard the lie in her voice. Because what else could she say? That she could feel ripples of awareness whispering over her skin whenever he looked at her? That she found his hard and rugged profile the most beautiful thing she'd ever seen and she wanted nothing more than to just sit and stare at it?

She broke the mould of her Cinderella evening by excusing herself long before midnight. As soon as the clock struck eleven she stood up and politely thanked them for a lovely dinner. Somehow she maintained her high-headed posture as she walked away from the terrace but as soon as she was out of sight, she began to run. Along the path leading to the beach she ran, straight past her cottage and down to the shoreline, glad she was wearing her practical sandals underneath the long dress. And glad too that the waves were pounding against the sand so that the heavy sound drummed out the beating of her thudding heart. Picking up the hem of her dress, she stood back, careful not to let the sea-water touch the delicate fabric as she stared out at the moon-dappled water.

She remembered how she'd felt when the supermarket had sacked her just before she'd flown to Lasia, when she'd been swamped by the sense of having no real place in the world. She could feel it now—because she hadn't really been part of that glamorous table, had she? She'd been the outsider who had been dressed up for the occasion in a stranger's dress. Had Ariston known how alienated she'd felt—or was he too busy reeling her in with his potent sexuality to care? Didn't he realise that what was probably just a game to him meant so much more to someone like her who didn't have his tight circle of friends, or wealth, to fall back on?

She felt stupid tears stinging her eyes and wondered if they had been caused by self-pity. Because if they were she was going to have to lose them—and quickly. Count your blessings, she told herself fiercely as she rubbed her eyes with the back of her hand. Just be glad you've been strong enough to resist someone who could never be anything more than a one-night stand.

But as she turned to walk back towards her cottage she saw a figure walking towards her—a man she recognised in a heartbeat, even from this distance. How could she fail to recognise him when his image was burned so powerfully onto her mind that she could picture him at the slightest provocation? His shadowy figure was powerful as he moved and the glint of moonlight in his eyes and the paleness of his silk shirt captured her imagination. She felt her skin prickle with instinctive excitement, which was quickly followed by a cold wash of dismay as he approached, because she'd tried to do the right thing. She'd done everything in her power to stay away from him. *So why the hell was he here?*

'Ariston,' she said steadily. 'What are you doing here?'

'I was worried about you. You left dinner so abruptly and I watched as you took the path to your cottage.' His eyes narrowed as they swept over her. 'Only no light came on.'

'You were spying on me?'

'Not really. I'm your employer.' His voice sounded deep above the soft lapping of the waves. 'I was merely concerned for your welfare.'

Her eyes met his. 'Is that so?'

There was a pause. 'Yes. No,' he negated and suddenly his voice had grown harsh. 'Actually, I don't know. I don't know what the hell it is. All I know is that I can't seem to stop thinking about you.'

Keeley saw the sudden change in him. The tension which stiffened his body, which she suspected mirrored the tension in her own. Just as she knew what was about to happen from the look on his face—a raw look of hunger which set off an answering need somewhere deep inside her.

'Ariston,' she whispered, but it sounded more like a prayer than a protest as he pulled her into his arms, into the warmth of his embrace, and she let him—ignoring the objections which were crowding her mind. And the moment he touched her, she was lost.

He drove his mouth down on hers and she heard his little moan of triumph as she kissed him back. Her lips opened and he slid his tongue inside her mouth to deepen the kiss. She swayed against him, her finger-nails digging into his chest through the fine silk of his shirt, and he circled his hips against hers in a move-ment which was unashamedly urgent. And now his hand was slipping inside the bodice of her dress so he could cup her braless breast with his fingers and she let him do that, too. How could she stop him when she wanted it so much?

His groan was muffled as he explored each diamond-tipped nipple and she could feel her panties growing moist. Was he going to do it to her now? Here? Push her down onto the soft sand without giving her time to object? Yes. She would welcome that. She didn't want anything to destroy the mood or the moment, because this had been a long time coming. Eight years, to be precise. Eight long and arid years when her body had felt as if it were made of cardboard, rather than respon-sive flesh and blood. Keeley swallowed. She didn't want time to have second thoughts about what was about to happen—she wanted to just go with the flow and be spontaneous. A rush of excitement flooded through her until she remembered what she was wearing and, un-locking her lips from his, she pulled away from him. 'The dress!' she stumbled.

He stared down at her uncomprehendingly. 'The dress?' he echoed dazedly.

'It's not mine, remember? I don't want to...to mark it.'

'Of course. You borrowed the dress.' Something hardened in his eyes as his gaze swept over her and his smile was tinged with a flicker of triumph as he picked her up and walked across the sand towards the cottage, before kicking open the door.

CHAPTER FIVE

ONCE INSIDE, ARISTON carried Keeley straight upstairs in a display of masculine dominance she found intoxicating. As he brushed hungry kisses over her neck and lips she was on such a delirious high of pleasure that she was barely aware of him lifting her arms above her head and peeling off her borrowed dress. Until suddenly she was standing in front of him wearing nothing but a pair of tiny thong panties. Half naked in the silver moonlight, she should have felt shy, but the look blazing from Ariston's eyes made her feel anything *but* shy. Tilting her chin, she felt the silky movement of her hair as it swayed against her bare back and a sudden sense of liberation rippled through her as she met his slow and appreciative smile.

'*Theos mou*, but you are magnificent,' he said, his body tensing as he cupped one of her breasts like a market trader calculating the weight of a watermelon.

And even that rather brutal gesture excited her. Every single thing about him was exciting right now—each nerve ending in her body feeling as if a layer of skin had been peeled away, leaving her raw and aching. His voice dipped approvingly as his gaze focussed on her tiny panties. 'It seems that beneath the often unexceptional clothes you favour, you dress in order to please your man.' He glittered her a smile. 'And I approve.'

His arrogance was breathtaking and Keeley wanted to tell him that his words were inaccurate on so many counts. That the tiny briefs were the only thing she *could* have worn under such a flimsy gown without getting a visible panty line and usually she wore a heavy-duty bra to contain her overripe breasts. But he was playing with her nipples again and it was such an unbearably sweet sensation that she didn't have the desire—or the strength—to break the fragile mood with stumbled words of explanation. Because during that short journey from beach to bedroom she'd known there was to be no turning back. It didn't seem to matter if it was right or wrong, it just seemed inevitable. She was going to let Ariston Kavakos make love to her tonight and nothing was going to stop her.

She lifted her gaze to his, watching as he began to unbutton his shirt, his eyes not leaving her face as he bared his hair-roughened chest.

'Play with your breasts,' he ordered softly. 'Touch yourself.'

The words should have shocked her but they didn't—maybe because he'd managed to turn them into an irresistible and silky command. Should she tell him that her sexual experience was laughably lacking and she wasn't sure how good she would be? But if she was going to do this, she needed to do it without any hang-ups. Tentatively, she spread her palms over the aching mounds and began to circle them as he'd demanded, and the weird thing was that once she'd banished her inhibitions, she started to *feel* sexy. She imagined it was Ariston's hands tracing erotic movements over her aroused flesh. She wriggled impatiently and her heavy eyelids fluttered to a close.

'No.' Another soft order rang out in the moonlit bedroom. 'Don't close your eyes. I want you to look at me, Keeley. I want to see your expression when I make you come. And believe me, I am going to make you come, *koukla mou*. Over and over and over again.'

Keeley's eyes widened because his words were so graphic. So *explicit*. She got the distinct impression he was deliberately demonstrating control over her. Was that the way he liked it? To be totally in charge? To tell her what to do and *show her who was boss*? Her heart started to race because he was naked now, his erection so pale and proud amid the dark curls—and even the daunting dimensions of *that* weren't enough to intimidate her. He walked over to where she stood, removing her hands from her breasts and replacing them with his lips, bending his head to kiss each nipple in turn, the tip of his tongue working expertly on the puckered flesh until she let out a small moan of pleasure.

'I like to hear you moan,' he said unsteadily. 'I promise I'm going to make you moan all night.'

'Are you?'

'Neh.' He tangled his fingers in the spill of her hair, anchoring her head so that she couldn't look anywhere except at him. 'Do you know how many times I have

imagined you like this, Keeley? Standing naked in the moonlight like some kind of goddess?'

Goddess? Was he crazy? A shelf-stacker from Super Save who was carrying too much weight? A wave of hysteria bubbled up inside her. She wanted to tell him not to say things like that but the truth was she liked it. She liked the way it made her feel. And why *shouldn't* she feel like a goddess for once when his words were painting pictures in her imagination which were increasing her desire? Because this was probably the way he did it. His method. Sweet-talking her into submission with his practised lines. Telling her the things she longed to hear, even if they weren't true. Presumably this was what men and women did all the time and it didn't mean a thing. Sex didn't mean a thing. That had been one thing her mother *had* taught her.

'Ariston,' she managed, through bone-dry lips.

'Have you dreamed about me too?' he murmured.

She supposed it would destroy the mood if she admitted that all the dreams she'd had about him were deeply unsettling. But why destroy the mood with an admission which no longer seemed relevant?

'Maybe,' she admitted.

He let out a low laugh of pleasure as he skimmed his hand over her tiny thong. 'I love that you blow so hot and cold,' he said. 'Did you learn long ago how to keep a man guessing?

Keeley bit her lip. His impression of her was a million miles away from the reality, but why puncture the bubble now? He obviously thought she was some kind of man-magnet and surely it would be a waste of time to try to convince him otherwise. Because she wasn't expecting any future in this. She knew that only a fool would expect a relationship with a man like Ariston, but her heart still clenched as she acknowledged just how fleeting it was going to be. And if his fantasies about her were turning him on, why not play the game? Why not scrabble up what little knowledge she had and work with it?

'Do you always waste so much time talking?' she purred.

Her softly spoken tease made the atmosphere change. She could sense a new tension in him as he picked her up and carried her over to the bed, not bothering to pull back the bedsheet as he laid her on it. His eyes were unfathomable as he stared down at her.

'Forgive me for not recognising your...' he slid his hand between her legs, pushing aside the panel of her panties with a murmur of acknowledgment as he flicked his finger over her slick, wet heat '...impatience.'

Keeley swallowed because now his finger was working with a purpose and she could feel the heat inside her building. She wanted him to kiss her again but the only area he seemed interested in kissing was her torso and then her belly and then...then... She sucked in a shocked breath as he pulled down her panties and moved his head between her legs so that she could feel the tickle of his thick hair brushing against her thighs. Her body was tensed for what was going to happen next but nothing on earth could have prepared her for that first sweet lick. She jerked on the bed and tried to wriggle away from the almost unendurable pleasure which was spiralling up inside her, but he was holding her hips so she couldn't move. And so she lay there helplessly—a willing prisoner of the Greek tycoon as layer upon layer of pleasure built to such a level of intensity that when it broke it felt like a swollen river bursting its banks and she screamed out his name.

As the spasms slowly ebbed away she felt a delicious warmth seeping through her body and opened her eyes to find him leaning over her, a trace of amusement curving the edges of his lips.

'Mmm…' he said softly. 'For a woman who blows so hot and cold, I didn't expect you to be quite so vocal. Are you always so sweetly *enthusiastic* when you come, Keeley—or are you trying to massage my ego by acting like that was the first orgasm you've ever had?'

Keeley wasn't sure how to answer. She wondered if it would be shameful to admit she'd never experienced pleasure like that before and wondered how he would react if he realised just how sketchy her sexual experience was. She licked her lips. Don't frighten him away, she told herself. Why shatter this deliciously dreamy mood with reality? Tell him what he expects to hear. Be the woman you've never dared be before.

'You shouldn't be so good,' she said lazily. 'And then I wouldn't be quite so…*vocal.*'

'Good? Are you kidding? I haven't even started yet,' he murmured.

She swallowed, and suddenly she felt out of her depth. 'I'm not…'

His gaze lasered into her. 'Not what, Keeley?'

She licked her lips again. 'I'm not on the pill or anything.'

'Even if you were, I always like to be doubly sure,' he said, his voice hardening as he groped around in the pocket of his trousers until he'd found what he was looking for.

Keeley watched as he slid the condom on and thought how *anatomical* this all seemed—as if emotion played no part in what was about to happen. She swallowed. Had she really thought it might be otherwise—that Ariston Kavakos might show her tenderness or affection?

'Kiss me,' she said suddenly. 'Please. Just kiss me.'

Ariston frowned as she made her breathless appeal and as he gave himself up to the kiss she'd demanded, his heart clenched. *Hell...* She was so...*surprising.* One minute the cool seductress and the next—why, she was almost *shy.* After making him wait longer than he'd ever had to wait for anyone, she was so sweet in her response. Had she learned at the knee of her mother how best to captivate a man? Had she discovered that keeping them guessing was the ultimate turn-on for men who'd seen everything, done everything and sometimes been bored along the way?

He felt as if he wanted to explode as he stroked her and kissed her and his heart was pounding as he moved over her, sucking in a deep breath of anticipation as, slowly, he entered her. And wasn't the most insane thing that he was almost *disappointed* at the ease with which he thrust into her slick, wet heat? Hadn't he been fantasising about her for so long that he'd allowed himself the ultimate illusion—and hadn't her wild reaction to her orgasm only reinforced that crazy notion? That maybe she was a virgin and maybe he was the first…

But his insanity lasted no longer than a second before he began to relax and to feast himself on all the soft and curvy flesh which was just there for the taking. She was so hot. So tight. He caught his hands under her thighs and hooked her legs around his back, enjoying her little squeals of pleasure as he increased his penetration. He drove into her hard and harder still, deliberately holding back until she could bear it no longer and called out his name again. And then she just went under, her body arching into a tight bow until she let it go with one long and shuddering cry. And wasn't *this* his fantasy? Not some woman she could never be, but Keeley Turner underneath him while he rode her, with those soft thighs tensing as she came all over again. He waited until her soft moans had died away and only then did he allow himself his own release, his heart clenching as the seed pumped hotly from his body and he reminded himself that *this* was what it was all about. The ultimate conquest of a woman who had been haunting him for years. A farewell to something which should have been finished eight years ago.

He fell asleep afterwards and when he awoke it was to find his lips touching one pouting breast. Barely any movement was needed to take the puckered nipple deep into his mouth and to graze it with his teeth and lick it, until she was squirming beneath him and before he knew what was happening he was inside her again. This time it was longer. Slower. As if it were all happening in some kind of dream. But his orgasm just went on and on and on. Afterwards he rolled onto his back, careful to allow her head to rest on his shoulder because women were very susceptible to rejection at times like this— and although he planned to wave her goodbye in the very near future, it certainly wouldn't be tonight. But he needed to think about what happened next because this was a situation which would need unusual levels of diplomacy. His fingertip skated a light survey over her belly and he felt her shiver in response.

'Well,' he whispered. 'I can't think of a more satisfactory end to the evening.'

Keeley nodded, trying not to show her disappointment. Of all the things he *could* have said and he came out with something like that. Why, he made her feel like an after-dinner brandy he'd consumed! She licked her swollen lips. But what did she expect? Words of admiration and affection? Ariston telling her she was the only woman for him and that he wanted a relationship with her? Of course not. It was what it was, she told herself fiercely. A one-night stand which wasn't supposed to mean anything. So she rolled away from him, shaking her tangled hair free as she attempted to find the level of sophistication which this kind of situation no doubt called for.

'Indeed it was,' she agreed coolly.

There was a short silence for a moment, during which he seemed to be mulling over his words.

'I'm surprised Santino didn't try to follow you down here to get to you before I did,' he said eventually.

It was such a random remark that Keeley frowned

as she turned her head to look at him, pushing back a handful of untidy hair. 'Why on earth would he have done that?'

He shrugged. 'I noticed how much attention he was paying you throughout dinner.'

'Did you?' she said, without missing a beat.

'I certainly did. And after you'd gone Santino and Rachel left pretty abruptly too. We could hear them arguing all the way back to their room.'

'And you thought…what?' she questioned softly as some inner warning system began to sound inside her head. 'Did you think it was about me?'

'I suspect it was. Your name was mentioned more than once.'

'And…what?' she demanded. 'Did you think I was hungry for a man, Ariston? Any man? That if Santino *had* arrived before you that I would be in bed with him?'

'I don't know.' There was a heartbeat of a pause as he lifted his eyes to hers. 'Would you?'

Keeley froze just before instinct kicked in and she longed to flex her fingernails over his skin and tear at his silken flesh. To inflict some kind of hurt on him—something which might mimic the searing pain which was clamping around her heart. She expelled the breath she'd been holding, bitterly aware of how little he thought of her. But she'd known that from the start, hadn't she? And had thought, what? That the growing sexual attraction between them would somehow cancel out his obvious lack of respect? That admitting him to her bed so quickly might make him admire her? What a stupid little fool she'd been.

'Get out,' she said, in a low voice.

'Oh, Keeley,' he said softly. 'There's no need to over-react. You asked me a question and I answered it truth-fully. Would you rather I told you a lie?'

'I mean it!' she snapped. He made to pull her back into his arms but she jumped out of bed before he could touch her. 'Get out of here,' she repeated.

He shrugged as he swung his legs over the bed and reached for his trousers. 'I wasn't intending to insult you.'

'Really? In that case, I think you ought to take a good, long look at the things you just said. You think I'm sexually indiscriminate, do you, Ariston? That one attractive man is pretty much the same as any other?'

'How should I know? You are your mother's daugh-ter, after all. And I've had enough experience of women to know what they are capable of,' he said rawly. 'I know just how unscrupulous they can be.'

Keeley reached for the cotton dressing gown which was hanging on a hook on the door and pulled it on, not daring to speak until she had tied the belt around her waist and her naked body was hidden from his gaze.

'Why *did* you seduce me, Ariston?' she questioned in a low voice. 'When you obviously think so little of me?'

He paused in the act of sliding on his shirt, the move-ment making his powerful muscles ripple beneath the silk fabric. 'Because I find you intensely attractive. Be-cause you lit a longing in me all those years ago which never really went away. Maybe now it will.'

'And that's all?'

His eyes narrowed. 'Isn't that enough?'

But instinct told her there was something more. Something he was holding back. And suddenly she needed to know, even though she suspected it was going to shatter her. 'Tell me the truth like you did before,' she said. 'Just...tell me.'

His eyes gleamed like silver in the moonlight, before he shrugged. 'It started out with wanting to have you for myself, for all the reasons I've just stated,' he said in a low voice. 'But also because...'

'Because what, Ariston? Please don't stop now. Not when this is just getting fascinating.'

He zipped up his trousers before looking up. 'Because I knew that my brother wouldn't be tempted by you, if he knew I'd had sex with you first.'

'Which naturally you would have made sure he knew?'

He shrugged. 'If I'd needed to, then yes. Yes, I would.'

There was a disbelieving silence before she could bring herself to respond. 'So it was...it was some kind of territorial thing? The ultimate deterrent to ensure that your brother wasn't tempted, even though there is no spark between me and Pavlos and there never has been?'

He met her gaze unflinchingly. 'I guess so.'

Keeley felt faint. It was even worse than she'd thought. Briefly, she closed her eyes before going into damage-limitation mode and that was something which came as naturally to her as breathing. The thing she was best at. She sucked in an unsteady breath. 'You do realise I'm going to have to leave the island? That I can't work for you any more. Not after this.'

He shook his head. 'You don't have to do that.'

'Really?' She gave a bitter laugh. 'Then how do you see this playing out? Me carrying on with my domestic work while you occasionally sneak down here to have sex with me? Or am I now supposed to abandon my uniform as if this was some bizarre kind of promotion and join you and your guests for dinner every night?'

'There's no need to overreact, Keeley,' he gritted. 'We can work something out.'

'That's where you're wrong, Ariston. We can't. There's no working out something like this. I won't be treated in this way and I won't spend any more time in the company of a man who is capable of such treatment. Tonight was a mistake—but we can't do anything about it now. But I'm not staying here a second longer than I have to. I want to leave tomorrow, first thing. Before anyone is awake.'

He'd finished buttoning up his shirt and the expression on his rugged face was hidden by a series of shifting shadows. 'You're aware that you need my co-operation to do that? That I own the airstrip as well as the planes—and no other aircraft is allowed to land or take off from here without my permission. I might not be willing to let you go so easily, Keeley—have you thought about that?'

'I don't care what *you* want, you'd just better let me go,' she said, her voice shaking now. 'Because I'm a strong swimmer—and if I have to make my own way to the nearest island, then believe me I will. Or I'll contact one of the international newspapers and tell them I'm being kept prisoner on the Greek tycoon's island—I imagine the press could have a lot of fun with that. Unless you're planning to confiscate my computer while you're at it—which, I have to inform you, is a criminal offence. No? So get out of here, Ariston—and prepare one of your planes to take me back to England. Do you understand?'

CHAPTER SIX

ARISTON STARED OUT of the vast windows, but for once the travel-brochure views of his island home failed to impress him. He might as well have been in a darkened cave for all the notice he took of the sapphire sea and silver sand, or the neglected cup of coffee which had been cooling on his desk for the last half-hour. All he could see was a pair of bright green eyes and a pair of soft, rosy lips—and pale hair which had trickled through his fingers like moonlight.

What was his problem? he wondered impatiently as he stood up with a sudden jerking movement which made the cup rattle. Why did he persist in feeling so *unsettled* when all should have been well in his world? Weeks had passed since Keeley Turner had fallen eagerly into his arms during a sexual encounter which had blown his mind but ended badly. She had flown back to London the next morning, refusing to meet his eye and saying nothing other than a tight-lipped goodbye before turning her back on him. But she had taken the money he'd given her, hadn't she? Had shown no qualms about accepting the additional sum he had included. He'd thought he might receive an angry email telling him what he could do with his money—wasn't that what he'd *hoped* might happen?—along with some furious tirade suggesting he might be offering payment *for services rendered*. But no. She was a woman, wasn't she—and what woman would ever turn down the offer of easy money?

And that had been that. He hadn't heard from her since. He told himself that was a good thing—that he had achieved what he had set out to achieve and bedded a woman whose memory had been haunting him for years. But infuriatingly, little had changed. In fact, it seemed a whole lot worse. Surely by now he shouldn't still be thinking about her, or the way it had felt to press his lips to her pulsating heat as she had orgasmed right into his mouth. Was it because he wasn't used to a woman walking away from him, or because he couldn't help admiring the tempestuous show of spirit she had displayed when she had stormed away? Or just because she'd been the hottest lover he'd ever had?

But after yet another disturbed night he found himself wondering where was the closure he'd been chasing and why he hadn't tried a little harder to keep her here a bit longer, so he could have got her out of his system. Should he have softened his answers to her questions with a little diplomacy and told her what she wanted to hear, instead of giving it to her straight? His mouth hardened. It didn't matter. He didn't like lies and it was too late to go back over that now. What was done was done.

At least Pavlos had announced his engagement to

the beautiful Marina, with a wedding planned for early next year. His brother was happy—he'd called him just last night from Melbourne and told him so, and Ariston felt as if his work was done. That all was well within the Kavakos dynasty—its future now ensured…if only this damned disquiet would leave him.

But it didn't leave him, despite a schedule spent travelling across much of Southeast Asia—and although he threw himself into his work even more single-mindedly than usual, he remained as unsettled as ever. Which was why he found himself making an unplanned trip to England on his private jet, telling himself it was always useful to pay an unexpected visit to his London office because it kept his staff on their toes. And besides, he liked London. He kept a fully staffed apartment there which he used at different times during the year—often when the summer heat of Lasia was at its most intense. But even in London he found himself struggling to concentrate on his latest shipbuilding project or enjoy the fact that the company had been featured in the prestigious *Forbes* magazine in a flattering article praising his business acumen.

He told himself it was curiosity—or maybe courtesy—which made him decide to call on Keeley, to see how she was doing. Maybe she'd calmed down enough to be civil to him. He felt the beat of anticipation. Maybe even more.

He had his car drop him down the road from her bedsit and when he knocked on the door, the long silence which followed made him think nobody was home. A ragged sigh escaped from his lungs. So that was that.

He could leave a note, which he suspected would find its way straight into the bin. He could try calling but something told him that if she saw his name on the screen, she wouldn't pick up. And that had never happened to him before either.

But then the door opened a little and there was Keeley's face peering out at him through the narrow crack—her expression telling him he was the last person she had expected to see. Or wanted to see. His eyes narrowed because she looked terrible. Her blonde hair hung in limp strands as if it hadn't been washed in days, her face was waxy white and she had deep shadows beneath her eyes. He'd never seen a woman who had paid such scant attention to her appearance—but then he'd never made an impromptu call like this before. 'Hello, Keeley,' he said quietly.

Keeley stiffened, her knuckles tightening over the doorknob as she stared into Ariston's searing blue eyes and a wave of horror washed over her. What in heavens name was he doing here—and how was she going to deal with it? Her instinct was to slam the door in his face but she'd tried that once before without success and, besides, she couldn't do that, could she? Not in the circumstances. She might despise him but she needed to talk to him and it just so happened that fate had scheduled that unwanted prospect without her having to arrange it herself. She found herself wishing she'd had time to brush her hair or put on clothes she hadn't fallen asleep in, but maybe it was better this way. At least she wouldn't have to worry about him making a pass at her when she looked like this. Why, he must be wondering what had possessed him to take someone like her to his bed.

'You'd better come in,' she said.

He looked surprised at the invitation and she understood why. After the way they'd parted he must have thought she'd never want to see him again. But no matter how much she wished that could be true, she couldn't turn him away—just as she couldn't turn the clock back. She had to tell him. It was her duty to tell him.

Before he worked it out for himself.

'So what brings you here today, Ariston?' she said, once they were standing facing each other in the claustrophobically small sitting room. 'Let me guess... Pavlos is back in London and you've decided to check whether or not I've got my greedy hooks in him. Well, as you can see—I'm here on my own.'

He gave a short shake of his head. 'Pavlos is engaged to be married.'

'Wow,' she said, feeling winded though she wasn't sure why. 'Congratulations. So you got what you wanted.'

He shrugged. 'My wish to see my brother happily settled with a suitable partner has been fulfilled, yes.'

'But if Pavlos is safe from my supposed clutches, then what brings you to New Malden?' She frowned. 'An area like this isn't exactly a billionaire's stomping ground, is it? And I don't recall leaving anything behind on your island which might need "returning".'

'I was in London and I thought I'd drop by to see how you are.'

'How very touching. Do you do that with all your ex-lovers?'

His mouth hardened. 'Not really. But then, none of my lovers have ever walked out on me like that.'

'Oh, dear. Is your ego feeling battered?'

'I wouldn't go quite that far,' he said drily.

'So now you've seen how I am.'

'Yes. And I don't like what I see. What's the matter, Keeley?' His frowning blue gaze stayed fixed on her face. 'You look sick.'

Keeley swallowed. So here it was. He'd given her the perfect opportunity to tell him her life-changing news. She was surprised he hadn't worked it out for himself and if he'd bothered to look harder at her baggy shirt, he might have noticed the faint curve of her belly beneath. She opened her mouth to tell him but something made her hesitate. Was it self-preservation? The sense that once she told him nothing was ever going to be the same?

'I have been sick,' she admitted, before the words came out in a bald rush. 'Actually, I'm pregnant.'

He didn't catch on, not straight away—or if he did, he didn't show it.

'Congratulations,' he said evenly. 'Who's the father?'

It was a reaction she should have anticipated but stupidly she hadn't and Keeley felt hurt. She wanted to tell him that only one man could possibly be the father but he probably wouldn't believe her and why should he? She hadn't exactly acted with any restraint where he was concerned, had she? She'd fallen into his arms—not once, but twice and made it clear she'd wanted sex with him. Why wouldn't a chauvinist like Ariston Kavakos imagine she behaved like that all the time? She licked her lips.

'You are,' she said baldly. 'You're the father.'

His face showed no reaction other than a sudden coldness which turned his eyes into sapphire ice. 'Excuse me?'

Was he expecting his cool question to prompt her into admitting that she'd made a mistake, and he wasn't going to be a daddy after all? That she was trying it on because he was so wealthy? The temptation to do just that and make him go away was powerful, but her conscience was more powerful still. Because he *was* the father—there was no getting away from that and the important thing was how she dealt with it. Suddenly, Keeley knew that, despite her morning sickness and ever-present sensation of feeling like a cloth which had been wrung out to dry, she now needed to be strong. Because Ariston was strong. And he was a dominant male who would ride roughshod over her to get what it was he wanted, if she let him.

'You heard me,' she said quietly. 'You're the father.'

His face darkened as he studied her and suddenly she got an idea of just how formidable an opponent he might be in the boardroom.

'How do you know it's mine?'

She flinched. 'Because you're the only one it could be.'

'I only have your word for that, Keeley. You were no virgin.'

'Neither were you.'

He gave a cruel smile. 'Like I told you—it's different for men.'

'You think I would lie about something like this?'

'I don't know—that's the thing. I know very little about you. But I'm a wealthy man. There are undoubted benefits to getting pregnant by someone like me. So was it an accident, or did you plan it?'

'*Plan* it? You think I deliberately got myself pregnant, just to get my hands on your money?'

'Don't look so outraged, Keeley. You wouldn't believe the things people would do for money,' he said, his gaze flicking over her coldly. 'Or maybe you would.'

'You seem to be very good at dishing out blame, but I'm not going to carry the entire burden.' She sucked in a deep breath as she walked over to the window sill. 'I always thought contraception was the joint responsibility of both parties.'

Ariston met her shadowed eyes and was surprised by a sudden wave of compassion—and guilt. How many times had he made love to her that night? His brow furrowed. Just twice, before she'd kicked him out of her bed and announced that she was leaving the island. Had he been careful that second time, or had he…? His heart missed a beat. No. He hadn't. He'd been so aroused that in his sleepy and already sated state he had slipped inside her without bothering to put on a condom. How the hell had that happened, when he was traditionally always the most exacting of men?

And hadn't it felt beyond blissful to feel her bare skin against his? Her slick wet heat against his hardness. Had some protective instinct made his mind shut down so that only just now was he remembering it?

His heart was thundering as he watched her, noting the way she had slumped against the window sill. When she leaned back like that he could see the curve of her belly and for the first time noticed that her already generous breasts were even bigger than usual. She was undeniably pregnant—so should he simply take her word that he was the father?

But memories of his mother—and many of the women in between—made him wary. He knew all about lies and subterfuge because they'd been woven into the fabric of his life. He knew what people would do for money. He had learnt caution at an early age because he'd needed to. It had protected him from some of the darker things which life had thrown at him and Pavlos, so why shouldn't he seek its protection now?

'You're right, of course. Contraception is the responsibility of the man and the woman,' he said. 'But that still doesn't answer my question with any degree of satisfaction. How do I know—or *you* know—that I'm the father of your baby?'

'Because…'

He saw her bite her lip as if she was trying to hold the words back but then they came tumbling out in a passionate torrent.

'Because I've only ever had sex once before!' she declared. 'One man, one time, years ago—and it was a disaster, okay? Does that tell you everything you need to know, Ariston?'

He felt a dark and primitive rush of pleasure. It all added up now. Her soft sense of wonder when he'd made love to her. Her disbelieving cries as she had come. These all spoke of a woman achieving satisfaction for the first time, not someone who'd been around the sexual block a few times. But what if she was lying? What if she was simply using the skills of an actress, learnt at the knee of her mother? His mouth hardened. Surely he owed it to himself to demand a DNA test—if not now, then at least when the child was born.

But her waxy complexion and tired eyes were making him stall and he was surprised by another wave of compassion. He forced himself to sift through the available facts and the possible solutions. Despite her lack of qualifications, she wasn't stupid. She must realise that he'd come at her with all guns blazing if he discovered he'd been bamboozled by a false paternity claim.

He glanced around the shabby little room, trying to impose some order on his whirling thoughts. Fatherhood had never been on his agenda. He accepted that he was a difficult man who didn't believe in love, who didn't trust women and who fiercely guarded his personal space—and those factors had ruled out the forced intimacy of marriage. The desire to carry on his own bloodline had always been noticeable by its absence and he'd always supposed that Pavlos would be the one to provide the necessary heirs to take the Kavakos empire forward.

But this disclosure altered everything. In a few short minutes he could feel something changing inside him, because if this was *his* child then he wanted a part of it. A big part of it. His heart clenched. For how could it be any other way? Why would he not want to stake a claim on his own flesh and blood? He looked into Keeley's wary eyes and thought this must be the last thing she wanted—an unplanned baby with a man she loathed. And no money, he reminded himself grimly. Her circumstances were more impecunious than most. So why not offer her the kind of inducement which would suit them both?

'So when were you going to tell me?' he demanded. 'Or weren't you going to bother?'

'Of course I was. I was just…waiting for the right time,' she said, with the voice of someone who had been putting off the inevitable. 'Only it never seemed to come.'

He frowned. 'Why don't you sit down in that chair? You don't look very comfortable standing there and you really should be comfortable, because we need to talk.'

Her chin jutted forward but she didn't defy him, though he noticed that she stared straight ahead as she made her way towards a battered armchair. Yet despite her unwashed hair and sloppy grey sweat-pants, Ariston couldn't help his body from reacting as she walked past him. He could feel the tautness and the tension hardening his muscles and the instinctive tightening low in his abdomen. What was it about her which made him want to impale her whenever she came near?

She sank down onto the chair and lifted up her face to his. 'So talk,' she said.

He nodded, sliding his hands into the pockets of his trousers as he looked at her. 'I don't imagine you wanted to be a mother,' he began.

She shrugged. 'Not yet, no.'

'So how about I free you of that burden?'

She must have misunderstood him because her arms

instantly clamped themselves around her belly as if she was shielding her unborn child and suddenly she was yelling at him. 'If you're suggesting—'

'What I'm *suggesting*,' he interrupted, 'is that I have you moved from this miniature hell-hole into a luxury apartment of your choice. That you are attended by the finest physicians in the land, who will monitor your pregnancy and make sure that you both maintain tip-top health. And after the birth…'

'After the birth…*what*?' she said, her voice dropping to a whisper, as if she'd suddenly got an inkling of what he was about to say.

'You give up your baby.' He gave a cold smile. 'Or rather, you give it to me.'

There was a pause. 'Could you…could you repeat that?' she said faintly. 'Just so I can be sure I haven't misunderstood your meaning.'

'I will raise the child,' he said. 'And you can name your price.'

She didn't speak for a moment and he was taken aback by the naked fury which blazed from her green eyes as she scrambled to her feet. For a min-ute he thought she was about to hurl herself across the room and attack him and wasn't there a part of him which wanted her to go right ahead? Because a fight-ing woman was a woman who could be subdued in all kinds of ways and suddenly he found himself wanting to kiss her again. But she didn't. She stood there, her hands on her hips, her breath coming quick and fast.

'You're offering to *buy* my baby?'

'That's a rather melodramatic way of putting it,

Keeley. Think of it as a transaction—the most reasonable course of action in the circumstances.'

'Are you out of your mind?'

'I'm giving you the opportunity to make a fresh start.'

'Without my *baby*?'

'A baby will tie you down. I can give this child everything it needs,' he said, deliberately allowing his gaze to drift around the dingy little room. 'You cannot.'

'Oh, but that's where you're wrong, Ariston,' she said, her hands clenching. 'You might have all the houses and yachts and servants in the world, but you have a great big hole where your heart should be. You're a cold and unfeeling brute who would deny your baby his mother—and therefore you're incapable of giving this child the thing it needs more than anything else!'

'Which is?'

'Love!'

Ariston felt his body stiffen. He loved his brother and once he'd loved his mother, but he was aware of his limitations. No, he didn't do the big showy emotion he suspected she was talking about and why should he, when he knew the brutal heartache it could cause? Yet something told him that trying to defend his own position was pointless. She would fight for this child, he realised. She would fight with all the strength she possessed, and that was going to complicate things. Did she imagine he was going to accept what she'd just told him and play no part in it? Politely dole out payments and have sporadic weekend meetings with his own flesh and blood? Or worse, no meetings at all. He met the green blaze of her eyes.

'So you won't give this baby up and neither will I,' he said softly. 'Which means that the only solution is for me to marry you.'

He saw the shock and horror on her face.

'But I don't want to marry you! It wouldn't work, Ariston—on so many levels. You must realise that. Me, as the wife of an autocratic control freak who doesn't even like me? I don't think so.'

'It wasn't a question,' he said silkily. 'It was a statement. It's not a case of *if* you will marry me, Keeley— just when.'

'You're mad,' she breathed.

He shook his head. 'Just determined to get what is rightfully mine. So why not consider what I've said, and sleep on it and I'll return tomorrow at noon for your answer—when you've calmed down. But I'm warning you now, Keeley—that if you are wilful enough to try to refuse me, or if you make some foolish attempt to run away and escape...' he paused and looked straight into her eyes '...I will find you and drag you through every court in the land to get what is rightfully mine.'

CHAPTER SEVEN

AS SHE PREPARED for Ariston's visit next morning, Keeley stared at her white-faced reflection in the mirror and gritted her teeth. This time she wouldn't lose her temper. She would be calm and clear and focussed. She would tell him she couldn't possibly marry him but that she was willing to be reasonable.

She washed her hair and put on a loose cotton dress and a sudden desire to impose some order made her give her bedsit an extra-special clean—busying herself with mop and duster. She even went down to the local market and bought a cheap bunch of flowers from the friendly stallholder who implored her to, 'Cheer up, love! It might never happen!'

It already had, she thought gloomily as she crammed the spindly pink tulips into a vase as she waited for the Greek tycoon to arrive.

He was bang on time and she hated her instinctive reaction when she opened the door to see him in an exquisite pale grey suit, which today didn't make him look remotely uncomfortable. In fact, he came over as supremely relaxed as well as looking expensive and hopelessly out of place in her crummy little home. She didn't *want* to shiver with awareness whenever she looked at him, nor remember how it had felt to be naked in his arms, yet the erotic images just kept flooding back. Was she imagining the faint triumph which curved those cruel lips of his—as if he was perfectly aware of the way he made her feel? *He can't make you do anything you don't want him to*, she reminded herself fiercely. You might be carrying his baby but you are still a free agent. This is modern England, not the Middle Ages. He can hardly drag you up the aisle against your will.

'I'm hoping you've had time to come to your senses, Keeley,' he said, without preamble. 'Have you?'

'I've given it a lot of thought, yes—but I'm afraid I haven't changed my mind. I won't marry you, Ariston.'

He said something soft in his native tongue and when he looked at her, he seemed almost regretful as he sighed. 'I was hoping it wouldn't come to this.'

'Come to what?' she questioned in confusion.

'Why didn't you tell me about your mother?'

She felt the blood drain from her face. 'Wh-what about my mother?'

His gaze slid over her. 'That she's living in a care home and has been for the last seven years.'

Keeley's lips folded in on themselves because she was afraid she might cry, until she reminded herself that she couldn't afford the luxury of tears—or to show any kind of vulnerability to a man she suspected would seize on it, as a starving dog might seize on a bone. 'How did you find out?'

He shrugged. 'The gathering of information is simple if you know who to ask.'

'But why? Why would you go to the trouble of having me investigated?'

'Don't be naïve, Keeley. Because you are the mother of my child and you have something I want. And knowledge is power,' he added as his sapphire eyes bored into her. 'So what happened? How come a middle-aged woman has ended up living in an institution where the average age is eighty, unable to recognise her only daughter when she visits?'

Without thinking, Keeley grabbed the arm of the nearest chair before sinking into it before her legs gave way, as they were threatening to. 'Didn't your investigators tell you?' she questioned hoarsely. 'Didn't they gain access to her medical records and tell you everything you needed to know?'

'No—they didn't. I don't think it's morally right to do something like that.'

'How dare you talk to me about *morals*?' she bit back. 'I'm surprised you even know the definition of the word.'

'So what happened, Keeley?' he questioned again, more softly this time.

She wanted to tell him it was none of his business but she suspected that wouldn't deter him. And maybe it *was* his business now, she realised, with a wrench to her heart. Because her mother was the grandmother of *his* child, wasn't she? Even if she would never realise that fact for herself. A sudden wave of sadness engulfed her and she blinked away another hint of tears before he could see them. 'So what do you want to know?' she questioned.

'Everything.'

Everything. That was a tall order. Keeley leant her head back against the chair but it took a couple of moments before she had composed herself enough to speak. 'I'm sure you don't need me to tell you my mother's fleeting fame as an actress was quickly replaced by the notorious reputation she gained after that...' she stumbled on the words '...that summer at your house.'

His mouth hardened, but he didn't comment. 'Go on.'

'When we arrived back in England she was approached by lots of tabloid newspapers and the tackier end of the magazine market. They wanted her to be a torch-bearer for the older woman who was determined to have a good sex life, but in reality they just wanted a gullible fool who could shift a few extra copies in a dwindling retail market.' She drew in a deep breath. 'She talked at length about her different lovers—most of whom were considerably younger. Well, you already know that. She thought she was striking a blow for women's liberation but, in reality, everyone was laughing at her behind her back. But she didn't notice and she certainly didn't let it deter her. And then her looks began to fade...quite dramatically. Too much wine and sun. One crash diet too many.'

She stopped.

'Don't stop now,' he said.

His voice was almost gentle and Keeley wanted to tell him not to talk that way. She'd misinterpreted his kindness once before and she wasn't going to make the same mistake again. She wanted to tell him that she could deal with him better when he was being harsh and brutal.

She shrugged. 'She started having surgery. A nip here and a tuck there. One minute it was an eyebrow job and the next she was having goodness knows what pumped into her lips. She started to look...' She closed her eyes as she remembered the cruelty of the newspapers which had once courted her mother so assiduously. The snatched photos which had been only marginally less flattering than the awful ones she'd still insisted on posing for, usually dressed in something cringe-makingly unsuitable—like leather hot pants and a see-through blouse. How quickly she had become a national laughing stock—her face resembling a cruel parody of youth.

And how ultimately frustrating that she had been too blind to see what was happening to her.

'She started to look bizarre,' she continued, not wanting to appear disloyal but now the words seemed to be rushing to get out because she'd never talked about it before. She'd kept it buttoned up inside her, as if it was *her* shame and *her* secret. 'She met this surgeon and he offered to give her a complete facelift, only she didn't bother to check out his credentials or to wonder why he was offering her all that work at such an advantageous price. Nobody was quite sure of what happened during the operation—only that my mother was left brain-damaged afterwards. And that she never recognised me—or anyone else again. Her capacity for normal living is "severely compromised" is how they described it.' She swallowed. 'And she's been living in that care home ever since.'

He frowned. 'But you visit her regularly?'

'I do. Every week, come rain or shine.'

'Even though she doesn't recognise you?'

'Of course,' she said quietly. 'She's still my mother.'

Ariston flinched at the quiet sense of dignity and grief underpinning her words. Maybe it was inevitable that they made him think about his own mother, but there was no such softening in *his* heart. Bitterness rose in his throat but he pushed it away as he studied the woman in front of him. She looked very different today, with her newly washed hair shining over her shoulders in a pale fall of waves. The shapeless sweatpants and baggy top were gone and in their place was a loose cotton dress. She looked soft and feminine and strangely vulnerable.

'Why don't you tell me what it is *you* want?' he said suddenly.

She met his gaze warily, as if suspecting him of setting up some kind of trap. 'I want my baby to have the best,' she said cautiously. 'Just like every mother does.'

'And you think that living here...' he looked around, unable to hide the contemptuous twist of his mouth '...can provide that?'

'People have babies in all kinds of environments, Ariston.'

'Not a baby carrying the Kavakos name,' he corrected repressively. 'How are you managing for money? Are you still working?'

She shook her head. 'Not at the moment, no.'

'Oh?' His gaze bored into her.

She shrugged. 'I found another supermarket job when I got back from Lasia and then I started getting sick. I eked out the money you paid me but...'

'Then how the *hell*,' he persisted savagely as her words tailed off, 'do you think you're going to manage?'

Keeley swallowed in a vain attempt to stop her lips from wobbling, before drawing on her residual reserves. She'd overcome stuff before and she could do it again. 'Once the sickness has improved, then I can start working more hours. If I need to I might have to move to a cheaper area somewhere.'

'But that would take you further away from your mother,' he pointed out.

She glared at him for daring to point out the obvious but suddenly she couldn't avoid the enormity of her situation. She hadn't even got a buggy or a crib—and even if she had, there was barely any space to put them. And meanwhile Ariston was offering what most women in her situation would snatch at. He wasn't trying to deny responsibility. On the contrary, he seemed more than willing to embrace it. He was offering to *marry* her, for heaven's sake. Whoever would have thought it?

But yesterday he'd wanted her to give him the baby, she reminded herself. *To take her child away from her.* Because he could. Because he was powerful and rich and she was weak and poor. He'd wanted to remove her from the equation—to treat her like a surrogate— and *that* was a measure of his ruthlessness. At least if she was married to him she would have some legal rights—and wouldn't that be the safest place to start from? Staring into the watchful brilliance of his eyes, she repressed a shiver as she realised what she must do. Because what choice did she have? *She didn't. She didn't have a choice.*

'If I did agree to marry you,' she said slowly, 'then I would want some kind of equality.'

'Equality?' he echoed, as if it was a word he'd never used before.

She nodded. 'That's right. I'm not prepared to do anything until you agree to my terms.'

'And what *terms* might they be, Keeley?'

'I would like some say in where we live—'

'Accommodation is the last thing you need concern yourself with,' he said carelessly. 'Don't forget, I have a whole island at my disposal.'

'No!' Her response came out more vehemently than she'd planned but Keeley knew what she could and couldn't tolerate. And the thought of the isolation of his island home and of being at Ariston's total mercy made her blood run cold. 'Lasia isn't a suitable place to bring up a baby.'

'I grew up there.'

'Exactly.'

There was a flicker of amusement in his brilliantine eyes before it was replaced by the more familiar glint of hardness. 'Let me guess, you have somewhere else in mind—somewhere you've always longed to live? A town house in the centre of Mayfair perhaps, or an apartment overlooking the river? Aren't these the places women dream about if money were no option?'

'I haven't spent my whole life plotting my rise up the property ladder!' she snapped.

'Then you are rare among your sex.' His gaze bored into her. 'Lasia is my home, Keeley.'

'And this is mine.'

'This?'

She heard the condescension in his voice and suddenly she was fighting for her reputation and what she'd made of her life. It wasn't much, but in the circumstances hadn't it been the best she could manage? Hadn't she struggled to get even this far? But what would Ariston Kavakos know of hardship and making do, with his island and his ships and the ability to click his fingers to get whatever he wanted? Even her. 'I want to stay in London,' she said stubbornly. 'My mother is here, as you yourself just pointed out, remember? I can't just up sticks and move away.'

He rubbed his forefinger along the bridge of his nose and Keeley watched as he closed his eyes, the thick lashes feathering blackly against his olive skin. Was he wondering how he was going to tolerate a life saddled with a woman he didn't really want, with a mother whose incapacity had been brought about by her own vanity? Was he now working out how to back-pedal on his hastily offered proposal of marriage?

His eyes flickered open. 'Very well. London it shall be. I have an apartment here,' he said, rising to his feet. 'A penthouse in the City.'

Keeley nodded. Of course he did. He probably had a penthouse in every major city in the world. 'Just out of interest, how long do you think this marriage of ours is going to last?'

'The tone of your voice indicates that you think a long-standing union unlikely?'

'I think the odds are stacked against it,' she said. 'Don't you?'

'Actually, no, I don't. Put it this way,' he added softly. 'I don't intend for my child to be brought up by any other man than me. So if you want to maintain your role as the mother, then we stay married.'

'But—'

'But what, Keeley? What makes you look so horrified? The realisation that I am determined to make this work? Surely that is only a good thing.'

'But how can it work when it isn't going to be a *true* marriage?' she demanded desperately.

'Says who? Perhaps we could learn to get along together. Something which might work if we put our minds to it. I have no illusions about marriage and my expectations are fairly low. But I think we could learn how to be civil to one another, don't you?'

'That isn't what I meant and you know it,' she said, her voice low.

'Are you talking about sex?' A trace of sardonic amusement crept into his tone. 'Ah, yes. I can see from your enchanting little blush that you are. So what's the problem? When two people have a chemistry like ours it seems a pity not to capitalise on it. I find that good sex makes a woman very agreeable. Who knows? It might even bring a smile to your face.'

Keeley felt both faint and excited at the way he was

expressing himself—and didn't she despise herself for feeling that way? 'And if I…refuse?'

'Why would you?' His gaze flicked over her body. 'Why fight it when submission is much more satisfactory? You're thinking about it now, aren't you, Keeley? Remembering how good it felt to have me inside you, kissing you and touching you, until you cried out with pleasure?'

The awful thing was that not only was he speaking the truth—but she *was* reacting to his words and there didn't seem to be a thing she could do about it. It was as if her body were no longer her own—as if he was controlling her reaction with just one sizzling glance. Keeley's nipples were pushing against her cotton dress and she could feel a newfound but instantly familiar tug of desire. She wanted him, yes—but surely it was wrong to want a man who treated her the way Ariston did. He had used her as a sexual object rather than someone he respected and something told her he would continue to do so. And wouldn't that leave her open to emotional wounding? Because something told her Ariston was the kind of man who could hurt. Who could hurt without even trying.

'But what,' she continued determinedly, 'what if I decided I couldn't stomach the idea of cold-blooded sex with a man like you?'

'Sex with me is never cold-blooded, *koukla mou*—we both know that. But if you were to persist in such stubbornness, then I would be forced to find myself a mistress.' His face darkened. 'I believe that's what usually happens in these circumstances.'

'In that parallel universe of yours, you mean?' she spat back.

'It's a universe I was born into,' he snapped back. 'It's what I know. I won't consign myself to a sexless future because you refuse to face up to the fact that we are having difficulty keeping our hands off each other,' he said. 'But I will not insult you, nor feel the need to take another woman to my bed if you behave as a wife should, Keeley. If you give me your body then I will promise you my fidelity.'

And then he smiled, a hard, cold smile which suggested he was almost *enjoying* her resistance. As if he were savouring the moment until he was able to conquer her. Or defeat her.

'It's up to you,' he finished. 'It's your call.'

Keeley's heart pounded. The way he spoke about marriage and sex was so *primitive*. He was autocratic and proud and he stirred her up so she couldn't think straight, but deep down she realised she had no other place to go. She remembered his warning about taking her to court to fight for the baby if she tried to oppose him. Some men might have made such a threat lightly, but she suspected Ariston wasn't one of them. But women had rights too, didn't they? He couldn't force her to remain in a marriage if it wasn't working. And he couldn't demand sex from her because it was his marital right to do so. Surely even he couldn't be *that* primitive.

'Very well, I will marry you. Just so long as you understand I'm only doing it to give my baby security.' She tilted her chin to meet the triumphant fire blazing from his eyes. 'But if you think I'm going to be some kind of sexual pushover just to satisfy your raging libido, then you're mistaken, Ariston.'

'You think so?' The smile which flickered at the edges of his lips was arrogant and certain. 'I am rarely mistaken, *koukla mou*.'

CHAPTER EIGHT

'Wow! I've NEVER seen a bride wearing red before!' exclaimed Megan. 'Is this some new kind of fashion?'

But before Keeley had a chance to answer the woman who'd lent her the ill-fated dress on Lasia, her brand-new husband leaned forward and spoke for her.

'It's an ancient Greek custom,' said Ariston smoothly, his words curling over her skin like dark smoke. 'Traditionally, the bride wore a red veil in order to ward off evil spirits. But I suspect Keeley has deliberately adapted the look and given it a modern twist by wearing a crown of scarlet roses to match her dress. Isn't that right, Keeley?'

Resenting his perception even more than the way he'd just butted in, Keeley looked up into the blue blaze of Ariston's eyes, trying not to react as he slipped his arm around her waist and pulled her closer, looking for all the world like a loving and attentive groom. How appearances could deceive, she thought bitterly. Because he was not a loving groom—he was a cold-hearted control freak who was positively *glowing* with satisfaction because an hour earlier he had slipped an embellished golden wedding ring onto her rigid finger. He'd got exactly what he wanted and she was now his wife, stuck in an unwanted marriage he was determined would last.

He dipped his mouth to her ear and she hated the involuntary shiver which trickled down her spine as his breath fanned her skin.

'Clever you for researching Greek customs so thoroughly,' he murmured. 'Am I the evil spirit you're trying to ward off, Keeley?'

'Of course!' she said, curving her mouth into a big smile, because she'd discovered she could do the appearance thing just as well as Ariston. She could play the part of the blushing bride to perfection—all it took was a little practice. And why spoil a day with something as disappointing as the truth? Why not let people believe what they wanted to believe—the fairy-tale version of their story—that the struggling daughter of a notorious actress had bagged one of the world's most eligible men?

In the back of her mind she'd wondered if her past might catch up with her and if Ariston would have second thoughts about marrying a woman with a history like hers. Yet when a newspaper had regurgitated the old story of Keeley's mother cavorting on the back seat of the ministerial limo and asked Ariston whether the tawdry behaviour of his new mother-in-law gave him any cause for concern, he had broken the habit of a lifetime and given them a quote: 'Old news,' he'd commented, in a bored and velvety drawl. 'And old news is so dull, don't you think?'

Which was kind of ironic when Keeley thought about

how much fuss he'd made about what had happened in the past. But she supposed her pregnancy changed everything. It made him overlook her mother's transgressions. It made him act proprietorially towards her, something which he made no attempt to hide. She could feel him stroking his finger across the front of her scarlet dress, lingering lightly over the curve of her belly as if it was his right to do so. And she guessed it was. Because he was pulling the strings now, wasn't he? Certainly the purse strings. He had given her a brand-new credit card and told herself to buy what she liked—to transform herself into the woman who would soon become his wife. 'Because I want you to *look* like my wife from now on.' His eyes had glittered like blue ice as he had spoken. 'Not some little supermarket stacker who just happens to be wearing my ring.'

His remark had riled her and she'd been tempted to wear her oldest clothes all the time and see how he liked *that*. Would such defiance make him eager to be rid of her and thus grant her the freedom she craved? But then she thought about her baby…and the fact that she was soon going to be a mother. Did she really want to be seen pushing her buggy around the fancy places which Ariston frequented, wearing clothes which had come from the thrift shop? Wouldn't that whittle away at her confidence even more?

But the disturbing thing was that once she'd started, she'd found it surprisingly easy to spend her billionaire fiancé's money. Perhaps there was more of her mother in her than she'd thought. Or maybe she'd just forgotten the lure of wealth and how it could make people do unpredictable things. During her childhood when they'd been flush, money had trickled through her mother's fingers like sand and sometimes, if she'd been feeling especially benevolent, she had spent some of it on her only child. But her gifts had always failed spectacularly. Keeley had been given impractical frilly dresses which had made her stand out from the other little girls in their dungarees. There had been those frivolous suede shoes, ruined by their first meeting with a puddle—and ribbons which had made her look like some throwback to an earlier age. No wonder she'd grown up to be such a tomboy.

But she took to her new credit card like a duck to water, shopping for her imminent role as Ariston's wife with enthusiasm and allowing herself to be influenced by the friendly stylist who had been assigned to her by the fancy department store. She bought new clothes chosen specially to accommodate her growing frame, as well as new underwear, shoes and handbags. And didn't she enjoy the feeling of silk and cashmere brushing against her skin instead of the scratchy qualities of the man-made fabrics she'd worn up till then? She told herself she was only doing what she'd been instructed to do, but the speculative rise of Ariston's dark eyebrows when his driver had staggered into the City apartment under the weight of all those shiny shopping bags had left her feeling…uncomfortable. As if she'd just affirmed some of his deeply held prejudices about women.

But money was liberating, she realised. It gave her choices which had previously been lacking in her life and that newfound sense of liberation encouraged her to buy the scarlet silk dress and matching shoes, secretly enjoying the stylist's shocked reaction when she explained it was for her wedding day.

'You're some kind of scarlet woman, are you?' the woman had joked drily.

And now, at the small but glittering reception, Keeley realised that Ariston's hold on her had changed and he was pushing her away by a fraction so his gaze could rake over her, those smouldering blue eyes taking in every centimetre of the scarlet silk which was clinging to her curves.

'Spectacular,' he murmured. 'Quite…spectacular.'

She felt exposed—almost naked—which hadn't been her intention at all. She felt aroused, too—and surely that was even more dangerous. She tilted her chin defiantly, trying to swamp the sudden rush of desire which was making her skin grow heated and her nipples hard. 'So you approve of my wedding dress?'

'How could I not approve? It would have been entirely inappropriate for such an obviously pregnant wife to wear virginal white.' He gave a slow smile. 'Yet despite your unconventional colour choice and what I suspect was your intention to rile me, let me tell you that you really do make a ravishing bride, Keeley. Glowing, young and intensely fecund.'

'I'll… I'll take that as a compliment,' she stumbled, the tone of his voice making her momentarily breathless.

'That's what it was intended to be.' His eyes narrowed. 'So how are you feeling, *wife*?'

Keeley wasn't quite sure how to answer, because

the truth was complex—and strange. For the first time in her life she actually felt *safe*—and cosseted. She realised that Ariston would never let anyone harm her. That he would use his strength to protect her, no matter what. But he wasn't doing it for *her*, she reminded herself. He was doing it because she was carrying the most precious of cargoes, and as custodian of his unborn child she merited his care and attention. *That* was why he was suddenly being so considerate—and if she read anything more into it than that, then she would be embarking down a very perilous road.

'I'm a little tired,' she admitted. 'It's been a long day and I wasn't expecting it to be such…such an occasion.'

He frowned. 'You want to skip the meal and go home?'

'How can I? It wouldn't look very good if the bride didn't turn up for her own wedding breakfast.'

'You think I care?' He reached out to stroke his fingertips beneath her eyes. 'Your welfare supersedes everything.'

'No, honestly. I'm fine.' The touch of his fingers was doing crazy things to her heart and as she noticed Megan hovering close by with a camera phone pointed in their direction, something made her want to maintain the whole myth of this marriage. Was it pride? She forced a smile as the phone flashed. 'Let's join the others,' she said. 'Besides, I'm hungry.'

But Keeley's reluctance to leave the reception wasn't just about hunger. She was dreading returning to Ariston's gleaming apartment as man and wife and not just because she'd found its vast and very masculine interior intimidating. She had been staying at the famous Granchester Hotel while all the necessary pre-wedding paperwork was completed, because Ariston had insisted that they would only share a home as man and wife. Which seemed slightly bizarre since her rapidly increasing girth made a mockery of such old-fashioned sensibilities. But at least it had given her some breathing space and the chance to get used to her new life without Ariston's distracting presence. She knew she couldn't keep putting off living with him but now the moment of reckoning was approaching, she was terrified. Terrified about sharing an apartment with him and unsure how she would cope. At times she felt more like a child than a grown woman who would soon have a child of her own. Was that normal? she wondered.

But she pushed her reservations aside as she sat down to the Greek feast which had been provided by the hotel and it was a relief to be able to eat after what seemed like weeks of sickness. She could feel her strength returning as she worked her way through the delicious salads, though she could manage only half of one of the rich baklava cakes which were produced at the end of the meal. Despite the relatively small guest list, it somehow managed to feel like a real wedding and Ariston had even asked if she wanted her mother there. Keeley had been torn by his unexpected suggestion. She had felt a wave of something symbolic at the thought of her mother witnessing her marriage, until a last-minute chest infection had put paid to the idea. And maybe that was best. Even if she *had* been aware of what was going on around her, what would her mum have cared about seeing her married, when she'd made such a mockery of marriage herself?

Keeley had wondered why Ariston hadn't suggested a short trip to the register office with the minimum fuss and no guests other than a couple of anonymous witnesses gathered from the street. Wouldn't that have been more appropriate in the circumstances? But his reply had been quietly emphatic.

'Maybe I want to make a statement.'

'A statement?'

'That's right. Shout it from the rooftops. What is it they say? Fake it to make it.'

'By putting your stamp on me, you mean?' she questioned acidly. 'Branding me as a Kavakos possession— just like you did the night you had sex with me?'

His eyes had glittered like sunlight on a dark Greek sea. 'Humour me, Keeley, won't you? Just this once.'

And somehow she had done exactly that. She'd even managed to smile when he stood to make a speech, his fleeting reference to shotguns getting an affectionate laugh, especially from his brother.

'It's funny,' Pavlos said afterwards, with a bemused shake of his head. 'Ariston always vowed he would never marry and he said it like he really meant it. I'd never have guessed there was anything going on between you two. Not after that day at the art gallery when you could have cut the atmosphere with a knife.'

And Keeley didn't have the heart to disillusion him. She wondered what he'd say if he realised that Ariston had bedded her simply to ensure that Pavlos would never want her for himself, and that she had been too stupid and weak to resist him. Yet his need to control had backfired on him because he was now saddled to a woman he didn't really want, though he hid it well. As he raised his glass to toast his new bride, Keeley should have resented his ability to put on such a convincing show of unity—but the reality was a stupid, empty ache in her heart as she found herself yearning for something which could never be hers. He looked like a groom and acted like a groom—but the cold glitter in his blue eyes told its own story.

He will never care for you, she told herself. So don't ever forget it.

During the drive to his apartment, she tugged the scarlet flowers from her head and shook little bits of confetti from her blonde hair. But she couldn't shake off her detachment as she and Ariston walked into the impressive foyer of his apartment building, where doormen and porters sprang to instant attention and a few men in suits shot her bemused glances. She hugged her pashmina around her shoulders in a vain attempt to hide as much of the scarlet dress as possible. Why on earth hadn't she changed into something more sensible first?

A private elevator zoomed them up to the penthouse suite, with its impressive views over many of London's iconic buildings and its seemingly endless suites of rooms. There was even a swimming pool and a gym in the basement—and the outside terraces were filled with a jungle of plants which temporarily made you forget that you were in the heart of the city. She had been there only once before—an awkward visit to oversee the installation of her new clothes in a large room which was now called her dressing room and where every item had been hung in neat and colour-coordinated lines by Ariston's housekeeper.

She hugged the pashmina as they stood in a hallway as big as her bedsit, where a marble statue of a man appeared to be glaring at her balefully.

'So now what do we do?' she said bluntly.

'Why don't you go and change out of that dress?' he suggested. 'You've been shivering since we left the reception. Come with me and I'll remind you where our bedroom is.'

Our? She looked up at him. Had he mentioned that to her before, or had she just not been concentrating? Probably not. His housekeeper had been hovering helpfully during her previous visit, so maybe it had only been alluded to. 'You mean we're going to be…sharing?'

'Don't be naïve, Keeley.' He glittered her a smile. 'Of course we are. I want to have sex with you. I thought I'd made that clear. That, surely, is the whole point of being man and wife.'

'But the vows we made weren't real.'

'No? Then we could make them real. Remember what I said about faking it to make it?' He gave an odd kind of laugh. 'And don't widen your eyes at me like that, *koukla mou*. You look like one of those women in an old film who has been tied to the railway line and only just noticed the train approaching. I don't intend behaving like a caveman, if that's what concerns you.'

'But you said—'

'I said I wanted to have sex with you. And I do. But it has to be consensual. You would need to give yourself to me wholeheartedly—and consciously,' he added with a cool smile. 'I'm not talking about one of those middle-of-the-night encounters, where two bodies collide…and before you know it we're having mind-blowing sex without a single word being exchanged.'

'You mean…' the tip of her tongue snaked over her top lip as she followed him along the corridor, to a room which contained a vast bed which reminded her of a sacrificial altar '…like the night our child was conceived?'

He gave a short laugh. 'That's exactly what I mean. But this time I want us both to be fully aware of what's happening.' There was a pause as he turned around to face her. 'Unless silent submission is what secretly turns you on?'

'I already told you—I have practically no experience of sex,' she said, because suddenly it became important that he stopped thinking of her as some kind of stereotype and started treating her like a real person. 'I…' She bit her lip and said it before she had time to think about the consequences. 'I'd never even had an orgasm before I slept with you.'

He looked at her and she could see a glint of something incomprehensible in his narrowed blue eyes.

'Maybe that's the reason why I'm not trying hard to seduce you,' he said unexpectedly. 'Maybe I want you to stop staring at me as if I was the big, bad wolf and to relax a little. Your dressing room is next door—so why don't you get out of your wedding dress and slip into something more comfortable?'

'Like…what?'

'Whatever makes you feel good. But don't worry,'

he said drily. 'I'm sure I'll be able to keep my hands off you, if that's what you want.'

'That's what I want,' she said, seeing his tight smile before he turned away and closed the door behind him. And wasn't human nature a funny thing? She'd been gearing herself up to fight off his advances, but the news that he wasn't actually going to make any left her with a distinct feeling of *disappointment*. She never knew where she stood with him. She felt as if she were walking along an emotional tightrope. Was that intentional—or just the way he always was around women? She undid the side zip of the red wedding dress, trying to get her head around the fact that this vast room with its amazing views over the darkening city was *hers*.

No. Not hers. His. He owned everything. The dress she stood in and the leather shoes she gratefully kicked off.

But not the child in her belly, she reminded herself fiercely as she walked into the gleaming en-suite bathroom. That child was hers, too.

Stripping off and piling her hair on top of her head, she ran a deep bath into which she poured a reckless amount of bath oil, before sinking gratefully into the steamy depths. It was the first time all day that she'd truly relaxed and she lay there for ages, studying the changing shape of her body as the scented water gradually cooled and she was startled by the sound of Ariston's voice from the other side of the bathroom door.

'Keeley?'

Instantly her nipples hardened and she swallowed. 'I'm in the bath.'

'I gathered that.' There was a pause. 'Are you coming out any time soon?'

She pulled out the plug and the water began to drain away. 'Well, I'm not planning on spending the night in here.'

She towelled herself dry and tied her damp hair in a ponytail. Then she pulled on a pair of palest grey sweatpants and a matching cloud-like cashmere sweater and found her way back through the maze of corridors to the sitting room, where the lights on the skyscrapers outside the enormous windows were beginning to twinkle like stars. Ariston had removed his tie and shoes and he lay on the sofa, leafing his way through a stack of closely printed papers. His partially unbuttoned white shirt gave a provocative glimpse of his chest and, with his long legs stretched out in front of him, his powerful body looked relaxed for once. He glanced up as she walked in, the expression on his shuttered face indefinable.

'Better?'

'Much better.'

'Stop hovering by the door like a visitor. This is your home now. Come and sit down. Can I get you anything? Some tea?'

'That would be great.' She thought how *formal* they sounded—like two total strangers who had suddenly found themselves locked up together. But wasn't that exactly what they were? What did she really *know* about Ariston Kavakos other than the superficial? She realised she'd been expecting him to ring a discreet bell and for his housekeeper to come scurrying from some unseen corner to do his bidding, just as she'd done on her previous visit. But to her surprise, he rose to his feet.

'I'll go and make some.'

'You?'

'I'm perfectly capable of boiling a kettle,' he said drily.

'But…isn't your housekeeper here?'

'Not tonight,' he said. 'I thought it might be preferable to spend the first night of our honeymoon alone and without interruption.'

Once he'd gone Keeley sank down on a squashy sofa, feeling relieved. At least she would be able to relax without the silent scrutiny of his domestic staff who might reasonably wonder why one of their number was now installed as their new mistress.

She glanced up as Ariston returned, carrying a tray, with peppermint tea for her and a glass of whisky for himself. He sat down opposite her and as he sipped his whisky she thought about all the contradictory aspects of his character which made him such an enigma. And suddenly she found herself wanting to know more. *Needing* to know more. She suspected that in normal circumstances he would bat off any questions she might have, with the impatience of a man who held no truck with questions. But these weren't normal circumstances and surely it wasn't possible to co-exist with a man she didn't really know? A man whose child she carried in her belly. She'd *humoured him* as he had requested earlier in the day, so wasn't it his turn to do the same for her?

'You remember asking whether I wanted my mother at the wedding?' she said.

His eyes narrowed. 'I do. And you told me she wasn't well enough to attend.'

'No. That's right. She wasn't.' She drew in a deep breath. 'But you didn't even mention your own mother and I suddenly realised I don't know anything about her.'

His fingers tightened around his whisky glass. 'Why should you?' he questioned coolly. 'My mother is dead. That's all you need to know.'

A few months ago, Keeley might have accepted this. She had known her place in society and had seen no reason to step off the humble path which life had led her down. She'd made the best of her circumstances and had attempted to improve them, with varying degrees of success. But things were different now. *She* was different. She carried Ariston's child beneath her heart.

'Forgive me if I find it intolerable to be fobbed off with an answer like that.'

'And forgive me if I tell you it's the only answer you're getting,' he clipped back.

'But we're married. It's funny.' She drew in a deep breath. 'You talk so openly—so unashamedly—about sex yet you shy away from intimacy.'

'Maybe that's because I don't *do* intimacy,' he snapped.

'Well, don't you think you ought to try? We can't keep talking about cups of tea and the weather.'

'Why are you so curious, Keeley? Do you want something to hold over me?' He slammed his whisky glass down on a nearby table so that the amber liquid sloshed around inside the crystal. 'Some juicy segments of information to provide you with a nice little nest egg should ever you wish to go to the papers?'

'You think I'd stoop to something as low as that?'

'You already did when you wanted to leave Lasia, remember? Or are you blaming a suddenly defective memory on your hormones?'

It took a moment or two for Keeley to recall her blustering bravado, spoken when she'd been swamped by humiliation and the realisation that he'd had sex with her for all the wrong reasons. 'That was then when you were intimating that you might not allow me to leave your island,' she retorted. 'This is now…and I'm having your baby.'

'And that changes things?' he demanded.

'Of course it does. It changes *everything*.'

'How?'

She licked her lips, feeling as if she were on trial, wishing her gaze wouldn't keep straying towards his hands and wishing they would touch her. 'What if our little boy…?' She saw his face change suddenly and dramatically. Saw the same look of fierce pride darkening his autocratic features, as it had done when the sonographer had skated a cold paddle over her jelly-covered bump and pointed out the unmistakable outline of their baby son. For a man who claimed not to do emotion it had been a startling about-turn.

'What if our little boy should start asking me questions about his family, as children do?' she continued. 'Isn't it going to be damaging if I can't answer a simple query about his grandma just because his daddy is uptight and doesn't *do* intimacy? Because he insists on keeping himself hidden away and won't even tell his wife?'

'I thought you said our vows weren't real?'

She met his eyes. 'Fake it to make it, remember?'

There was a pause. He picked up his glass and took a long mouthful of whisky before putting it down again. 'What do you want to know?' he growled.

There were a million things she could have asked him. She was curious to know what had made him so arrogant and controlling. Why he possessed a stony quality which made him seem so *distant*. But maybe the question she was about to ask might give her some kind of insight into his character. 'What happened to her, Ariston?' she questioned slowly and watched his face darken. 'What happened to your mother?'

CHAPTER NINE

ARISTON'S HEART PUMPED violently as he looked into the grass-green of Keeley's eyes. And although deep down he knew she had every right to ask about his mother, every instinct he possessed urged him not to tell her. Because if he told her he would reveal his inner self to her, and that was something he liked to keep locked away.

He understood where his aversion to intimacy stemmed from but was content to maintain that state of affairs. He made the rules which governed his life and if other people didn't like them, that was too bad. His demanding lifestyle had suited him perfectly and, although his lovers had accused him of being cold and unfeeling, he'd seen no reason to change. He'd been self-sufficient for so long that it had become a habit.

Not even Pavlos knew about the dark memories which still haunted him when he was least expecting them. Especially not Pavlos—because hadn't protecting his brother been second nature to him and the highest thing on his list of priorities? But here was Keeley, his new and very pregnant wife, her face all bright and curious as she asked her question. And this wasn't some boardroom where he could quash any unwanted topic at a moment's notice, or a lover he could walk away from without a backward glance because she was being too intrusive. This was just him and her—a woman he was now legally tied to—and there was no way he could avoid answering.

He stared at her. 'My mother left us.'

She nodded and he could see the effort it took her to react as if he'd said nothing more controversial than a passing reference to the weather. 'I see. Well, that's... unusual, because usually it's the man who goes, but it's by no means—'

'No.' Impatiently he interrupted her. 'You want the truth, Keeley? The plain, unvarnished truth? Only I warn you, it's shocking.'

'I'm not easily shocked. You forget that my own mother pretty much broke every rule in the book.'

'Not like this.' There was a pause. 'She sold us.'

'She *sold* you?' Keeley's heart began to slam against her ribcage. 'Ariston, how is that even possible?'

'How do you think it's possible? Because my father offered her a big, fat cheque to get out of our lives and stay out, she did exactly that.'

'And she...never came back?'

'No, Keeley. She never came back.'

She blinked at him uncomprehendingly. 'But...*why*?'

Behind the hard set of his lips, Ariston ground his teeth, wishing she would stop now. He didn't want to probe any more because that would start the pain. The bitter, searing pain. Not for him, but for Pavlos—the little baby whose mama didn't want him enough to fight for him. He felt his heart clench as he started to speak and the bitter words just came bubbling out.

'I'm not saying my father was blameless,' he said. 'Far from it. He'd been brought up to believe he was some kind of god—the son of one of the wealthiest ship-owners in the world. He was what is known as a *player*, in every sense of the word. At a time when free love was common currency, there were always women—lots of women. From what I understand my mother decided she couldn't tolerate his infidelities any more and told him she'd had enough.'

'Right,' she said cautiously. 'So if that was the case, then why didn't she just divorce him?'

'Because he came up with something much more at-tractive than a messy divorce. He offered her a king's ransom if she would just walk away and leave us alone. A clean break, he called it. Better for him. Better for her. Better for everyone.' His mouth twisted. 'All she had to do was sign an agreement saying that she would never see her two sons again.'

'And she…signed it?'

'She did,' he affirmed grimly. 'She signed on the dotted line and went to live a new life in America, and that was the last we ever saw of her. Pavlos was…'

There was a pause and when he spoke it was in a voice devoid of all nuance. A voice, thought Keeley, which was enough to break your heart in two.

'Just a baby,' he finished.

'And you?'

'Ten.'

'So what happened? I mean, after she'd gone.'

He stood up, picking up his papers and stacking them on a nearby table, carefully aligning all the corners into a neat pile before answering her question. 'My father was busy celebrating the completion of what to him seemed like the perfect deal—being completely rid of an irritant of an ex-wife. In his absence he employed a series of nannies to look after us, but none of them could take the place of our mother. Even though I was a child I suspected that most of them had been chosen on account of their looks, rather than their ability to look after a confused and frightened little baby.'

He stared into space. 'I was the one who took care of Pavlos, right from the start. He was my responsibility. I wasn't going to risk anyone else getting close to him and leaving him again. So I bathed him and changed his nappies. I taught him how to swim and to fish. I taught him everything I knew—everything that was decent and good—because I wanted him to grow up to be a normal little boy. And when the time was right, I insisted he go to school in Switzerland because I wanted him as far away from my father's debauched lifestyle as possible. That's why I encouraged him to become a mariner afterwards, because when you're away at sea you don't get influenced or seduced by wealth. There's nothing around you but the wind and the ocean and the wildness of nature.'

And suddenly Keeley understood a lot more about Ariston Kavakos. What had seemed like an overprotective attitude towards his younger brother and his need to control now became clear, because as a child he had seen their lives dissolve into total chaos. That explained his reaction when he'd seen her with Pavlos because for him she had been her mother's child, and a harmful influence. He must have seen all his hard work threatened—his determination that Pavlos should have a decent, normal life about to go up in smoke.

And she understood why he had threatened to fight her for their child too, no matter how ruthless that might seem. Because Ariston didn't actually *like* women, and who could blame him? He was under no illusion that women were automatically the *better* parent who deserved to keep the child in the event of any split. He had seen a mockery made of the so-called maternal bond. He'd fought to protect his own flesh and blood in the shape of Pavlos, she realised—and he would do exactly the same for their own son.

Yet could his mother have been all bad? Wasn't he in danger of seeing only one side of the story? 'Maybe she couldn't have withstood your father's power if she'd attempted to fight for custody,' she ventured.

His voice was like stone. 'She could at least have *tried*. Or she could have visited. Wrote a letter. Made a phone call.'

'She wasn't depressed?' she said desperately, casting around for something—anything—to try to understand what could have motivated a woman to leave her baby behind like that. And her ten-year-old son, she reminded herself. Who had grown into the man who stood before her. The powerful man whose heart was made of stone. Had everyone been so busy looking out for the motherless little baby, that they'd forgotten his big brother must also be lost and hurting?

'No, Keeley, she wasn't depressed. Or if she was she hid it well behind her constant round of partying. I wrote to her once,' he said. 'Just before Pavlos's fifth birthday. I even sent a photo of him, playing with a sandcastle we'd built together on Assimenos beach. Maybe I thought that the cute little image might bring her back. Maybe I was still labouring under the illusion that deep down she might have loved him.'

'And?'

'And nothing. The letter was returned to me, unopened. And a couple of weeks later we found out that she'd taken a bigger dose of heroin than usual.' His voice faltered by a fraction and when he spoke again it was tinged with contempt. 'They found her on the bathroom floor with a syringe in her arm.'

Keeley rubbed her hands together, as if that would remove the sudden chill which had iced over her skin. She wasn't surprised when Ariston suddenly walked over to the window, his powerful body tense and alert, his broad shoulders looking as if he were carrying the weight of the world upon them. She wondered if he was really interested in gazing out at the tall skyscrapers, or whether he just didn't want to expose any more of the pain which had flashed across his shuttered features despite his obvious attempt to keep it at bay.

'Poor woman,' she said quietly.

He turned back to face her; his habitual composure was back and his eyes were as cold as a winter sea.

'You defend her? You defend the indefensible?' he iced out. 'Do you think that everybody has a redeeming feature, Keeley? Or just if it happens to be a member of your own sex?'

'I was just trying to see it from a different perspective, that's all.' She sucked in a deep breath. 'I'm sorry about what happened to you and to Pavlos.'

'Save your words.' He began to walk across the vast sitting room towards her. 'I didn't tell you because I wanted your sympathy.'

'No?' A shiver ran down the length of her spine as he approached. 'Then why *did* you tell me?'

He had reached her now and Keeley's breath caught in her throat because he was close. Close enough to touch—and she wanted him to touch her. So much. He was towering over her and she could detect the anger simmering darkly from his powerful frame.

'So that you recognise what is important to me,' he husked. 'And understand why I will never let my child go.'

She looked up at him, her heart beginning to pound. Yes, she could understand that perfectly, but where did that leave her? Old sins cast long shadows—was she to be punished for the sins of his mother? Would she be simply another woman for him to despise and mistrust—another woman to regard with suspicion? He'd told her unequivocally he wouldn't tolerate a sexless marriage and would take a mistress if he was forced to do so. But he had also promised her his fidelity if she took him as her lover, and she believed him. Why was that? Because she wanted to believe the best in people, or because she was empty and aching and wanted to reach out to him in the only way she suspected he would let her?

She shifted her gaze from the distraction of his handsome face to the hands which were clasped tightly in her lap. She studied the shiny golden ring which sat beneath the gleaming diamonds of her hastily bought engagement ring and thought about what those bands signified. Possession, mainly—but so far there had been no physical possession. He'd put his arm around her after the ceremony but that had been done purely for show. Yet despite everything she wanted him. Maybe even more than ever before—because didn't the things he'd told her just now make him seem more *human*? He'd revealed the darkness in his soul and she'd come to understand him a little better. Couldn't they draw closer to one another as a result? Couldn't they at least *try*?

She wanted to taste the subtle salt of his skin and to breathe in all his masculine virility. She wanted to feel him inside her again. And it was her call—he'd already told her that. She ran her fingertip over the cold diamonds. She could act all proud and distant and drive him into the arms of another woman if that was what she wanted, but something was making that idea seem repellent.

She snaked her tongue over bone-dry lips, because the alternative was not without its own pitfalls. Was he aware that she was crippled with shyness at the thought of trying to seduce a man as experienced as him? All they'd shared so far had been a mindless night of passion with the sound of the sea muffling their cries. It had happened so spontaneously that she hadn't had to think about it—while the thought of having sex now seemed so *calculated*. Was she expected to stand up and loop her arms around his neck—maybe shimmy her body against his, the way she'd seen people do in films? But if she tried to pretend to be something she wasn't—wouldn't he see right through that?

'Ariston?' she said, lifting her gaze to his at last in silent appeal.

Ariston read consent in the darkened pools of her green eyes and a powerful surge of desire shafted through him. He had revealed more to her than to another living soul and instinct told him it would be better to wait until he had fully composed himself before he touched her. Until the dark and bitter memories had faded. But his need was so strong that the thought of waiting was intolerable. How ironic that this woman carried his child and yet he scarcely knew her body! He'd barely explored the lushness of her breasts or stroked the bush of blonde hair which guarded her most precious of treasures. His heart was hammering as he pulled her to her feet and all he could feel was her soft flesh as she melted against him.

'A real marriage?' he demanded, tilting her chin with his fingers so that she could look nowhere but at him. 'Is that what you want, Keeley?'

'Yes,' she said simply. 'Or as real as we can make it.'

But as he pulled the ribbon from her ponytail, so that her hair fell in a pale waterfall of waves, Ariston knew he must be honest with her. She needed to realise that the confidences he'd shared today were not going to become a regular occurrence. He'd told her what she needed to know so she could understand where he was coming from. But she needed to accept his limitations, and one in particular.

'Don't expect me to be the man of your dreams, Keeley,' he husked. 'I will be the best father and husband that I can and I will drive you wild in bed—that much I promise you, but I can never love you. Do you understand? Because if you can accept that and are prepared to live with it, then we can make this work.'

She nodded, her lips opening as if to speak, but he crushed her words away with his kiss. Because he was done with talking. He wanted this. Now. But not here. He saw her startled look of pleasure as he picked her up and began to carry her towards the bedroom.

'I'm too heavy,' she protested, without much conviction.

'You think so?' He saw her eyes widen as he kicked open the bedroom door and too late he realised this was the kind of thing that women built their fantasies around. Well, that was too bad. He could only be the man he really was. Hadn't he warned her what he was and wasn't capable of? He laid her down fully clothed on the bed, but when her fingernails began to claw at his shoulders he gently removed them. 'Let me undress first,' he said unevenly.

His fingers were trembling like a drunk's as he unbuttoned his shirt and he noted that aberration with something like bemusement. What power did she have over him, this tiny blonde with her moon-pale hair and those green eyes which were forest-dark with desire? Was it because beneath that ridiculous fluffy sweater she carried their child—was it that which made him feel powerful and weak all at the same time?

He saw her eyes dilate as he dropped the shirt to the floor and stepped out of his trousers, yet the kind of flippant question he might *usually* have asked about whether she was enjoying the floorshow didn't seem appropriate. Because this felt…different. He felt the hard beat of rebellion. Surely those meaningless vows he'd made earlier hadn't got underneath his skin?

'Ariston,' Keeley whispered and suddenly she was feeling confused—wondering what had caused his face to darken like that. Was he having second thoughts? No. She swallowed. She could see for herself that was definitely not the case, and though she should have been daunted by all that hard, sexual hunger—the truth was that she was shivering with anticipation.

She raised her lips but his kiss was nothing but a perfunctory graze as he slid off the velour sweat-pants and pulled the voluminous sweater over her head, so she was left in nothing but her underwear. And she was glad she'd allowed the stylist to steer her towards the fancier end of maternity lingerie to buy a matching set of underwear which had cost the earth. The front-clipped lilac silk bra clung to her breasts and the matching bikini briefs made her legs look much longer than usual. As his dark gaze raked over her, the look of appraisal on his face made her feel intoxicatingly *feminine*, despite her shape.

His hand starfished darkly over one breast and as she felt the nipple tighten so presumably did he, because a brief smile curved his lips.

'I want you,' he said unsteadily.

'I want you, too,' she whispered.

He leaned over to skim down her little bikini briefs. 'I've never had sex with a pregnant woman before.'

Lifting her bottom to assist him, Keeley gave him a reproachful look. 'I should hope not.'

'So this is all very...' he undid the front fastening of her bra so that her breasts came spilling out and bent his head to capture one taut tipple between the controlled graze of his teeth '...new to me,' he rasped.

'New to me, too,' she moaned, her head falling back against the pillow.

He took his time. More time than she would have believed possible given his obvious state of arousal. His body was taut and tense as he stroked his fingertips over her skin—as if he was determined to reacquaint himself with this new, pregnant version of her body. And, oh, didn't she just love what he was doing to her? He palmed her breasts and traced tiny circles over her navel with the tip of his tongue. He tangled his fingertips in her pubic hair and then stroked her until she squirmed. Until every nerve ending was so aroused she didn't think she could bear it any more. Until she whispered his name on a breathless plea and at last he entered her. Keeley moaned as he filled her with that first thrust and he stilled immediately, his eyes shuttered as they searched her face.

'I'm hurting you?'

'No. Not at all. You're...' Some instinct made her thrust her hips forward so that he went deeper still— because surely that was safer than telling him he was the most gorgeous man she'd ever seen and she couldn't quite believe he was her husband. 'Oh, Ariston,' she gasped as he began to move inside her.

And Ariston smiled because this was a sound with which he was familiar. The sound of a woman gasping out his name like that. He forced himself to concentrate on her pleasure, to make this wedding-night sex something she would never forget. Because a satisfied woman was a compliant woman and that was what suited him best. His self-control was almost at breaking point by the time she shattered around him, her fleshy body spasming with release, and it was only then that he allowed himself the luxury of his own orgasm. But he was unprepared for the way it ripped through his body like a raging storm or for the raw, almost savage sound which was torn from his throat as he came.

CHAPTER TEN

A SOFT GLOW crept beneath Keeley's eyelids and in those few blurred seconds between sleeping and waking, she stirred lazily. Replete from pleasures of the night and with the musky scent of sex still lingering in the air, she reached out for Ariston—but the space beside her on the bed was empty, the sheet cold. Blinking, she reached for her wristwatch and glanced across the bedroom. Just after six on a Saturday morning and there, silhouetted by the light flooding in from the corridor, was the powerful figure of her husband, fastening his cufflinks. She levered herself up the bed a little. 'You're not going into work?'

He walked into the bedroom, one of the cufflinks catching the light and glinting gold. 'I have to, I'm afraid.'

'But it's Saturday.'

'And?'

Keeley pushed the duvet away, telling herself not to make waves. Hadn't they just had the most amazing night, with the most amazing sex—and hadn't those hours of darkness felt like perfect bliss? So what if he went to work when most of London was still fast asleep and getting ready for the weekend? She told herself that Ariston's dedication to work was the price you paid for being married to such a wealthy man. But it was hard not to feel disgruntled because it would have been nice to have spent the morning in bed for once. To have done stuff like normal newly-weds—moaning and giggling about crumbs in the bed or debating whose turn it was to make the coffee.

But she wasn't a normal newly-wed, was she? She was the wife of a powerful man who had married her solely for the sake of their baby.

She forced a smile to her lips. 'So what time will you be home?'

Reaching for his jacket, Ariston glanced across to where Keeley lay, looking delectably rumpled and oh-so-accessible. Her heavy breasts were spilling over the top of a silky nightgown, which somehow managed to make her look even more decadent than if she'd been naked. She must have slipped it on again during the night, he thought, swallowing down the sudden dryness which rose to his throat. A night when she had been even more sensual than usual, her uninhibited response to his first careless advances leaving him deliciously dazed afterwards.

He'd arrived home with an armful of flowers impulsively purchased from a street seller outside his office, a vibrant bouquet which bore no resemblance to the long-stemmed stately roses usually ordered by one of his secretaries to placate her when he had been held up by a meeting. And Keeley had fallen on them with delight, burying her nose in the colourful blooms and going to the kitchen to put them in water before his housekeeper had shooed her away and taken over the task.

His heart clenched as he remembered the soft flush of colour to her cheeks and the bright glitter of her eyes as she'd risen up on tiptoe to kiss him. He had pulled her onto his lap after dinner, playing idly with her hair until she'd turned to him in silent question and he'd carried her off to their bedroom with a primitive growl of possession. Had he once told her that he didn't play the caveman? Because it seemed that he'd been wrong. And he didn't like being wrong.

He watched as she tucked a lock of hair behind her ears, the movement making her breasts strain even more against the shiny satin of her nightgown, and he forced himself to look away. To align the pristine cuffs of his shirt beneath his suit jacket as if that were the single most important task of the day.

Was she aware of her growing power over him? A shimmer of unease iced over his skin. She must be. Even someone as relatively innocent as her couldn't be oblivious to the fact that sometimes he didn't know what day of the week it was when she turned those big green eyes on him. Perhaps she was trying to extend that subtle power. Perhaps *that* was the reason for the sudden look of determination which had crossed over her sleep-soft face.

'Ariston?' she prompted. '*Must* you go?'

'I'm afraid I must. Anatoly Bezrodny is flying over from Moscow on Monday and there are a few things I need to look at before he arrives.'

There was a pause as she snapped on the bedside light and pleated her lips into a pout which was just begging to be kissed. 'You spend more time at the office than you ever do at home.'

'Perhaps you'd like to dictate the terms of my diary for me?' he questioned silkily. 'Speak to my assistant and have her run my appointments past you first?'

'But you're the boss,' she protested, undeterred by his quiet reproof. 'And you don't have to put in those kind of hours. So why do it?'

'It's *because* I'm the boss that I do. I have to set an example, Keeley. That's why you have a beautiful home to live in and lots of pretty things to wear. So stop pouting and give your husband a kiss goodbye.' He walked over to the bed and leaned over her, breathing in the sexy, morning smell of her. 'You haven't forgotten we're having dinner out tonight?'

'Of course I haven't.' She lifted her lips to his. 'I'm looking forward to it.'

But he thought the kiss she gave him seemed dutiful rather than passionate, which naturally challenged him—because nothing other than complete capitulation ever satisfied him. Framing her face with his hands, he deepened the kiss until she began to moan and he was sorely tempted to give her what she wanted, until a swift glance at his watch reminded him that his car would be waiting downstairs.

'Later,' he promised, reluctantly drawing away from her.

After he'd gone, Keeley lay back against the pillows, blinking back the stupid tears which had sprung to her eyes. What *was* her problem—and why was she feeling so dissatisfied of late? It wasn't as if she hadn't known what she'd been getting herself into when she'd married Ariston. She'd known he was a workaholic and he'd never promised her his heart. He'd been honest from the start—some might say brutally so—by telling her he could never love her. And she had accepted that. *He was giving as much of himself as he was capable of giving*—that was what she told herself over and over. She closed her eyes and sighed. It wasn't his fault if her feelings for *him* were changing…if suddenly she found herself wanting more than he was prepared to give. And allowing those feelings to accelerate was fruitless; she told herself that too. She would be setting herself up for disappointment if she kept on yearning for what she could never have, instead of just making the most of what she *did* have.

So she ate the delicious breakfast prepared by Ariston's cook and told his driver that she didn't need him that day. She thought the chauffeur seemed almost *disappointed* to be dismissed and, not for the first time, she wondered if Ariston had asked him to keep an eye on her. No. She picked up her handbag and checked she had her mobile phone. She mustn't start thinking that way. That really *was* being paranoid.

She thought about going to look at the autumn leaves in Hyde Park, but something made her take the train to New Malden instead. Was it nostalgia which made her want to go back to where she used to live? To stare at the world she'd left behind and try to remember the person she had been before Ariston had blazed into her life and changed it beyond recognition? She found herself walking down familiar streets until at last she reached her old bedsit, and as she stood and looked up at the window she wondered if she was imagining the surreptitious glances of the passers-by. Did she look out of place with her quietly expensive clothes and extortionately priced handbag as she chased the ghosts of her past?

She ate lunch in a sandwich bar and spent the afternoon at the hairdresser's before going home to get ready for dinner, but she was unable to shake off her air of heaviness as the housekeeper let her in. She didn't know what she'd expected from marriage to Ariston, but it certainly hadn't been this increasing sense of isolation. She'd known he was tricky and distant and demanding, but she'd...well, she'd *hoped*.

Had she thought that living together and having amazing sex might bring them closer together? That what had started out as a marriage of convenience might become, if not the real thing, then something which bore echoes of it? Of course she had, because that was the way women were programmed to think. They wanted closeness and companionship—especially if they were going to have a baby. She knew she'd broken down some invisible barrier after he'd told her about the heartbreak of his childhood and she'd prayed that might signal a new openness. After the passion of their wedding night, she'd waited for that openness to happen. And then she'd waited some more.

And now?

Careful not to muss her hair, she pulled a silky black evening dress over her head. Now she was being forced to accept the harsh reality of being married to someone who barely seemed to notice her, unless she was naked. A man who left early each morning and returned in time for dinner. Who slotted in time with her as if she was just another appointment in his diary. Yes, he accompanied her to all her doctor's appointments and murmured all the right things when they saw their baby son high-kicking his way across the screen. And very occasionally they drove out to the countryside or watched a film together—small steps which made her hope that non-sexual intimacy might be on the cards. But every time her hopes were dashed as those steel shutters came crashing down and he pushed her away—Mr Enigmatic who was never going to make the mistake of confiding in her again.

Ariston arrived home in a rush and went straight to the shower, emerging from his dressing room looking a vision of alpha virility, in a dark dinner suit which matched the raven thickness of his hair. He walked over to the dressing table where she sat and began to massage her shoulders—bare except for the spaghetti straps of her black dress. Instantly she felt the predictable shimmerings of desire and her nipples hardened.

'Ariston,' she said huskily as his fingers dipped from her shoulder to caress her satin-covered ribcage.

'Ariston, what? I'm only making up for what I didn't have time for this morning. And how can I prevent myself from touching you when you look so damned beautiful?'

She clipped on an opal earring. 'I don't feel particularly beautiful.'

'Well, take it from me, you are. In fact, I'm tempted to carry you over to that bed right now to demonstrate how much you turn me on. Would you like that, Keeley?'

Did the leaves fall from the trees in autumn? Of *course* she would like it. But using sex as their only form of communication was starting to feel dangerous. The contrast between his physical passion and mental distance was disconcerting and…unsettling. Each time he made love to her it felt as if he were chipping away a little piece of her, and wasn't she worried that soon there would be nothing of the real Keeley left? That she would become nothing but an empty shell of a woman? She fixed the second earring in place. 'We don't have time.'

'Then let's make time.'

'No,' she said firmly, rising to her feet in shoes which probably weren't the most sensible choice for a pregnant woman, but this was the first time she'd met Ariston's colleagues and, naturally, she wanted to impress. 'I don't want to arrive with my cheeks all flushed and my hair all mussed, not when I've spent all afternoon at the hairdresser's.'

'Then perhaps you should skip the hairdresser's next time,' he commented drily as he glanced at the elaborate confection of curls piled high on her head. 'If it puts you in such a bad mood.'

It was one of those stupid little rows which spiralled up out of nowhere and Keeley knew she ought to dispel the atmosphere which was still with them when they got into their car. She wasn't going to improve matters by sulking, was she? Laying her carefully manicured hand on his knee, she felt the hard muscle flex beneath her fingers.

'I'm sorry I was grumpy.'

He turned towards her, the passing street lights flickering like gold over his rugged features. 'Don't worry about it,' he said smoothly. 'It's probably just your hormones.'

She wanted to scream that not everything involved her wretched *hormones*—but she was aware that such a reaction would make a mockery of her words. She stared down at her baby bump instead, before lifting her gaze to his. Why not tell him about what else had been bugging her lately—a practical issue they could address and which might improve the quality of their lives? 'Ariston.'

'Keeley?'

She hesitated. 'Do we have to have quite so many staff?'

His eyes narrowed. 'I'm not quite sure what you mean.'

She shrugged a little awkwardly and began to fiddle with her jewelled handbag. 'Well, we have a housekeeper, a cleaner, a cook, a driver and a secretary—as well as that man who comes once a week to water all the plants on the terrace.'

'And? It's a big apartment. They all have their necessary roles in my life.'

She didn't correct him by reminding him that it was her life, too. Choose your battles carefully, she reminded herself. 'I know that. I just thought that maybe I could, you know…help.'

'Help?' He furrowed his brows. 'Doing what?'

'Oh, I don't know. Chores. *Stuff.* Something to make me feel like a real person who's connected with the world, rather than some sort of mindless doll who gets everything done for her. A bit of cleaning, perhaps. Maybe even some cooking.' She bit her lip. 'But when I offered to peel some potatoes for Maria the other day, she acted like I'd threatened to detonate a bomb in the middle of the kitchen.'

He seemed to be picking each word carefully, like someone selecting diamonds from a barrel of stones. 'Probably because she didn't think it was appropriate.'

'And why wouldn't it be?'

'Because…' He sucked in a breath and made no attempt to hide his sudden irritation. 'You are not on my staff, Keeley, not any more. You are now the mistress of my household and I would prefer it if you acted that way.'

She sat up ramrod-straight. 'You sound like you're *ashamed* of me!'

'Don't be absurd,' he clipped out. 'But it isn't possible to flit between the two worlds—you must realise that. You can't be peeling potatoes one minute, and asking someone to serve you tea the next. You need to be clear about your new role and demonstrate it to everyone else, so nobody gets confused. Do you understand?'

She swallowed. 'I think I'm getting the general idea.'

He caught hold of her hand. 'And things will probably settle down once you've had the baby.'

'Yes, probably. At least that's something I *can* do,' she said lightly.

There was a pause as he circled his thumb over her palm. 'Though we will need a nurse, of course,' he added.

At first she thought she must have misheard him. 'I'm sorry?' she said, but her heart had started to race with some dark and nameless fear as she looked into his face.

'A nurse,' he reiterated. 'A nursery nurse, I believe they're called.'

'But...' She could feel tiny little beads of sweat pricking at her forehead. 'I thought since you'd been so hands-on with Pavlos, you wouldn't want us to have any outside help with the baby. Was I wrong about that too, Ariston?'

She saw his face darken. Was he angry at the mention of his brother's name—for her daring to bring up a subject he had very firmly closed on the night of their wedding?

'Obviously, you will do the lion's share but I shall be out at work for most of the day.'

'And?' she questioned in confusion as his voice tailed off.

His eyes briefly caught the gleam of lights as the car slid to a halt outside the restaurant. 'And we will need a nurse who speaks Greek, so that my son will grow up speaking my tongue. For that is vital, given the heritage which will one day be his.'

His words were still reeling around Keeley's head as they entered the upmarket Greek restaurant—one of very few in central London, or so Ariston informed her as they were led towards the best table in the room. But she didn't care about the stunning *trompe l'oeil* walls painted with bright blue skies and soaring marble pillars, which made you feel as if you were standing in the middle of an ancient Greek temple. She was so reeling at this latest bombshell that she could barely take in the names of Ariston's formidable-looking colleagues or their beautiful wives, who, to a woman, were sleek and dark and polished. She recited their names silently in her head, like a child learning tables. Theo and Anna. Nikios and Korinna.

And of course they all kept slipping into Greek from time to time. Why wouldn't they, when it was their first language? Even though they seamlessly switched to English to include her, Keeley still felt like a complete outsider. And this was what it would be like when she had the baby, she realised as she stared down at her glass of melon juice. She would be on the periphery of every conversation and event. The English mother who could not communicate with her half-Greek child. Who remained on the outskirts like some silent ghost. She swallowed. Unless she did something about it. Started being proactive instead of letting everyone else decide her destiny for her. Since when had she started behaving like such a *wuss*? If she didn't like something she ought to change it.

The men were deep in conversation as Keeley looked

across the table at Korinna, who was playing with her dish of apple sorbet instead of eating it.

'I'm thinking about learning Greek,' Keeley said suddenly.

'Good for you.' Korinna smiled before lifting her narrow shoulders in a shrug. 'Though it's not an easy language, of course.'

'No, I realise that,' said Keeley. 'But I'm going to give it my very best shot.'

She was just returning from the washroom when she crossed paths with the young waiter who had been looking after their table all evening, and he moved aside to let her pass.

'You are enjoying your meal, Kyria Kavakos?' he questioned solicitously.

'Oh, yes. It's delicious. My compliments to the chef.'

'You will forgive me for intruding?' he said, in his faultless English. 'But I couldn't help overhearing you saying you wanted to learn Greek.'

'I do. I'm just trying to work out the best way to go about it.'

He smiled. 'If you like, I could help. My sister is a teacher and she's very good. She teaches at the Greek school in Camden but she also gives private lessons and is very keen to expand. Would you like her card?'

Keeley hesitated as he offered her a small cream card. She told herself it would be rude to refuse such a kind offer and that perhaps this was an example of fate stepping in to help her. They said that working one-to-one was the best way to learn a new language and this could be an empowering gesture on her part. Wouldn't it be a brilliant surprise for Ariston if he realised she was making an effort to integrate into a culture which was so important to him?

She would show him what she was capable of, she thought. And he would be proud of her.

'Thank you,' she said with a smile, taking the card from the waiter and slipping it into her handbag.

CHAPTER ELEVEN

ARISTON LET HIMSELF quietly into the apartment to hear the unmistakable sounds of someone slowly reciting the Greek alphabet. He stood very still. They were coming from the music room, which was situated at the furthest end of the penthouse, and they were being spoken by a voice he didn't recognise. He frowned as he heard a second voice stumble over the letter *omicron*—traditionally a difficult letter for non-Greek speakers to pronounce—and suddenly realised that it was his wife who was now speaking. He began to walk along the corridor and the sight which greeted him took him completely by surprise. A beautiful young Greek girl wearing a sweater and a very short denim skirt was standing outlined against one of the giant windows and his wife was sitting near the piano, reading aloud from a textbook. They looked up as he walked in and he saw uncertainty cross over Keeley's features as her words died away.

The smile he gave was intended to be pleasant but his words didn't quite match. 'What's going on?' he questioned.

'Ariston! I wasn't expecting you.'

'Apparently not.' He raised his eyebrows. 'And this is?'

'Eva. She's my Greek teacher.'

There was a pause. 'I didn't know you had a Greek teacher.'

'That's because I didn't tell you. It was going to be a surprise.'

'Look, I can see you must be busy.' Eva was looking at each of them in turn and beginning to gather up a stack of papers before thrusting them hastily into a leather briefcase. 'I'd better go.'

'No,' said Keeley quickly. 'You don't have to do that, Eva. There's still half an hour of the lesson left to run.'

'I can always come back,' said Eva in a bright voice which suggested this was never going to be an option.

Ariston waited as Keeley showed the teacher out, listening to the sound of her rapid returning footsteps before she marched into the room and glared at him.

'What was *that* all about?' she demanded.

'I could ask you the same question. Who the hell is *Eva*?'

'I told you. She's my Greek teacher—isn't that obvious?'

'Your Greek teacher,' he repeated slowly. 'And you found her…where?'

She sighed. 'She's the sister of the waiter who served us the night we went to the Kastro restaurant. He overheard me saying to Korinna that I wanted to learn Greek and so he gave me Eva's card on my way back from the washroom.'

'Run that past me again,' he said. 'She's the *sister* of some random waiter you met in a restaurant?'

'What's wrong with that?'

'You're seriously asking a question like that?' he demanded. 'Think about it. You don't even *know* these people!'

'I do now.'

'Keeley,' he exploded. 'Don't you realise the potential consequences of inviting *strangers* into my home?'

'It's my home too,' she said in a shaky voice. 'Or at least, it's supposed to be.'

With an effort he altered the tone of his voice, trying to dampen down the anger which was rising up inside him like a dark tide. 'I'm not trying to be difficult, but my position is not like that of other men. I happen to be extremely wealthy. You know that.'

'Oh, yes—I know it. I'm never likely to forget it, am I?' she retorted hotly. 'What do you want me to do, Ariston—go around checking that Eva hasn't pocketed one of your precious Fabergé eggs?'

'Or maybe,' he continued, as if she hadn't spoken, 'maybe introducing you to the Greek teacher was simply a clever diversion and the pretty-boy waiter has designs on you himself?'

'You think he has designs on me?' She stood up and gave a disbelieving laugh as she angled her palms over the curve of her belly. 'Looking like *this*? How dare you? How *dare* you say such a thing to me?'

Ariston let her words wash over him but instead of being irritated by her defiance, all he could think about was how ravishing she looked in her anger. Her blonde hair was spilling wildly around her face and her green eyes were spitting emerald fire and automatically he reached out to pull her into his arms. That first contact made her pupils dilate and although she had started beating her hands furiously against his chest, she moaned when he started to kiss her and she moaned some more when he palmed her nipple and felt the tip pushing hungrily against his hand. She kissed him back and her kiss was hot and hard and angry, but the beating of her fists became less insistent. He levered her closer, and jutted his hips so that she could feel just how hard he was and she writhed against him in furious frustration.

Slipping his hand underneath her dress, he felt her bare thigh and as he began to stroke his fingers towards her panties his desire went right off the scale. Just like hers. He could hear the unsteady rush of her breath as she scrabbled at his belt, and as she slipped the notch free he felt as if he might explode. He was rock-hard and the unmistakable scent of her arousal was in the air as his slowly moving fingers reached her panties to discover they were damp. So damp. He groaned again, and so did she as he pushed the taut panel aside and slicked his finger over her honeyed flesh, confident that sex would dissolve the tension between them as it always did. Couldn't he show her who was boss and wouldn't her hungry body accept that, the way it always did? Her arms wound themselves around his neck and he was about to pick her up and carry her over to the *chaise-longue* when suddenly he came to his senses.

'No,' he said suddenly, his heart pounding in protest

as he removed her hand from his trousers and pushed her away.

It took several moments before she spoke and when she did she looked at him in confusion. 'No?'

'I don't want you, Keeley. At least, not right now.'

'You don't?' she questioned, before giving a disbelieving laugh. 'Are you quite sure about that? Isn't that the way you like to settle any kind of disputes we have?'

He suppressed a ragged groan before forcing himself to step away from her. 'I'm not making love to you when we're in this kind of mood,' he said, his voice thick. 'I'm angry and so are you, and I fear I might be more...*physical* with you than I should be.'

'And?'

'And that's probably not the best idea given that you're pregnant.'

Keeley stared into his shuttered features as desire drained from her body, like water from the bathtub, and in its place came a horrible sinking realisation. Because no matter what she did or what she said—no matter how hard she tried or how long they stayed married—Ariston would always remain in command. She could learn Greek until the cows came home but it wouldn't make any difference. She could even try to find out more about ship-owning, but she would be wasting her time. Because what she wanted didn't count. It was what *Ariston* wanted which counted and it always would, because he ruled the roost and had been allowed to do so for years.

He liked her to know her place and to run everything past him first. He didn't like strangers in the house and now she knew that, she would be expected to respect his wishes. Her home had become her prison and her husband the rigid jailer. And the reason he didn't want to make love to her right now was nothing to do with his fears about her pregnancy. The expression on his face was as dark as the time he'd told her about his mother and suddenly she understood why. Because he didn't like the way she was making him react, she realised.

He didn't want to lose control or to be seen to lose control.

And she realised something else, too. That if she stayed, she would spend the rest of her life sublimating herself to *his* desires and *his* whims. The one thing she had asked for when she'd agreed to marry him hadn't materialised. They would never be equals—and what kind of an example would that be for her son?

Smoothing her hands over her hot cheeks, she stared at him. 'I'm done with this, Ariston,' she whispered hoarsely.

He narrowed his eyes. 'What are you talking about?'

'You. Me. Us. I'm sorry. I can't do this any more. I can't stay in this…this *mockery* of a marriage.'

His smile was cruel. She hadn't seen him look at her that way in a long time, but now she was reminded of the essential ruthlessness which lay at the very core of him.

'But you don't have any choice, Keeley,' he said silkily. 'You're pregnant with my child and there's no way I'm letting you go.'

She met the quiet fury in his eyes. 'You can't stop me.'

'Oh, I think you'll find I can,' he said. 'I have the

experience as well as the wherewithal. You have nothing while I have everything. I can get the full weight of any international court to rule in my favour in a custody battle—don't ever doubt that—though it's a path I'd rather not take. So don't make me, Keeley. Why don't we just calm down and recalibrate?' He fixed his steely blue gaze on her. 'Perhaps I *was* a little unreasonable—'

'Perhaps?' she demanded and she realised something else, too. That people didn't interrupt Ariston. His power had allowed him to build a wall around himself so high that nobody ever dared try. He'd made up all the rules and everyone else was supposed to just fall in and obey them. And everyone always had—until now. She was the only one who had dared to step out of line, but he couldn't wait to make her step right back in it again. 'You don't get it, do you?' she said shakily. 'This isn't a marriage, Ariston. It's a farce and a prison—and I'm not just talking about your lack of trust or the jailer-like behaviour you've demonstrated simply because I had the temerity to invite someone home!'

'Keeley—'

'No! You will hear me out. You will. Do you want to hear the reality of what it's like being married to you? Of how great it really is? You spend long hours in the office—and when you're back, at best you tolerate me. Guaranteed orgasms and the occasional trip to the theatre don't add up to intimacy, but I guess I shouldn't be surprised, because you don't *want* intimacy. You told me that yourself and at the time I thought I could live with it, or maybe even change it—but now I know I can't. Because you don't care about me, Ariston—

all you really care about is your baby. Sometimes you make me feel like a character in a science-fiction film, someone who is growing your child so that you can take him away from me just as soon as he's born! As if I'm nothing but a damned incubator!'

'Keeley—'

'Will you stop trying to interrupt me?' she yelled. 'When I mentioned that we were completely outnumbered by staff and spoke of my desire to help with a little housework, you looked at me as if I was some kind of freak. So what am I supposed to do all day? Haunt the shops like some well-dressed mannequin while I blitz your credit card?'

'Lots of women do.'

'Well, not me. If you must know, it bores the hell out of me. I had a brief love affair with excessive spending before we got married, but I'm over it now. It's an empty, meaningless existence. I'd rather give the money to charity than keep buying more overpriced handbags!'

'Keeley—'

'I haven't finished,' she continued icily. 'You speak Greek and I can't, which means I would always be the outsider—and when I do use my initiative to take lessons, I get accused of having the hots for my teacher's brother!'

'I hear what you're saying,' he said, sucking in an unsteady breath. 'And I realise I overreacted. Of course you must have lessons if you want them, but at least let me choose someone suitable to teach you. You can't just sign up with the sister of someone you've bumped into at a restaurant.'

'Why not?'

'Because they haven't been vetted,' he gritted out.

It was the final straw and it was at that point that Keeley knew there could be no going back. And no going forward either. Her heart was pounding fit to burst but somehow she kept her voice steady. 'So what am I supposed to do—be stuck in here while you vet anyone I might wish to see? Do you want to build barriers around me as high as the ones you've built around yourself?'

'*Now* who's overreacting?' he demanded.

'I'm not.' She shook her head. 'I thought things might change a little once we were married—but instead of the closeness I foolishly hoped might happen, all I get is anger and suspicion! I feel sorry for you, Ariston,' she added quietly. 'To view the world in such a cynical way means you'll never be happy and that will inevitably spill over into all our lives. And I'm not having any child of mine brought up in an atmosphere like that. I don't want our son to grow up knowing only distrust and cynicism—or to wonder why Mummy and Daddy never show each other any real affection. I want him to have a healthy view of the world, and that's why I'm leaving.'

'Just try,' he challenged softly.

She gave a nod of bitter understanding as she met his darkened eyes. 'Is that your way of saying you'll cut off my funds? Are you going to play the financial tyrant in addition to the emotional one? Would you really go that far, Ariston—after everything you've been through yourself? Well, go right ahead—be my guest! But if you do that I'll go straight to a lawyer and get them to slap a maintenance order on you. Or I'll sell *these*.' She pointed a shaking finger at the cold diamonds which flashed on her fingers, and then at the glittery tennis bracelet which was dangling from her wrist. 'Or *this*. Or if need be, I'll go to the papers. Yes. I'd do that, too. I'd sell my story and tell them what it was like being married to the Greek tycoon. I'd do anything to make sure you don't take my baby away, no matter how much you offer me to disappear from your life. Because I would never ever walk away from my baby and no amount of money could induce me to.' She sucked in a deep breath before her next words came out with a quiet intensity.

'I am not your mother, Ariston.'

She saw him flinch as if she'd hit him, but nothing was going to stop her now. 'Now, if you'll excuse me,' she said, her voice trembling, 'I'm going to pack my things and move out. And if you try to stop me, I'll... I'll call the police!'

His expression was unfathomable as their gazes clashed and she knew she'd pushed him as far as she possibly could. All the things she'd said had needed to be said and she'd meant every word of them, but that small glimmer of hope inside her refused to die. Could he read it in her eyes? Could he see the yearning she suspected still lingered there? The hope that maybe this showdown had cleared the air once and for all and he would let her get close enough to be the wife she really wanted to be. To show him all the love which was in her heart and maybe break down some of those formidable barriers he'd erected around his own. She swallowed. He might not ever be able to love her back, but couldn't he relax enough to *like* her and to *trust* her?

But the moment he opened his mouth she knew she had been wishing for the stars.

'I think, given your current state of hysteria, that you might be better to sleep on it. I will give you some space by moving into a hotel tonight—and hopefully, by morning, you might have calmed down a little.' His voice suddenly softened. 'Because getting yourself into this kind of state can't be good for the baby, Keeley.'

It was the final twist of the knife and Keeley wanted to howl with frustration. And sorrow. That too. She was glad he cared for his unborn son, but suddenly she needed him to care for her, too—and he was never going to do that. Quickly, she turned away from him, terrified he would see the heartbreak on her face or witness the tears which had begun to stream from her eyes as she stumbled her way towards the bedroom.

CHAPTER TWELVE

THE OCTOBER SKY was grey and brooding and Ariston was staring into space when the intercom on his desk buzzed and the disembodied voice of Dora, his assistant, spoke.

'I have Sheikh Azraq of Qaiyama on the line for you on one, Ariston.'

Restlessly, Ariston tapped his finger against the surface of the desk. He had been waiting for the call to confirm a deal he'd worked hard for. A deal which had the potential to increase the company's portfolio by many millions of dollars. He was about to accept the call when his mobile phone started ringing and he saw the name which was flashing up on the screen. Keeley. He felt the urgent crash of his heart and the sudden tightening of his throat.

'Tell the Sheikh I'll call him back later, Dora.'

'But, Ariston...'

It was rare for his assistant to even *attempt* to remonstrate with him but Ariston knew the reason for her unusual intervention. Sheikh Azraq Al-Haadi was one of the most powerful leaders of the desert lands and one who would not take kindly to his refusal to accept a phone call which had taken many days of planning to organise. But one thing he knew without a shadow of a doubt was that talking to Keeley was more important. His tapping ceased and Ariston's hand clenched into a tight fist as satisfaction hardened his lips into a smile. Was she regretting her decision to walk out on him? Finding that life wasn't quite so straightforward without the protection of her influential husband? Had she realised that he'd been right all along and that his concern about her associates had sprung solely from a need to protect her? He allowed himself a beat of anticipation. He would accept her back, yes, but she must understand that he would accept no similar tantrums or hysteria in the future—for all their sakes.

'Please tell the Sheikh I will move heaven and earth to arrange another call,' he said firmly. 'But for now I have someone else I need to speak to, so don't disturb me until I say so, Dora.'

He snatched up the mobile phone and clicked the connection, but took care to keep his voice bland and noncommittal. 'Hello?'

There was a breathless kind of pause. 'Ariston,' came the soft English voice which made his heart stab with a strange kind of pain. 'You took so long to answer that I thought you weren't going to pick up.'

Something inside him was urging him to make an attempt at conciliation but the anger he'd felt when she had carried through her threat and walked out on him had not left him.

'Well, I'm here now,' he said coolly. 'What is it you want, Keeley?'

The tone of her voice altered immediately and the stumbled apology he had been expecting was not forthcoming.

'As I'm having private healthcare, my obstetrician has fitted in an extra check-up for me and I'm due for a scan tomorrow,' she said, her voice now as cool as his. 'And I thought you might like to come. I realise it's very short notice and you might not be able to clear your diary in time—'

'Is that why you left it so late to invite me?'

He heard the unmistakable sound of a frustrated sigh. 'No, Ariston. But since you haven't bothered answering any of my emails—'

'You know I don't like communicating by email,' he said moodily.

'Yes, I realise that.' There was a pause. 'I just… I wasn't sure whether or not you'd want to see me. I thought about sending you a photo once I'd had the scan done, then thought that wouldn't be fair and so I—'

'What time,' he interrupted brutally, 'is it happening?'

'Midday. At the Princess Mary hospital. Where we went before—you remember?'

'I'll be there,' he said, before the voice of his conscience forced the next question from his lips. 'How are you?'

'I'm fine. All good.' He could hear her swallowing. 'The midwife is very pleased with my progress and I—'

'I'll see you tomorrow,' he said, and terminated the conversation.

He sat staring into space afterwards, angry with himself for being so short with her, but what the hell did she expect—that he would run around after her like some kind of puppy? He stared at the sky, whose dark clouds had now begun to empty slanting rods of rain onto the surrounding skyscrapers. After their blazing row he'd spent the night in a hotel to give her time to cool off, returning the following morning and expecting her to have changed her mind. In fact, he'd been expecting an apology. His mouth hardened. How wrong he had been. There had been no contrition or attempt to make things better. Her mood had been flat yet purposeful as she had repeated her determination to move out.

He'd tried being reasonable. He had not opposed her wishes, giving her free rein to move into her own place, telling himself that, if he gave her the freedom she thought she wanted and the space she thought she needed, it would bring her running right back. But it hadn't. On the contrary, she had made a cosy little nest out of her rented cottage on Wimbledon Common, as if she was planning to stay there for ever. During his one brief visit, he had stared in disbelief at the sunny yellow room, which she had made into a perfect nursery by adorning the walls with pictures of rabbits and such like. A shiny mobile of silvery fish had twirled above a brand-new crib and in the hallway had stood an old-fashioned pram. He had looked out of the window at the seemingly endless green grass of the Common and his heart had clenched with pain as he acknowledged his exclusion. And yet pride stopped him from show-ing it. He had given a cool shake of his head when she had offered him tea, citing a meeting in the city as the reason why.

She had told him she would be fair and that he could have paternal visiting rights as often as he liked and he believed her, but the idea of living without his son made his heart clench with pain. And yet the thought of an ugly legal battle for their baby had suddenly seemed all wrong.

Why?

Why?

He slept badly—something which was becoming a habit—and he was already waiting when Keeley ar-rived at the hospital, failing to hide the shock on her face when she saw him.

'Ariston!' Her cheeks went pink. 'You're early!'

'And?'

She looked as if she wanted to say something more but smiled instead, except that, as smiles went, it didn't look terribly convincing. Her mouth seemed strained but he thought he'd never seen her looking more beauti-ful, in a green velvet coat which matched her eyes and her fair hair hanging over one shoulder in a thick plait.

'Shall we go up to the scanning room?' she said.

'As you wish,' he growled.

The appointment couldn't have gone better. The ra-diographer smiled and pointed out things which didn't really need pointing out—even to Ariston's untutored eye. The rapidly beating little heart and the thumb which was jammed into a monochrome mouth. He could feel the salt taste of unwanted tears in the back of his throat and was glad that Keeley was busy wiping jelly from her stomach, giving him enough time to compose himself.

And when they emerged into the quiet London street it felt as if he had stepped into another world.

'Would you like lunch?' he questioned formally.

'I...no, thank you.'

'Coffee, then?'

She looked as if she wanted to say something important but although she had opened her lips, she quickly closed them again and shook her head. 'No, thanks. It's very kind of you but I'm off coffee at the moment and I'm...tired. I'd rather get home if it's all the same with you.'

'I'll have my driver drop you off.'

'No, honestly, Ariston. I'll get the bus or the Tube. It's no bother.'

'I'm not having you struggling across London on public transport in your condition. I will have my driver drop you off,' he repeated in a flat tone which didn't quite disguise his growing irritation. 'Don't worry, Keeley. I'll take a cab. I wouldn't dream of subjecting you to any more of my company since you clearly find the prospect so unappealing. Here. Get in.'

He pulled open the door of the limousine which Keeley hadn't even noticed and which had drawn to a smooth and noiseless halt beside them. He was watching her as she slid onto the back seat, the scent of leather and luxury seeming poignantly familiar as she stared into Ariston's blue eyes—those beautiful blue eyes which she had missed so much. Her mouth dried. Should she tell him to come round some time? Would that send out the wrong message—or maybe the real message—that it wasn't just his eyes she had missed?

'Ariston,' she began, but he had closed the car door and given an almost imperceptible nod to his driver as the powerful machine pulled away.

And Keeley turned round, slightly ungainly with her baby bump, wanting to catch a glimpse of his face as the car pulled away. Was she hoping for one of those movie endings, where she would surprise a look of longing on *his* face and she could yell at the driver to stop the car, and...

But he was walking away, striding purposefully towards a black cab which had just switched off its yellow light, and Keeley turned away, biting her lip as the limousine took her southwest, towards Wimbledon.

She was doing the right thing. She was. She kept telling herself that over and over. Why sit through a torturous lunch or even a cup of coffee when Ariston had a face like dark granite? He didn't love her and he never could. He was an unreasonably jealous and controlling man. He might have the power to turn her to jelly whenever he so much as looked at her but he was all the things she despised.

So how come she still wanted him with a longing which sometimes left her breathless with regret for what could never be?

And she was doing this for their baby, she reminded herself. Building respect between them and forging a relationship which would demonstrate what two adults could achieve if they only put their minds to it.

The journey to her cottage took for ever and in truth it would have been quicker getting the train, but the moment she walked up the path to her little house she could feel a slight lifting of her mood. Wimbledon Common had been one of those places she'd always drooled about when she'd lived in New Malden. She used to take the bus there on her day off. It had a villagey feel and a pond, plus lots of lovely little shops and restaurants. She'd seen other pregnant mothers giving her cautious smiles when she was out and about and she wanted to reach out and make friends, but something was holding her back. She shut the front door with a bang. She didn't want to let anyone close because then she would have to explain her circumstances and tell them that her brief marriage was over. Because if she admitted it to someone else, then she would have to accept it was true.

And she didn't want it to be true, she realised. She wanted...

She bit her lip as she batted the dark thoughts away. She didn't dare express what she wanted, not even to herself. All she knew was that she couldn't go back to that old way of living. Of feeling like a pampered doll in someone else's life. A decorative asset to be brought out whenever the situation merited it. She wanted to *connect* with the real world—not sit in her gilded penthouse and look down on it. And most of all she wanted a man who wouldn't make out that feelings were like poison—and you should avoid them whenever possible.

She lit a fire in the grate and had just made a pot

of tea when there was a ring on the bell. She peered through the peephole, shocked to see Ariston standing on her doorstep, his hands shoved deep in the pockets of his trousers, his face a dark glower. She pulled open the door and there he was, his black hair ruffled by the October wind and his jaw all shadowed.

Her heart missed a beat. 'Ariston,' she said, wondering if he could hear the slight quaver in her voice. 'What…what are you doing here?'

His shuttered features looked forbidding. 'Can I come in?'

She hesitated for only a moment before stepping aside to let him pass. 'Of course.'

She wasn't going to do that thing of offering him tea—of pretending this was some kind of social call. There wasn't going to be any of that fake stuff which just wasted time and meant nothing. She would hear him out and then he would go. But a shiver of apprehension whispered over her because an impromptu visit like this didn't bode well—not when his expression was so serious and so *brooding*. Had he decided he was being too soft with her and now that she was showing no signs of moving back, he was going to retaliate? Maybe instruct his lawyers to reduce the generous amount of income she was receiving—to shock her into seeing sense. Was he going to starve her out to make her come back to him? It was an unpalatable thought until she thought of one which was even worse.

That he didn't want her back.

Pain and panic rushed through her like a hot, fierce tide. What if he'd decided that life was easier without a wife who was constantly nagging him because he stayed late at the office? If he'd decided he'd had enough of domesticity and wanted to get back on the party scene. That she had been right all along and the marriage simply wasn't working.

'What do you want, Ariston?' she said, in a low voice. 'Why are you here?'

Ariston stared at her and the trilingual fluency of a lifetime suddenly deserted him. On the way here he'd worked out exactly what he was going to say to her but all the words seemed to have flown straight out of his head. But he knew what he wanted, didn't he? He was a man who was skilled in the art of negotiation. So wasn't it time to go all out and get it?

'I'm going to reduce my hours,' he said.

She looked taken aback, but she nodded. 'Okay.'

'Because I realise that you're right.' He rubbed his fingers over the faint stubble of his chin as if only just realising he'd forgotten to shave that morning. 'I've been working too hard.'

He looked at her expectantly, waiting for the praise which such a magnanimous gesture surely merited and for her to fling herself into his arms to thank him. But she didn't. She didn't move. She just stood there with her green eyes wary and her pale hair glowing in the thin autumn light which was streaming through the window.

'And your point is, what?' she questioned.

'That we'll spend more time together. Obviously.'

She gave an odd smile. 'So what has brought about this sudden revelation?'

He frowned, because her reaction was not what he had imagined it would be. 'I allowed myself to accept that the Kavakos company is in the black and is likely to stay that way for the foreseeable future,' he said slowly.

She screwed up her nose. 'And hasn't it always been?'

Raking his fingers back through his hair, he shook his head. 'No. I think I told you that when my father died, I discovered he'd blown most of the family fortune. For a while it was touch and go whether or not we'd make it. Suddenly I was looking into a big black hole where the future used to be and I had so many people relying on me. Not just Pavlos but all the staff we employed. People on Lasia whose livelihood depended on our success. People in cities all over the world.' He sucked in a deep breath. 'That's why I put the time in— long hours, every day, way past midnight. It took everything I possessed to turn things around and get the company back on an even keel.'

'But that was then, and this is now—and Kavakos is arguably the biggest shipping company in the world.'

He nodded. 'I know that. But hard work got to be such a habit that I let it take me over. And I'm not going to do that any more. I'm going to spend less time at the office and more time at home. With you.' He looked at her. 'That's all.'

The silence which followed seemed to go on and on and when she spoke her voice was trembling.

'But that's not all, Ariston,' she said. 'The reason you work so hard isn't because you've developed some kind of *habit* you can't break or because secretly you live in fear that all your profits are going to disappear overnight. It's because at work you're the one in charge and what you say goes. And you like to be in control, don't you? Work has always provided you with an escape route. It's there for the taking when your wife wants to get too close or tries to talk about stuff you don't want to talk about.'

'Are you listening to a word I've just said?' he demanded. 'I've told you I'll reduce my hours, if that's what it takes to get you back.'

'But don't you realise?' she whispered. 'That's not enough.'

'Not *enough*?' he echoed, his blue eyes laced with confusion. 'What else do you want from me, Keeley?'

And here it was, the question she'd wanted him to ask ever since he had carried her to their bedroom on their wedding night. A no-holds-barred question which would make her vulnerable to so much potential pain if she answered it honestly.

Did she dare?

Could she dare not to?

She'd once vowed never to put herself in a position where she could be rejected again, but that was a vow she'd made when she'd been hurt and humbled. All these years later she was a grown woman who would soon have a baby of her own. And it all boiled down to whether she had the courage to put her pride and her fears aside and to reach out for the one thing she wanted.

'I want your trust,' she said simply. 'I want you to believe me when I tell you things and to stop imagining the worst. I want you to stop trying to control me and let me have the freedom to be myself. I want to stop feeling as if I'm swimming against the tide whenever I try to get close to you. I want ours to be a marriage which *works*—but only if we're both prepared to work at it. I want us to be equals, Ariston. True equals.'

His eyes narrowed as he nodded his head. 'You sound like you've given this some thought.'

'Oh, I've given it plenty,' she said truthfully. 'Only I wasn't sure if I'd ever get the chance to say it.'

There was another silence and the haunted expression on his face tore at Keeley's heartstrings for she saw her own fears and insecurities reflected there. It made her want to go to him and hug him tightly—to offer him her strength and to feel his. But she said nothing. Nothing which would break the spell or the hope that he might just reveal what was hidden in his heart, instead of trying to blot it out and hide it away, the way he normally did. Because that was the only way they could go forward, she realised. If they both were honest enough to let the truth shine through.

'I didn't want to let you close because I sensed danger—the kind of danger I didn't know how to handle,' he said at last. 'I'd spent years perfecting an emotional control which enabled me to pick up the pieces and care for Pavlos when our mother left. A control which kept the world at a safe distance. A control which enabled me to keep all the balls spinning in the air. I was so busy protecting my brother and safeguarding his future, that I didn't have time for anything else. I didn't want anything else. And then I met you and suddenly everything changed. You started to get close. You drew me in, no matter how hard I tried to fight against it, and I recognised that you had the power to hurt me, Keeley.'

'But I don't want to hurt you, Ariston,' she said. 'I am not your mother and you can't judge all women by her standards. I want to be there for you—in every way. Won't you let me do that?'

'I don't think I have a choice,' he admitted huskily. 'Because my life has been hell without you. My apartment and my life are empty when you aren't in them, Keeley. Because you speak the truth to me in a way which is sometimes painful to hear—but out of that pain has grown the certainty that I love you. That perhaps I've always loved you—and I want to go on loving you for the rest of my life.'

And suddenly she could hold out no longer and crossed the room as quickly as her pregnant shape would allow. She went straight into his arms and at last he was holding her tightly and she closed her eyes against the sudden prick of tears.

'Keeley,' he whispered, his mouth pressed hard against her cheek. 'Oh, Keeley. I've been dishonest with myself—right from the start. I felt the thunderbolt the first time I set eyes on you and I'd never felt that way about a woman before. I told myself you were too young—way too young—but then I kissed you and you blew my world apart.' He pulled away and stroked an unsteady finger over her trembling lips. 'It was easier to convince myself that I despised you. To tell myself you were cut from the same cloth as your mother, and that I only wanted sex with you to extinguish the burning hunger inside of me. But you just kept igniting the flames. When you became pregnant—a part of me was exultant. I couldn't decide if it was destiny or fate I needed to thank for a reason to stay close to you. But then came the reality. And the way you made me feel was bigger than anything I've ever felt before. It felt...'

'Scary,' she finished, pulling back a little so that she could gaze deep into his eyes. 'I know. Scary for me, too. Because love is precious and rare and most of us don't know how to handle it, especially when we've grown up without it. But we're bright people, Ariston. We both know what we don't want—broken homes and lost children and bitter wounds which can never be completely healed. I just want to love you and our baby and to create a happy family life. Don't you want that too?'

Briefly, Ariston closed his eyes and when he opened them she was still there, just as she always would be. Because some things you just knew, if only you would let your defences down long enough for instinct to take over. And instinct told him that Keeley Kavakos would always love him, though maybe not quite as much as he loved her.

He pulled her closer, his breath warm against her skin. 'Can we please go to bed so we can plan our future?' he questioned urgently.

'Oh, Ariston.' She rose on tiptoe to wind her arms around his neck, and he could hear the relief which tinged her breathless sigh. 'I thought you'd never ask.'

EPILOGUE

'So, HOW ARE you feeling, my clever and very beautiful wife?'

Keeley lifted her gaze from the tiny black head which was cradled against her breast, to find the bright blue eyes of her husband trained on her.

How was she feeling? Tough question. How could words possibly convey the million sentiments which had rushed through her during a long labour, and which had ended just an hour ago with the birth of their son? Joy, contentment and disbelief were all there, that was for sure—along with a savage determination that she would love and protect their new baby with every fibre of her being. Baby Timon. Timon Pavlos Kavakos. She smiled as she traced a feather-light fingertip over his perfect, olive-skinned cheek.

'I feel like the luckiest woman in the world,' she said simply.

Ariston nodded. He didn't want to contradict her at such a time, but if luck was being handed out—then surely he was its biggest recipient? Watching Keeley go through labour had been something which had taught him the true meaning of powerlessness and silently he had cursed that he was unable to bear or share her pain with her. Yet hadn't it been yet another demonstration of his wife's formidable strength—to watch her cope so beautifully with each increasing contraction? A wife who was planning to join him in the family business, just as soon as the time was right. He remembered her reaction when he'd first put the idea to her and his tender smile in response to her disbelieving joy. But why wouldn't he want his capable and very able wife working beside him, with hours which would suit her and their son? Why wouldn't he want to enjoy her company as much as possible, especially since her command of Greek was getting better by the day?

But she'd told him that these days she studied his language with a passion born from wanting to fit in and not because she was terrified of being left out. Because she was determined to speak the same language as their child. And because family was more important than anything else. A fact which had been drummed home by the sudden death of her mother, a death which in truth had filled Keeley with a sad kind of gratitude, because Vivienne Turner was at peace at last. And it had focussed their minds on the things which mattered. They had decided to make their home on Lasia—on that exquisite paradise of a place, with its green mountains and sapphire sea and skies which were endlessly blue.

Ariston thought how beautiful she looked lying there, still a little pale and exhausted after her long labour, her blonde hair lying damply against her cheeks as she smiled up at him trustingly. 'Would you like to hold your son now?' she whispered.

A lump instantly constricted his throat. It was what he'd been waiting for. In fact, it felt as if he'd been waiting for this moment all his life. A little gingerly at first, Ariston took the sleeping bundle from her, and as he bent to kiss the baby's jet-black hair a fierce wave of love rushed over him. He was used to holding babies because he used to hold Pavlos most of the time—but this felt different. Very different. This child was *his* flesh. And Keeley's. Timon. The pounding of his heart was almost deafening and the lump in his throat was making speech difficult, but somehow he got the words out as he looked into the tear-filled eyes of his wife.

'*Efkaristo,*' he said softly.

'Thanks for what?' she questioned shakily as he put his free arm tightly around her shoulders and drew her close.

'For my son, for your love—and for giving me a life beyond my wildest dreams. How about that for starters, *koukla mou*?'

She was trying to blink them away but the tears of joy just kept rolling down her cheeks and Ariston smiled as he kissed each one away, while their son slept contentedly in his arms.

* * * * *

CLAIMED FOR THE GREEK'S CHILD

PIPPA ROSCOE

For Laurie,

Who put up with me in New York for six weeks
while I disappeared off to my writing table on
the roof of our apartment at stupid o'clock in
the morning, with my rocket fuel coffee, a fan
instead of air-conditioning and a dental crisis!

Although Pin-Up Girl cocktails, an American
Football game, incredible food, a trip to Boston
and Christmas decorations at Macy's hopefully
made up for it!

New York, and this book, wouldn't have been the
same without you. Xx

PROLOGUE

Three years ago

'MR KYRIAKOU? WE'LL be landing in about twenty minutes.'

Dimitri gave a curt nod to the stewardess on board the Kyriakou Bank's private jet. He wasn't capable of more than that. His jaw was clenched so tightly it would have taken a crowbar to pry it open. The only thing that had successfully passed his lips since his boarding the plane had been a whisky. Only one. That was all he would allow himself.

He glanced out of the window and, although he should have been seeing the soft white clouds that hovered above the English Channel, instead he saw the slope of a beautiful woman's shoulder. Naked, exposed...vulnerable. Beneath the palm of his hand he could feel the silky texture of her skin. His fingers twitched at the memory.

He ran a hand across his face, rubbing at the exhaustion of the last year, allowing the stubble of his jaw to scratch at the itch that made him want to turn the plane around. To go back to the bed where the beautiful woman lay—probably still asleep. He'd snuck out like a thief. An analogy that caught in the back of his throat, and for an awful moment he thought he might actually choke.

He couldn't fathom what he'd been thinking. But that was the problem. He *hadn't* been. Despite the knowledge that this day had been coming, the knowledge of exactly what would greet him the moment the plane touched down in the States, Dimitri had needed one night. Just one night...

Yesterday, he'd left Antonio Arcuri and Danyl Nejem Al Arain—his best friends and fellow members of the Winners' Circle Racing Syndicate—behind at the Dublin Race Series and allowed instinct to take over. As he'd slid into the driver's seat of the powerful black supercar the thrust of the engine met the need for freedom coursing through his veins. He'd followed the road out of the small city, past the huge doors of the Guinness brewery, through dark streets, along roads that slowly found their way into rolling green countryside. It was only then that he'd felt able to breathe. Only then that he'd been able to block out what was to come.

Unconsciously he'd manoeuvred the sleek, dark car down impossibly windy roads, allowing only the thrill of the powerful machine beneath him to fill his senses. Something was driving him—he wasn't willing to give it a name.

Dimitri had slowed only when the car's petrol light came on. He'd found himself in a small village and, if it had had a name, he hadn't noticed. An old pub with a black sign and peeling paint defiantly stared down an even older church at the opposite end of the one street that divided the village. He followed the road to the end, where, instead of finding a petrol station, he came to a large gravel drive in front of a small bed and breakfast.

To Dimitri the Irish were known for two things: hospitality and whisky. And he was in great need of both. As he turned off the ignition he was hit with a wave of exhaustion so intense he wasn't entirely sure that he could make it out of the car. He sat back and pressed his head angrily into the back of the seat. He'd run and he hated himself for it. All this time, this planning… Frustration at the shame he was about to bring to Antonio and Danyl… It hurt Dimitri in a way he hadn't imagined, hadn't thought possible after all he'd endured in his thirty-three years.

He allowed that anger to propel him from the car and over to the door of the bed and breakfast, the sound of his fist pounding on the door jarring even to his own ears. He glanced at his watch for the first time in what felt like hours and was surprised to find that it was so late. Perhaps the proprietor was asleep. He looked back to the car, wondering how much further it would get, wondering whether he should turn back, when the door opened.

The moment he caught her large green eyes looking up at him he knew he was doomed.

She let him in, quietly, one finger to her lips and the other hand making a 'gently, gently' motion. She beckoned him through to a small seating area decorated with just about everything that he'd expected a small Irish bed and breakfast to have, but his gaze narrowed on the small wooden, clearly well-stocked bar.

'You're after a room?' she almost whispered.

Was he?

'Just for the night.'

Her eyes assessed him, but not in the sexual way he was used to from beautiful women. It was as if she were doing mathematics—on his expensive clothes, a watch that was probably worth half a yearly intake for this place, the car outside. He wasn't offended.

Dimitri took out his wallet and removed all the euros he had in it. What did it matter to him? He couldn't take them where he was going. He placed the thick bundle of notes on the bar.

'No, sir. That's not...that's not necessary. It'll be sixty euros for the night, an extra five if you'd like breakfast.'

The Irish lilt to her voice was a little surprising to him. Her skin wasn't the light, freckled complexion that had populated the racecourse back in Dublin—it was closer to his own Greek colouring, only without the benefit of the sun she seemed pale. For a moment he allowed himself to imagine this woman on a Greek island, sun-kissed and glorious, the sun's rays deepening the natural promise of her skin tone. Long, dark tendrils of hair had been swept up into a messy pony-tail that should have made her look young, rather than chaotically beautiful. Loose tendrils from a grown-out fringe played along her jawline, accentuating her cheek-bones and contrasting with the lighter golden tones in hauntingly emerald-coloured eyes.

Forcing his attention away from her, he looked at the bottles behind the bar. Scanning them, he was slightly disappointed. If he'd had a choice, none of them would have been it. But beggars couldn't be choosers.

'No breakfast. But I'll take a bottle of your best whisky.'

Again, her eyes were quick and assessing. Not calcu-lating. That was it. That was what was different about her. There wasn't anything selfish in her gaze, nothing judgemental. She was simply trying to figure him out. As if making up her mind, she slipped behind the small bar, not even looking at the obscene amount of money she was yet to touch, and she pulled down two cut crystal glasses housed in a hidden shelf above the counter. The way she resolutely ignored the money made him wonder if he'd offended her and a shadow of guilt stirred within him.

She placed the two glasses on the wooden bar top, waiting for his reaction, to see if he would object to her joining him. It was his turn to assess. She'd barely said two words to him. She looked to be in her early twenties. The white shirt she wore as a uniform was ill-fitting, as if made for someone bigger than her. The worn name tag sewn onto the shirt pocket said 'Mary Moore'. She didn't look much like a Mary. But he skimmed over these small details in preference of one: there was something behind her eyes. Something that called to him.

He nodded, allowing her to proceed. Instead of reaching for one of the bottles behind her, she bent beneath the bar and pulled out one that was more expensive. The good stuff saved for special occasions. Well, he supposed this *was* a special occasion.

She poured the amber liquid into each glass and, when finished, pushed one glass towards him and picked up the other.

'*Sláinte,*' she had said.

'*Yamas,*' he'd replied.

And they both drank deeply.

The plane banked to the right as it prepared to come in to land. Whether it was the drink from the night before, or the one from two hours ago, he could still taste whisky on his tongue, he could still taste *her*. As the plane descended towards the runway, images flashed through his mind. The first taste of her lips, the feel of her heart beating beneath the palm of his hand, her perfect breasts, her thigh as he moved it apart from the other. The feel of her wrapped around him and her thrilled cry as he sank deeply into her. The ecstasy he found as they climaxed together, swathed in each other. The memory of the scream he'd silenced with an impassioned kiss was drowned out by the roar of the backward thrust of the small jet engine as they came in to land at JFK.

Even the air stewardess seemed reluctant to open the cabin door. Her smile was sad as he disembarked, as if she too knew what was about to happen. But she couldn't. Only he, and perhaps two others in the whole world, did—the lead investigator, and whoever it was who had *really* perpetrated the crime.

At the bottom of the small metal steps stood about twenty men in blue windbreakers with yellow initials marking them to be FBI agents. Gun belts with hand-cuffs and batons carefully held in place sat heavily around each man's waist.

He stepped down towards the tarmac. Looking straight into the eyes of the lead agent, Dimitri Kyriakou, international billionaire, held out his hands before him—as he'd seen done in movies, as he'd known he would have to do long before this flight, long before last night—and as the steel handcuffs were clasped around his wrists he forced his head to remain high.

CHAPTER ONE

Present day

> *Dear Dimitri,*
> *Today you found me.*

DIMITRI GUIDED THE car down roads he'd travelled only once before. Headlights pierced the night, picking out slanting sheets of rain and wet shrubs lining the road. His mind's eye, however, ran through images of his now very much *ex*-assistant's horrified face as words like 'Sorry', 'I didn't know' and 'It was for the best… for the Kyriakou Bank' stuttered from the man's lips.

Fury pounded through Dimitri's veins. How had this happened? *How?*

In the nineteen months since his release from that godforsaken American prison, he'd sweated blood and tears to try and find the culprit responsible for setting him up to take the fall for one of the most notorious banking frauds of the last decade. Not only that, but also to bring his—*his father's*—family-owned bank back to its former glory.

And finally, one month ago, after the arrest of his half-brother, Manos, he'd thought all his troubles had ended. He'd thought he could put everything behind him and focus on the future. He thought he'd be finally able to breathe.

Until he'd received notification of unusual activity on a small personal account he'd not looked at in years. He'd set up the alerts the moment he'd resumed his position on the board of governors and had hoped that he'd never receive one.

But two days ago he had.

And he'd been horrified to discover that, unbeknownst to him, his assistant had arranged payment to a woman who had claimed Dimitri had a daughter. It had happened before, false accusations seeking to capitalise on his sudden unwelcome and erroneous notoriety after his arrest, demands for impossible amounts of money from scam artists. But this time...

Was it some perverse twist of fate that this discovery had coincided with the second leg of the Hanley Cup? That he should be drawn back to Dublin not only for the Winners' Circle, but also because his assistant had transferred the ridiculous sum of fifty thousand euros to a money-grabbing gold-digger who had—

The sound of his phone ringing cut through his thoughts like a knife.

'Kyriakou,' he said into the speaker set in the car.

'Sir, I have the information you...for...'

'Yes?'

'It's...rush... So I cannot guarantee...disclosure.'

'You're breaking up, Michael. The signal out here is terrible,' Dimitri growled, his frustration with this whole mess increasing. 'Can you hear me?'

'Yes, sir... Just about.'

'Look, you can email me the file and I'll look at it later, but for now, just top-line thoughts will do.'

'Mary Moore...years old... One daughter—Anna,

no father on the…certificate. Arrests for drunk and disorderly…disturbing the peace.'

Dimitri let out a curse. He couldn't believe it. The woman who had come apart in his arms was a drunk? Had a criminal record? *Dammit*.

'Okay. I've heard enough. Get me your invoice and I'll ensure the payment is—'

'Wait, sir, there's…you need…'

'The signal's breaking up now. I'll read the full file when I can access emails.'

With that, Dimitri ended the call, not taking his eyes from the road once. If he thought he'd been angry before, it was nothing compared to the fury now burning through his veins. He glanced at the man sitting silently in the passenger seat of the car—the only man outside of the Winners' Circle he trusted. David Owen had been his lawyer for over eighteen years.

'Legally, at this moment, there's actually very little you can do,' David said without making eye contact. 'All you have is the request for fifty thousand euros and a grainy black and white photo of a little girl.'

And it had been enough. Enough for Dimitri to recognise that the little girl was his. He'd looked exactly the same at her age—thick, dark, curly hair, and something indescribably haunted about her large brown eyes. Dimitri acknowledged that that might have been fanciful on his part. But surely, with an alcoholic criminal as a mother, that was a given.

'You have no actual proof that the child is yours.'

'I don't need it. I know it. *Know* that she is my blood. The timing fits, and, *Theos*, David, you read the email, you saw that picture too.'

David nodded his head reluctantly. 'We could engage Social Services, but that would cause publicity and scandal.'

'No. I will not have any more scandal attached to the Kyriakou name. Besides, it would take too long. The reason you're here is to help me get what I want without any of that. I can't afford for the press to find out about this yet. The mother is clearly only in it for the money. A little legal jargon will help grease the wheels, so to speak.'

The satnav on his phone told him to take the next left. How on earth Dimitri had found his way to that little bed and breakfast three years before, he had no idea.

'Are you sure you want to do this? As I said, legally your position is not the strongest.'

'She lost her right to any legal standing when she tried to blackmail me,' Dimitri bit out.

How could he have been so deceived? *Again?* How could he have let that happen?

Throughout his wrongful imprisonment, fourteen months incarcerated and locked behind bars like an animal, he'd held up the memory of that one night, of *her*, as a shining beacon in the darkness. A moment completely for him, known only to them. He'd lived off the sounds of her pleasure, the cries of ecstasy and that first, single moment—the moment when he'd been shocked, and ever so secretly pleased, to find that she had been a virgin—he'd drawn it deep within him, hugged it to him and allowed it to get him through the worst of the time he'd spent in prison.

Had he been deceived by her innocence? Had she *really* been a virgin? But even he had to acknowledge that thought as inherently wrong. It may have been the only true thing about Mary Moore. But the rest? She'd lied. She'd kept a secret from him. And she'd live to regret it for the rest of her life. Because nothing would prevent him from claiming his child.

Anna gasped as the rain pelted down even harder. It snuck beneath the neck of the waterproof jacket she'd slung around her shoulders the moment she got the phone call. She hadn't had the presence of mind to bring an umbrella though. She dug her hand into the pocket and pulled out the only protection she had with her against the elements. And the irony of that was enough to poke and prod at the miserable situation she was in.

She pulled the large, thin envelope from her pocket and held it over her head as the paper ate up the rain in seconds, and water dripped down her jacket sleeve and arm, to eagerly soak the cotton of her T-shirt.

It didn't matter if the letter got wet. She knew it word for word by now.

We regret to inform you...owing to late payments...as per the mortgage terms...right to repossess...

She was about to lose the small bed and breakfast she'd inherited from her grandmother, the place where both she and her mother had been born and had grown up. It might never have been the future that she had imagined for herself, but it was the only one she could cling to in order to support her child. How had her mother managed to keep this from her? Mary Moore was barely functioning as it was. But—Anna supposed—that was the beauty of being an alcoholic. Even in her worst state, her mother managed to hide, conceal, lie.

Through the pounding of the rain, Anna could hear

the raucous sounds of music and shouts coming from the only building with signs of life on the road. Light bled out from the frosted windows, barely illuminating the wet benches in the courtyard. Anna braced herself for what was guaranteed to be a pretty bloody sight.

She pushed open the door to the pub, and the men at the bar stopped talking and turned to stare. They always stared. The colour of her skin—the only thing her Vietnamese father had left her with after abandoning them before her birth—had always marked her as an outsider, as a reminder of her mother's shame. She shook out the letter, put the sodden paper back into her pocket and ran a hand through her hair to release the clusters of raindrops still clinging to the fine strands. The smell of warm beer and stale cigarettes defiantly smoked even after the ban hung heavy on the air.

She locked eyes with the owner, who stared back almost insolently.

'Why did you serve her?' Anna demanded.

The owner shrugged. 'She had the money.' As if in consolation, Eamon nodded in the direction of the snug.

She could hear sniggers coming from the men who had turned their backs to her and anger pooled low in her stomach. It was a hot, fiery thing that moved like a snake and bit like one too.

'What, you've never seen a drunk woman before?' she demanded of the room.

'She's not a woman, she's a—'

'Say that word and I'll—'

'That's enough,' Eamon interrupted, though whether for Anna's sake or for his peace and quiet, she couldn't tell.

She stepped through to the snug. Her mother was sitting alone in the empty room, surrounded by round wooden tables. She looked impossibly small, and in front of her, next to a newspaper, was a short glass filled with clear liquid—probably vodka. Anna hoped for vodka; gin always made it harder. She took a seat next to her and pushed down her mounting frustration. Anger never helped this situation.

Mary looked worse than the last time she'd seen her. From the day Amalia was born, Anna knew she couldn't allow Mary to continue to live with them. She wouldn't take the risk that her drunken outbursts could harm her daughter. She'd arranged for her mother to live with one of the only family friends Mary Moore had left. And their exchanges ever since had been loaded and painful.

'What happened, Ma? Where did the money come from?' Anna hated the sadness in her voice.

'I thought I'd be able to pay off some of the mortgage... I thought...just one drink... I thought...'

'Thought what, Ma?' Anna couldn't imagine what her mother was talking about, but she was used to the circulatory nature of conversations when she was in this state. The small flame of hope she'd nursed in the last few weeks as her mother had stayed sober and even talked of rehab spluttered out and died on a gasp.

'Even when he got out of prison, I thought he was guilty...but when they arrested his brother...'

Oh, God. She was talking about Dimitri.

Her mother nudged at the newspaper. Beside the main article was coverage of the forthcoming Dublin Horse Race, with a black and white picture of three men celebrating a win in Buenos Aires. Her eyes couldn't help but be drawn straight to one man: Dimitri Kyriakou.

'And he has all that money...so...' Mary Moore's

words were beginning to slur a little around the edges.
'So I did what you never had the courage to do.'

'What did you do, Ma?'

'A father should provide for his child.'

A million thoughts shouted in her mind. She, more
than anyone, knew the truth of her mother's statement.
But she *had* tried to garner his support…she *had* tried
to tell him once about his daughter: nineteen months
ago, on the day she, along with the rest of the world,
discovered his innocence. She'd called his office and
had been met with a response that proved to her that
the man she'd spent one reckless night with, the man to
whom she had given so much of herself, her *true* self,
had been a figment of her fevered imagination.

'Ma?'

'At least you picked one with money…he was willing
to pay fifty thousand euros in exchange for our silence.'

Sickness rose in Anna's stomach. Pure, unadulter-
ated nausea.

'Jesus, Ma—'

The slap came out of nowhere.

Hard, more than stinging. Anna's head rang and the
buzzing in her ears momentarily drowned out the shock.

'Do *not* take His name in vain, Anna Moore.'

In that one strike, years and years of loneliness, anger
and frustration rose within Anna. She locked eyes with
her mother and watched the righteous indignation turn
to guilt and misery.

'Oh, Anna, I'm so—'

'Stop.'

'Anna—'

'No.' Anna put her hand up, knowing what her ma
would say, knowing the cycle of begging, pleading and

justification that would follow. But she couldn't let it happen this time.

Had Dimitri really paid a sum of money to reject their daughter? A hurt so deep it felt endless opened up in her heart. The ache was much stronger than the throbbing in her cheek.

Anna rubbed her chest with the palm of her hand, trying to soothe the pain that she knew she would feel for days, possibly even years. *This* was what she'd wanted to avoid for her daughter—the sting of rejection, the feeling of being unwanted...unloved. She wouldn't let her daughter suffer that pain. She just wouldn't.

Anna looked at her mother, seeming even smaller now that she was hunched in on herself. The sounds of familiar tears coming from her shaking body.

Eamon poked his head around the entrance to the snug. There was pity in his eyes, and she hated him for it. She hated this whole damn village.

'I'll make sure she's okay for the night.'

'Do that,' Anna said as she walked out of the pub with her head held high. She wouldn't let them see her cry. She never had.

Anna didn't notice that the rain had stopped as she made her way back to the small family business she had barely managed to hold on to through the years. All she could think of was her little daughter, Amalia. Her gorgeous dark brown eyes, and thick curly hair. Sounds of her laughter, her tears and the first cries she'd made on this earth echoed in her mind. And the miraculous moment that, after being placed in her arms for the first time, Amalia opened her eyes and Anna had felt...love. Pure, unconditional, heart-stopping love. There was nothing she wouldn't do for her daughter.

The day she'd discovered that she was pregnant with

Dimitri's child was the day that his sentence had been handed to him by the American judge. She'd almost felt the gavel fall onto the bench, as if it had tolled against her own heart. She'd never wanted to believe him guilty of the accusations levelled at him, the theft of millions of dollars from the American clients of the Kyriakou Bank, but what had she known of him then? Only that he was a man who liked whisky, had driven her to the highest of imaginable pleasures and left her bed the following morning without a word.

Hating to think that her child would bear the stigma of such a parent, she'd determined to keep the identity of Amalia's father to herself. But when she'd heard of his innocence? And tried to get in touch with him? Only to hear that she was just one of several women making the same 'claim'? She practically growled at the memory. Her daughter wasn't a claim. Amalia had been eight months old, and from that day she'd promised to be both mother and father to her child. She'd promised to ensure that Amalia would be happy, secure and know above all that she was loved. She wanted to give her daughter the one thing she had never had growing up after her own father had abandoned his pregnant wife.

As she walked up the path towards the front of the bed and breakfast she could see a small minibus in the driveway. The three customers who had checked in earlier that day were stowing their bags in the back.

Mr Carter and his wife saw her first.

'This is absolutely unacceptable. I'll be adding this to my review.'

'What's going on?' she demanded, her interruption momentarily stopping Mr Carter's tirade.

'We booked with you in good faith, Ms Moore. I suppose the only good thing is that we're upgrading to the hotel in town. But really. To be kicked out with no explanation at ten thirty at night… Not good, Ms Moore. Not good.'

Before Anna could do anything further, her customers disappeared onto the bus. She jumped out of the way as it backed out of the drive, leaving only one man standing in front of the door to her home.

Dimitri Kyriakou. Looking just as furious as she felt.

Dimitri had been pacing the small bar where he'd first met Mary Moore. Somewhere in the back of the building a member of Mary's staff was holding his daughter in her arms and looking at him as if he were the devil.

From inside, he heard the irate conversation from one of the customers. She'd returned.

In just a few strides Dimitri exited the bar, passed along the short hallway and out through the front door, just in time to see the bus departing.

He'd let anger drive him out here, but he was stopped in his tracks the moment he caught sight of the woman who had nearly, *nearly*, succeeded in separating him from his child.

Tendrils of long, dark hair whipped around her face, her green eyes bright with something he could recognise. Anger was far too insipid a word for the storm that was brewing between them. She looked…incredible. And he hated her for it. She was better than any of his imprisoned dreams could have conjured. But wasn't that how the devil worked? Looking like the ultimate temptation whilst cutting out a soul?

'What are you doing here? And what have you done to my guests?' she demanded.

The hostility in her tone was nothing he'd ever imagined hearing from her lips. But he was happy to hear it. Happy to have it match his own.

'We need to talk; they were in the way. I got rid of them.'

Money was an incredible thing. It had been both his saviour and his destroyer, but this time he was going to use it to help him get what he wanted...what he *needed*.

The woman holding his daughter moved into the hallway behind him, drawing Mary's attention. He watched as the mother of his child rushed past him, forcing him to back out of her way, and swept their daughter up in her arms.

They made a striking image, Mary's dark head buried in the crook of their daughter's neck. He'd so desperately wanted to hold his child the first moment he set eyes on her. But the woman employed by Mary had raged that she wouldn't let her be held by a stranger. *Christe mou*, was this how he started as a father? Being denied the right to hold his child? Anger crushed his chest.

'Thank you, Siobhan. You can go now.'

'If you're sure?' the young girl asked, casting him a doubtful look. After a quick nod of reassurance from the woman holding his child, the girl brushed past him, letting loose a low tut as she did so.

Dimitri locked his gaze with Mary's. If looks could kill...

It was all Anna could do to take him in. Dimitri filled the entire doorway, looking like the devil come to collect his dues. Tall, broad and mouthwatering. Anger slashed his cheeks and made a mockery of the taut bones of his incredible features. The long, dark, hand-made woollen coat hung almost to his knees, covering a dark blue knitted jumper that, she knew, would stretch across his broad shoulders perfectly. Broad shoulders that she'd once draped with her hands, her fingers, her tongue. Even the sight of him drove away the bone-deep chill that had settled into her skin from the rain. Her body's betrayal stung as it vibrated, coming to life for the first time in three years, just from his proximity. Desire coated her throat while heat flayed her skin.

He looked as if he'd just stepped from the pages of a glossy magazine. And there she was, soaking wet, an old, hideous luminous-green waterproof jacket covering ill-fitting jeans and a T-shirt that was probably indecently see-through from the rain. But it was his eyes, shards of obsidian and hauntingly familiar, so like the ones she'd seen every single day since her daughter had been placed in her arms. Though they had never been filled with such disdain.

'You have five minutes.' His voice was harsh and more guttural than she remembered. Cursing herself silently, she forced her brain into gear.

'For what?' Anna asked, thinking that this was an odd way to start the conversation she'd spent years agonising over.

'To say goodbye.'

'Goodbye to who?'

'Our daughter.'

CHAPTER TWO

Dear Dimitri,
I didn't mean for it to be like this.

INSTINCTIVELY ANNA CLUTCHED Amalia tightly to her chest.

'I'm not saying goodbye to my daughter!'

'Don't play the put-upon mother now.'

Dimitri had taken a step towards her and Anna took a step back.

'You,' Dimitri continued, 'who only two days ago blackmailed me with news of her. The transfer has been made, but I've come to collect. Because there's no way I'm leaving my daughter in the care of an alcoholic, debt-ridden liar and cheat.'

Anna's head spun. So much so, it took her a moment to realise that he had somehow mistaken her for her mother.

'Wait—'

'I've waited long enough.'

Anna watched, horrified, as another man appeared in the doorway. A man who had 'legal' stamped all over him. It didn't make a dent in Dimitri's powerful tirade.

'Mary Moore of Dublin, Ireland. Mortgaged up to the hilt, with three drunk and disorderlies, one child and no father's name on the birth certificate. You should have been on the stage,' Dimitri spat, his anger infusing his words with misplaced righteousness. 'The woman I met that night three years ago was clearly nothing more than a drunken apparition...with consequences. That consequence—'

'Don't you *dare* call my child a consequence,' she hissed at him, struggling not to raise her voice and disturb Amalia, who was wriggling in discomfort already.

'That consequence is why I am here,' he pressed on. 'Now that I am aware of her existence, I shall be taking her with me. If it's money you need, then my lawyer here will draw up the requisite paperwork for you to sign guardianship over to me. Though I wouldn't normally pay twice for something, I will allow it this time.'

'Pay twice for *something*? You're calling my daughter "something"?' Anna demanded furiously.

His words provoked her beyond all thought. Blood pounded in her ears; injustice over his awful accusations sang in her veins; fury at his arrogance, anger at his belief that she would do just as he asked lit a flame that bloomed, crackled and burned.

'I am sure that it would be possible, *Mr Kyriakou*, almost easy for you, even, to have your lawyer draw up paperwork, to hand over ludicrous amounts of money, money that would be *yours*, I'm sure, not taken from the clients of the Kyriakou Bank...' she paused for breath, ignoring how his darkened eyes had narrowed infinitesimally, before continuing '...were I Mary Moore.'

His head jerked back as if he had been slapped.

'Mary Moore is guilty of all the things you have lambasted her for. She is the one who contacted you demanding money for her silence. But I. Am. Not. Mary. Moore. I'm *Anna* Moore. And if you raise your voice to me in front of our daughter *one more time*, I'll throw you out myself!'

In her mind she had been shouting, hurling those words against the invisible armour he seemed to wear about him. But in reality she had been too conscious of her daughter, too much of a mother to do anything that would upset her child. But she had caught Dimitri on the back foot—she could see that from the look of shock, then quick calculation as he assessed the new information. And she was determined to press her advantage.

'I will call the police if I have to,' Anna continued. 'And with your record—even expunged—I think you'll find that they'll side with me. At least for tonight.'

The smirk on his cruel lips infuriated her.

'My lawyer would have me out in an hour.'

'The same lawyer that told me he'd pay me off, *"just like the last one"*, when I tried to tell you of our child's birth?'

Dimitri spun round to look at David in confusion. But David seemed just as confused as he. 'It wasn't me,' his friend said, shaking his head. 'I don't know anything about that.'

'What? When did this happen?' he demanded, already beginning to feel unsteady on the shifting sands beneath his feet.

'When you were first freed from prison nineteen months ago, I called your office. You may like to think that I purposefully kept my daughter from you, but I did try to reach out to you,' Mary—*Anna*—said from over his shoulder. Reluctantly he turned back round to look her in the eye, needing to see the truth of her words. 'He referred to himself as Mr Tsoutsakis. It's not something I'm likely to forget.'

'*Theos*, that was my ex-assistant and, I assure you,

he will never work again,' Dimitri swore, still trying to wrap his head around the fact that Anna had tried to reach him for something other than bribery or money.

'I don't care who it was. I was told, in rather specific terms, that I would be paid off, just like the other hundred or so women calling to claim they had carried the heir to the Kyriakou Bank. I had—and still have—no intention of taking money from you, or depriving whatever number of illegitimate children you fathered before, or since, your imprisonment of any child support.'

'There are no other children,' he ground out. 'When I…when I was arrested certain…women sought me out, claiming that I had fathered numerous children unrelated to me.' Their sordid attempts at extortion had snuffed out the last little flame of hope he'd had in human decency. To use a child in such a way was horrific to him. In total four women had jumped on the wrong bandwagon, assuming he'd pay for their silence. But none of them, neither his two ex-girlfriends nor the two strangers who had claimed an acquaintance with him, had realised that he would never, *never* let a child of his disappear from his life. Dimitri resisted the urge to reach out to Anna. 'I swear to you. There were no other women, no other children.'

'And I'm supposed to just believe you?' Her scorn cut him to the quick. 'So, this is your lawyer? Tell me, *Mr Lawyer*, what would the courts say to a man who turns up at ten thirty at night making false accusations of alcoholic behaviour, costing me three bookings and irreconcilable damage to my professional reputation, threatening to take my daughter away from me and trying to blackmail me?'

And, finally, it was then that their daughter started to cry.

'You're making her upset,' Dimitri accused.

'No, *you* are,' she returned.

Feeling the ground beneath him start to slip further, Dimitri pressed on, ignoring his own internal warning bell.

'It's neither here nor there. You need to pack. Get your things—we're leaving,' he commanded. Even to his own ears he sounded obtuse. But he couldn't help it. It was this situation…his childhood memories clawing their way up from the past and into the present making him rash, making him desperate.

'I'm not going anywhere and I really will call the police if you try to force me. You clearly don't know the first thing about parenting if you're expecting it to be okay to just upend a child at ten thirty at night.'

'And whose fault is that?' he heard himself shout, immediately regretting his loss of control. Nothing about this situation had gone as he'd intended and that there was a grain of truth in her last accusation struck him deeply.

David shifted in the hallway, drawing their attention.

'My recommendation is to sleep on this a little. Clearly there has been a series of misunderstandings and we each need time to reflect on the new information we all have. Dimitri, we should take the car back to Dublin and return in the morning.'

'I'm not leaving my daughter,' Dimitri growled.

'Ms Moore, is this something that you are happy to accommodate?'

Dimitri almost couldn't look at her, didn't want to gauge her reaction. When he'd walked into this, he'd been so sure. Sure of his plan, of his information, of the situation. Yet the moment she'd revealed that she wasn't Mary, but Anna, he *knew* she wasn't lying. He'd felt the truth of it settle about his shoulders and, looking at it now, he was relieved. The woman who had given birth to his daughter wasn't an alcoholic. Hadn't been arrested. The woman he'd slept with and spent years dreaming about… Layers and layers of cloudy images began to shift, and when he opened his eyes he looked at Anna and they became clear.

Anna was looking down at her daughter, rocking her gently in her arms as she settled their child, making soothing noises that seemed to satisfy the girl…his daughter. And he held his breath before her pronouncement. He felt, rather than heard, her sigh.

'I'll put him in one of the recently vacated rooms. I'm not comfortable with the way he's done things.' It irked him that she was directing her conversation to David rather than him, but he had to be fair. It was justified after the accusations he'd hurled at her. And Dimitri knew a thing or two about wrongful accusations. 'But we do,' she continued, 'need to talk and figure out where we go from here.'

Dimitri followed David out to the car, assuring David that he wasn't such a monster as to cause harm or fear to his daughter or the mother of his child, especially given that she was clearly not the woman he had thought from the report. He took several deep breaths of cool night air before returning to the small bed and breakfast. Peeking into empty rooms on the ground floor, he felt like a trespasser in his daughter's home and hated it.

He followed the soothing sounds of a gentle lullaby that contrarily only fuelled the anger within him. How many nights had he missed the simple pleasure of putting his daughter to bed, knowing that she was safe, cared for…loved? He paused on the threshold of a dusky-pink room, gently lit by a softly glowing night light.

Dimitri looked at the nearly sleeping child in the crib. She was peaceful and angelic. He knew that was a cliché, but he couldn't think of any other words to describe his daughter. It was the first time he'd really *seen* her, not hidden by the shoulder of a stranger or buried in her mother's arms. Her skin was dark, like both her parents', but the eyes—they were his. He knew that Anna hadn't seen him yet, her body hadn't stiffened the way it had every single time he'd come within a foot of her. But she was far from relaxed, and he deeply regretted that their adult emotions had come to interfere with his child's sleep.

How had this mess happened? She'd been shocked by Dimitri's accusations, his presence…all of it. For nineteen months, she'd forced herself to abandon the hope that he might come for her. The hope that her daughter wouldn't grow up feeling that same sense of rejection that felt almost a solid part of Anna. But that was the thing—Anna's father hadn't just been absent, it wasn't a passive thing…he had walked away. Had actively chosen to leave her and her mother behind.

She pushed at the adrenaline still pounding through her veins, desperately fighting the need to flee. Instead, she clung to the words she'd spoken to the lawyer. They really did need to find a way forward, now that he knew about Amalia, now that he claimed to *want* their child. Wasn't that what she'd dreamed of when she first reached out to him? Never would she have chosen to raise her daughter without a father in her life…the way she had been raised.

As Anna watched her daughter in the crib, she marvelled at how she'd got so big. She was twenty-seven months old and before lying down on the soft mattress

Amalia had held on to the bars and looked at Anna with big brown eyes. Anna had reached out and smoothed a soft curl of hair from Amalia's forehead. She'd bent down and whispered a promise to her child.

'It will be okay, sweetheart. It will.' She'd hoped that she wasn't lying.

Anna waited until she heard the sounds of her daughter's breathing slow. She waited until she knew she couldn't put it off any more and turned to leave the room.

But Dimitri stood in the doorway.

How many times had she imagined him standing there? How many times, during Amalia's sleepless nights, the teething, the crying…the times when Anna had been so exhausted she couldn't even weep? What would she have given to see him standing there, a support, a second hand, anything to help take away some of the weight of being a single parent?

But when she'd heard the lawyer—the assistant, as she now knew—dismiss her claims as one of the many women who had called Dimitri, she'd realised that she hadn't known Dimitri at all. The disbelief and incredulity in Tsoutsakis's voice had been the reminder she'd clung to each and every night that she had been right to hang up the phone, to end the conversation before she could reveal any more of herself, of her daughter.

But now? What did it all mean? That it hadn't been Dimitri who had outright rejected his daughter. That he was innocent of the imprisonment that had made her sure she couldn't let a criminal be the father of her child. Now that he was here, standing before her.

'I don't even know her name.' Anna read a whole host of emotions in that one sentence: pain, regret… anger.

'Amalia. Her name is Amalia.'

For a second, he looked as if he had been punched in the chest… He closed his eyes briefly but when they opened he wore a mask.

'She's mine.' It was a statement rather than a question. But for all his seeming arrogant certainty, she could tell that he needed to hear it from her. It was as if he was holding his breath.

For just a moment, Anna considered lying. It would all go away. Dimitri would leave and go back to Greece, or America, or wherever he'd come from. Life could return to normal, she'd continue to manage the bed and breakfast, continue to handle her mother's alcoholism, continue to raise her daughter on her own. But she couldn't do it. She knew what it was like to grow up in this small village without a father, with the stigma of being discarded and unwanted. She knew the questions that were sure to come from her daughter's lips because they had come from her own.

Where's my daddy? Didn't Daddy want me? Did he not love me?

His eyes darkened impossibly as she made him wait for her answer.

'Yes. She's your daughter.'

'How?' he bit out. 'We were careful. Every single time. We were careful.'

It was a question she had asked herself time and time again during her pregnancy. Forcing herself to relive that night, the intimacies they'd shared, trying to find the exact moment that their daughter had been conceived.

'Protection fails sometimes,' she said, echoing the words of the female doctor who had looked at her with pity.

Anna followed him out into the hallway, ensuring Amalia's door stayed open just an inch.

He spun round to face her.

'How could you? How could you keep this from me?'

This was the argument that she'd expected. The one she'd rehearsed in the dead of night when she'd known, somehow, that he *would* return and come to claim his child. This was the reason that she had poured hours and months into writing letters—documenting her thoughts, experiences, feelings from the day Amalia was born. Letters that had never been sent, nor read by the intended recipient, because they had been addressed to the father of her child. And this man? This man she did not know.

'You left my bed and within hours were arrested for massive financial fraud. How could I subject the precious child I carried to a man I barely knew and who was in prison within months?'

'I was *wrongfully* imprisoned,' he bit out.

'I didn't know that at the time! And the moment I did find out, I was...' She actually growled her frustration. 'You know what I was told.' She tried to take a calming breath. 'Look, let's talk about this in the morning. We both need sleep, or at least I certainly do.' She stopped short of adding 'please' to the sentence. Instinctively she knew that any sign of weakness would be like blood in the water to a shark. She waited, her breath held, until the almost imperceptible nod of his head signalled his agreement.

Anna led Dimitri down the hallway to a room. Admittedly it was the smallest room she had to offer, but right now Anna was going to take any small victory she could. Did it make her petty? Perhaps. But she was too tired to care.

Only she hadn't been prepared for the sight of his large build in the small room. She hadn't braced herself for the memories that rushed to greet her of the last time he'd spent the night under this roof.

He'd swept into her life when she had been at her lowest, when she had felt helpless against the failings of *both* her parents. When all she'd wanted was something for herself. Just for once. One night that wasn't about being responsible or putting someone else's needs above her own.

She'd told herself that she would stop at one drink. She'd told herself she'd stop at one kiss, one touch…and after he'd given her pleasure she had never imagined possible she'd told herself she only wanted one night. But that had been a lie.

Until she'd woken, alone. The dull ache that took up residence in her heart that morning robbed her of the pleasure and the reckless need for one stolen night. In that moment she was cured of any selfish want she'd ever have, and she'd promised never to lose herself like that again. But she had never regretted that night. And she never would. For it had brought her Amalia.

Dimitri looked around the small room. It was little bigger than the cell he'd had in prison, but the exhaustion in Anna's eyes had struck a nerve. He'd come here, all guns blazing, expecting to sweep in and take his child away from a mother who couldn't care less about his child. What he'd seen instead was a beautiful woman who was fiercely protective of her child. A woman who had raised a child alone, just as his own mother once had. Perhaps he should take the time to work this new information into his plans, before trying again. As if sensing his resolution, Anna backed out quietly from the small room, and Dimitri sat heavily on the surprisingly comfortable mattress.

David was probably helping himself to a whisky from the hotel's minibar right now, Dimitri thought as he pulled off his shoes. But he wouldn't have changed places with the man. He was sleeping less than twenty metres from his daughter. From his own child. And he knew that he'd never let her out of his sight again.

A loud crashing sound from below jerked Dimitri from the fitful sleep he'd fallen into. Terror raced through his bones for just a second, until he saw the faint outline of flowery wallpaper and felt the soft mattress beneath him. He wasn't back in prison. No one was about to get hurt. He waited for a moment to get his breath back, for the painful sting of adrenaline to recede from his pores.

But then the crash sounded again, and his daughter started to cry. *What the hell?*

He launched out of the bed and into the hallway, where he met Anna.

'Anna, what—?'

'Go back to bed,' she whispered harshly. 'Please, just—'

Another crashing sound came, this time accompanied by the sound of breaking glass.

He caught a look of panic passing across Anna's features before she disappeared down the stairs. Amalia was starting to cry in earnest now, and he went into her room. Did he pick her up? Would that make her stop, or cry even harder?

Her poor little face was already red, with big, fat tears rolling down her cheeks. The ear-piercing screams of his daughter caught in his heart and he reached down and picked her up, ignoring the stab of hurt as she tried to pull away from him, her strength surprising him.

He held her against his chest and followed Anna's

footsteps down to the hallway and the bar below, thinking he was ready for whatever he would find down there. But he wasn't.

Anna was on the floor, kneeling before a small red-haired woman, who was trying to shake Anna off.

'Please, Ma. You need to go.'

'You left me with that man—'

'You know Eamon, Ma.'

Dimitri watched as Anna's mother tried to get out of the chair, pushing Anna away and nearly succeeding, until Anna stood and took her by the shoulders.

'Ma, please. It's late and you've woken Amalia.'

For a moment, that seemed to do the trick. 'My precious Amalia…' But the moment she caught sight of Dimitri standing with her granddaughter, any hold that Anna might have had on her mother disappeared.

She knocked Anna off balance and she fell awkwardly on her knee. Mary took two uncertain steps towards him and Dimitri instinctively turned to protect his daughter, angling his body away from the drunk woman. He held out his arm.

'Enough!' His strong command brought the older woman to a standstill. 'Anna, take Amalia upstairs.'

Anna looked for a moment as if she was about to argue, but clearly thought better of it.

She took her daughter from him, their skin brushing against each other's for the first time since that night three years before. Ignoring the waves of little pinpricks that rushed over his hands, Dimitri watched as Anna disappeared up the stairs, her last glance at them uncertain and worried.

Dimitri stared at the woman in front of him, seeing very little trace of Anna's colouring, but for just a moment he could see reflections of what must have once made the older woman beautiful, especially in the startling moss-green eyes looking back at him.

Dimitri wasn't a stranger to what alcohol could do to a person and what kind of chemical prison it could be. Some responded to gentle persuasion, but the time for that had passed.

'I'm going to get you some water, and you're going to sleep down here on the sofa.' There was no way he was going to let her upstairs near his child or her daughter. Mary made one last effort to complain, but he saw that off with a raised eyebrow.

'Do not test me, Mrs Moore. You've done enough damage tonight.'

She just hadn't realised how much yet.

As Mary reluctantly lay down on the sofa, Anna stuck her head over the bannisters. He raised a hand to stop her from coming further down the stairs, knowing that her reappearance would spark another round from the woman on the sofa.

Anna's eyes were sad as she mouthed the words 'thank you' to him and disappeared. And just for a moment he felt sorry for her. Because she had no idea what was about to happen.

He waited until Mary Moore fell into a comfortably drunk sleep and pulled out his mobile. David answered on the second ring.

'I need you to do a couple of things for me. I need indefinite management cover for the bed and breakfast and a list of rehab clinics as far away from this village as humanly possible, and I need both by ten a.m. tomorrow.'

'Sure thing. Anything else?'

'Yes. Tell Flora to get the house prepared for anything a two-year-old might need. And after that, I want you to start working on a watertight prenup.'

CHAPTER THREE

Dear Dimitri,
How could you do such a thing?

ANNA FLIPPED OUT the bed sheet, the whipping sound it made before it settled over the mattress making her wince. She was exhausted, having barely slept the night before. Every time she'd closed her eyes she'd seen Dimitri standing between her and Amalia as if it were a prophecy foretelling how she would, from now on, see her daughter—at a distance and with him separating them. If not that, then she'd been tortured by the memories of her own pleasure as Dimitri had teased orgasm after orgasm from her innocent body.

But when she woke, all she could think of was her mother. It had been years since Mary had turned up at the bed and breakfast that far out of control. A twinge cramped her stomach. This hadn't been the life she'd wanted. Once she'd dreamed of escaping the small village, whose inhabitants had been hostile towards them from the moment Mary had been forced to raise her child alone. Anna had fantasised about studying art and sculpture, perhaps even at the University of Glasgow. It had been a hope that she'd cherished as she'd worked at the bed and breakfast saving every penny she made to put towards tuition fees. That Anna had somehow managed to follow in her mother's footsteps—becoming, instead, another single mother—had sealed their fate. Undesirable. Unwanted. The cautionary tale that locals told their children. And what a cautionary tale it was. Only the masochistic would want Dimitri Kyriakou arriving on their doorstep to claim what he felt he was owed.

By the time the sun had peeked around her curtain that morning, she'd realised she needed a plan. She needed to take back the control that was slipping through her fingers like hot sand.

This was the last of the rooms that needed cleaning after the hasty departure of her guests the night before. If she was lucky, she'd be able to pull some new clients from the horse racing meeting in Dublin in a few days' time.

Thankfully her mother had left before Anna had brought Amalia down for breakfast. It was the one showdown she hadn't been prepared for. Where her mother was concerned, Anna realised that she no longer had any defences left. How could her mother have done that, knowing Amalia was in the house? Clearly all the talk of rehab—the apparent reason she'd taken the money from Dimitri in the first place—was a... Anna wasn't ready to call it a lie, more of a thin spider's web of fiction that broke under the weight of addiction.

Rehab had been a mythical promise she'd heard over and over again throughout the years. A place the woman wearing her mother's skin would go, and upon her return would be her real mother gifted back to her. The mother who had once been a bright, powerful, creative woman with a deep well of love to give and not enough pools in which to store it. But her mother was one problem. Dimitri was another.

There were a hundred different ways she'd imagined their reunion, and not one of them came remotely close to what had happened the night before. Recalling the night they'd spent together three years before, she re-alised that she'd been wearing her mother's shirt—the one with the name Mary Moore sewn onto the pocket. And, with her mother's record, would *she* not have stormed in like a Valkyrie, ready to retrieve her child from such a woman? The way that no one had done for her?

She felt, rather than heard, a presence behind her. Siobhan was downstairs with Amalia, so there was only one person it could be. Only one person had ever had that effect on her body. It had been the same way the first time she'd laid eyes on him. A feeling that the world had ever so slightly tilted on its axis, a feeling that nothing would ever be the same again. It started on her forearms, as if she were held there between powerful hands, raising the hairs beneath the imaginary touch. It licked up her spine and across her neck. And then Anna cursed herself for being fanciful.

'What are you doing?' Dimitri asked, sounding as sleep-deprived as she.

'Preparing the rooms. I may get some walk-ins later. The weather is good, and the races are on…' She trailed off, knowing that she had to address what had happened with her mother. 'About last night—'

'Does she live here?'

'My mother? No.' Anna shook her head vehemently, instantly understanding his concern. 'No. It's been years since she turned up here like that.'

'Who else do you employ here?' It wasn't perhaps the question she'd expected. She'd imagined Dimitri would haul her over the coals for her mother's appearance. Anna was still trying to gather her thoughts from the breakneck speed of his inquisition. She still hadn't turned to face him. She needed just a moment more to gather her strength.

'Siobhan helps out when we're at capacity. Which we would have been today, had not all my customers been removed to a hotel in Dublin.' With this she finally turned to take in the broad expanse of the man who had no damn right to look that good after a night in the smallest room she had.

Instantly regretting it, she turned back to the room, picked up the cleaning basket and made her way into the en suite bathroom. She put on the rubber gloves and spread a healthy squirt of bleach on the scrubber as if she could clean away either the sight of him or him completely.

She got onto her knees, realising that this was perhaps the most ridiculous way to have a conversation, but, needing something to do with her hands other than throttle the man behind her, she pushed on.

'I've been thinking, and I would like you to have a relationship with my—*our*—daughter.' She told herself it was the smell of the bleach that had her stomach twisting and turning worse than any morning sickness she had experienced. 'I'd be happy to grant visitation rights, but you must understand that we will be staying here. My life is here and so is my daughter's. I will not uproot everything she's ever known.'

There. She had managed to get the words from her mind to her mouth without crying, or sounding weak. She needed him to agree to this.

For a moment, just as he had done the night before, he felt almost sorry for her. She had no idea that her life was about to change irrevocably. But from the first time he'd heard of his daughter, Dimitri knew that he wouldn't settle for visitation rights. He wanted his daughter with him. All the time.

He was man enough to admit that the knowledge that he currently didn't have any legal rights to his child was nothing short of terrifying. The fear that had gripped him in those first moments of this shocking discovery had been nothing like anything he'd ever experienced. *Nothing.* Even when he'd arrived at his father's house at the age of seven for the first time, not knowing if he'd take him in. Even before that, when the police filling the tiny apartment he'd shared with his mother were saying unintelligible things that he struggled to make sense of years after they had left his life. None of it scratched the surface of the deep well that opened up when he realised that there was a tiny life out there, his flesh and blood...

'I don't want you to miss out on things,' Anna was saying as she furiously scrubbed at the toilet, before picking herself up off the floor and turning—still with her back to him—to the sink.

'You don't want me missing...' His sentence trailed off as incredulity hit him hard. 'What, like the first sonogram? The first sound of my daughter's heartbeat? Tell me, Anna,' he said, reaching out to pull her around to him, so that he could look her in the eyes, so he could see the truth written there in them when she answered his next question. 'Does my daughter even know the word *Daddy*?'

He regretted touching her the moment his fingers hit the bare skin of her arm beneath her short T-shirt. He tried to ignore the flames that licked out at him from just one touch; he tried to ignore the rush of memories he'd held at bay for the last two days. He had to. Instead, he focused on the mounting horror in Anna's eyes.

'What? Did you think I wouldn't have wanted to be part of those things? *Christe mou*, Anna, did you even think of me at all?'

Dimitri cursed again, but this time silently. He hadn't want to reveal that much. He needed to get this back on to an unemotional level if he had any hope of persuading her to his cause. But the more and more he thought of all the things he had missed out on, all of the things Amalia would have grown up with, the stigma of being illegitimate in a sternly familial culture…and at how he hadn't been able to protect her from that… He knew how much damage could be done to a child when they were unwelcome, unwanted…

So, no. No. He'd never put his daughter through that. He would do what he had to do. Because that was what Dimitri did. He put aside anything that would prevent the required outcome. He cut off the thoughts of the past, his mother, his half-brother's betrayal, thoughts of the time he had spent wrongfully incarcerated in prison. They had no place here. Here was his daughter. And the mother of his child. And he needed them in Greece.

'This is getting us nowhere,' he said, looking around the small bathroom. 'Can we… Do you have coffee? Can we sit and have a proper conversation, when you're not…?' He gestured towards the cleaning products and the hideous yellow gloves Anna was wearing.

The smell of coffee seemed to have a calming effect on his nerves, but the moment the insipid, thin liquid hit his tongue he regretted it. Dimitri kept his eyes trained on Anna, who had yet to stop moving, either around the small bathroom she'd been cleaning or the impressive, sleek chrome kitchen he'd been surprised to find tucked away from the main part of the old cottage.

He supposed the small staff area could pass as cosy and compact. But while he sat pressed up against the wall, his long legs barely fitting beneath the wooden table, his patience finally wore thin.

'Sit down,' he demanded.

Anna stilled, freezing against the command, but finally she slipped—easily—into the seat opposite him. Though her body had finally stopped moving, her eyes seemed to take everything in but him.

'I want you to come to Greece.'

Ah. That did it. Anna's gaze zeroed in on his.

'No.'

'No?' he asked, his eyebrow raised.

She let out an incredulous laugh. 'How can I go to Greece? I have a business here, my mother, my...life is here, Dimitri. I can't.'

This was nothing he hadn't expected, but the email he'd received from David that morning had confirmed that everything was in place. In fact, in just five short minutes Anna would see how pointless her arguments would be. He didn't want to use her mother's behaviour from the night before against her. But even if Mary didn't live under the same roof she was still an influence on his daughter's life, she could still put his daughter at risk. So he *would* use it if Anna forced him to. First he'd try a softer approach. And if that didn't work...

'Anna. The situation you're in can't be easy. The bank is about to take all this away from you.' He ignored the small gasp of shock that fell from her mouth.

'How do you—?'

'And between Amalia and your mother, dealing with all that alone—'

'I haven't been alone—'

'—must have been incredibly trying. All the work that you have to do here… You must be exhausted. It certainly can't allow you the time you'd like to dedicate to our daughter.' That there was no interruption this time told him all he needed to know. 'I want to pay off the mortgage—in your name. I will also pay for your mother to go to a rehab clinic. Anna, your mother needs help. Proper help. And I can provide that.

'A lovely couple is ready and willing to run the bed and breakfast in your absence, just for a short time, whilst you come to Greece. There, Amalia can get to know me, get to know her Greek heritage, her family.' Forestalling her objections, he pressed on. 'Anna, it's something that you deserve—time away from this place, to relax and to spend time with your daughter without having to worry about keeping the roof together over your heads.'

Anna's head spun. In her wildest dreams she had wanted this. She had wanted someone to sweep in, take care of everything, to resolve all her financial worries, to help with her mother, to allow her to focus solely on her daughter. In her deepest heart, she'd even wanted that person to be Dimitri. Like the fairy-tale prince and the happy-ever-after that she had never thought was possible. But, just like in all good fairy tales, Dimitri's offer was surely too good to be true. Like the poisoned apple, or the spindle needle's prick, there was always a price to pay. And, just like the miller's daughter, there was no way she would hand over her child.

But for a moment Dimitri's eyes had softened, and she'd seen glimpses of the man she'd met that night three years before. The man she'd written secret letters to in the dead of night. The man who three years ago had looked at her as if she was the one thing that could save him. And that night, she'd felt the same of him. That night, she'd needed him. Was it possible that she needed him now too?

'I also want to apologise,' he pressed on. 'Last night, I thought the worst. It was a combination of shock to discover that I was a father, and fear of just how much I had missed. Anna,' he said, reaching out to take her hand in his, the rough, tanned skin caressing hers with surprising softness, 'please, give me the chance to make up for my actions. I want the chance to make things right, to get to know my daughter—to get to know Amalia.'

Of all the things he'd said, it was *this* that truly undid Anna. The small crack in her heart that had appeared the day she'd held her daughter in her arms, alone in the hospital room without anyone to share that moment with, opened just a little wider. Because it was the one thing that her father had never wanted of her.

Could she do it? Could she hand over everything to Dimitri and just walk away? Years of having to be the responsible one, having to make the decisions and do what needed to be done, cried, begged and pleaded for her to say *yes*. But the sensible part of her, the cautionary part of her, feared that it would come at too high a price.

Anna thought of her mother. Of how she had been the night before. Of how many times Mary had promised, sobbed and agonised over her own demons. Anna could never afford to send her mother to a rehab clinic—certainly not the kind that Dimitri's money could afford. If it had just been about her and Amalia, perhaps she might have found the strength to say no. But she knew that she'd never forgive herself for not allowing her mother one more chance.

'How long would it be for?' Anna asked, hating the sound of hope in her own voice.

'Not long. A week; two if needed.' If she thought it odd that he hadn't met her eyes as he spoke, it was buried beneath a layer of hope, and a feeling of exhaustion so deep that she clung to his offer like a drowning man clung to the shore.

And when she said yes she ignored the little voice in her head that told her that she'd just signed her life away.

The next few days passed in a blur. Anna had met with the couple that David—Dimitri's lawyer—had found. They seemed kind and were understanding of the situation. They'd had a small hotel themselves but had passed it on to the next generation in their family and were now travelling around Ireland. Anna, to her surprise, liked them. She'd imagined she would feel resentful, but their care and passion for her own business eased the way considerably.

Dimitri had arranged for a car to take Anna and Mary to the rehabilitation clinic. And, once again, Anna had felt that odd sense of surprise. Through the four-hour journey her mind had built up images of a cold, locked-down concrete facility, but instead she discovered a place that rivalled some of the most expensive hotels in Dublin. Being reunited with her mother after that fateful night had seen her mother spiral into the guilty cycle that Anna was familiar with. But there was something else in her mother's eyes now—hope. A hope that Anna tried so hard not to nourish in her breast, but the air of change was upon them and it was contagious.

The clinician they met at the entrance explained that she and Mary were not to have contact for at least a month. Explained why and how this helped with Mary's recovery process and that it was vital for Mary to have the time to focus on herself. Anna would be allowed to call the centre to find out how her mother was doing and was assured that Mary would be in very good hands. Her mother hadn't even looked back as she passed through the glorious white doors to the centre.

And, now that David had appeared with Amalia's and her passports—hers had expired since she'd last used it—Dimitri had gone out. It was strange, because Anna had almost become used to his presence, even if he felt like a jailer. The weight of his constant gaze, as if he couldn't allow her out of his sight for more than five minutes, had been a pressure she hadn't realised was there. So instead of Dimitri, David sat with her in the small staff area, talking through the process and getting her to sign financial documents to do with the bed and breakfast. And once again she pushed down the inner voice that warned her she was handing over complete control of her life to Dimitri Kyriakou.

Dimitri hadn't even made it two miles from the B & B before he'd pulled over on a quiet country road. He was supposed to be in Dublin at the race series for the second leg of the Hanley Cup; he was supposed to be with the two other members of the Winners' Circle, Antonio and Danyl—men who were more family to him than any blood relation could ever be. But the invisible thread tying him to his child, to Anna...it didn't stretch that far yet. If Anna knew, or even suspected, what was about to happen, she'd run and take his daughter with her. He just couldn't take the risk.

Tomorrow they would be on his private jet and once they were in Greece, once they landed on *his* soil, the power would be all his. But tonight? Tonight, though he couldn't be there in body, there was no way in hell that he would miss the second race in the Hanley Cup.

He stared at the screen of his tablet, blocking out the sounds of the driving rain, casting the outside world in a blur.

He watched the build-up to the race live, glad that the storm hadn't yet reached Dublin. Nineteen months ago, just after his release, the Australian female jockey Mason McAulty had approached them in a London hotel with such an outrageous proposal it had momentarily silenced all three members of the Winners' Circle. She'd promised to win each of the three legs of the Hanley Cup riding one of their syndicate's horses; a feat which hadn't been achieved in twenty years.

As the camera panned up to the viewing box reserved for the Winners' Circle, Dimitri caught sight of Antonio's brooding Italian face, the grim set to his lips only softening when Emma Guilham—his PA turned fake fiancée, turned very much *real* fiancée—stepped up beside him. Dimitri had often wondered what might have happened had he not been able to convince Antonio to step back from his path to revenge and embrace the one that led him to Emma. Dimitri realised with a start that counselling his friend had been oddly prophetic. He'd certainly not imagined himself to ever consider matrimony. He'd never thought he'd need to.

The high-pitched siren sound of the race starting called his attention back to the horses on the screen. McAulty was riding a new horse from their syndicate, Devil's Advocate, a gorgeous dark brown thoroughbred. Horse and rider seemed as one as they fluidly spun round the sweeps and curves of the course.

The familiar taste of adrenaline hit the back of his throat, his heart racing as if it were he on the horse and not Mason. After a strong start she'd been pushed back into third place, but she was passing her competitor, quickly checking behind her, urging Devil's Advocate on and gaining on the second.

Dimitri, his heart in his mouth, watched from nearly seventy miles away as they rounded the last bend and looked towards the stretch of flat before the finish line. Mason was still in second place… And then, incredibly, he saw her flash the briefest of smiles and a burst of speed exploded from Devil's Advocate, at first inching his way to pass the lead horse then leaping ahead to a thundering victory.

The noise from the tablet was deafening. His phone started ringing in his pocket and as the camera panned to Antonio and Danyl in the box he saw Danyl turning away with a phone pressed against his ear.

'Did you see? We won!' his friend exclaimed the moment that Dimitri answered.

'Yes, it was a great race,' replied Dimitri, his voice controlled and belying the momentary pleasure coursing through his veins.

'Where are you?'

'Dealing with something.'

'Something? That sounds intriguing even for you, my friend.'

'It's nothing I can't handle on my own,' he said, hoping to God that he was right.

'You know we'd help. Anything.'

Dimitri felt a smile grace his lips. 'I know you'd try to move mountains, Sheikh, and think yourself capable of it, but…'

'You only need ask, Dimitri.'

'Actually there is something. I'd like you and Antonio to come to Greece.'

'You know we wouldn't miss the charity gala—'

'It's not that. It's…for my wedding.' It was the first time that Dimitri had said it out loud. He might not have told Anna yet, nor got her agreement, but he would on both counts. He didn't miss the shocked silence from the other end of the phone. And it took a lot to shock this sheikh.

'Of course we will come. When?'

'Soon. The moment I know, you'll know.'

'Does she have a name?'

'Anna. It's…complicated.'

'You once said nothing would cause you to take a wife, unless…'

Dimitri cursed his friend's quick mind.

'It happened just before I was arrested. My daughter, Amalia, she's twenty-seven months and—' he couldn't prevent the sigh from escaping his lips '—she's incredible.' For the first time, the first real time, he let it sink through his skin, into his bones, deep: he was a father.

'Congratulations, Dimitri,' his closest friend replied, the sincerity in his tone soothing some of the fears he'd had about sharing the news of his new-found family. 'I cannot wait to meet them.'

He nodded, unable to shift the thanks from his mind to his mouth, instead changing the subject. 'How's Mason doing?'

There was a barely perceptible pause before his friend replied, 'She's fine. She's planning to return to Sydney tomorrow.'

'Already? I don't think she's even left the back of the horse yet,' Dimitri said, scanning his tablet for the current footage of the racecourse.

'She's…quite determined.'

Dimitri let out a huff of air, thinking that the description could equally be applied to Anna.

'Good luck with that,' he said to Danyl as much as himself.

'Why would I need luck? Mason is nothing to me, other than our jockey.'

Dimitri wasn't so sure of that and signed off not too long later. He switched off his tablet and listened for a moment to the pounding of the rain, wondering how it was that he could still hear his own heartbeat ringing in his ears. In just a few more hours, Anna and Amalia would be on Greek soil. And then he'd have everything he'd need.

It was late by the time they eventually arrived at Dimitri's island home just off the coast of mainland Greece. Anna had spent the last hour putting a fractious, overly excited Amalia to bed and walked through the adjoining door into the considerably larger room that was to be hers. Was this what Dimitri's life was like? In Ireland one day, Greece the next?

Was it normal to feel so disorientated—so nauseous—from even such a short flight? Or was it the fact that she'd handed over the keys to her business, her security, her life to strangers and followed the father of her child to Europe?

She hadn't been prepared for the pack of paparazzi awaiting the arrival of the private jet. Oh, Dimitri had warned her of it; she just hadn't taken him seriously. Closing her eyes now, she could still see the strobe of flashbulbs in the dark. If she listened hard she could still hear the rapid-fire questions, most in Greek, but a surprising few in English.

'Is it true that you carried the heir to the Kyriakou Bank?'

'Is that the child?'

'Where have you been all these years?'

'Why did you hide...?'

Ignoring the swell of emotions in her chest, Anna focused on how her body still vibrated from the boat trip from Piraeus, the boat that Dimitri had piloted himself, standing tall and proud at the wheel, as if he were a marauding pirate rather than an international tycoon—an image that had fired her fevered imagination and brought too many memories of that night from three years ago to the surface.

The powerful speedboat thrilled Amalia as it crested waves and cut through the water as if it were air, but it had only made Anna's heart sink further. Who had the money for such a boat? But then she had seen the house Dimitri had brought her to...

The large, low-hung moon picked out sleek, modern lines that winked at her in the night, hinting at a luxury that felt surreal. She'd glimpsed an infinity pool beyond a patio that opened out to the elements, partitioned off by a plastic rail with a gate—clearly a new addition, since it stood out like a sore thumb. While it touched her that Dimitri had thought of Amalia's safety, she wondered if perhaps that was how *she* seemed, painfully and obviously out of place.

Questions burst through her mind as she wondered if she had denied her daughter by not trying hard enough to tell Dimitri about their child. When they entered his house, toys fit for a princess, still in their boxes, littered the living room and guilt swirled in her stomach. What would Amalia's life have been like if she'd had this from birth? Rather than working all hours in the day, could she have given Amalia finer clothes, better toys and, more importantly, more of herself? She'd done the best she could, she told herself sternly.

'I came to see how you were settling in.'

She closed her eyes against Dimitri's intrusion. Yes, that had been what she'd told him before disappearing into the room she had been given. But explaining that she just needed some space, from him, from his presence, seemed too much like weakness.

'My things have been put away.'

'I have people to do that.'

Yes, thought Anna. *I was one of those people until a few days ago.* But now? It was only for a few days, she told herself. Amalia would get to spend time with her father, and then she and Amalia would return to the bed and breakfast. So she'd better not get used to this. Because he had an island, and she had a bed and breakfast…because she still was *one of those people.*

'Flora?' she asked.

'Yes.'

Anna had instantly liked Dimitri's housekeeper and could tell the older woman was kind, generous and loving.

She opened her eyes, because not being able to see him only made it worse. His smell, unique and distinctly male, assaulted her senses. From the first moment she'd laid eyes on him, she'd known that she was in trouble. It was as if her body, her soul, had immediately identified him as her undoing. But she wasn't here for him, or for her. She was here for Amalia, so that her daughter could get to know her father. Nothing more.

'Thank you,' she said. Finally breaking the silence that had almost become too much.

'What for?' Dimitri sounded genuinely surprised.

'For everything?' she said, shrugging her shoulders and finally turning to take him in. He'd changed out of his cold-weather clothes, and her heart stopped. Even more devastating, he stood there in dark blue linen trousers that moulded his powerful legs and hugged his lean hips. A light blue shirt, rolled back at the sleeves, revealed firm, tanned forearms and Anna forced herself not to bite her lip.

Her fingers itching to reach out, she searched for a distraction instead. She picked up the small clay sculpture she'd wanted to take to Amalia. Even as a small baby, when the palm-sized sculpture had seemed twice as large in her little hands, Amalia had loved to hold it, grip it, even try to gnaw on it. Throughout it all, the little glazed clay piece had never broken.

She turned it in her hands, rubbing the smooth line of the larger oval shape entwined with a smaller one. She had made it years ago, and she'd never shaken the feeling that the piece had been oddly prophetic: mother and child, cast, glazed and fired long before she'd met Dimitri and started out on this path alone. Or perhaps it had reflected her and her own mother—in a maternal embrace she had long forgotten.

Dimitri frowned, noticing her busy hands.

'What's that?'

'Oh...nothing...it's...' Anna let out a huff of gentle laughter. She shrugged and held it out to him.

When he took it into his large hands, it looked dwarfed by them. She saw him studying it, turning it in his hands, relishing the feel of the smooth tempered blue glaze around the edges.

'It's beautiful,' he said simply and she felt the truth of his words to her soul.

'Thank you,' she replied, trying to press down the

surprising shock of sentiment that rose from the simple compliment.

He paused and she was intrigued as she watched the play of emotions crossing his dark features as he realised what she meant.

'You made this?'

'Yes. Just after finishing school. I'd hoped to... I wanted to go university to study art and sculpture, but...' She trailed off. Her mother, him, her daughter, the bed and breakfast...

Rather than filling the silence, Dimitri just stared at the sculpture in his hands, his thumb working over the edges of the two strangely comforting shapes. He pressed it back into her hands, and Anna was confused by the frown still marking his brow. He was hovering... and she didn't quite know why.

'Do you have our passports?' she asked. Anything to fill the strange, awkward silence. 'I wasn't given them back when we landed.'

Something dark passed over Dimitri's features, and the sick feeling that Anna had been trying to ignore rose fully in her chest.

'I have them.'

'I'd like them back.'

'I'm afraid that's not possible.'

'What do you mean?' Anna asked, her heart in her mouth.

'I'm not giving them back to you.'

'But—'

'No buts. You are now in the position that I was in only a few hours ago. You are on Greek soil, and Amalia is my child.' His eyes darkened, and the atmosphere between them became heavy with tension. 'You cannot be trusted to raise my daughter in a safe environment.

Your mother proved that quite successfully that first night. If you want any kind of rights over your child, if you wish to take her back to Ireland, then you will have to marry me.'

'Marry you?' Anna sputtered as she tried to comprehend what he was saying. 'Marry you? Why would I...?' Shock was short and sharp in her mind. Fear sliced through her like a knife. He thought she couldn't be trusted to take care of her child? All she had *ever* done was take care of Amalia. Everything, she'd done everything, sacrificed everything for her. And her mother...? Betrayal thick and fast spread through her. All her instincts were to take her daughter and run. But where to? And who would help her? She was on an island in a country she didn't speak the language of, and where she knew literally no one. How had she been so stupid? How had she allowed herself to trust this man? This man who, right now, she didn't even recognise.

Dimitri could see the fear in her eyes. He knew what it was like to feel trapped and helpless. But he couldn't allow himself to feel sorry. Not for a minute.

'I'm not reneging on my offer. I will take care of your mother, and your business, should your mother ever want to return and continue to run it. But for now you will agree to marry me, giving me legal rights over my child. I will accept nothing less. And you will not get your passports back until you do.'

'Get out!' she shouted. 'Just get out.'

CHAPTER FOUR

Dear Dimitri,
Will you ever trust me?

ANNA DIDN'T KNOW how she'd slept the night before, unless it was some kind of biological form of self-preservation. She opened her eyes to strange surroundings. Light filtered through the floor-to-ceiling windows that offered the most incredible view of sea and sky. Her head hurt and her mouth was dry. Water. She needed water. She looked over at the side table beside the bed and caught sight of the clock.

Ten thirty a.m.? Shock crashed through her, propelling her up from the bed. She slipped on the sheets and tumbled off the mattress onto the floor. Where was Amalia? Why hadn't she heard her daughter? She was in the room next door and would have heard her, *should* have heard her by now.

She ran to her daughter's room, but it was empty. Had he taken her? Had he left her in this house on her own on the island? His threats from the day before rang in her ears as she headed for the stairs that led to the ground floor.

Her bare feet slapped the cold marble floor and, as she took the stairs two at a time, she slipped and lost her breath. Her feet struck air, gravity pulling her down so hard and so fast she had no time to prepare for the biting pain that struck her leg and back. Her teeth snapped together, cutting into the soft flesh of her tongue. She thrust out her hand to try to break her fall as bone met marble and distantly she was surprised not to hear a crack.

Shouts and cries came from somewhere else in the house and when Anna opened her eyes she saw the horrified look on Flora's face, her arms reaching towards her. Arms that Anna batted away, unthinkingly, blind to all but the only face that she needed to see. Her daughter's.

She tried to stand from where she had fallen, her shaking legs barely holding her up. She reached out to the wall to try and hold herself up but couldn't understand why it kept moving further and further away.

'*Theos mou*, Anna!'

'She wasn't in her room,' she managed to get out.

'Anna, you need to sit down. Are you okay?'

She pushed past Dimitri and painfully made her way to the table where Amalia was sitting in a high chair, now red-faced and howling. Anna poured herself into a seat and her heart finally settled as she put her hand on her daughter's arm, as she could feel her daughter, could see that, although upset, her daughter was there and was okay.

Only then did the hurt and pain of her own body start to come into focus.

'I… I didn't know what you'd done with her, where she was…' Anna started shaking now, whether with fear for her child or shock from the fall she didn't know.

Dimitri had come to the table, watching her, and he was saying something that Anna couldn't quite hear.

'...okay? Are you okay?' he demanded. He'd crouched down in front of the chair, bringing him eye level with her, looking at her as if he expected something from her, and Anna resolutely ignored the concern in his eyes.

'Okay? Seriously?' An avalanche of adrenaline hit her. There were too many emotions crashing through her body to distinguish—fury, anger, shock, pain, fear. 'You don't do that! Ever! You never do that to a woman who has spent the last two years raising a child on her own. What the hell were you thinking?'

Dimitri stood there and she hated him. She weakly struck out at his chest. As her voice became louder and louder Amalia started to cry harder and harder.

'After the stunt you pulled last night...' Anna trailed off.

Dimitri turned and said something to the housekeeper, who was looking at Dimitri as if he were the devil. Flora's furious stream of Greek made Anna feel just a little bit better.

'I'm going to call the doctor,' Dimitri announced, reaching out to help her as she picked up Amalia, clearly worried that she wouldn't be strong enough. One look from Anna stopped his hand mid-air. Anna pulled her daughter onto her lap and hugged her fiercely. He had no idea how strong she could be for her daughter.

'I'm fine. I don't need a doctor.'

His pulse hadn't even begun to settle yet. When he'd seen Anna fall everything had stopped. Including his heart. It must have hurt, and it would be a miracle if she'd not broken a bone. His daughter's crying was just beginning to subside and as he looked Anna over he could see a nasty grazed bruise beginning to appear on her calf. Across her slim arms, similar red, angry welts painted her skin and guilt clenched his stomach so tight, worse than anything he'd ever experienced.

Flora came back into the room and gave him a look that could have stopped Hades in his tracks. She placed two bags of frozen vegetables on the table beside Anna, waited for Anna to meet her gaze and cocked her head in the universal body language of *are you okay?* When Anna finally replied in the affirmative, Flora nodded to herself once, rubbed Anna on the arm gently and held her hands out to take the now silent Amalia.

Dimitri watched, fascinated, as Anna handed over their daughter to his housekeeper in a way she'd never done with him. Flora took Amalia out into the garden, making sure to stay where they could both be seen by Anna.

Shame and guilt hit him hard. He'd wanted to spend some time with his daughter. He'd even wanted Anna to get some proper rest. He knew what she'd been through in the last few days, what *he'd* put her through. And look what had happened. He wanted to pace, he wanted to run, do something with all the feelings that were coursing through his body in that moment. But he didn't. Because Anna was at the table, and most likely in considerable pain. Frozen peas weren't good enough. He needed to call a doctor.

'I'm truly sorry,' he said, taking the seat next to her, still fearful that she might break into a thousand pieces.

'I don't know you,' she said as if she were talking to a stranger. 'We spent one night together nearly three years ago, and after that? You show up out of nowhere, threaten me, bring me to Greece and are presently engaged in forcing me to marry you. What did you expect me to think when I woke to find my daughter gone?'

'I…' Dimitri was struggling to find the words. Words that would somehow make her understand. 'I just wanted to spend some time with my daughter,' he said, hating the weakness, the vulnerability in his voice. 'I know you might not credit me with this, but the moment I saw our daughter, that is how I felt. Terrified that you would take her away from me. That I would never have access to her. The reason I want us to marry is so that we have *equal* rights. Not because I want sole custody. I am not so much of a monster that I would rip my daughter away from her mother.'

'As you intended when you came to my bed and breakfast and tried to take my daughter from me?'

'As I intended when I thought that the mother of my child was an alcoholic, willing to use my child to blackmail me for money, a mother who I thought—*at that time*—was a threat to my daughter's safety.' Dimitri ran a hand over his face. This wasn't getting them anywhere. 'Please, let me call a doctor for you. That was a really hard fall.'

Anna looked at him accusingly. As if the fall had been his fault. As if this whole sorry mess was his fault. And he had to acknowledge the truth of it. He followed her gaze as she turned her attention to Amalia outside with Flora.

'I didn't know what to do when she started crying,' he confessed. 'She'd been so quiet and happy until…'

'She's good with strangers because of the bed and breakfast. She's used to seeing different faces.'

Dimitri couldn't stop the anger that rose within him quickly and eagerly, eating up the space that she had given him.

'I'm not a stranger, Anna.'

'Oh,' she retorted with fake surprise. 'Have you explained that to our twenty-seven-month-old daughter? She's bright, but genetics may be a little above her age range.'

He barely restrained the growl that almost choked him.

Anna stood on still shaking legs. 'I'm going to go and take a shower.' Dimitri watched her struggle to get to her feet for barely a second before he stood and swept her into his arms. He'd done that the night they'd come together and had forgotten how impossibly light she was.

'What are you doing?'

'Am I hurting you?' he asked, before taking another step.

'No,' she said into his chest. Instead of pulling away, as he had expected her to do, she leaned into him just a little, and he ignored the shift that he felt beneath his ribcage, pushing away the swift and sudden arousal that had caught him by surprise. She must have been in considerable pain. He'd seen American football players take less hard hits than she had. That was what he told his mind, but his body seemed to have its own thoughts.

He was only wearing a thin T-shirt, the temperature in Greece considerably hotter than the cold dampness of Ireland that had seeped into his bones and not let go until he'd returned Anna and his—*their*—daughter to his home on this island. The thin material offered no protection against the feeling of her skin against his. Everything in him screamed at him to take her straight to his bed, but he wasn't that much of a bastard.

He walked back up the stairs to her room and gently slid her down the full length of his body, torturing himself, punishing himself with what he could not have, and settled her gently on the floor.

His arms were still around her and she looked up at him, the golden flecks in her large green eyes flaring. Their breaths caught at the same time. He was chest-to-chest with her, barely an inch between them. It was the closest they'd been since that night.

As she exhaled, he breathed in deeply, and he was half convinced that he could taste her on his tongue. It would take nothing at all to close the distance, to take her lips as his traitorous body had wanted to do since he'd laid eyes on her just those few days ago in Ireland. Need coursed through his veins with lightning speed, tightening muscles all over his body.

And in her eyes, he could see it too, that need, that want. Anna's breathing became light little puffs of air against his cheek, ratcheting up his arousal to impossible heights. Begging, pleading almost for him to take her.

His fingers gripped and flexed, trying to find the space where skin met skin and, instead of letting her go as his mind was shouting at him to, he pulled her closer, the inch of air between them became a centimetre and…

'I should have that shower.'

When she looked back at him some of the anger, the pain had returned to her eyes and somehow he forced his body to let her go. He straightened and walked away, out of the room, out of the house, and kept on walking until he had his body under control once more.

Anna woke for the second time that day, disorientated and—this time—in pain. Her leg throbbed and her shoulder and arm hurt from where she'd tried to break her fall. As she rose to get up from the bed Flora came in, her arms flapping and a string of Greek accompanying the glass of water and painkillers she thrust into her hands.

Anna took them and drank down the water thankfully. Slowly she tried to get up again and this time succeeded. From the time on the clock, she'd hoped that her daughter would have been put down for her nap. As she looked into the room, Amalia's soft little breaths assured her that she was okay. She made her way back down to the kitchen area, and asked Flora where Dimitri was. The older woman scowled and with a shrugging of her shoulders went back to preparing a feast fit for a king.

She was in Greece, it struck her fully for the first time. After Dimitri had told her that she wouldn't get their passports back unless she married him, it had short-circuited all thoughts about the incredible place he had brought them to.

Once again she felt adrift. She watched on helplessly as Flora pottered around the kitchen, occasionally bringing delicious things for her to try. And, as much as she wanted to be excited by the lovely food, she longed for the time when, only yesterday, she would have been able to go to her fridge and prepare lunch with the things that she and Amalia were used to eating. And then she felt ungrateful. Not to Dimitri, but to Flora, who was becoming increasingly attentive the more uncomfortable Anna was feeling.

Dimitri came in from the pool area, looking windswept and mouthwateringly handsome. He had changed from the T-shirt he'd been wearing earlier in the day and replaced it with a white linen shirt that hung slightly open at the neck showing swirls of dark hair on his chest. Just a brief foray out into the sunshine had turned his skin a golden brown, and his dark eyes, heavy with concern, poked and prodded at the memory of the moment they had shared just before her shower. His hands were jammed into the pockets of his tan trousers, and bare feet padded their way towards her.

Anna felt a blush rise to her cheeks. She would have kissed him. The man who had brought her to Greece and taken away her freedom. The man who was threatening to keep her daughter here without her permission.

'Flora, this smells delicious,' he said in English, clearly for her benefit.

Flora grunted in response, shrugging her shoulders at him, the way she had done when Anna had asked after him earlier. Anna just about raised a smile for the female solidarity in the kitchen.

'How are you feeling?' he asked her. As stubborn as she had a mind to be, she couldn't ignore him completely. Even Flora seemed to hold her breath to see if she would answer him.

'Stiff. Sore. But okay,' she said eventually and Flora turned her attention back to pulling a tray of roast tomatoes from the oven.

'Have you been awake long?'

'Not very. Flora has been taking care of me,' she said, smiling over at the housekeeper, who had taken to humming along to herself while she cooked. She pressed two glasses of cold white wine in their direction. Anna frowned. 'I'm not sure that's a good idea. I've just taken two painkillers.'

Flora hushed her and said something in Greek, which Dimitri translated. 'She says it's fine, you've only had ibuprofen. A little wine won't hurt.' He paused and smiled as Flora continued. 'She said you need to relax.'

Anna let out a huff at that. Dimitri picked up the two glasses of wine and gestured for her to follow him outside. Flora caught her casting a worried glance up at her daughter's room, and with a *'Nai, nai, nai,'* she shooed her outside after Dimitri.

The view that she walked out to was breathtaking. A pergola spread out from the sides of the house, where beautiful tendrils of pink bougainvillea picked up the last rays of the sun as it sank into the welcome arms of the horizon. To her left an infinity pool stretched out towards the sea. Only the pool tiles gave the water a slightly lighter shade of aquamarine, allowing her to pick out the edge of the patio and the start of the sea beyond it.

Dimitri pressed a glass slick with condensation into her hands. The cool drink would be a welcome relief from the heat of the day. But she couldn't quite bring herself to take a sip of the light-coloured liquid.

She needed to find the strength to ask the questions that had been crying out in her mind since the night before. Since he'd made that awful demand.

'I do want you to know your daughter. Really I do. But I don't understand why I have to marry you in order for that to happen.' She ignored the darkening of his eyes and pressed on. 'I'd be happy to amend the birth certificate, I'd be happy to discuss joint custody—'

'It's not enough,' Dimitri ground out, trying to suppress the rage he felt. Knowing that it had as much to do with the present as it did the past. 'All that legal wrangling…if something happened to me, or if something happened to *you*, I would not want my child's future to be dependent on lawyers.'

'Dimitri, nothing's going to—'

'You don't know that!' he barked, cursing himself for his loss of control. 'You cannot know that, Anna. I was only seven years old when my mother died.' His own words had shocked him. He'd had no intention of revealing his past, but now that he'd started he couldn't seem to stop. 'She'd been in a car accident on the way back from her shift as a waitress in the local restaurant. I'd come home from school, was watching TV, when the police knocked on the door.' In his mind he was back in their small one-bedroom apartment in Piraeus, the sound of the fist against wood something he'd never forget. Ever. His memories skipped over the moment of shock, of pain…and instead called to his mind the confusion…of not knowing what would happen. Of being numb to almost everything, even his grief, other than the fear of what would happen to him now. 'It took my mother's sister two months to track my father down. The father I'd never met before. A family I knew nothing about and who, aside from my father, knew nothing about me.' He'd been thrust into a world of impossible money and luxury, where the corridors echoed with arguments, and shouts, always accompanied by his name.

'So yes, Anna, we might not know each other, and yes, marriage might seem extreme to you, but you will marry me because I know that you'll do what's needed to protect our child.'

She had watched him with solemn eyes and he turned away as something horrifyingly like pity shone there.

'I know—'

He couldn't prevent the dismissive huff that fell from his lips as he turned back to her.

'I know,' she repeated, 'how important that is… My father was… My father left us before I was born.'

'Then you understand why we must marry.'

Anna shook her head sadly, the long, dark, layered tendrils of her hair framing her face and shoulders. 'Dimitri, your father wasn't married to your mother, yet he took you in. My father *was* married to my mother and it didn't stop him from leaving us.'

Dimitri frowned, remembering his investigator's report on Mary Moore. 'But there is no father named on your birth certificate.'

'It was the only way my mother could find to hurt him the way he'd hurt her. And before you ask,' she said, throwing up a hand between them as if to ward off an attack she'd known would come, 'I couldn't have put you on Amalia's birth certificate without you being there. And you were...'

'In prison.'

She nodded. 'I'd like some time to think about this. Perhaps we could talk tomorrow?'

Dimitri's jaw clenched as he remembered what tomorrow would bring.

'Sadly I don't think that will happen. Tomorrow we have a family party to go to.'

The next morning Anna found herself wearing a sumptuous silk dress that would have kept the bed and breakfast away from the bank manager for at least two more months. The dress had appeared in her room as if magicked there by fairies—though, in reality, probably just by a very well-paid assistant. She, Amalia and Dimitri had been swept up in yet another limousine from Piraeus after the short boat ride from the island, and she was now staring, wide-eyed, as the limo pulled up the drive of one of the biggest villas she had ever seen.

If Dimitri had been concerned by the press lining the street outside his family's home, he hadn't shown it. Her eyes still stung from the camera flashes, even through the tinted windows. Her ears still hurt from the yells, demands for a sound bite, even though she'd not understood the Greek words.

But all of that was pushed aside by the sheer magnitude of the Kyriakou estate. To say it was enormous would have been a gross understatement. But she couldn't help but find the ostentatiousness slightly distasteful. Calling to mind Dimitri's words from the night before, she wondered how this must have been to a little boy whose mother had worked as a waitress. The loss he must have felt at such a young age... The thought of it made her chest ache. Her heart. She couldn't even begin to imagine it.

'This is where you grew up?' she asked Dimitri, unable to hide the awe in her voice. 'After leaving your mother's?' She waited so long for an answer, she was unbuckling Amalia from her seat when she heard his reply.

'Yes.'

By the time she had retrieved Amalia from the car, Dimitri was standing beside a brand-new pushchair she had once lusted after. A pushchair that had felt a million miles out of her reach but had been obtained with less than a blink of Dimitri's dark eyes.

Amalia was struggling in her arms, refusing to get into it.

'It's okay. You're better off carrying her anyway,' Dimitri stated. 'My family will want to pass her around. I hope that you're okay with that?'

The tone of his voice issued a challenge she knew she had no hope of winning. And besides, this was why she had come to Greece, she reminded herself. To allow Amalia to get to know her family. Of course, that was before she had been threatened with blackmail to marry a man she hardly knew but was beginning to see glimpses of. So much had happened in the last twenty-four hours, it was hard to focus on that salient event. And today, she was supposed to smile and lie to that same family about what she was doing in Greece.

She hadn't even agreed to his demands yet, but sensed that he, as with all else, simply expected her compliance. Anna felt swept along by the tidal wave that was *Dimitri*. With no choice, no decision-making necessary, all she could do was hope to come out the other end able to breathe.

She followed him up the stone stairs that led to an impressive set of large doors, open on their hinges. A wall of cool air hit her the moment she stepped over the threshold, as did the sounds of a large outdoor party in full swing. They passed through a cream marble foyer, with room after room shooting off the corridor, each decorated in styles that ranged from tasteful to outrageous. But it was when they reached the doorway to the garden that her feet slowed to a stop. Even Amalia had stopped wriggling. Anna tried to prevent the gasp that fell from her lips, but clearly failed. It was like a scene from a magazine spread of the rich and famous—only she didn't recognise any of the people.

A tall, thin, attractive woman approached with a wide smile and a twinkle in her eye. She introduced herself as Nella, Dimitri's cousin, and drew them towards a circle of women and children sitting under a large white awning.

Within seconds, the whole of Dimitri's family had descended upon them, all speaking at the same time, pinching cheeks, giving hugs, and a litany of comments in both English and Greek complaining of how skinny both Anna and Amalia were. Amalia was quickly removed from her embrace and replaced with a plate of food and a glass of wine.

Even though Dimitri stood behind her, silent and brooding, as if reluctant to let them out of his sight, Anna couldn't help but smile as her daughter lapped up the attention lavished upon her, while she answered yet another question about why she didn't have red hair or pale skin. *Yes*, she was Irish, but she was *also* Vietnamese. Unsurprisingly this didn't seem to help the confusion much. *No*, she couldn't possibly eat another bite; she was almost popping out of the brand-new dress. As would Amalia, if she wasn't careful.

In a small corner of her heart, Anna had to acknowledge that everyone was lovely and welcoming. All the aunts and uncles, cousins and children were loud and brash and exactly how she'd once wanted Amalia's family to be. With a few glances at his chiselled profile she stuck to the story that Dimitri had woven from the space in between truth and fiction: that they had met three years ago and had wanted to keep their relationship quiet because of the legal problems. She voiced the lies time and time again because his family all seemed so hopeful that something good had come from such a difficult time.

Anna had never really given much thought to the ramifications of Dimitri's half-brother's actions. She hadn't even had the chance to find out what *he* felt about the whole thing. What that kind of betrayal must have done to him. That thought probed painfully at the thin layer of guilt hiding beneath the outrage she struggled with from his high-handedness.

Dimitri's cousin Nella drew her back from her thoughts by telling her that she was too pale, that she needed more sun to make her skin shine. Whether it was because she had spent years hating the very thing that had marked her as so different in Ireland, or whether it was because she liked the straight-talking Greek girl, she promised herself that she would make an effort with Nella, as something about her made her think that they could be really good friends.

Seeing Anna tucked safely under the wing of his cousin, Dimitri turned to observe the rest of the party, trying to see it with fresh eyes. Women in richly coloured clothes—turquoise, red, white, royal blue—assaulted the eyes, but not as much as the incredible amount of expensive jewellery that hung around necks, dripped from ears and fingers. Deeply tanned men in linen suits wore watches that screamed money, sunglasses that hid boredom or jealousy, or both.

He'd recognised Anna's initial look of wonder, curiosity and even a little bit of fear and with an amused laugh he didn't really feel, he realised that he must have looked like that the first time he'd come here.

'Is it hard being back here after what happened with your brother?'

He hadn't realised that Anna had stopped speaking with Nella and come to stand beside him.

'Half-brother,' Dimitri instantly replied. As if that made it more understandable. As if that made the betrayal somehow less. He hadn't wanted to admit to her that this was the first time since Manos's arrest that he'd been home. The first time that he'd seen his father and stepmother in person. It was a weakness, and he hated it.

Only his father could throw such a lavish party in the face of such an enormous family scandal and get away with it. Nowhere on the faces of the guests did he see concern or embarrassment. The only intrigue came from the rabid reporters clamouring at the gates. And he wondered if it was exactly this kind of self-delusion, this ability to ignore something so wrong, that had allowed Manos to get away with what he did.

A waiter passed with a tray of champagne flutes, and, unthinking, he took one and drank down half of the serving. When Anna politely declined he raised an eyebrow, forgetting that she couldn't see it behind the large frames of his sunglasses.

'You can drink if you want. I'll only be having this one.' He needed all his wits about him with the exchange he was about to have with his father.

'That's okay, I don't really drink.'

Of course she wouldn't. Mary Moore had probably seen to that. But then the memory of their first night together surfaced again, unbidden. The taste of whisky on her lips, unable to mask the sweetness of her mouth.

'When we met—'

'Darling,' a voice interrupted his train of thought. 'You're here,' scolded Eleni Kyriakou in English, as if they hadn't already been here some time. And 'darling'? When had she ever called him that? he wondered, not even bothering to scour his memory. He turned to take in the vivid array of patterned silks that adorned his stepmother. There was an almost forced happiness in her eyes—as if that could cover the deep discomfort they had both felt long before Manos's arrest.

'Eleni,' he acknowledged, knowing that it was better to meet her head-on than avoid her.

'And this,' she said with more warmth than he'd ever heard before, 'must be Amalia. My beautiful granddaughter.'

Dimitri scanned Anna's face for any signs that she might have been upset by the subtle snub, but her features were schooled. Good. She'd need to keep them that way if she was to survive this afternoon.

Guilty. When was he going to stop feeling guilty? *Christe mou*, perhaps he was the one who needed to toughen up. He was doing what he had to in order to claim his child. Anna had made decisions that had brought this upon herself. That was what he needed to remind himself. His only interest in her went as far as 'I do', and nothing further.

Before he could stop her, Eleni was reaching out to take Amalia from Anna's hands and he saw the brief flash of something pass across Anna's eyes, but Eleni was so focused on their child she missed it. Assuring himself once more that Anna would be just fine, he extricated himself from the situation and went in search of Agapetos Kyriakou, his father.

Swift, powerful steps took him back into the house that held such painful memories. He'd been putting off this confrontation for as long as possible, but now… it couldn't be avoided. He wasn't surprised to find his father in the study, but he *was* surprised to hear his lawyer David's clipped British accent coming from the speaker phone.

'I refuse to discuss this without my client present.'

'I'm here,' Dimitri ground out, stepping into the room, clearly surprising the two men attempting to go behind his back. 'What is going on?'

His father at least had the grace to look discomfited, which was about as far as Agapetos had ever managed in his presence. Nikos, his father's lawyer, launched into a fast-paced litany of Dimitri's errors, but he interrupted.

'English, please. David doesn't speak Greek.'

'And that is your fault for hiring an English lawyer,' Nikos bit back in English, his father staying silent for once.

'What did he say?' David asked through the phone's speaker.

'Nikos was calling me seven shades of a fool for not having a DNA test done before bringing Anna and Amalia here,' Dimitri explained, the fury he felt making his tone harsh. 'I will make this clear once and for all. I would *never* allow my child to grow up knowing that her place with me was determined only by a positive test. Or growing up thinking that she's only worth her DNA.'

'Then you *are* a fool,' stated Nikos.

'She is my daughter. I know it. And, as her father, it's my job to protect her from pain. Whether financial *or* emotional.'

Nikos looked as if he was about to reply, when his father cut him off.

'If my son says that she is his, then she is his.'

It was as if a bucket of ice-cold water had been thrown over him. The hairs rose on his arms, and breath locked in his lungs. Never, *ever* had his father shown such confidence in him before. He stared at Agapetos, though the older man refused to meet his gaze, whether from discomfort at the emotional statement, or… Dimitri didn't know what else it could have been. His entire life he'd been waiting, hoping for a sign of kindness, affection, even just support from his father, and it happened now? Did he feel guilty over Manos's actions?

'Leave us,' Agapetos ordered his lawyer. There was a brief battle of wills, but eventually Nikos left the room, leaving him alone with his father. Feeling as if the ground had shifted beneath him, Dimitri waited.

'You will marry her?'

'I'm doing everything in my power to ensure that happens.'

'Good. That is good.'

Dimitri frowned. He'd expected his father to say the words Nikos had uttered, not this. Not his desire to see him married with a child.

'I'd...' His father took a deep breath and pressed on. 'I'd like to see this as a new beginning. A fresh start... for all of us. Anna and Amalia included. I'm not saying it will be easy, but I'd like to try.'

Dimitri could only nod, as his father swept an arm over his shoulder the way he had seen him do with Manos time and time again.

'Then I'd like, very much, to see my granddaughter.'

Anna watched the two men leave the room from the shadowed enclave beside the study. She had gone in search of Dimitri after feeling his absence too long and had paused the moment she'd heard David's voice on the phone asking what was being said.

She had listened, her heart in her mouth at Dimitri's simple words, his resolute defiance of the man he called Nikos... They had struck her as something incredible. There was so much loaded into Dimitri's response, Anna struggled to unpick it. His love for his child and the trust he had in her, trust that she had taken for granted. He'd asked her only once if Amalia was his daughter. That was all it had taken.

She wanted that for Amalia. A father who would care for her, protect her, stand up for her. Again, the bittersweet slice of pain each time Dimitri said or did something good reminded her of the lack that she had grown up with. She knew how easy it was for a father to turn away from his child, to fail in that one duty, even to replace that child with another family...

As Dimitri's wife, that wouldn't happen. As Dimitri's wife, she would be ensuring that her daughter was protected, cared for and loved even. She might not be able to expect those things for herself, but she *would* secure them for her daughter. What she would, however, secure for herself was protection. For her heart.

CHAPTER FIVE

Dear Dimitri,
Today I made a deal with the devil.

DIMITRI PACED THE length of the patio, moonlight his only companion as Anna settled their daughter in her bedroom. He knew that she had something on her mind, having been quiet the entire journey back from his father's house. And that suited him fine. He was still reeling from his father's behaviour. He had cooed over his grandchild in a way Dimitri never imagined Agapetos had done with either him or Manos. Was it possible that they could have the fresh start his father had promised? Could he forgive the hurts of the past? Could he push away the difficult memories and feelings that he associated with his father, his childhood?

Anna came out onto the patio and hovered behind a seat at the large handcrafted table he'd bought from one of the local tradesmen. He watched as she ran her fingers over the fine grain of the wood, the moonlight glinting off the slight curls in her long, dark hair.

'I...' She paused, seeming to struggle over what she had to say. She pressed on again. 'I will marry you.'

It was not what he'd expected. In fact, he had returned to the house, ready to counter her objection to marrying him with more threats and more anger. So it took Dimitri a moment to catch up with the elation that was coursing through his body.

'But I have a few conditions.'

This was a different Anna to the one who had sat in the small staff area of her B & B, the one who couldn't meet his eyes. This Anna was the Anna he'd met that night three years before. Calm, assessing, in control. As if muscle memory moved within him, the taste of arousal pierced his tongue. She was glorious again. He wasn't concerned about her conditions, but he would let her voice them. Negotiation was about give and take. But what she didn't yet know was that Dimitri intended to take everything that he wanted.

'We need to agree to stop all the games. All the blackmail.'

'*Nai*—yes. This can be done.'

'I'll sign a prenup. Whatever you need. But I want to move forward from a place of equality. You have—' she paused infinitesimally '—all the power. And that's not okay. I am Amalia's mother. If we marry, you will never have sole custody of my child.'

'Understood. And agreed.'

'If the current caretakers of the bed and breakfast prove themselves, and if they are happy to do so, they can continue in my absence until we hear what my mother would like to do with the business. Until then, Amalia and I will stay here in Greece.'

'Good.'

'I want to be able to visit Ireland and spend time there each year.'

'Absolutely. It's important that all aspects of her heritage are available to her. I will have brochures of possible homes here by the morning.'

'I want to learn Greek,' she said, taking him by surprise. 'I won't be cut out from conversations between you and my daughter. This marriage will only work if we communicate openly.'

'We will find someone right away.' Why was she agreeing so suddenly? Where was the catch?

'And…' Was that a blush he could see paint her cheeks? 'And I will not be sharing a bed with you.'

'What?'

'This will be a marriage on paper, one with legal rights, but I will not share your bed.'

'You expect me to live like a monk, and you a nun?' he demanded, his body crying out to reject her preposterous stipulation.

'I have very few expectations of you, Dimitri. I just don't want to find out about it. The possibility of it is one thing, but knowing it? I'd rather not.'

That cut him deeply. He had never made claims of sainthood and certainly had his fair share of experience, but he would never treat his wife the way his father had treated either his stepmother or his own mother.

'Hear me now, Anna. I would never disrespect my wife, or the mother of my child in that way. Ever.' His words were binding, the promise ringing in his own ears. If Anna was taken aback by the vehemence in his tone, Dimitri didn't see it. 'But if you think this marriage will be left outside the bedroom, you are very much mistaken.'

He wanted, so much, to go to her, to lean into the area of heat surrounding her body. To relish it. But he didn't. He left the table between them, allowed her the space and clarity to fully understand his words. But despite the distance, desire was thick on the air around them and the little flare of the pulse at her neck told him all he needed to know.

'I won't sleep with you,' she whispered, her voice trembling as she struggled to hide her attraction to him.

'You would deny yourself the pleasure we shared? I still remember the cries of your ecstasy as you came apart in my arms. As you begged me for more. Deeper, harder, again and again. The way your eyes opened as I met every single one of your requests.'

The way her eyes opened now, wide but unseeing, lost in the memory his words had conjured, her sharp inhale as her body swayed towards him. His own arousal was painfully hard, pressing against the material of his trousers, and the sight of her own desire, the way her nipples had hardened, peaked against the thin silk of her dress, was the only satisfaction he had at that moment.

'Tell me, Anna… Do *you* remember?'

She inwardly cursed as a shaky breath left her lungs, feeling it was as much an answer as he needed. *Of course* she remembered. His simple words had plunged her into an arousal that she felt in every single part of her body. The present clashed with the past as she felt his caress on her skin, relished the memory of him within her, filling her, completing her in a way she had never imagined. She felt now her skin flush, her erratic heartbeat flutter, even though he was still standing on the other side of the table. She hated that her body made a mockery of her words. Betraying her in the most fundamental way.

Yes, she wanted to cry. She *did* remember. She *did* want to reach out, to touch him, feel the weight of his punishing kisses, the way that only he made her body come alive. But it was the greater risk, the one to her heart, that she was truly fearful of. And *that* was why she couldn't let herself be with him. She couldn't let him in at all. Because if she did, she wasn't sure that she would survive it.

'I will make you this promise, Anna.' His voice called to her as she struggled with the intoxicating feelings of her desire. 'I will not seduce you with fine words and wine, I will not come to your door. Not once. And I will *not* touch you against your will.'

Anna jerked a breath of air into her lungs—had she done it? Had she got him to agree to her condition?

'I won't have to.' Dimitri pulled his head back, just enough to meet her eyes. '*You* will come to me. You will beg *me* to touch you. To take you as I did that night, over and over again. You will plead with me to pleasure you, to find the release that only I have given you. And I will, Anna. I assure you that I will. But *you* will be the one to come to *me*.'

Weeks slipped through Anna's fingers like sand. She had settled into a strange routine with Dimitri, who spent his mornings with her and Amalia at breakfast, and returned after the sun had set. She had learned to both long for and resent those hours. He hovered in the background as if he were some dark angel, waiting for her to make a mistake. He was there with her when her daughter woke in the night, watching her soothe Amalia's tears. He shared Anna's joy as Amalia would race along the patio, holding herself up at the plastic railing fencing off the swimming pool.

Occasionally he would surprise her with a visit in the afternoon, a brief swim with Amalia as she splashed and giggled in the water. But when Amalia was asleep he was there, waiting for Anna to come to him. She resented the sense of satisfaction she felt coming off him in waves whenever he was near, as if he smugly knew more about herself, her body, than she did.

Each night she would lie awake, listening to the quiet house, imagining him in his bed, the sound of his breathing, the slip-slide of his skin against his sheets. It was a slow torture as she fell into fevered dreams of his body, his touch, his caress, the feel of him moving deep within her. And each morning she woke more exhausted than the day before. He had stayed true to his promise. He had not touched her, nor come to her, but she felt as if she was being watched, hunted, slowly entrapped by her own desires.

Anna put the phone back in its cradle. Her mother's therapist had informed her that Mary had requested to stay on yet another month, refusing contact with Anna even though she was entitled to that now. It hurt and it surprised her to find that her mother still had access to parts of her heart that would cause such pain.

But she wanted to let her mother know about her marriage personally, rather than reading about it in the headlines of a newspaper. The therapist had agreed to pass on a letter, should Mary Moore feel up to reading it.

That she wouldn't be at the wedding...well. Anna still couldn't quite tell how she felt about it. She thought of the wedding more in an abstract way, as if it was something simply to be done. An event to be planned, rather than a marriage or a future way of life.

But as she began the letter, her hand automatically began to spell out Dimitri's name...and she thought of the hundreds of pages she had written to him over the years, telling him of something Amalia had done, telling him of the joys and the tears she had shed, Amalia's first bath, first steps, first words, first smile, second teeth and second words, second falls and third. To tell him of the moment she had truly realised that she was a mother. The well of love that had almost brought her to her knees. All of that she had wanted to share with the father of her child. But the man she was marrying? He was not the same man she had written to over the last few years. She needed to be realistic. Now, more than ever, was not the time for fantasies and could-have-beens.

Pushing thoughts aside, she focused on the letter in front of her. Anna's hands shook a little as she committed the words to the page.

Dear Ma,
I'm getting married... I have decided to stay in Greece. The lovely couple running the bed and breakfast are taking good care of it for us. You'd like them, Ma.

I wish you could see Dimitri's house. It's incredible. One day I hope that you will. Amalia is getting big! She's outgrown almost all of the clothes I brought with us.

And I've been learning a little Greek. Flora, Dimitri's housekeeper, has been teaching me a phrase a day, along with some of the most delicious recipes...

Dimitri paced the length of his Athens office. How was it that, on the cusp of achieving everything he had wanted, he suddenly felt trapped? Trapped by the marriage he had brought upon himself. He cursed out loud into the empty room, the words bouncing off the sleek chrome and dark wood that surrounded him. When he had been in prison, he had longed to come back to his office. The place where he was in control. He had longed to stand once again in his house, looking out on to the open sea, but somehow he couldn't shake the feeling that he had swapped one cage for another.

He rubbed at his ring finger, the phantom itch that had started the moment that Anna had agreed to his proposal. What did he know about marriage? His own father had been a bastard and had abandoned his mother, the young waitress he had ruthlessly seduced, then discarded, just like he had his son. Even if he had softened at the party just weeks ago, Dimitri couldn't ignore the way he had been his entire life until that point. Agapetos's own marriage had been based solely on a business deal, rather than any finer feelings, and it had kept his entire family in a state of misery throughout Dimitri's life. Was that what would become of him and Anna? Would she come to resent him for forcing this upon them? Would *he*?

He was no better off than when he was stuck in that prison, where testosterone mixed with anger, impotence and helplessness. Where desperation made men weak, and bullies strong. Where fear was a feral animal stalking the hallways, beaten, bruised and bloodied.

His only release was the short moments he would steal with his daughter. Her laughter was a panacea to the chaotic thoughts that filtered through his mind almost constantly. Whether it was breakfast, where Amalia would rain down an Armageddon of culinary destruction, or the evenings, where he would watch over Anna as she soothed her daughter's night-time tears, he still felt like an outsider. But the thing that had surprised

him the most was the fear of somehow causing damage
to the small life they had created together.

He couldn't turn to Agapetos, couldn't trust the fragile bond that had begun to form with his offering of
peace. He couldn't turn to Antonio and Danyl, who
hadn't the first clue of parenting. Antonio was busy
making plans for his wedding to Emma. Danyl had
the weight of an entire country on his shoulders, and
Dimitri was reluctant to add to that. No. To all intents
and purposes, Dimitri was alone in this. And that was
the only real way he knew how to be. He had long since
learned that he couldn't rely on others to help bear his
burden. So instead, he became a man on the verge of
the perfect marriage to the mother of his child. That was
the image he needed to maintain, and perhaps if he told
himself that enough times he might start believing it.

'Mr Kyriakou?' The intercom buzzed with his new
assistant's voice. 'The Sheikh of Ter'harn and Antonio
Arcuri are here to see you.'

Before she had even finished speaking, Danyl had
stormed into his office, laden with two bottles of dark
amber liquid in each hand, Antonio swiftly following
behind.

'You didn't think you could get married and miss
out on the stag, did you?'

The doorbell rang just as Anna put the letter to her
mother in an envelope. Flora had offered to post it for
her, Anna's limited Greek most definitely *not* up for
ensuring its secure delivery. The sound of voices from
the hallway and an unaccountably flustered Flora surprised her. Frowning, Anna rounded the corner to see
Dimitri's stepmother, Eleni, in the doorway, with what
looked like an army of people and clothes behind her.

'Mrs Kyriakou?' asked Anna, unaware of her plans to visit.

'Ms Moore,' she said, still failing to make eye contact as she brushed a piece of imaginary lint from her chic designer suit.

'Anna, please call me Anna' was all she could reply as Eleni Kyriakou pushed her way into the house that suddenly felt a million times smaller as it filled with uniformed people dragging racks of covered dresses into the open-plan living area.

'Anna,' Eleni finally relented. If there was a superior 'sniff' to be heard, Anna was sure it was covered by the cacophony of voices that filled the room.

Amalia stirred in her high chair at the table, craning her neck to take in what new exciting delights had surrounded her. In an instant, all the formidable uniformed minions turned into gushing women, pinching her cheeks and thighs and exclaiming happily in Greek. Flora descended, shooing them away, retrieving Amalia and sending Anna a look that told her categorically that she wasn't paid enough to deal with Eleni Kyriakou.

Eleni looked longingly after her granddaughter and Anna felt a little burst of pity for the older woman. Until she turned her assessing gaze on Anna.

'You are in need of a dress, I believe,' the older woman stated. Anna took a closer inspection of the covered garments on the racks. Wedding dresses.

It wasn't as if Anna had ever really imagined her wedding day, what she would be wearing, or how— even—she would be choosing the dress, but it had never involved the overbearing stepmother of Dimitri Kyriakou. In fact, Anna had thought that perhaps she might spend the day in Athens and pick something from a retail store. But the names in gilt lettering on the covers of these dresses were some of the most expensive designers she had ever heard of. And then there were names of designers she hadn't heard of, whose clothes were guaranteed to be priceless.

Within seconds she was being manhandled out of her light clothes, and standing before her soon-to-be mother-in-law in little more than her underwear. Anna knew that her body had regained her pre-baby figure fairly easily after a diet of sleepless nights and hard working hours at the bed and breakfast, but still she seemed only just to pass muster.

The dispassionate assessment of her physique made her feel like a mannequin, as gown after gown was relieved of its covering. The sheer number of dresses and styles almost overwhelmed her, although some called for instant dismissal, especially the one that made her think of Little Bo Peep. Taffeta was discarded as impossible, tulle too heavy for the heat and, although Anna was surprised to find herself quite liking the shorter, nineteen-fifties-style skirt, Eleni Kyriakou dismissed it with a flick of her red nail-polished finger. Finally one of the younger stylists timidly brought forward her offering while the others were distracted. She cast one quick glance in their direction, before pressing it into Anna's hands and shooing her off behind the screen that had been erected in the living room for what little was left of her modesty.

As her fingers reached out to the exquisite lace detail of the plunging bodice, a thread of excitement wound through her. The skirt was long, and pure oyster-coloured silk, flaring out into a seamless fishtail. Exquisite lace detail was sewn onto the barely visible material of sleeves that would cover her arms down to her wrists. Anna almost groaned out loud when she saw the hundreds of little buttons at the back but was pleasantly surprised to find a concealed zip hidden beneath them. She stepped into the cool, silky skirt and lifted the bodice over her breasts, realising that she'd have to discard her bra.

As she pulled the zip, she cast a glance at her reflection in the window—the nearest mirror was in the hallway. The bodice lay flat against her stomach, and the plunging neckline revealed enough to be sexy but hid enough to be respectable. Her sun-bronzed skin glowed against the oyster colour of the silk. She swept her hair up in a band and a spark of excitement ignited within her. *This* was the one. She knew it. She could feel the rightness of it settle about her as the silk skirts swirled about her bare feet.

Tentatively she stepped out from behind the screen, just in time to see Flora, returning to the house with Amalia, stop dead in her tracks. All conversation in the room halted midsentence. For a second Anna worried that she'd made a huge mistake, until everyone started talking at once, oohing and aahing after the gown.

Anna felt a smile spread over her mouth, and even Eleni appeared to be satisfied.

After the assistants had removed all the dresses from Dimitri's house and Anna was back in her own clothes, she sat at the table to have coffee with Flora and Eleni. Anna had expected Eleni to leave with the magic she'd summoned that morning, but she hadn't.

'Your mother?' Eleni asked her, slightly uncomfortably. 'She is not able to come?'

'No, she's…she's having medical treatment.'

'And your friends?'

Anna didn't really want to explain how she couldn't have asked the few friends that had survived her job and her child to pay for the extraordinarily expensive air fare to Greece in the summer months. Nor how she would have explained to them the events of the last few weeks.

Eleni nodded as if she somehow understood. 'Nella, Dimitri's cousin, told me that the English have a tradition in weddings. I'm not sure if it's the same for Ireland...' Anna was too busy wondering when her English had got so good to try to understand where this was going. Eleni looked to Flora. It was the first time that Anna had seen her anything less than poised and, well, rude, frankly.

'Something old, something borrowed...' said Eleni, producing the most exquisite pearl-encrusted bracelet. The colour of the pearls matched her dress perfectly, and Anna felt the stir of emotion within her breast.

'New and blue,' Flora said, less articulately, placing a beautiful blue lacy garter beside the pearls.

Anna was overcome in an instant. She felt tears pressing against her eyes. It was a silly tradition, one she hadn't even given a second thought to, but that these two women had made such an effort to make it happen... She felt so grateful to Nella for thinking of such a thing, and somehow managing to convince Eleni to be part of it. Around the table sat three generations of women, all brought together by Dimitri, and Anna, who had not once felt that kind of female solidarity or emotional support before, was so very touched.

'Not all weddings...start the same way,' Eleni said, still not quite able to make eye contact with her. 'But Dimitri, he is a good man. He will care for you and your child.' Her words soothed Anna's unspoken fears, just a little, and made Anna wonder at Eleni's own marriage. 'We do what we have to, for our children, *nai*?'

Eleni's burst of honesty made Anna bold. 'Does Dimitri know that you think he is a good man?'

Eleni paused before continuing, clearly wondering how much to reveal of their relationship.

'Dimitri's childhood with us was…not easy. His father is…*not* easy,' she said honestly. 'It may have been easier for Dimitri to see me as…as…' she seemed to be struggling, whether with the English language, or something far harder '…very different to his own mother. And when he came to us I was worried about my own son, Manos. And now with what has happened…'

Flora's tutting interrupted Eleni, who shot a dark look at the older woman. No matter what her son had done, and how he had done it, Eleni was still his mother. Anna knew that bond. Knew what she would do for her daughter.

'But there is a goodness in Dimitri. I know that.'

Anna could only hope that Eleni was right. Because she was about to commit her life and her daughter to Dimitri Kyriakou.

CHAPTER SIX

Dear Dimitri,
Today I wore your ring.

THE CHURCH WHERE they were to be married was like
something out of a film. It was on a small jut of land
reaching out to the sea, accessible only during low tide.
The small building's roughly hewn hunks of blondstone
melted into the sand behind it and were surrounded by
sea and sky.

The late afternoon sun still providing a pure golden
light and heat, the way it never did in Ireland, made
Anna feel as if it were something from a dream rather
than the day that she committed her life to Dimitri.

Because the church was so small and the number of
guests so large, the wedding was held outside, in front
of the old building. A large erected awning provided
guests with shelter from the blaze of the sun. Rows and
rows of chairs had been placed in the courtyard, and
numerous pots of bay trees, shaped small and round,
bordered the aisle. White silk bows had been tied to
the backs of chairs, and Anna was grateful to Eleni for
all the work she'd put into the wedding. Since the day
she had brought the wedding dresses to the house, the
two women had found a balance. Eleni was still for-

midable and not a woman to be crossed, but Anna had found respect there.

Anna hovered, alone, just out of view from the guests and the man who stood waiting at the top of the aisle. She felt an ache in her chest. There was no father to walk her down the aisle. No friends eagerly waiting to see her exchange rings, no family to witness her join herself to another person before guests, the priest, the sun and sky. She was so surprised to find *want* in her breast. The want that made her ache and tears press against the backs of her eyes. The want that made her wish so very much that she was doing this for love. That the man who would place his ring, his ownership, on her truly loved her. She had seen so many different versions of Dimitri over the last few weeks: the demanding, uncompromising man; the vengeful angel; the father to her child…the seducer, full of the dark promises he'd made her that night she'd agreed to be his wife.

She peered around the pillar that had been her protection until now, looking up at the large, sprawling family, all talking away and creating more noise than she could have expected for such a solemn event. Seated at the front, beside Eleni and her husband, was Flora with Amalia, happily babbling away with the older woman.

This was why she was marrying Dimitri. Not because of flowery words and promises she would neither have trusted, nor believed. Happy-ever-afters were for other people. Anna was making a life for her daughter, providing her and even her own mother with a security that she was simply not capable of by herself. This was what forced her to put one foot in front of the other as she began the long walk down the aisle to the man she would spend the rest of her life with.

* * *

As Dimitri saw Anna walk towards him, something stirred within his chest. She looked...alone. She had no one to walk with her, no one amongst the guests. Had he done that to her? Guilt poked and prodded painfully somewhere deep within him. She had no one to protect her...protect her from him. He had told himself time and time again why he was doing this, why *she* had forced him to do this.

But could he blame her? Her actions and decisions had been in defence of their child. Protecting her from a man who had been imprisoned, and was then said to have fathered a whole brood of illegitimates across the globe. Would he have not chosen to cut a person like that from his daughter's life? Within his own realisation, he could only hope that one day she too might understand what had brought them to the altar.

Now, seeing her make slow and steady progress towards him, he made a silent vow. The moment his ring was on her finger, she would be his to protect, just as he protected their daughter. The weight of that silent promise was heavier than anything he'd ever experienced. And for a moment he thought he'd felt it settle about his shoulders like a physical thing. Until he realised that it was Danyl, his best man, standing beside Antonio, his other best man, having thrown an arm about his shoulder.

'She is a thing of beauty, my friend.'

Yes, Dimitri acknowledged, she really was. The low neckline of the dress, exposing the deep tan of her skin, teased and hinted at a sensual promise that she had yet to offer him. The swirls of lace detail covering her chest and arms drew his gaze across her upper body, and the soft silk skirts kicked out each time she took a step closer to him. Desire pooled low in his stomach. The dress hugged every curve of her body, clinging tightly to her chest and arms, but the low neckline made his hand itch to slip beneath the fabric and feel the softness of her breast. She was the last woman he had touched, and she would now be the last woman he would ever touch. And he *would* touch her. He would have her. But *only* when she came to him.

The light caught on the tiny diamond earrings in her ears, making them sparkle in the setting sun. That was how he had imagined her during those dark days in prison, the light that pierced the darkness around him, the one memory he had clutched to him. If he had imagined her wearing a white dress, about to take his ring, he had purposefully removed the thought from his mind the day he'd thought she'd used him for money.

As she drew level with him he caught a momentary look of uncertainty, of doubt, but it was replaced with determination in a heartbeat. He knew the strength of will required to force away demons, and that called to him.

As the priest began, Anna turned to Dimitri, hoping that her eyes expressed the thanks she felt at the service being conducted in English. But as the words wrapped around her heart, she felt full of a kind of sadness rather than joy. Dimitri's voice rang with such sincerity as he promised to love her, to honour her above all else, and she wondered whether that could ever be true.

Lost amongst the words and her feelings, she almost missed the moment when the priest pronounced them man and wife. Dimitri turned then, giving her one last breath before his head lowered to hers and his lips claimed her for eternity.

The kiss was everything, overpowering and all-consuming. His lips unlocked hers, and the moment she felt his tongue against hers she was lost. Her arms came up around his neck of their own volition, clinging to him as if he were her only lifeline. Desire drenched her from head to foot as he brought her body against the hard muscles of his chest, pressing her breasts against his steel torso. She felt his thighs against hers, through the thin material of the silk skirts, and the evidence of his own desire pressed between her hips, shocking her, making her lose her breath to his mouth, the kiss, to him.

She was oblivious to everything but Dimitri...until the first spattering of something hit her back and caught in her hair. Then another wave of the tiny little bullets pelted her arms and back again. That was when she heard the cries from the guests and looked up to find rice caught in Dimitri's thick, dark curls.

'Did no one warn you?' he asked, his eyes serious, belying his playful tone.

For a second she thought 'no'. No one had warned her about such a kiss. The kind that battered away the walls around her heart, the kind that destroyed her promises not to share his bed.

And then she realised he meant the rice. She'd helped Flora, Eleni, Nella and many more female family members fill hundreds of little bags full of rice rather than confetti. She hadn't expected them all to be used, but the rice was working its way under the lace, catching in her hair as much as Dimitri's. His dark, midnight-blue suit had little white dustings from where the rice had been slung at him.

In a second she was caught up by the wave of emotions coming from the guests—the joy and happiness was palpable on the air. Through the noise she heard Amalia squealing with delight and turned to see her scooping awkward fistfuls of rice and raining them down on Flora's skirts. The laugh she couldn't prevent fell from lips still bruised from Dimitri's kiss, and she realised that she was still encased in his arms.

'That's the first time I've heard you laugh since that night three years ago, *agapi mou*,' he said for her ears only. The laughter subsided and she looked at him with sombre eyes, until another wave of rice hit them yet again, and Dimitri raised his arms about her as if to protect her from the onslaught. That one small action touched Anna more than she could ever have imagined, soothing some of the ache that lay in her heart.

The chaos from the dance area of the incredible hotel holding the reception was something to behold. Dimitri looked on as Antonio stood with his phone pressed to his ear, presumably whispering sweet nothings down the phone to his fiancée, who had been unable to make the trip. Danyl looked bored as he entertained yet another hopeful candidate for the position of his wife. The dark-haired woman beside him looked more interested in Dimitri's cousin than Danyl, he thought ruefully.

The place beside Dimitri at the head of the table was empty, his father having made his excuses to leave almost the moment dessert had been served. Anna was just bidding his stepmother a surprisingly fond farewell, Eleni's fingers brushing over the pearl bracelet Anna was wearing, a smile in his stepmother's eyes Dimitri had never seen before. Eleni caught his gaze just before she left, nodding at him in a way that poked at something in his chest.

All the guests seemed to be having a wonderful time.

Flora was at her table with the now sleeping Amalia resting against her shoulder. It reminded him that Anna had no one for her here and prompted his question to her.

'Would you have wanted your mother to be here? Or, your…?' He trailed off, realising how crass it was to bring up her father.

Anna turned to him as surprise was replaced by the heavy sigh that escaped her lips. 'My mother would have probably made a scene, and… I made my peace with my father's absence three years ago.'

He frowned at the timing, but her words provoked a different thought.

'Is that why you didn't try harder to tell me about Amalia?' He knew his angry words were wrong the moment they left his lips. Hurt slashed her cheeks pink.

'I thought we put all this behind us when I agreed to marry you. If not—'

'No. I'm sorry. I shouldn't have said that,' he admitted. 'Please, we were talking about your father…'

'The night we met, I had just come back from trying to find him.'

The woman he had met that night in Ireland had been… He'd thought she was resolved, absolutely sure of herself. Had he got it wrong? Had that night been one in which he'd seen what *he* wanted to see, rather than the truth? Had the woman he'd sought to exorcise his own demons been already shattered by those of her own? A woman defined by *his* needs rather than hers? He was almost afraid to find out.

'About three weeks before we met, I'd found some letters that were kept in the attic I was hoping to renovate for the bed and breakfast. All had been returned to the sender. Recognising my mother's handwriting, and the first name on the envelope, I realised the letters must have been written by my mother to my father.'

'Did you read any of them?'

Anna frowned, taking a sip of water from the glass in front of her before answering. 'I didn't feel that I could. These were my mother's letters. If they were full of hate and anger, I didn't *want* to read them. If they were full of love and need, I *couldn't* read them. But I had my father's full name and address. I used them to find that my father owned a small restaurant in London. It had recently won an award, which was why it was so easy to find.'

Her eyes had lost some of their sparkle, and she gazed over his shoulder as if seeing some imaginary scene.

'Without telling Ma, I booked myself a flight to London, using some of the savings my grandmother had left me—those Ma hadn't been able to drink away,' she explained sadly.

'It didn't go well?' Dimitri asked, pulling her back to the present.

'I went there believing that if he saw me there would be some kind of innate biological recognition. In my head, he would start to cry, embrace me, take me back to his home, perhaps even find a way to help me to help Ma.'

The pain in her voice as she expressed such simple hopes from her father cut through him like a knife. Anna looked out, seemingly unseeing of the guests, of the night sky that had descended to cover the deep sea beyond.

'He was busy. The restaurant was packed full of people, and the staff, clearly members of his family—his *new* family—were run off their feet. He glanced at me briefly, not really taking me in. Just trying to find some-where out of the way to put a single diner. The ease he had with the people around me, his distraction... I didn't feel able to speak to him. I just... I sat where he directed me to sit and watched them together. Laughing, joking, shouting even, as someone got an order wrong from the kitchen. But I was on the outside looking in. I didn't even order any food. They'd forgotten about me in the busyness of the restaurant and I just...slipped away.

'By the time I got back to Ireland, my mother had convinced herself that I wasn't coming back and had drunk her way through most of the bar. That was why I was wearing her shirt the night you came to the bed and breakfast. I wasn't supposed to be working, but she was in such a state that I couldn't have let her anywhere near the guests. I'd just welcomed the last couple when you arrived on the doorstep. I nearly didn't let you in,' she added ruefully.

He looked at her, unable to voice the fear that he'd taken advantage of her that night, but he didn't have to. Yet again, she read his thoughts as if he'd said them out loud.

'Don't look at me like that. I knew what I was doing that night. It was reckless, and foolish, but I wanted it. You. That night, I wanted you.'

That night. Not now. But in that moment he could tell that they were both imagining what their lives might have been like had she not let him in. But Anna seemed to skip over the thought quickly.

'I feel so stupid for thinking that my father might have been able to recognise me on sight. I suppose that it's a childish fantasy,' she said, and because she'd turned her head away he nearly missed the question that fell from her lips. 'Is that how you felt when you first saw Amalia?'

Dimitri could tell that she was both hopeful and fearful of his answer. And he wasn't sure how to reply. Saying yes would acquit him in her eyes but would damn her father. And he couldn't bring himself to do such a thing on their wedding day.

But it was too late. She'd seen it in his eyes, he could tell.

'I'm pleased you had that. It's an incredible moment when you see your child, hold her for the first time, recognise that burst of love that tells you that you would do anything, *anything* to protect her. That your world has irrevocably changed and there is this little person in the centre of it all. That the purpose of your life is now them.'

'Do you understand, then,' he pressed on, 'why I did what I did? Why we needed to marry?'

'I understand it,' she admitted reluctantly. 'But I will never forgive you for doing it the way you did.'

The cool night air bit into her arms as the boat took them back from the hotel on the mainland to Dimitri's island home. Little lights marked the jetty for the boat and the wind loosened tendrils of hair about Anna's face, causing her to hold them back so she could see her footing.

Flora bid them goodnight, but she was still holding Amalia in her arms as she made her way back to her small home at the foot of the hills beneath the sprawling mansion that was to be their home.

'Where is Flora taking Amalia?' Anna asked Dimitri, a sense of dread pooling in her stomach.

'Back to hers for the night. All the bedding and things that Amalia will need was moved this morning.'

Fury cut through her. 'Without consulting me? You arranged for my daughter—'

'*Our* daughter,' he cut sternly into her sentence.

'To spend the night somewhere else, without my knowledge?'

He stopped in his tracks and turned back to her, standing steady on the wooden jetty, being gently rocked as the boat made its way back to the mainland shore. 'What outrages you more? That you weren't consulted on the whereabouts of your daughter, or that you no longer have a barrier to stop you from acting on your desires?'

His taunt was as cruel as it was accurate.

'Don't change the subject. You failed to consult me on where our child would spend the night. You can't do that.'

'And how,' he said, running a hand over a face that suddenly seemed exhausted, 'do you think I felt, about all the decisions you kept from me?'

'But this is new for you!' she cried into the night. 'I've been doing everything on my own, every day, because you went to prison, because your assistant led me to believe that there were hordes of women out there like me.'

She gulped in a breath of cool air and that was all the time he needed to undo her completely.

'There is no one out there like you.'

'Because I'm the mother of your child?' she demanded, both terrified of and eager for his answer.

'No, not just that.'

For just a moment, he loomed over her in the darkness, blocking out the light of the moon until all she could see was him. All she could see was the desire in his eyes. And then he turned and left her standing on the jetty, watching his white shirt disappear over the crest of the hill that led to the house.

Damn him.

By the time she had summoned the courage to return to the house, she had realised the truth of his words. The courage she had needed was not for fear of him...but of herself. Of just how much she wanted to give in to her desire for Dimitri, to relish the pleasure she knew he could give her.

Dimitri was at the drinks cabinet, his tie hanging loose at his neck, the glass of amber liquid nearly to his lips when he turned to look at her.

'Did you want one?' he bit out reluctantly.

'I don't.'

'Because of your mother?' he asked, curiosity ringing in his tone.

'Haven't we had enough of my personal life for one day? I'm going to bed. Alone,' she tossed at him over her shoulder.

'Not interested in consummating the marriage, then?'

'You've blackmailed me into wearing your ring. Now you want to blackmail me into your bed?' she demanded, turning back to him, still dancing around the edges of want, need and self-denial.

'I told you before, I wouldn't have to.'

'You're arrogant.'

'And you're stubborn,' he threw back at her.

His eyes locked with hers and she felt it, that thread of electricity that joined them, that cried to the world of their attraction.

'There you are, standing as if full of anger and righteousness. But it's neither of those things, Anna, is it?' he demanded. At his very words she felt the cords that tied her to those feelings begin to fray, slowly breaking, thread by thread. 'Inside, you're quivering with desire.' He took a step towards her, only increasing the tremors she felt break across her skin. 'Your pulse is racing, not with injustice, but need.' She tried to slow her breathing, but the flutter she felt at her pulse points was undeniable. 'Your cheeks are flushed, not with fury, but arousal. There,' he said, his fingers hovering above the lace that barely covered her breasts, 'your own body is straining towards me, desperate for my touch.'

She batted away his hand, but her heart wasn't in it.

He looked at her with assessing eyes, as if not quite understanding why she would fight this so much, why she would deny them both the pleasure they so desperately wanted.

'What are you so afraid of?' he asked.

It was the softness of his voice in the darkened room that undid her. That buried its way into her chest, lodging on the aching breath that shuddered from her lungs. If he'd been angry—if he'd shouted—she would have used it to fuel her indignation. But he hadn't. His words were like a verbal key, unlocking her soul and baring her to him.

In the deepest reaches of her heart, she knew what it was. She knew that she was terrified that she wouldn't just be giving her body to Dimitri, but more… Her heart.

But the words wouldn't come. Some innate sense of self-protection prevented her from revealing such a weakness. She looked up at him, swathed in the shadows of the room, marvelling at how the light from the moon cast him in silver finery, lighting the sharp angles of his face, making his dark eyes seem to almost glow. He was stunning, powerful…irresistible.

If she'd thought he'd turn away from her silence, she was wrong.

Instead, he pressed closer to her, crowding her, tempting her.

'Ask for what you want, Anna. It is your right.'

'As your wife?' she spat at him, desperate to cling to anything she could use to maintain the barriers she had put around her heart three years before, longer even. The barriers he was bashing through with the force of a storm.

'No. *Theos*,' he growled. 'As a *woman*.'

It was as if he had let loose a battle cry to everything feminine inside her, begging, pleading with her to reach for him, to take what she wanted. And it was so tempting in the darkness of the empty island home. What he was asking her. What he was telling her to demand from him. He was right—she had been using their daughter as an excuse, as a shield from the simmering tension that had always, *always* been there between them. It seemed like the simplest of things, but Anna felt the decision like a pendulum, swinging either way, weighed down, but pushing them forward to an undeniable conclusion.

Dimitri could feel her need, so strong he could almost taste it. He cursed himself to hell and back because by illuminating her desire for him he had served to increase his own. His arousal pressed hard against the dark linen trousers he had worn for the wedding.

Her eyes flared and he could see her wavering. He could feel the struggle going on inside her, he could see it in her sea-green eyes. He'd promised her that *she* would beg—the irony was not lost on him. In that moment he would have given almost anything to have her succumb to him. In that moment, it was he who was poised on the brink of begging.

'You did that first night,' he reminded her. 'You demanded everything from me and I gave it willingly and I would not refuse you this, ever. So—' Dimitri took a step towards her '—you want me?' he demanded.

She looked almost mutinous, but finally said the word he'd been longing to hear. 'Yes.'

'Say it.'

'I want you.'

The thrumming that had unsettled the air about them stilled. She could still walk away. And he honestly couldn't have blamed her, but he saw her fingers hesitantly reached for the back of her dress. *Christe mou*, he was going to die if she had to undo all those buttons. He closed his eyes and heard the sound of a zip sliding down its fastener.

When he opened them again he watched the slow slide of the dress as it slipped, first from her shoulders, revealing her naked chest, the slopes of her breasts perfect as they rose and fell in time with her rapid breathing. She pressed the dress over her hips and it fell from her waist, pooling in a white silk puddle at her heeled feet.

Her chin rose defiantly as she stood there in nothing but her shoes and a white silk thong. He took her in all at once, the sight of her nearly undoing him completely. He felt the tremors of his own arousal begin to threaten his control.

'All of it. Take it off.' He gestured towards her thong. He watched her eyes widen a fraction. Good. It was good to see her as unsettled by this thing between them as he was. A masochistic part of him wanted her to stop. To refuse his last demand. Because if they took this step...there would be no going back. He would be making her his wife, in more than name only. And once he had what he wanted, he wouldn't let go.

Her thumbs slid down her hips and hooked under the thin lace of her underwear. Fire burned his lungs and Dimitri realised that he'd forgotten to breathe. This was what she did to him. As if she knew it, her hands hovered at her sides, waiting, taunting almost.

'Take. It. Off.'

His voice shredded the last of her uncertainty and he watched, heart in mouth, as she slid the flimsy material down over her hips, lifting long, lean, tanned legs, sweeping it down over her ankles, and she tossed it to the side.

'Say it,' he commanded.

'I've already told you... I—'

He shook his head slowly.

'You bastard.'

'That may be, but I still want you to say it.'

She started to tremble then—not with fear, no. Desire and want was clearly written in her gaze and satisfaction spread through him to see her as much at the mercy of their attraction as he. She bit her top lip as if to prevent her from saying the one thing he needed to hear. The one thing that would start what they had both wanted from the very first moment they had laid eyes on each other.

He wanted to take that lip within his own teeth. He wanted to lave it with his tongue, taste her cries as she found her pleasure in his arms. It was an all-consuming want that he wouldn't be rid of until he had her beneath him again.

He closed the gap between them with the last step he would take.

'Say it.'

Her white teeth loosened their grip on the plump pink lip.

'Please,' she whispered on a ragged breath.

He reached for her then, drawing her to him as his lips crashed down against hers, pressing her body entirely against his. Her lips opened to him, his tongue filling her mouth, meeting her own. *Christe mou*, he'd only once ever found this feeling before, only with her.

He lifted her from the pooled silk at her feet, drawing a gasp from her that he felt down to his soul. Her legs came up around his waist, his hands went down to the backs of her thighs, glorying in the soft skin he felt there, and he pulled her against him and she gasped again when she must have felt his desire.

Through the thin material of his trousers he could feel the heat of her; he wanted to touch her, taste her. His clothes were too much. He needed them gone.

He walked them up the stairs to his bedroom, the one she'd never been in. He kicked open the door and realised that someone had been in here since he'd left. He let her legs go, sliding her down the length of his body, and took in the rose petals scattered across his silk sheets, the tiny candles that had been placed around the edges of the room providing little star lights casting the barest of shadows.

He took it all in dispassionately because his sole focus was Anna. As he took one step forward she retreated, until her legs were pressed against the mattress of his bed. She nearly fell back, but he held her in place. Trembling. She trembled at his every touch.

She sat down on the mattress and he went to his

knees before her, taking her calves in his hands as one by one he undid the little shoe straps around her ankles.

Her eyes never left his, locked together by wanton curiosity and need. Her hands balled the silk sheets of his bed in her fists as if to stop her reaching for him and Dimitri felt the cord of his desire for her tighten.

Her small fingers slowly reached up to the loosened tie, slipping the material away from the knot and sliding it slowly, torturously, from around his neck, tossing it aside just as she had done with her panties.

Her hands, hot, pressed against his chest, either side of the buttons, before turning their attention to releasing the small buttons from their holes. *Christe mou*, this was taking too long.

His own hands came up to either side of his shirt and he tore at the material, sending buttons flying, and cast the ruined garment from his torso.

Her eyes widened again in satisfaction as he stood, making quick work of his belt, sweeping off his trousers and briefs in one go. And he stood there, tall, naked, needing and wanting.

Anna felt her mouth dry the instant he stood above her, glorious and powerful, his bronzed skin glinting in the glow of the tiny lights that littered the room. It was dark enough to see his features, and the storm behind his unrelenting gaze. They stared at each other for an impossible moment, two gladiators about to do battle.

They moved together at the same time, Dimitri coming towards her, her moving up off the bed towards him. Their bodies crashed together, his powerful arms reaching around her, pulling her against him. The cry of pleasure falling from her lips as she felt the entire

length of his naked body against her own was stopped
only by his kiss.

His hands roamed over her body, the same way they
had done three years before, touching, moulding, feeling
every part of her. Her back, her thighs, her breasts. God,
the things he was doing to her breasts. He leaned her
back over his arm, his tongue playing with her hardened
nipple, wringing another cry from her mouth, as his
clever fingers taunted the other. And it wasn't enough.
The need to feel him, inside her, was so utterly overwhelming.

'Dimitri…please.' The words came unbidden from
her own mouth, her voice husky with a desire that she
was almost ashamed of.

'What is it you want, *agapi mou*? How is it you'd like
me to take you? To please you?'

The words caught in the back of her throat. She didn't
know how to do this. How to express what it was that
she wanted. She wanted…everything. She wanted him
to touch her, she wanted him to taste her…she wanted
to taste him. But the words wouldn't come.

As if he sensed her inability to speak, a small smile
curved that sinful mouth and he pressed her back into
the soft mattress, moving with her, allowing her to feel
the weight of him against her, over her. He leaned on
one arm, trailing his free hand across her neck, between
her breasts, down over the stomach that had borne their
child. As if the same thought had struck him, he bent
to press kisses against the slight swell of a stomach that
had been almost perfectly flat three years before. Was
he taking in the changes that pregnancy and birth had
wrought on her body? Did he find them distasteful? But
his kisses soothed her fears, driving heat and sparkles
of sensation across her skin. His hand continued fur-

ther down her body, gently pressing her thighs apart. And then he found the heart of her.

Her hand flew to his, not knowing whether she was going to push him away or press him to her. It felt incredible, the pleasure he was wringing from her. She felt her back rise from the mattress, her chest eagerly reaching for his own. But instead of satisfying her desire he pulled back, raised himself to take her in. He took her hand in his other and pressed it over his as he continued to caress her intimately.

Gasps rained down from her lips as he thrust a long finger deep within her. One, then two, filling her, but it wasn't enough. His lips came down on hers as his tongue echoed the movements of his quick fingers. Her skin was alive, and her breath came in pants. Words, unspoken before, freed by the pleasure he was giving her, fell into the room. Begging words, pleading words she'd have had the sense to prevent if she were in control of her body, of her mind. But she wasn't.

The hard jut of him pressed against her stomach and she shifted her hips, wanting him, needing him inside her. She was so close to an orgasm, the little lights of the room turning into starbursts in the edges of her mind. But then he stopped, and her heart did too.

She had a moment of uncertainty, until he pressed her thighs further apart and plunged into her deeply in one swift motion, bringing her to completion, bringing her out of her mind. A small well of hysteria bubbled deep within her, and for a second Anna lost all sense of time, all sense of place, and only Dimitri remained, the feel of him as her muscles held him in place within her.

Just when Anna thought she'd found her breath, he started moving, slowly, languorously almost, but deeply, so deeply, she couldn't tell where she ended and he began.

Even three years before she hadn't felt anything this incredible, the power of him turning her helpless, and she gave herself over to him completely. Again and again he brought her to the brink of yet another orgasm, and just before she could fall he would slow the punishing rhythm, as if testing the very limits of his own control. Minutes gave over to sensation, time gave over to pleasure and only when she felt him harden even more did she find the truth of their joining. He stilled, biting his bottom lip as if preventing the same cries she'd given freely from escaping. She felt him shudder and release himself into her at the very same moment she fell into the abyss.

CHAPTER SEVEN

Dear Dimitri,
I wanted more. More than you were willing to give.

THE SOUND OF Amalia's laughter woke Anna from her sleep. Her body ached in a way she'd only known once before and she stretched out beneath the sheets, loosening her muscles. She didn't have to open her eyes to know that Dimitri had left their bed. Had left the room. For a moment, her heart stuttered and she was back in her bed in Ireland three years before. Confused and disorientated. Only this time, she didn't run through the small bed and breakfast looking for him, wondering where the man she'd given her virginity to was. Wondering if he would ever come back. This time, Anna knew that—even though he had left her bed—he would be having breakfast with their daughter, as he had done every single day since they had arrived in Greece.

But it didn't mean that she was any less confused. Last night, Anna had asked him for what she wanted and he had given it to her. Again and again throughout the night they had reached for each other. She had given him the thing that he had told her she would: her body. *But*, she lied to herself, *only her body.*

She came down the stairs and what she saw held her back. Dimitri was holding Amalia in his arms, gibbering away in a nonsensical mix of English and made-up words that Dimitri pretended to understand perfectly. Amalia thrust out a fist and grabbed hold of Dimitri's dark hair, and instead of brushing her aside he simply laughed.

Was this what she had kept her daughter from? Not the pain and hurt she had promised herself over and over again, but the love of her father? A small, but very powerful, part of her wondered whether instead she had actually been protecting herself. The sight was so striking, it took her a moment to see that Dimitri was dressed in a suit, as if he were…

'You're going to work?' she couldn't help herself from asking. 'The day after our wedding?'

Flora grumbled from the kitchen, as if understanding not the words, but the sentiment.

'The bank doesn't stop just because I got married, Anna,' he said as if scolding a child. 'I have meetings to attend and a charity function to organise.'

Amalia, as if noting the change in tone around her, started to fuss. He walked over to Anna and placed Amalia into her arms.

'I'll be back, but most likely late, so don't wait on dinner for me.'

With nothing else said, he left the house. The sense of concern she'd felt earlier grew into a living, breathing animal in her chest. Now that she had given him what he wanted, was he going to retreat? Was this how their marriage was going to be? Shame and foolishness taunted her fragile heart.

It had taken Dimitri three sentences to cut through whatever fantasy she had clung to from the night before.

It had taken less than thirty seconds for pain, sharp and acute, to slice through laughably thin armour, poking and prodding at old wounds.

Instantly she began to question what she'd done wrong, what she'd said to make him leave. The familiar pins and needles shivering across her skin, vibrating within her chest, reminded her of her childhood, when she would wait at the school gates for the imaginary figure of her father to come and get her. But he never had. Anna had promised herself that she'd not feel like this again. And she wouldn't. She slowly pulled each block of stone back into place around her heart, refusing to mistake sensual intimacy with emotional intimacy. She may have the security of wearing his wedding ring, but she knew from experience that a gold band didn't mean a thing.

Dimitri found himself pacing the length of his office yet again. Through the glass frontage he had watched as the sun set over the Athens's skyline, as he tried to focus on the numbers for the last financial quarter rather than the memories of losing himself in Anna's arms. Each of the seven days since their wedding had been the same. He would leave for work after breakfast with Amalia, the moment that Anna appeared from their bed. He wouldn't return home until the sun had long since set and would find Anna asleep on the sofa, or in a chair in the living room amidst a pile of second-hand English paperback books. He would pick her up and take her back to his room, where they would make love long into the early hours of the morning.

But they had barely exchanged a word. It was as if their life was playing out in silence. As if he was afraid of what he would reveal, or what she would ask of him: the one thing he didn't even know if he was capable of.

Dimitri could count the number of people he trusted on one hand. Antonio and Danyl were the closest thing he had to a family. His father had been cold and distant his entire life up until recently, and Dimitri still wasn't sure he could trust the changing tide of their relationship. But it was Anna who was threatening to undo him. Seeing Anna with Amalia, it hurt. Watching her prepare his daughter's food, watching her soothe away her tears, it reminded him of his mother. And all the memories he'd sought to suppress for years were coming to the surface.

Little things, like the way his mother had made the best, sweetest baklava—so big it resembled a loaf and had to be cut with a bread knife—the way that she had put a plaster over his knee when he had fallen. The way that, even after her long day at the restaurant, she would still find the energy to read to him at night. The feel of having her there, the comfort and the love that she had wrapped around him, protecting him from the bad things of the world. Protecting him from his father's absence and rejection.

And those were the memories he didn't mind so much. But it was what came after that shook him to his soul. The shock, the pain when all of that was taken away in a heartbeat. When the policeman had stood in the hallway to their apartment asking the seven-year-old Dimitri if he had any other family. It was the weeks, the months that followed—that was what he didn't want to remember.

At the age of seven he'd made himself an island, realising that no one else could protect him. And that was the very reason why the charity event he was holding with the other members of the Winners' Circle in Kavala tomorrow night was so important.

* * *

Returning to the island, early for once, he felt fresh from the boat trip that had blown away the dark thoughts of his day. He hovered in the hallway to the kitchen, steeling himself against the childish giggles of his daughter and Anna's laughing response, and he wondered if he would ever get used to the sounds of such domesticity. Whether he even deserved them.

The moment Anna saw him, she cut him an almost accusatory look.

'You're back,' she stated with an undertone he couldn't quite decipher.

'Yes, it is my home,' he stated before being able to stop the defensive tone from creeping into his voice. He tried not to wince at her hurt reaction. When did his own home become such a minefield? He bit down against the flare of irritation. 'We are travelling to Kavala tomorrow.'

'Are you?' Anna replied, purposefully misunderstanding him, Dimitri was sure.

'*We* are attending a charity gala dinner there.'

Flora swooped in, prepared to clear the field for the battle she had realised was to come. Amalia went willingly into her arms and Flora retreated outside to the garden.

'I'm sure you will have a wonderful time.'

'Anna,' he bit out.

'Dimitri,' she returned.

He cursed. This could go on all night.

'I'm not going,' she repeated.

He searched her tone for a hint of anger, or defiance, but was surprised to find there was none. Just a simple statement of fact.

'You have to be there.'

'Why? Why do you want me there?'

Such a loaded question. One he wasn't yet prepared to search his soul to answer. 'The press will be there. And it's expected that you—as my wife—will be too.'

Anna felt her stomach clench and she instinctively pressed a hand to soothe it. So it wasn't because he actually wanted her there. No. It was for appearances' sake. She could feel the ridges and tension almost vibrating from her forehead. Why was it that everything Dimitri did or said seemed to continually feed into years-old insecurities?

For a whole week she'd said nothing, betrayed none of her feelings, terrified of making this strange stalemate situation worse. These briefly exchanged words were the most they'd said to each other since the morning after the wedding.

'If that is the only reason you would like me there, then I'm afraid I shall have to decline.'

'Have to... Anna, I'm not joking about this. You are coming with me.'

'Until you give me a good enough reason, I'd rather spend that time with our daughter.'

She'd thought he'd stalk out. Leave. Yet again. But there was something anchoring him to the spot. And for just a moment she glimpsed a side of Dimitri she hadn't been privy to yet. Gone was the amused, indignant man, gone was the patronising husband. He stalked towards her in just a few long strides, towering over her with broad shoulders that blocked out the setting sun, his eyes as dark as the night promised to be. The demand she had laid at his feet loosening the bonds around his secrets.

'You want to know? Fine. I didn't go straight from my mother's home to my father's.'

It took a moment for Anna to orientate her mind to how that might fit in with the charity event, but Dimitri pressed on while she struggled to keep up.

'As I said before, it took my mother's sister two months to track down my father. But during that time, I was put into the care system. My mother's sister couldn't take me in—she lived nearly five hundred kilometres from Piraeus in Kastoria. Her work wouldn't allow her to take more than a few days away, and she couldn't afford to lose her job.

'So it was decided that I should be put into the care system, until something suitable could be arranged. What I didn't know at the time was that the "something suitable" was code for until my father could be persuaded to take me in.

'The people managing the unit were kind, or as kind as they could afford to be. The first day, my jacket was taken—and trust me, my mother wasn't rich, so it wasn't expensive by any standards. But, when I did nothing, my shoes were taken the next day. It's funny what you cling to as a child. Amalia has her sculpture, I had only clothes—small things that my mother had worked hard for and were my only reminders of her. Pieces of her were being taken away from me, bit by bit, and I did nothing to stop it from happening.

'Each day, I asked the adults what was happening, where I would be going, when I would be going. And each day they said, come back tomorrow.

'Two months is a lifetime for a seven-year-old boy. Friendships made, fights lost… Most of the boys had grown up on the streets, tough, mean, clever. There was one kid who tried every day to run away, desperate to go back to where he'd been. But that wasn't an option for me. There was nowhere for me to go back to.'

Dimitri took in a breath. It shuddered in his chest, as if the memories were shaking him to his very core. There had been no protection then. No Danyl or Antonio—the friends he wouldn't meet until university. At the time, his seven-year-old self had thought that he was numb. Numb with grief, numb to the chaos and tension that he'd lived and breathed…but it had scarred him deeply. And only now, forcing himself to recall this time, did he realise how close to prison it had been. How they had both been tinged with the same fear, the same raw vulnerability. His life had not been his own, in either situation. And both times had forced him to realise that there was no one out there who could protect him. He had to protect himself.

'I soon learned that if I didn't fight back, if I let that soft heart form friendships with unworthy people, people who would lie, steal and cheat their way through the care system, I wouldn't survive.'

He let out a huff. 'I know that sounds dramatic, I know I would have continued to live, breathe, be fed. But…the boy my mother raised? Not so much. So I became tough. I fought for what little belongings I had, fought to keep the things that reminded me of her. I promised myself that I would never be in that situation ever again.'

I promised myself that I'd never let anyone be my weakness again, his inner voice concluded. Until Manos. Until that one thread of hope had formed and been severed.

'When my father finally took me in, I had the best that money could buy—education, clothes, the biggest house I'd ever seen. It didn't matter that Manos hated me on sight, that my father barely spared a thought to me other than how he could turn me into an asset for the Kyriakou Bank. It didn't matter my father's wife watched me like a hawk, as if I'd do something eventually to hurt her child. It only mattered that they gave me access to the tools that would allow me to ensure I was never beholden to another. I worked hard at school, at university in New York.'

The memories of meeting Antonio and Danyl softened features he hadn't realised had become rock-hard.

'And the moment I had enough money, enough power to create a charity for homeless children, I did. Antonio and Danyl helped too. Because none of us ever wanted a child to feel that same sense of helplessness, that same uncertainty. So once a year there we hold a gala. This year it is in Kavala, and we—you and I—*will* be there.'

Dimitri refused to turn to Anna. Refused to see the pity he knew would be there in her eyes. He'd never wanted her to look at him in that way. He *never* wanted to see that from her.

'Why didn't you just tell me how important this was, and *ask* me to come with you?'

Unbidden, the words that came surprised even himself. 'I didn't want to risk that you'd say no.'

He felt her small hand reach his elbow and gently pull him about to face her.

'You have to trust me, Dimitri. If I knew how important this was, then of course I would come with you. But trust works both ways, Dimitri. You can't demand truth and fidelity from me, and not give it in return. So if there is something that I don't want to do or, in fact, *do* want, then you have to trust me too.'

But, in the darkest reaches of his heart, he knew that this was what he was most afraid of.

* * *

Anna shifted uncomfortably in the back of the limousine taking them to the gala at the exclusive hotel in Kavala, the same limousine that would pick them up at the end of the night and return them to his apartment nearby.

Had it only been last night that Dimitri had opened himself up to her? She felt as if years had passed. She was beginning to see through the mask that Dimitri wore to the child, the vulnerable boy who'd been lost and needed, *deserved*, kindness. Beneath his words she'd felt his pain, and was finally beginning to understand his need to secure certain things for their daughter. She'd once so easily dismissed his notion that something might happen to her, or to him. For her it was hypothetical. For him it had been real. A lesson hard learned.

She felt that they'd made a step forward last night. That slowly they were forging connections she both longed for and feared. But she also knew that he was holding something back. Because he was speaking of a childhood pain, not the pain of the present that she could see hovering around him like an aura.

Flora and Amalia had stayed back at the island, neither Dimitri nor Anna willing to upset Amalia's routine for just one night. A few hours ago, Amalia had played with diamonds and pearls as if they were plastic bricks, Anna's heart lurching as she saw her daughter's chubby fist gripping enough jewels to support them for a lifetime. The same expensive jewels that now hung around her neck like a noose.

The cool silks of a turquoise dress skittered over her skin like a caress—one that she hadn't received from Dimitri since their conversation the night before. She had marvelled at how the beautiful colour had sat against her sun-darkened skin. Never before had she seen the colour of her skin as anything other than something that marked her as different, that reminded her constantly of her father's absence from her life. But here, in Greece, it came to life; *she* came to life. *Stunning* was how Dimitri had described her one night. *Beautiful*, another, and more recently *his*. But the night-time words were left in the dark, and the day...?

She had darkened her eyelashes with liner and mascara, accentuating features she now wanted to own, to shine as if both her appearance and her emotional scars had made her who she was today. She'd dusted the lids of her eyes with a golden shadow, bringing the vivid green of her irises to light. Was it Dimitri's confession, his struggles with his past, that had helped her find her own strength? The fact that this incredible, powerful man, with his own dark secrets, could be proud and confident? *If only he had chosen her for herself...*the unwelcome secret voice of her heart whispered.

Brushing that thought aside, and focusing on an inner sense of confidence, she proudly walked up the red carpet that lined the steps to the incredible hotel built within an old imaret in the port town halfway between Thessaloniki and Istanbul. As they passed through the high, sweeping archways she ignored the flash of the press's cameras, the questions called out to Dimitri. She followed his actions, smiled when he smiled and, when he turned to her and claimed her lips with his own, shock momentarily gave way to desire, inflaming hopes of what might come after the gala.

The moment they entered the gilded ballroom, sound hit her like a wave, a thousand voices in a hundred languages echoing off the stone walls and marble floors, but all hushed in an instant, turning to greet Dimitri like a long-lost friend. After the fourth introduction, Anna stopped trying to remember people's names, instead taking it all in and falling back into warm greetings she was well versed in from her experience at the bed and breakfast.

When Dimitri guided her towards yet another group of people she felt herself smile as she recognised the man that stood in the centre of a tightly knit group. The sheikh who had been at their wedding, the royal she had been almost too scared to speak to, now greeted her with warmth the moment his eyes lit on hers.

'Dimitri, so kind of you to join us,' said the heavily accented voice with mock reproach.

'I knew that this evening would be doing well in your more than capable hands, Danyl.'

'Anna, lovely to see you again,' Danyl said, bypassing Dimitri's compliment.

The lack of formality between her husband and the prince drew only the slightest of frowns from the two dignitaries, who made excuses and left the small group. Anna's eyes were drawn to the cool beauty pressing herself against the sheikh. In Anna's mind, she was exquisite. Ice-blonde hair, perfectly swept back, as if ready and waiting for a crown, topped a face with the palest of skin. Milk and honey was the first thing that came to Anna's mind.

'Allow me to introduce Birgitta Svenska,' Danyl said without making eye contact with the woman, his tone as bland as if he were reading off a restaurant menu. Anna thought she saw a brief flash of hurt in Birgitta's features.

'A pleasure,' the woman said in cultured tones that betrayed no hint of a Scandinavian accent. Her gaze remained cool and assessing, until she took in Anna's husband. Calculation turned to appraisal, and Anna was surprised by the fierce streak of possessiveness that ran across her shoulders.

'Any sign of Antonio?' asked Dimitri as if he too had somehow passed over the European beauty.

'He couldn't make it. He sends his apologies. Emma's morning sickness has kept her in their apartment in New York.'

Anna smiled. 'You should tell her to try ginger tea. It certainly worked for me.'

Dimitri turned to her. 'You had morning sickness?'

'Yes, Dimitri. Oddly enough, it's actually quite common,' she replied, gently mocking him. Though her tone had clearly done nothing to assuage the sting reflected in his gaze.

'I hadn't expected her to be experiencing it so soon. He only just called to tell me the news,' he said, turning back to the Sheikh of Ter'harn. 'Anything new from Australia?' Dimitri asked.

'Nothing you cannot find out for yourself, Dimitri.' It was then that Anna was reminded of the sheikh's true power, the look in his eyes enough to quell an army. Her husband responded only with a raised eyebrow.

'She is fine,' Danyl reluctantly admitted.

'She?' Anna couldn't help querying.

'It has been the talk of the racing world,' scolded Birgitta, as if somehow Anna's ignorance was a fatal flaw. 'The Winners' Circle syndicate is trying the impossible with a female jockey. Three wins on the Hanley Cup hasn't been achieved since…'

'Mason's father,' concluded Danyl.

Birgitta eyed her companion with speculative eyes before enquiring after the Kyriakou Bank's recent success, effectively shutting the sheikh and Anna out from the conversation. Danyl's only reaction was an amused quirk of his lips, before turning his powerful attention to Anna.

'How is your daughter?'

'Well, thank you. She's thriving in Greece.'

'As are you, it would seem.'

Anna smiled at the compliment, letting it warm her, but she still couldn't help but glance at the intimate way Birgitta was conversing with her husband.

'Don't worry, Anna. He only has eyes for you.'

Anna cocked her head to one side, considering his words. Before she could contradict his statement, Danyl pressed on.

'I have never seen him with any woman the way he is with you. And it is good. As it should be. I cannot say that he's the easiest of men.'

'No. He's not.'

'But he is very much worth it. Once his loyalty is earned, it is steadfast. As is mine. So should you need anything, Anna, *anything*, just say.'

The sincerity in his tone touched her. It made her happy that Dimitri had people like Danyl in his life, after the loneliness of his childhood. And now, it seemed, perhaps she did too.

Birgitta politely excused herself from the conversation with Dimitri and disappeared. In an instant, Danyl's whole demeanour changed. He ran a hand over exhausted eyes.

'Another potential bride?' queried Dimitri.

'She certainly seems to think so. I feel like a prize bull.'

Anna felt a smile lift the corners of her mouth at the easy admittance of the powerful royal before her, but quietly retreated from the personal tenor of the conversation.

Dimitri watched Anna slip away into the crowds, dark intent swirling in his stomach. The first time he had laid his eyes on her that evening, clothed in the gentlest of turquoise silk, he had wanted to order her back into the room, strip her of her dress and lock her in. The only thing that had stopped him was the shock of his own caveman-like reaction.

'You seem tense. Certainly more tense than usual,' Danyl remarked.

'It's… We're staying at the apartment here tonight.'

'And you haven't been back since Manos's arrest.'

'No,' Dimitri replied, casting his eyes around for a drink, for anything to distract him from the direction of this conversation.

'Perhaps it is a good thing that Anna is with you.'

'I think it may be *because* Anna is with me.'

'She's a good woman, Dimitri.'

'She's not just a woman. She's the mother of my child.'

'Is that all? You have the look of a man in more than lust, Dimitri.'

'You know me better than that, Danyl.'

'But does Anna?'

Anna came from the bathroom stall out into a beautiful, Ottoman-styled bathroom. Large mirrors adorned high arched walls covered in exquisitely detailed tiles in shades of blue and white. As women bustled around the room she was almost surprised not to see them in period dress.

As she washed her hands she caught sight of Birgitta at the basin beside her.

'So you are Dimitri Kyriakou's new bride.' The statement was accompanied by such a deep study, Anna wondered if Birgitta was trying to understand why Dimitri had chosen her.

'Yes, I suppose that would be me. Unless he has another one squirrelled away that I don't know about.'

With a slight inclination of a perfectly smooth shoulder, Birgitta sidestepped Anna's attempt at humour. 'Though I wouldn't expect it of Kyriakou, there are certainly some men out there I wouldn't put it past.'

Anna honestly couldn't tell if Birgitta was being funny or not. 'You mean Danyl?'

An arched eyebrow reminded Anna that she was speaking of royalty on a far too familiar basis.

'If the Sheikh of Ter'harn were married, I doubt very much that I would be here.'

With no trace of self-pity in her tone, Anna couldn't help but marvel at the woman's apparent stoicism.

'Oh, don't look at me like that,' Birgitta continued in a weary tone. 'I know what my role is here tonight. *Danyl*,' she said, 'needs a bride. My family need me to make a good marriage.' Another shrug of her beautiful shoulder punctuated her concluding statement. 'We— wives or *potential* wives—are nothing more than conveniences and possessions. We make of it what we will. And don't misunderstand me—I will make the most of this.' The determination in Birgitta's tone made Anna reassess the woman in an instant. She only hoped that Danyl knew what he was getting into.

But her words had struck a chord within Anna. She certainly hadn't been a convenience for Dimitri, she knew that much. But the determination, the idea that she could make something of this, rather than sit passively by and let things happen to her... Hadn't that been what Dimitri had said to her the night of their wedding? That she needed to ask for what she wanted?

Was she so terrified, she thought sadly, that she had truly stopped asking for things for herself, for her future? Was she so convinced that she would be rejected, or left, abandoned, that she had stopped even *thinking* of her future, of herself?

As she re-entered the ballroom she located Dimitri easily amongst the throngs of people. The breadth of his strong shoulders drew her to his innate power. As if sensing her, he turned, his eyes finding her in a heartbeat. The hairs on Anna's arms rose, goosebumps raining down over her skin at the sensual promise of his gaze.

She wasn't willing to allow this marriage to simply happen to her. If she wanted to make their marriage work, then she couldn't live in fear, or hold herself back. She needed to have faith in both her husband and herself, faith that he wouldn't leave her and faith that she was good enough to make him stay. And, with that thought ringing in her ears, she took a glass of champagne from the nearest waiter, taking a deep drink and allowing the bubbles to explode in her throat, sparking excitement and something like hope deep within her.

CHAPTER EIGHT

Dear Dimitri,
Today I found you. The real you.

DIMITRI HAD DELIVERED the keynote speech about the poverty that was affecting Greece's families, the orphanages that were filled not just with orphans, but also with children with loving parents who had turned them over to the state because they simply couldn't care for them whilst holding down the myriad jobs they needed to take to keep a roof over their heads. He'd highlighted the plight of just a few small families, giving voice to the crisis that affected so many, and he'd felt righteousness ring in his voice—a righteousness that he so rarely felt about his own business these days, aside from the need to compensate for Manos's awful actions.

He'd tried to avoid thoughts of his half-brother's betrayal for so long, but now that the limousine pulled up to the apartment he hadn't stepped foot in for over three years, he wondered if Anna could sense the dark thoughts that were descending upon him. One look at Anna, who had shifted in her seat to look up at the large building towering over the port's skyline, the silks of her skirt rising up against perfect thighs, and Dimitri struck down the well of arousal firing within him, instead focusing on Danyl's insightful question.

No, he thought. Anna didn't understand his difficult feelings about love, didn't understand how it had been routed out of him by his father's aloofness and his mother's death. Didn't understand how it had been impossible for him to let a woman get close to him. How impossible it still was. He cursed himself, thinking that he should tell her. Warn her. But the words wouldn't come.

'This is yours?' she asked, awe evident in her tone. From any other woman, he'd find it jarring, a leading question that instantly became calculating. But no matter how much he searched her voice, he couldn't accredit Anna with that.

'Yes,' he bit out gruffly into the night as he escorted her from the car.

He entered the foyer, pulling out the key card for the lift access to the penthouse apartment, feeling rather than seeing Anna follow on his heels. Mirrors lined the lift, rose-gold lighting turning Anna's skin an even more delectable shade. Standing so close, he could smell her perfume in the air, warmed by her body. His hands itched inexplicably, desperate to reach out. As if she sensed that need somehow, she leaned ever so slightly towards him and for a moment he fought against the desire to step back, to create some kind of distance... the distance that was with them before he'd taunted her on their wedding night. Before he'd laid a challenge, a demand, at her feet.

He should have let her have her paper marriage, because ever since that moment, his brain had seemed to stop functioning and instead he was immersed in feelings, wants and needs he'd been able to prevent for years.

The doors to the lift opened up directly onto the foyer of the apartment.

Dimitri didn't know what he'd expected. Owing to his brother's use of it, he'd somehow imagined the walls to be painted black…evidence of drugs and prostitution perhaps—the things that he had bought with other people's money. Perhaps broken TVs and plates from one of Manos's legendary tantrums.

Anna swept past him, deeper into the apartment.

'This is lovely,' she said, looking around the open-plan kitchen and living room. And it was. It didn't have any incredible floor-to-ceiling windows wrapping around the apartment, but the balcony leading from the master suite could be seen through the windows of the living room.

But, despite the incredible view, it wasn't enough. It didn't feel open enough. The walls were beginning to press down on him, as if his whole being was shaken with the need for air, for the open sky. Memories of his time in the care system, of the small, bunk-bed unit in the prison, each thought scratched against him like barbs, drawing thin lines of blood invisible to the eye.

He needed a drink. He needed his bed. His bed, alone. Not with her. Not with the wife whose very presence was taunting him—the woman whose image he had clung to as if his sanity depended on it as he had lain in prison listening to the sounds of the other prisoners, hundreds of men all breathing the same air. He needed to stop all these chaotic thoughts.

He didn't realise that he'd been pacing the room until he felt Anna's gentle hand on his forearm, stopping him almost midstride.

'What's wrong?' she asked, concern easy to read in her eyes.

'Go to bed, Anna,' he ordered, hating that his own words sounded so harsh.

'No,' she said, cocking her head to one side as she looked at him, as if she was trying to understand a puzzle.

'I need you to leave.'

'I'm not going anywhere.'

The growl that emerged from lips thinned by anger and something else Anna couldn't quite identify should have been chilling, but instead it fired her own determination to understand her husband. She could see the pain, the fury emanating from him. So, instead of turning and fleeing, she stepped towards Dimitri's potent frame, relished the powerful vibrations coming off him in waves, allowed them to fill her, to imbibe her with that same sense of energy and power.

'What is it?' she demanded.

The indecision in his eyes tore at her heart. If he couldn't trust her, then what would that mean for their marriage? Because that was what she had begun to think of it as. Not just some blackmail scheme to access his daughter…but a partnership. But if she couldn't get Dimitri to see that, she didn't know how much longer they'd be able to go on.

'It's… Ever since…'

Anna was shocked. She'd never seen her husband speechless before, grasping for words. Even in his fury he was eloquent and impossible.

'It's okay,' she assured him, closing the distance between them, placing her hand on his arm—the muscles beneath her palm locked tight.

'It's not okay. None of it's okay, Anna.' He spun out of her hold and left her standing in the living room. But she wasn't going to let him get away that easily. She followed him through the side door—ignoring the palatial master suite—and out onto the balcony, where Dimitri was now standing, fingers gripping the balustrade, the white of his knuckles clashing with the stone.

'You're not going to let this go, are you?' he demanded.

'No.'

Dimitri turned to see her standing, strands of her dark hair caught on the gentle breeze, proud, immovable, determined. She had changed. It was as if after their wedding night she had taken something within her, inside her, keeping her strong, making her fearless. Or perhaps she had always been that way, and he had only just seen it now.

If he were any kind of man he would match her strength, and that was enough of a thought to loosen the words that had clogged his throat in the living room, that had stuttered to a stop before escaping.

'I don't like being in enclosed spaces. It's too much like being in prison.' He looked at Anna, this woman who wanted more from him, demanded more from him…but just how much he was willing to give he wasn't sure any more. 'White-collar crime. That's what they call it in America.'

'Why did you go to prison there and not in Greece?'

'The clients Manos chose to steal from were American, and he did it through the American branch. He believed that the Greeks had lost too much already. It was, apparently, the only altruistic thought he'd ever had—but don't for one second take him as a Robin Hood figure. He couldn't have been more of a cliché if he'd tried, using the money to fund his drug addiction, prostitution, a lifestyle even more lavish than this,' he said, gesturing to his stunning apartment.

He was surprised when Anna came to stand beside him, desperate to cling to the warmth of her body heat, allowing it to warm him as his words, memories, turned him cold.

'You were in prison for fourteen months,' she said, more of a prompt than a query.

'Between being released on bail and the court case, I spent a total of four hundred and twenty-seven days in prison.'

'But you were innocent.' Her outrage was a pale echo of the one he had nursed for what felt like years now.

'Yes, but so was every single man in there.' Her frown drew a grim smile from his lips. 'It's what they all said.'

'But for you it was true.'

'I remember the first time the lead investigator's questions changed. They had enough evidence to convict me, but I had two very good witnesses for one occasion when it was simply impossible for me to have taken the money.' An unspoken question rang loud out into the open air. 'No, Anna, not bedfellows. Antonio and Danyl. Even the FBI couldn't argue with the Sheikh of Ter'harn.'

'So why didn't they let you go?' Anna demanded.

'They needed time; they would need me to follow the court case through, until they had enough proof to bring down the real perpetrator. The Americans take financial crime very seriously and they didn't want to risk him escaping their justice again.'

Anna took all this in with wide-eyed shock. If he

hadn't experienced the whole sorry mess himself, he could almost have felt sorry for her.

'What did you do, while you were in there?'

At first nothing came to his mind, a blank wall protecting him from that time. Initially he'd thought his innocence would protect him. Not from the other prisoners, but from his own mind. 'Not much, is the answer to that question. I read.' He shrugged as if it were nothing, as if he hadn't spent hours, days, climbing the walls...nursing a secret fear that he'd never get out, that the FBI had lied to him. That he'd spend the rest of his days there. 'It's funny what your mind will do to you when you have no control over your day, your time. I spent time in the gym, trying to work off some of the energy that I suddenly had. And when I couldn't escape my body, I escaped into my mind. I... I thought about you,' he finally admitted. Hours and hours, losing himself in that night they'd had together. Holding the memory of her as a beacon against the darkness that had sometimes seemed to overwhelm him.

'What did you think about me?' Anna was almost too scared to ask.

'I could show you if you want,' he taunted, the gleam turning his eyes darker than burned caramel. But she refused to let him distract her.

'Later perhaps,' she replied, softening the rejection with a smile. She knew there was more. It wasn't just that this proud, powerful man had been caged like an animal. She sensed, somehow, that it wasn't the imprisonment that had really hurt. She needed to go deeper, poke deeper; *he* needed her to.

'And when you got out?'

The taunt dropped from his eyes, his gaze once again

out to the silent night sky, whilst inside a storm raged within him.

'Everything was both the same and different. I had initially fooled myself into thinking that it had been some high-level executive stealing from the company. My father had promised that he would provide the FBI with all the help they needed, and when the FBI first came to tell me they had identified the criminal I was relieved. I was actually fool enough to think that my father and brother had saved me. That all the time during my childhood, when I felt on the outside looking in, when I felt…when I was made to feel like an imposition, like an imposter…it all disappeared. For just a moment, I felt that I had family and that they had put aside their feelings and somehow found proof that had saved me from imprisonment. I felt love for them, the tendrils of connection… And when the FBI revealed that it was Manos I was struck dumb.' It was as if an axe had come down on the roots of his foundations.

Even though Anna had known the outcome, that it had been Manos's betrayal that had put him in prison, she felt the echo of his first moment of shock cut through her like a knife.

'I had been betrayed by a man who shared my blood. Not just betrayed, for that implies some kind of implicit wrongdoing on my part. He actively laid paperwork that set me up.'

She could see the pain of that hurt, she knew that pain, had borne it every day with her mother. But Dimitri's actions, although poorly motivated, had enabled her mother to find the help she so very much needed. And now Anna wondered if she could help Dimitri heal some of that pain, those hurts…that betrayal.

'Ma's drinking…it was hard. Each time she would

promise to stop, and I would go through the stages of grief, denial, anger. Each time it was harder and harder to forgive, because each time it felt like a greater betrayal. Each time it *was* a betrayal. But it seems that the rehab centre is working for her. She'll be coming out soon and she's really trying this time. And I want to thank you for that. I wouldn't have been able to provide her with that kind of help.'

He was watching her, wary. She had to tread lightly and feared that, even if she did, he could see what she was coming around to. He was like a panther, sleek, powerful, ready for fight or flight.

'And that's why this time it's important for me to be able to forgive. Her drinking is a disease. It's not something she can help; it's not a choice.'

He turned away from her, back to the skyline of Kavala.

'Manos had a choice. It wasn't a disease. He chose to steal money, chose to set me up.'

Pressing down the hurt she'd felt as he turned away from her, she once more placed a hand on his arm. 'I could imagine that your brother might have felt inadequate next to you. Clearly your childhood with your father was difficult…but is it the same now?'

Dimitri frowned. 'He's been…different, recently,' he reluctantly acknowledged.

'Relationships aren't static things, always staying one particular way. If there is hope for you and your father, could there be hope for you and Manos? I'm not saying that Manos is nice or even worth your sympathy—not at all. But sometimes when someone acts unnecessarily horribly towards another person, it's not about that other person, but about them. Which means that he might be at least worth your understanding.'

Anna's heart was in her mouth. She hoped, so much, that her words were getting through to him. Because he carried too much. He held too much within him, bottled up. It needed to be released if they were ever to have a chance.

Her chest ached and she resisted the urge to rub away the pain. But it wasn't the same kind of pain that hurt and lashed out. It was the kind of ache that grew and grew until it overshadowed everything. It was huge and terrifying, because in that moment she realised that she loved him.

The Dimitri who had spent one wild night with her in Ireland. The Dimitri who had been wrongfully imprisoned and so much more damaged by his half-brother's betrayal... The Dimitri who had forced her into marriage, and the one who had also opened her eyes to her own strength, her own desires and needs. The Dimitri who, she realised, had never really known comfort and understanding from the very people he should have first received it from.

This time, she allowed her body to take over. Casting all thought aside, she let her heart guide her hands and her actions. She wanted, *needed*, to show him as much as she could that she did love him, that she could and would give him that comfort, that support. She might not yet be able to put it into words, and even had she been able to she wasn't sure that Dimitri was ready to hear them, but this...she could do.

She took his hands, still clenched around the balustrade, in her own, gently releasing the iron grip he had on the stone. She pressed his palms against the bare skin beneath the V of the silk folds of the dress, allowing him to feel the beat of her heart. She reached up to him, to his jaw, relishing the feel of the stubble shadowing the harsh lines of his face.

Dark eyes, full of suspicion and surprise, watched her every move.

'Anna—'

'I don't want to go to bed, Dimitri.'

'I don't want this, Anna.'

'Do you want me to tell you what *you're* feeling? What *your* body is saying to me? Is it *my* turn, Dimitri?'

The sense of her own arousal gave a strength to her words that surprised her. She allowed it to fill her, to empower her. He shook his head again, but this time he didn't speak. She closed the distance between them. She felt rightness settle around her, making her movements sure.

She started with his tie, the crack of the silk as she snapped it away from his neck and threw it to the ground the only sound accompanying their harsh breaths. She pushed the black silk jacket from his shoulders, revelling in the feel of the superfine white shirt covering his powerful chest, the muscles there a solid wall.

She slid buttons through holes all the way down, slipping aside the shirt and glorying in the feel of his flesh beneath her palms. Was this how he had felt on their wedding night? Powerful and conquering? How had she gone all these years without this feeling? How had she allowed herself to become so afraid of her own desires?

Her hands went to the buckle on his trousers and were immediately halted by Dimitri's.

'Be careful, *monadiki mou*. Once you start this…'

'I have no intention of stopping,' she whispered into his ear, pressing her chest against his. She pulled back and barely had the chance to prepare herself for the bruising kiss that crashed down on her lips.

Their tongues warred for dominance, for control, but this time Anna was determined not to back down. Not to give over control to Dimitri. She pushed him back against the stone balcony, lifting the silk skirts of her dress over one thigh as she anchored her knee around his hip, pressing her core, the heart of her, against him, relishing in the hard length of his arousal. She shifted, moving their centres until she could almost feel him, through his trousers, through the silk of her dress, just where she wanted him, needed him, to be.

Dimitri's guttural curse escaped their kiss and his hands came around the curves of her hips, dragging her even further against him. Their groans mingled, just before he pulled away.

'You're killing me, Anna.' His dark eyes gleamed in the night. 'You're tearing me apart.'

Before Anna could say that he was putting her together again, that he was healing over the cracks in her heart, he took the silk straps of her dress and tore the material from her body, exposing sensitive flesh to the cool night air.

Her bare breasts heaved against his chest, his hand diving to the thin scraps of lace of her panties, his expert fingers finding the heat of her, pleasuring her, torturing her as she shifted in his embrace. It was as if he was trying to wring those same emotions from her with his seduction, tearing at her very being. His other hand had come down on the top of her thigh, anchoring it beside him, refusing to let her retreat, keeping her open to him, to his expert manipulation of her body.

It was an exquisite torture, but it wasn't enough. She wanted to give him this, for her, for him, for them. She needed to.

She let go of the grip she had on his neck with one

hand, trailing her fingers down his chest, catching on the dusting of dark swirls covering his torso, letting it guide her hand further down to beneath his trousers. She relished the feel of his hardened length, wrapping her hands around the base of him, glorying in the flare she saw in his eyes, the moment of indecision she read there. Her breath caught in her throat while she waited. Would he push her away? Would he allow *her* to pleasure *him*?

The back of Anna's hand brushed against the back of his, and their eyes locked in an instant. She told herself not to look away, refusing to close her eyes against the pleasure she was giving him as she stroked up and down, the way his bronze eyes darkened, the way a deep flush rose to his cheeks. Briefly she wondered what it was that Dimitri saw, how she looked, but as his long, lean finger plunged deep into her a gasp fell from her lips and she felt his satisfaction vibrate from his very soul. He thought he'd won this game of wills, this wicked contest of seduction. But he had severely underestimated her.

Using his distraction against him, she pulled away and, bending before him, still clad in her high heels and thong, she took him into her mouth. She let a smile play at her lips as curses littered the air, some in English, some in Greek… She didn't care. She felt empowered by his reaction. From the periphery, she could see his hands gripping the stone balcony, she could feel how his powerful, muscular thighs trembled, his hips beginning to shift beneath her.

'Anna…' His voice was practically a growl.

Reluctantly she let him go, but that didn't mean she was ready to let him take the lead. She drew herself up the length of his body slowly, stepping out of the reach of his arms. She watched as he kicked his trousers away from his legs, stepping out of them, fully naked. She took him in, powerful, proud, unashamed of his nakedness beneath the stars, open to the elements. With any other man, she imagined it would make them vulnerable, but with Dimitri it made him glorious.

'What game are you playing?' he demanded.

'No game. No playing. This is real and this is me, and what I want,' she said, knowing the words to be truer than any others she'd spoken to him.

A rush of emotion hit Dimitri's chest hard. In all the different moments that he'd seen her, he'd never seen Anna like this. The closest to it was the night that they had spent together three years before, the night they'd conceived their child. But here, Anna was incredible. The woman that would have hidden from him, would have needed him to draw her out of herself, to put words to the desire and attraction she felt, was now owning it, not asking for something she was afraid of, but demanding it for herself.

His own nakedness didn't shame him, it never had, and now he wanted Anna's. And if Anna thought that her lacy thong protected her in some way...she was wrong. An errant thought ran into his mind, the same way it had done on their wedding day... *Who would protect her from him?*

She took a step back towards him, having only moments ago retreated from his reach. She took his large hand in her smaller one, flattened the fist he had unknowingly made it into and returned it once again to the centre of her chest, the flat plane in between the two perfect mounds of her breasts.

She pressed his rough palm against her smooth, silky skin and Dimitri forced his body under control.

He wouldn't allow the shakes that had racked his body the moment her mouth had found him to happen again. The sight of her, before him, on her knees, had almost undone him.

But he could tell, now, from her eyes, from her tone, that this was something she craved—no, needed. An undercurrent of change was shifting beneath the surface of her skin, and he was drawn to it, fascinated by it and unable to take his eyes away from her.

He brought a hand up to her cheek, unable to resist the need to trace his fingers across her skin, his hand cupped her jaw, and once again he dipped the fingers of his other hand beneath her panties and into the seductive wet heat between her legs. *Christe mou*, she was so ready for him.

He spun her in his arms, bringing her back against his chest, her bottom cradled between his hips. His fingers stroked her, wringing cries from her mouth and tremors from her body. The heat of her body, flush with his, stoked the flames of desire that licked every inch of his skin.

Never before had she come so alive in his arms, never before had she unleashed the control she held about her like armour. She was stripped of everything and relishing it. It fired his blood, settling deep within him. The sound of her breath, pants littering the air about them, came quicker and more urgently, her pleas flung into the night, begging and wanting, the very thing he had taunted her with before now serving only to increase his own need, his own arousal.

He pressed his finger, one first then a second, deep within her and she cried out, reaching her own completion, falling forward and catching herself on the stone balcony. He held her body as she shuddered, each time her core gently tightening around his fingers.

It wasn't enough. It would never be enough. Now it was his turn, now it was what *he* needed.

He pressed his hands between the backs of her thighs, spreading her open to him, catching his curse before it could be let loose. She was incredible. He ran his hands over the curves of her backside, dipping his hands between her legs, casting his thumb out to catch the overly sensitised flesh and revelling in the way it sent a jolt through Anna's body, as she reached out to hold on to the stone balustrade.

He plunged deeply into her until there was nowhere left to go, and failed utterly to prevent the feral growl he unleashed into the air about them. The feel of his skin inside her, the easy glide as he slowly withdrew almost completely, before thrusting back again, quick, hard, deep. It still wasn't enough. As if sensing it too, she spread her legs wider, leaning back into him until she rested against his own thighs.

He thrust into her again, and again, never tiring of the feeling he was chasing, never tiring of the need to bring them together to an explosive completion. Once again, he drew his hand over her perfect breast, feeling the weight of it against his palm, moulding it, his fingers playing with her hardened nipple, forgoing the pleasure of taking it into his mouth, utterly overwhelmed with the intense passion her body was giving him. He dipped his fingers into the dark curls at the apex of her thighs, his thumb smoothing over her once again.

Her hot, fevered hand reached for his hip, grasping, pulling him into her more deeply, as if she was driven as much by this insanity as he. He wanted her to feel what he was feeling, that same sense of madness that was consuming them, that same sense of what they had become. It was exquisite torture as he pushed them almost to the brink, forcing himself to keep them there, hovering on the edge of the infinite nothingness of their own completion.

All about them, heavy on the air, their cries rang out into open air, the sound of his skin striking against hers the most intensely arousing thing he'd ever heard. All those nights in prison, never had he imagined the truth of their coming together, never had he been able to taste the strength of need, almost choking him now as he pushed them closer and closer to the edge.

That was his last thought, before his final thrust pushed them into oblivion.

Whether moments, seconds or hours had passed before his presence of mind came back, Dimitri couldn't have said. Anna was cradled in his embrace, all strength in her body lost. Picking her up in his arms, he walked them through to the bedroom, passing the bed and continuing on into the bathroom. Still with her in his arms, he walked into the large, glass-fronted shower and turned the handle, waiting for the water to become hot before he put her down on unsteady legs.

The intensity of their lovemaking seemed to have robbed them both of words. He poured gel into his hands, pressing it into her skin, her muscles, soothing away the aches he imagined she might have, over her breasts, between her legs, down her thighs. When she did the same for him, Dimitri pulled her back into him, desperate to once more claim that same completion.

He turned the shower off, covered her with a towel and dried them both before leading her to the bed. The entire time her eyes had watched him, his hands, his actions with an intensity that scared him. Something between them had shifted tonight, and he wasn't sure what that meant. Wasn't sure he even wanted to look too closely at it.

Just before sleep could claim him, Anna asked a question that surprised him. She wanted a honeymoon. Not to go anywhere, but just some time with him and Amalia alone on the island. Without Flora, without work… And, just before he fell into a deep sleep, he was pretty sure that he agreed.

CHAPTER NINE

Dear Dimitri,
I never guessed. I could never have imagined it
could be like this.

DIMITRI KNEW INSTINCTIVELY that he'd made a terrible mistake. Whether it was three days ago when he'd agreed to Anna's request for a honeymoon, or three minutes ago when he'd gone to war with his demanding daughter over breakfast. He had spectacularly underestimated the calming influence Flora had on Amalia. Spectacularly. The heat from the night before had been stifling and Amalia had woken up pitching to throw a fit. He empathised.

For the first time in months, years almost, he had nothing to do, or at least nothing he was familiar with. This 'honeymoon' idea of Anna's had exiled him from his business, business that had taken him two days to wrap up. His father had been almost gleeful to be rid of his brooding, obsessive need to pull their company back from the brink of the destruction Manos had caused. Encouraging him to enjoy his honeymoon, his wife and his daughter, his father had almost smiled as he had bid him farewell. Dimitri shook his head at the memory— wondering at the new tentative bonds of their relationship, amazed at the way it had begun to soothe some of the past hurts.

Had he really been that punishing at work? He cast his mind back over the months since he had come out of prison, all the days merging into one: fraught meetings with the board, impossible targets reached, devastated clients soothed and brought back into the fold—and all of which was done at an adrenaline-pounding pace. The trip to the Buenos Aires horse race last month and then one to Dublin, the only time away that Dimitri had allowed himself.

And he'd liked it like that, because it had kept him from thinking…from focusing on Manos's betrayal. But since the night in Kavala, since the night he'd opened up to Anna, shared some of his past, and his pain, he'd felt…lighter. And that scared him. Because he was simply not used to it. Since the age of seven, he'd been solely reliant on himself. And now he was beginning to trust the bonds that had been woven between him and Anna. But what scared him the most was that Anna had been right.

The moment that she had suggested speaking with his half-brother, a sense of ease opened up in his chest— his chest that had been in a vice-like grip ever since Manos was charged with the fraud and cover-up. Perhaps it was because for the first time he didn't feel as if he was facing his brother alone—that he had Anna and Amalia to return to, to share some of the burden with. Having Anna's support…it was different to the kind offered by Danyl and Antonio. It was healing. And he only hoped that he could do the same for her.

He turned from the kitchen table when Amalia cried out loud, forgetting the cup of coffee he carried. The searing heat as the hot liquid spilled from the rim of his cup drew a loud curse from his mouth.

Anna chose that exact moment to come into the kitchen and in once glance seemed to take in both his burned hand and furious mood, along with her daughter's loud, plaintive, dry-eyed crying.

'Can you do something about that?' he demanded roughly, distracted by the burn and thrusting his hand under the cold-water tap. He caught her raised eyebrow and instantly realised his mistake.

'Did you just call my daughter "that"? Really?' she demanded.

'Come on, Anna, I didn't mean it like that and you know it.' To his own ears he sounded exasperated.

'One of you in a mood I can handle, but both you *and* Amalia? Too much. As you have gone to such extreme lengths to "claim" your child, as you so artfully put it, this is what it's like, Dimitri. This was why I wanted a honeymoon. You wanted a wife and child—here we are. And now, I think, it's your turn to find out what parenting is truly about. Not just the happy breakfast times, but the hard times, when there's no reason other than our daughter's own demanding personality—one that I can only imagine she inherited from you—for her to throw a tantrum.'

'Did you even take a breath during that nice little speech?'

'Did you even think to ask what Amalia liked for breakfast?'

That stopped him in his tracks. 'What do you mean?'

'Figure it out, Dimitri. I'm going for a swim.'

Dimitri felt the anger and helplessness rise within him. 'You can't just leave me.'

'Yes, I can. There's nothing stopping you from being

a father—you're perfectly capable of seeing to her food, her health and her safety. Now you need to learn how to do the hard stuff.'

Dimitri watched, horrified, as Anna stalked out of the house and down to the beach with a towel tucked under her arm and her head held high. He cast another look at Amalia, who by this point had stopped crying, as if she was as shocked as he that she would be left with him.

He left the counter and approached his daughter with caution. Each eyeing the other with deep suspicion, Dimitri stepped closer to the table where she sat in the high chair. He had watched Flora every morning, presenting Amalia with that same breakfast. He was sure that he'd done everything the same way that she had. He leaned forward to the little pot of prepared breakfast Flora had left him in the fridge with a label on it, but the label had been smudged. He dipped his little finger into the grey goo and tasted it, pulling a face as the paste hit his tongue. *Theos*, that was awful. What had Flora been thinking?

He reached for a glass of water to drown out the foul taste, and locked eyes with his daughter.

'Okay, Amalia, I defer to your better judgement. That was vile. Now, what else is there around here that you might like?'

As Anna made her way back up from the beach she was wondering if she'd made a terrible mistake. She'd wanted this time to just be a family unit without Flora, to prove to Dimitri, to prove to herself that they could make this work. That she had been right to trust Dimitri with her heart.

But what if she'd left her daughter with him and he'd

failed? Her footsteps gathered speed, and by the time she reached the crest of the hill on which the house stood her heart was in her mouth and she was half terrified at what she might find.

But it was her daughter's laughter and infectious giggles that she heard first. Then the splash of water and, to her greatest surprise, a deeply voiced laugh. It stopped her in her tracks. She'd never heard Dimitri laugh. And for a second that was almost one of the saddest thoughts she'd ever had.

As she reached the flattened area of garden she saw Dimitri and Amalia in the infinity pool. He was holding her above his head, Amalia with her arms encased in little float bands, laughing hysterically as he swooped her in and out of the water. And suddenly she felt guilty for doubting him.

She walked back into the house to change and couldn't help the smile that formed upon the sight of the kitchen. Half-eaten fruit, breads and pastries littered the surfaces as if some grand eating competition had happened in her absence.

By the time she had showered, was dressed and leaving the room that had become solely used for her clothes, she heard Dimitri settling Amalia down in the living room to play. This time it was Anna who hovered in the doorway as Dimitri's gentle tones were soothing his daughter's excitement and redirecting her attention to the small building blocks she loved so much. It wouldn't be long before Amalia grew out of such easy distraction. It wouldn't be long before she was off to playgroup and then school. And for a moment her vision of the future jarred, because it had always been in Ireland that she had imagined those things to happen. But now the location had shifted to Greece.

Dimitri looked up and found Anna standing in the doorway, her usually open expression unreadable.

'I think Flora might have set me up.'

'I think Flora might have been teaching you a lesson.'

'You knew?' he demanded.

'I guessed,' Anna said with a shrug of her delicate shoulder and the faintest trace of a smile playing at her mouth.

'And you didn't think to warn me?' he replied, his tone readily losing the heat of anger and instead becoming filled with the warmth of humour.

'You're big enough and ugly enough to handle it,' she assured him.

As she passed him he reached for her hips and drew her towards him, leaning over her to crowd her, teasing her as she tried to bend out of his reach.

'You think I'm ugly?' he said, his head cocked to the side, the entire length of his body flush with hers.

'Hideous. Terrible. A monster,' she said as he punctuated her taunts with a kiss upon her neck. This Dimitri? This teasing, playful, impossibly sexy man? Simply irresistible.

'I am *not* a monster,' he mock growled as he pulled her into a kiss. A kiss that wasn't a punishment, wasn't demanding, but giving, generous and spine-tingling.

She met his growl with a groan of pleasure but batted him away and went to the fridge to prepare a snack.

'What time did you want to leave for Piraeus?'

'Forget it. We can cancel. Let's just go to bed. It's nearly dark anyway.'

'Dark? Dimitri, it's eleven in the morning!'

'No, Anna, did you not hear that? It was the nightingale, not the lark.'

Anna let out a gasp. 'How dare you corrupt Shakespeare to your own ends?'

Dimitri shrugged a nonchalant shoulder. 'If it would help my cause I'd—'

Anna cut him off with a kiss. His megawatt charm was more devastating than any of his previous anger or righteous indignation. The look in his eyes made her hope, dared her to believe that this was how things could be. And for the first time in three years Anna desperately wanted to throw caution to the wind, to seize this day, this moment, this feeling for herself.

Dimitri's phone pinged twice, alerting him to new emails, and he swept it up quickly and checked. If there was something secretive about it, the look of surprise, then of satisfaction, that flashed in his eyes smoothed over any misgivings. He looked…happy. That was what it was. For the first time since she'd met him…he seemed happy. And she couldn't help but feel that she had contributed somehow, she had helped him reach that state.

'Something important?'

'Two somethings, but I'll explain later,' he assured her, his eyes sparkling. 'Now, we have to get going,' he said, whisking Anna and Amalia up in a whirlwind of excitement and happiness.

Five hours later and Dimitri was worried. It had been an almost perfect day. They'd taken the boat into Piraeus and his car had picked them up and whisked them off to Athens, to galleries and the Parthenon. He'd laughed at Anna's sheer delight at a simple lunch of souvlaki, washed down with an ice-cold beer. The easy way she had with both Amalia and him was touching him deeply after the past few months fraught with tension and pent-up frustration. But his plans for his surprise for Anna were now complete, and for the first time he was beginning to doubt his decisions.

He'd wanted to give her something, anything, to help show her that she had given him such a gift. Just before they'd left for Athens, David had emailed to say that Manos had agreed to his visit request. He'd shared that information with Anna in the restaurant, and the smile she had greeted the news with had only inflamed the hope in his heart. It had felt right that he should receive that news today—when his plans for Anna had been underway in his home.

It had been a big project, and Dimitri had paid handsomely to have the changes to his home made and completed in just a few hours. He worried that he'd missed something, forgotten something that Anna might need. But he knew that wasn't what really concerned him. The greatest worry was that he'd got it horribly wrong. That the surprise might not quite be something that Anna would welcome. And that fear? It was almost as great as the one he'd felt about her not agreeing to their marriage.

'Are you okay?' Anna asked as the boat docked at the jetty. The sun was readily setting and Amalia was tired, wriggling in her arms, after such an exciting day.

'*Nai*. Let's…let's put Amalia to bed, and then…then we can…'

Why was he finding it so hard to get out a simple sentence?

'Then we can…?'

'Have the rest of the evening to ourselves,' he concluded, not having to fake the desire he felt at the idea of having Anna all to himself. Spending time with Amalia was incredible, but he'd missed three years of Anna too and now he just couldn't get enough of her.

Instead of leading them into the living room, Dimitri led Anna, still carrying Amalia, straight up to the bedroom. If she went anywhere else, if she even turned on the lights, then the surprise would be blown.

When Anna went towards her room he nearly shouted for her to stop. She turned back at him, laughing.

'Really, Dimitri. What on earth is going on?'

'I...'

How had she made him so tongue-tied? Was it her or was it what he so desperately wanted to show her? he wondered.

'Come with me?' he asked, the uncertainty in his voice making him cringe inwardly. He wanted so badly to do something for her. To show her all the things that he seemed incapable of saying.

He took her by the hand and led her back downstairs. The sunset bled through the windows, lighting the living room and door to the study in orange hues. He paused outside the room that was once his study, marvelling at how easy the decision had been to give up his space in his home, once he'd given it up in his heart.

His hand paused on the door handle. For just a moment he took a breath. Looking back to Anna, he could see the beginnings of concern in her gaze. He shook his head; he didn't want her to be worried. He pushed open the door and stepped back for her to see.

For a moment Anna was too distracted by Dimitri, by the hesitancy written across his powerful features, to look into the room. But, following his gaze, she turned to look at what had once been an office and was now...

Speechless, she took a tentative step into what was now, from just a glance, an incredible art studio. The desk and computer had been removed and in their place were long wooden benches lining two walls. On the third wall was a stack of shelves full of huge, plastic-wrapped slabs of clay, and so many different-coloured glazes she didn't know where to begin. Her fingers reached out to touch the spindle of chicken wire she could use as a frame, rasps and rifflers, wire-end modelling tools, cutting tools and some she didn't even know the names of.

She stepped further in and saw the pottery wheel in the middle of the room, cast in shadow from the setting sun, through the huge French windows leading out to the patio, where she saw...

'Is that a kiln?' she nearly cried. 'You installed a kiln?'

'Is it the wrong kind? I didn't know—'

His words were cut off by a fierce kiss that ended all too quickly as Anna darted around the room, looking at all the bits and pieces Dimitri had somehow amassed in the last five hours.

'This is incredible!' she exclaimed on a sigh. 'But what happened to your office?'

'I moved it. To the room that you were in,' he said, not meeting her gaze, as if afraid of her reaction. 'I thought... I wanted you to be with me in my room, *our* room.'

Anna didn't know where to start, what to think, to say.

She was utterly speechless. She knew that things had been better between them since Kavala, but this? This was more than she could have imagined. Already her fingers itched to rip open the packets of clay, to pour over the different-coloured glazes and...the kiln?

She turned to Dimitri, her cheeks almost aching from the smile and wonder she felt. 'What did I do to deserve this?'

'You... I wanted to give you something that had been taken away from you. I wanted you to know that you can still reach for your dreams, that you can still have them. That Amalia, your desires and I aren't mutually exclusive.'

It was then that the cracks in the armour around her heart shattered completely. She rushed to him and pulled him into a kiss that hopefully expressed all the things she was unable to say. Her hands reached for his neck, drawing him to her, moulding his shoulders with her fingers, desperate for more, for that last little bit of him that was just out of reach.

She pulled back, sensing the uncertainty there.

'Do you like it? Is it okay?' he asked, his voice gravelly.

'It's perfect. It's amazing,' she said, looking about her. 'You didn't have to get *everything*,' she said with a little laugh.

'I didn't want to miss anything.'

His words nudged at her. Nudged at a memory from when he had first found her and Amalia. Of just how much he had missed of Amalia's first years. And she wondered whether perhaps he might finally be ready to read the letters she had written to him over the years. Because finally, here, standing before her in a room he had created just for her, was the man she had always dreamed of. The real Dimitri.

'You didn't,' she assured him. 'You didn't miss a single thing. But there is just one thing left for me to see.'

He frowned his question to her.

'My new room,' she said, smiling, pulling him back into a deep kiss.

CHAPTER TEN

Dear Dimitri,
How could you do it? How could you break my
heart?

SHE DIDN'T KNOW how to speak to Dimitri, the Dimitri she married. So instead Anna wrote to the man who was the father of her child. The man she'd been writing to since the day her daughter was born. The man of her imagination.

But for the first time since she'd started writing the letters it was hard, almost impossible, to put pen to paper. For the man of her imagination was blurring into the man she loved, with his faults, his anger, his pain, but also the love she could see he felt for their daughter, the love that she had hoped he might feel for her.

A week ago he'd flown to America to see his half-brother. It was supposed to be for only two days, but he'd emailed her to explain that he'd extended his stay. She'd tried to tell herself that she was imagining the distance that had sprung up between them. That what she was feeling was just a relic of long-ago hurts.

The last two weeks before that, the incredible time they'd spent together since that day in Athens, had been…like a dream. Anna couldn't remember laughing so much, loving so much. The Dimitri she'd seen had been playful, charming and utterly devastating. So she clung to that dream, rather than her fears. She clung to the image of the three of them, united as a family, and poured it into the first sculpture she'd made in nearly four years.

Every night since Dimitri had left she'd come to her studio after putting Amalia down for bed, and moulded, shaped and smoothed out her dreams and hopes for the future. She hadn't known quite what it was she was making—her fingers moving instinctively over the cold clay until it warmed beneath her hands—until after nearly six days she'd finally stepped back and seen what she'd created.

It was the sister of the first clay piece Dimitri had seen, all those weeks ago when they'd first arrived in Greece. Only this one was different. Instead of two orbs, there were three, all joined by a sweeping arc, binding the figures together, encasing them in an embrace. Her hope. Her family.

'It's happening now.'

Dimitri slammed the phone down in his office. He had to get himself under control. But ever since the night he'd visited Manos... He clamped down on those feelings. He couldn't allow them to jeopardise what he was about to do. For once, he was actually fearful of his own self, of the sheer fury that coursed through his veins. He feared that it was too much for him to control.

He was afraid that whatever twisted kind of love he felt for his father that could remain after what his half-brother had told him would make him weak. And would make him unable to do what he had to do.

He waited until almost all the staff in the office had

left, before stalking down the empty corridor of the offices to his father's suite. He didn't want anyone else dragged into this mess. Before he entered his father's room, he looked back down the opulent halls of the empire of his family. He almost let go of a guttural sarcastic laugh that was threatening to escape from his tightly pressed lips.

These people weren't his family. They may have given him blood, paid for his education, but that didn't make them family. To think that he had actually believed his father, hoping for a fresh start, hoping for the connection he'd wanted almost his entire life. No. The only people he could rely on were himself and his true brothers, Antonio and Danyl. He had called them last night, explaining everything. They had offered him whatever he needed. But they couldn't help him with this. No. He was alone.

A small, Anna-sounding voice echoed in his mind. *What about me?*

And he shoved it away with all the force he could muster.

Dimitri pushed his way into his father's office, closing the door behind him. He took in his father, a man who had grown to almost monstrous proportions in the last few days. So it was with surprise that he took in the wizened features of the man who had given his blood to him. Looking at him now, Dimitri saw a small old man who deserved neither kindness nor forgiveness.

'Did we have an appointment? You know I have a meeting with the shareholders to prepare for.'

His father was yet to look at him. Did he know? Did he know why Dimitri had come here today?

'It can't wait.'

With a frown, Agapetos Kyriakou lifted his head to finally look at his son.

'What is it?'

'I went to see Manos last week.' His father should have played poker. Nothing in his face betrayed fear, not even a twitch at the mention of his sons sharing a conversation. No. He was too good for that. Dimitri pressed on. 'I went because I wanted to find some kind of resolution with my brother. The same kind I had thought I'd found with you. I wanted to see if there was something, anything there of a relationship I could salvage. Imagine my surprise at what Manos revealed to me.'

Agapetos's eyes narrowed, suspicion clearly painted across his features. Dimitri needed his confession, not just to reveal his crime that it was *he*, not Manos, who had laid evidence leading to Dimitri, but because he needed to hear it from his father.

'I just want to know why.'

'Why what?'

'Why you did it.'

'Did what? Dimitri, I don't know what you're talking about. You seem a little unsettled. Perhaps you should go back to Anna.'

'That's the last time you ever say her name.' Dimitri's fury was ice-cold. It raised goosebumps on his own skin and he clenched his hands into fists, balled at his sides. 'Do not ever speak of her or my child again. Because you'll never see them. You'll never get to infect them with your lies or your bitterness.'

Instead of seeing his fury reflected in Agapetos's eyes, Dimitri was cut short by the sight of tears. As if all the fight, the power, the vitriol had fled from his father's body.

'So he told you.'

'Yes, he told me. I thought you had done absolutely everything you could possibly do to me. I thought that nothing you could do would surprise me any more—but I was wrong. And what *really* gets to me is that I should have known. Of course my brother wasn't capable of laying down a paper trail that led to me. He was barely capable of getting up in the morning.'

Dimitri didn't know how, but he was now standing right in front of the desk, towering over his father, who was shrinking back in his chair and almost shaking.

'I didn't have a choice,' he said, tremors racking his voice. 'My son is weak,' he continued helplessly. 'He could never have survived a prison sentence—I don't think he will even now. But you?' he said, looking up at Dimitri. 'You are your mother's son. Strong, fierce and capable. The only way I could save one son was to sacrifice the other. I had to cover up Manos's theft, I had to lead them to you because no one else had access to the top-tier accounts. I tried, Dimitri. I just couldn't allow that soft, weak boy to languish in prison.'

'But why offer your olive branch at the party?' Dimitri demanded, giving vent to his deepest pain, the greatest betrayal. 'How could you even stomach to do it, knowing what you had done? Was it because you wanted to make up for your actions, or because you were afraid that I would keep digging, that I would un-cover your involvement?'

Agapetos was almost sobbing. Tears ran down creases in his cheeks; red eyes, the irises bright blue, peered up at him. Seeking what—forgiveness?

'You want me to believe that you did this out of some kind of familial love? That you were trying to protect him? That it was some form of altruism?'

'Yes.' The need, the desperation in his father's tone

could have swayed him. It could have saved his relationship with his father, his brother... It could have but for one ultimate truth. And that truth nearly undid Dimitri.

'But you loved neither of us enough to sacrifice yourself.'

The hitch in his father's breath was enough for Dimitri to know how right he'd been, the glint of selfishness in the man's watery eyes all the confirmation he'd ever need.

Dimitri had thought he'd feel powerful, he thought he'd feel as if he'd righted some incredible wrong. But instead, all he felt was empty, exhausted and devastatingly betrayed. So much more so having let himself hope...hope for a future, a relationship with his father, the kind he'd always wanted, no matter how badly treated or ignored. This was the death knell on that hope, and it made him feel like the vulnerable seven-year-old he'd never wanted to be again.

He left his father, tear-stained and miserable, in his office. Dimitri didn't even stop to collect his bag from his own office. For all he knew, his computer was still on.

The silence of the lift grated on his frayed nerves. His shirt scratched against his chest, and he wanted to escape. He left the foyer of the offices and crossed the street with powerful strides, fury making his steps long. He approached the unmarked blue van and pounded on the back doors.

They swung open as Dimitri reached inside his shirt and pulled the wire from beneath the cotton, ripping away the small pieces of tape securing the tiny microphone from its moorings.

'You got what you need?' he demanded of the FBI

agents who had heard everything. His father's confession, his family's dirty laundry...the pain.

The man in the windbreaker nodded, and Dimitri stepped back as agents poured out of the van and entered the offices of the Kyriakou Bank, ready to arrest his father.

Dimitri turned and walked away as he heard one of the men ask about him giving his statement.

'Not now,' he shouted over his shoulder and stormed deeper into the city.

Dimitri's feet were sore. Not just aching but bruised and battered, since the handmade Italian leather shoes were unable to withstand the furious pounding as he had walked through Athens down to Piraeus. His heart felt cold, the way it had done when he'd heard of his mother's death. Was he grieving again? His confrontation with his father certainly felt like grief. It scratched at him, ate at his skin, his bones. Dimitri's mind was full of anger and pain, and he pounded the pavement the way that the rain had battered his home less than a week before.

The streets had changed in the last few years. Graffiti marked buildings that had once seemed magnificent. Posters with anti-austerity jargon were clumsily pasted over advertising for expensive clothing, anger vibrating up from the very foundations of Greece. Poverty had spewed out people into the corners of streets and back alleys, each face peering out of the gloom showing the darkest of circumstances. It matched him, matched his mood. No one dared approach him, such was the sheet of armour his fury and pain had created.

If the private-boat captain thought anything strange about his appearance nine hours after dropping him off

that morning, he said nothing. They surfed the sea in
silence as the sleek motorboat cut through the waves
between the harbour and his island, the mindless hum
of the engine providing a constant grinding drone that
churned his thoughts.

For the first time in years Dimitri felt the plush,
leather-lined seats, the chrome and steel of the boat an
outrageous luxury, jarring against his humble origins
with his mother. Was this how Anna had felt? Pulled
from her quiet, small life, and thrust into his obscenely
rich world?

When had he become immune to it? To the money
and lavish lifestyle? A lifestyle that his brother and father had been so desperate to protect at all costs. It had
taken two years for the Kyriakou Bank to survive the
last scandal. What would it take to ride this one out?
And for the first time in years, Dimitri wondered if
he shouldn't just let it all burn to hell. But somewhere
in him remained the last threads of his pride, and the
determination to succeed that had seared his soul was
clamouring to get out.

He stalked into the kitchen, where Flora and Anna
were talking. Flora took one look at him, scooped up
Amalia and disappeared.

And there stood Anna. A vision in white, the pristine
sundress so pure, so innocent, he almost couldn't look
at it, at her. All he knew was that he needed to protect
her and Amalia from what was about to happen. Protect them in the way that his father—his family—had
never done for him.

And in that moment a small, terrible part of him
blamed Anna. Blamed her for lifting the lid on this
greater betrayal. Blamed Anna for making him think
that he was better off with her and his daughter in his

life, when all along he should have known. Should have trusted the knowledge and the simple fact that he was better off alone.

'I have arranged for you to return to Ireland.'

'What?' Her shock was so sincere, so confused, it hurt. Hurt a part of him that he had thought long since gone from his father's machinations.

'Your mother is due to leave the facility in the next few days. It would be good for you to be there when she does.'

'What's going on… What happened?'

What happened? The question cut through him, and he wanted to scream, *Everything. Everything happened.*

'My father has been arrested.'

Anna started across the kitchen, coming towards him, comfort, sorrow, confusion, all warring within her gaze. He held up a hand to ward her off. He couldn't do this if she touched him. He had known what would need to be done, and his father had been only the first step. But this second step was the only way he could protect Anna and their daughter.

'There is going to be a huge scandal. Bigger than any that have come before. The press will be camped out on my doorstep, and it will be nasty.'

My doorstep, not *ours.* That was the moment Anna realised Dimitri was truly sending her and their daughter away. Her head was spinning. She had been trying to tell herself that she'd imagined his withdrawal, but she hadn't. Clearly she hadn't.

'I don't care,' she replied, clinging to her love for him, to the tentative bonds they'd formed before he'd gone to see his brother, before…this. 'I don't care if the hounds of hell come after you. I'm staying. *We're* staying,' she said, desperate to remind him that it wasn't just her he was getting rid of, but their daughter too. 'This is the worst of *for better or worse*. And I won't just leave you.'

'I don't need you here. I need to focus on what is about to happen. You are just a distraction.'

He felt an arm on his elbow and he was spun round with more force than he could credit her with.

'How could you say that?' she asked, her voice hoarse. 'I've seen you as many things over the last few years—'

'What? As a criminal?' he demanded, almost afraid of the answer. 'A liar?' he pushed, hurting himself just as much as he was hurting her.

'No. I've seen you as the man who came to me one night, needing nothing more than I was willing to give. The man who was willing to go to prison, even though he knew it was wrong. As the man who showed me that I could reach for the things that I wanted in life, the man who encouraged me to do so.'

Something shone in her eyes, making them bright, making her words batter against the armour he so desperately needed. But he couldn't look at it. Couldn't bear to.

'Well, I'm glad you got something out of it. But it's time for you to leave.'

'I won't.'

'Yes, you will!' he shouted. 'I'm trying to protect you!'

'No, you're not, you're trying to protect yourself. I love you,' she said simply. 'I love you. And I want to be here for you. Please. Let me be.'

Had he even heard her? Had he heard her declaration of love, or had he just chosen to ignore it? 'Dimitri,' she cried.

He shook his head, as if rejecting her, as if refusing to accept her love for him.

'My feelings for my father and my brother made me weak, left me open to…' *to the pain*, he said, concluding the sentence in his head—not ready to admit such a thing to anyone but himself.

'Love isn't a weakness. Love is strength. Let me share that strength with you now,' she pleaded.

'No. You're only saying that because you're so desperate to cling to anyone that won't abandon you, leave you like your father,' he growled.

The hurt in her eyes created a chasm where his heart had used to be.

'If you do this you are no better than my father. You will be making the same mistake he did,' she accused. In an instant, fire whipped up around him, his fury, his helplessness, causing him to lash out with unspeakable anger.

'And what chance did you give your father, Anna? Did you speak to him? Tell him about yourself? No. You walked away from him without telling him who you really were. You didn't give him a chance because he'd failed at the first hurdle, failed to not instantly recognise you. Just like you failed to really try to tell me about our daughter. Tell me, Anna, is it easy to walk away and blame others for leaving you?'

Pain lashed across her heart as his whip-harsh words rained down upon her. Nausea swelled in her stomach and her head swam. She reached out an arm to steady herself on the table in the kitchen.

'How could you say that?' she demanded.

'Is it not the truth?' he said with a shrug, as if it were simple, as if it were true. Horrified, she pressed a shaking hand to her lips.

'No,' she said, her voice wavering, no longer truly confident of what she had believed her entire life. 'No,' she said with a strength she no longer felt. 'But I will not subject my daughter to this, to you. You want me to protect my child? Then I will,' she said, turning away from him. Turning away from the accusations and the hateful words.

Anna packed with numb fingers. She filled the small suitcase she had brought with her with only the clothes she had come to Greece with. The lavish designer dresses, the trouser suits and glittering jewels lay untouched in the room. She went to the table and picked up the letter she had started to write to Dimitri, to the father of her child. But that man was, and always had been, a figment of her imagination. And she refused to share those thoughts, those words with a man who would turn his back on them. Who would get rid of them if they were an inconvenience.

What was it in her that made people turn their backs on her? She had married Dimitri in order to provide her daughter with someone who wouldn't repeat the same cycle of accidental neglect. But there had been nothing accidental in the words Dimitri had hurled at her that night. Each one calculated to force her from his life. Each one a barb, sticking in her heart, making her wonder if he was right. If all this time it had been she who had walked away.

She had come to Greece with her daughter, and with dreams of Amalia getting to know her family. But now? Dimitri had become her world. The pain she felt eclipsed everything that had come before it. He was sending her away. Having let her into his life, having shown himself to be everything that she had ever needed, he was throwing her away. Even her father had had the decency to remove himself before she could ever know him. But Dimitri had been cruellest of all. He had shown her what her life could really be, full of love, and family...

She put the small number of belongings she had brought with her back into her suitcase and looked around the room, her gaze falling on the passports for her and her daughter almost accusingly. Her heart warred with her head. She wanted to stay. She wanted to be there for Dimitri. Through all the cruel words he had sent her way, she could see the pain and anguish that racked him so fully.

Flora, with tears in her eyes, had told her that the boat would be coming for her in one hour. So easy, so quick was it for Dimitri to remove her from his presence. Pride told her to leave, that Dimitri had burned his bridges, but her poor heart begged her to stay. Told her that he would change his mind. That he would come after her. But she knew that hope. She had felt that same hope over and over again, with her father, with her mother. It had no place here.

It was only as the private plane taxied on the runway, her daughter safely in the seat beside her, having slept through the whole awful mess, that she realised that Dimitri hadn't come for her. And that he never would.

CHAPTER ELEVEN

Dear Dimitri,
You gave me hope...

ANNA LOOKED OUT at the fields that ran behind the bed and breakfast that had once been her home, remembering that night in Kavala, the words Dimitri had said. *Everything was both the same and different.*

Her mother was in the kitchen with Amalia, and Anna had stepped outside for fresh air. She needed a moment to take it all in. They were selling the place. Her mother, understandably, wanted a fresh start. She needed, they *all* needed, to leave the village that had been so cruel and full of so many painful memories. Her mother had rented a small house by the sea, and some of the money from the sale would provide a strong future there for her.

The day she had met her mother from the institution Mary had asked Anna for her forgiveness. She had said how sorry she was for the weight she had placed on Anna, for the hardness and difficulty she had put upon them. She had spoken of her love for Anna and Amalia, and Anna forgave her completely. They knew that it wouldn't be easy, that her mother was an alcoholic and that there would always be an addiction there, but her mother had promised to do her best to fight for her sobriety every single day. Anna had never seen her mother as strong, but this time she truly felt there was a difference. In the last month, she had seen her mother fight with an energy she had felt missing in herself.

They had spoken about her father and it was difficult for Anna to hear that her mother had felt betrayed when she reached out to her father. That Mary had felt terrified that Anna wouldn't come back, would have chosen the man who had rejected them both, over her. Anna had warred with herself, feeling guilty that she had sought him out, but angry that her mother hadn't been able to understand. At the time. There were hurts on both sides, and they wouldn't just disappear, but they both had to work through them. Her mother's rehabilitation didn't just overwrite all the pains of the past, but they were both willing to try and resolve them now.

But Anna hadn't forgotten the way the ground beneath her had shaken when Dimitri had thrown his hurtful accusations her way. From the moment the words had fallen from his lips, Anna had wondered, chest aching, whether he'd been right.

And deep down, with a very long, very hard look within herself, she realised that he was right.

Yes, her father had left, and there was no denying that. But when she'd gone to London three years before...she had left before she'd given him a chance. And she hated that. Hated both herself and Dimitri for showing her that about herself.

But in the last three weeks she had decided to do something about it.

A week ago she had called the number for the restaurant owned by her father. Although she had warred with the idea of going to London in person, she felt that her first tentative steps towards a relationship with him should be made gently. She had braced herself for all possibilities—rejection, anger, hurt…but she had hoped for love. And this time she had been right. Soon she would arrange a time to go to London and meet her father. But first…

Looking out over the fields, Anna clutched her mobile in a tight fist. For seven days she had tried to reach out to the Sheikh of Ter'harn. She almost laughed at herself. She, speaking to the ruler of a country she hadn't even heard of more than two months ago. Naturally her calls had gone unanswered. Initially. But every day she had called five times, because she needed his help. She honestly didn't think she could put her plan into motion without it, and she refused to drum up some fake injury to Amalia to get Dimitri's attention. So every day she had spoken to the same assistant, but unlike last time she refused to be ignored, dismissed or lied to. Every day the same assistant explained that she couldn't speak to Danyl.

Until today.

Dimitri ran a hand over his face, his palm passing over what had long stopped being stubble and was now nearly a full beard. He sat heavily down at the wooden table on the patio and looked out to a sea that was about to swallow the sun whole.

He was thankful. The night suited him better ever since Anna and Amalia had left the island.

You loved neither of us enough to sacrifice yourself. His own words had run over and over again in Dimitri's head in the past few weeks. If he'd known how much it would hurt to sacrifice himself, his own feelings, he might have forgiven his father. Might have.

But he needed to remain strong. The media circus

that had descended on the Kyriakou Bank had been nothing short of a plague. Ironically it was the fact that he'd been instrumental in bringing down his own father that had allowed the board of governors to stay true and faithful. And if nothing else, the Greeks loved a family tragedy.

Perhaps he had been most surprised by Eleni Kyriakou. She had come to see him and asked for his forgiveness. She hadn't known the actions that her husband had taken, and surprisingly became a bridge between him and the fragmented people that considered themselves his family.

But every time the word 'family' entered his mind, images of Amalia flashed over the pain—Amalia at breakfast throwing food at him, in the pool throwing water at him. But the place he couldn't allow his mind to wander was to Anna. Every time it did, he tried to cling to the old wound of hurt that she had kept her daughter from him, but it wouldn't stick. Because this time it was him, keeping himself from Amalia, from Anna.

He wondered what they were doing now. David had told him about the sale of the B & B. But, aside from the news that her mother was renting a small house by the sea, he knew nothing. And, having experienced life with his daughter, with Anna, he was even more tortured by their absence. By the loss of them.

Two days after they had left, he had finally faced the studio he had created for Anna. He'd been unable to stop himself from entering a place he'd begun to think of as *hers*. Unable to prevent himself from desperately seeking out any remnants of her, a trace of her that showed she hadn't just been a figment of his imagination.

There on the bench had been a completed sculpture. It had stopped him in his tracks, his fingers itching to reach out and caress the smooth lines of the three orbs, linked within a band, a bond, joining the three figures he'd come to imagine were Anna, Amalia and himself.

Over the last three weeks his hands had learned the shape, the feel of the solid fired clay, the silky green-blue glaze that covered it. He had clung to it, almost the same way that Amalia had clung to Anna's first sculpture. The one that had shown him a hint of her hopes and dreams. The ones he'd so very much wanted her to fulfil.

Dimitri heard the door to his house open and close and couldn't even bring himself to find out who had arrived. A bottle of whisky was placed on the table beneath the pergola on the patio and Danyl poured his tall frame into the seat opposite him.

Dimitri scoffed. 'When it was Antonio's turn I brought coffee.'

'Then perhaps it's best that we know what the other needs. Because you're going to need more than coffee.'

'Why are you here?' Dimitri demanded. 'Don't you have a country to run?'

'I do. But friends are more important. You are more important.'

'I'm touched. Deeply. Truly. You can go now,' Dimitri said, reaching out for the bottle of whisky. As if anyone could dismiss a sheikh so easily—as if he could dismiss Danyl so easily.

'Not yet.'

'I'm better off alone,' Dimitri growled.

'You've never been alone, Dimitri—you have me and Antonio.'

'It's different.'

'Why?'

'Because…' He searched for a way to express his feelings without hurting his friend and failed. He could only find an honest reply in the deepest part of his heart and hope that Danyl would understand. 'I could survive without you both. I don't think I could survive if she left me.'

'So you pushed her away?' Danyl asked, no hint of anger or hurt from Dimitri's easy dismissal of the fellow members of the Winners' Circle.

'I had to. Look at what I did to her, Danyl… Blackmailing her into marriage, holding her and her daughter hostage to my whims. All my talk of protection, and the one person they should have been protected from was me. She is better off without me.'

'I do not believe that. Not for one second. And neither does she.'

Danyl placed a small package on the table, and Dimitri stared at it, frowning at the stack of letters, unable quite yet to reach out and take them. He studied Danyl as he poured two rather unhealthy measures of amber liquid into two glasses and didn't say a word as Danyl placed one in front of him before heading back into the house.

Hesitantly he reached for the small shoebox packed full of letters, each envelope bearing his name, each one headed with a date. He ran his fingers over the fine spines, the last letter dated only weeks before.

'This will take me years,' he tossed over his shoulder to his friend, who had retreated.

Tentatively he reached for the first one, pulling it free from the sealed envelope, and his heart stopped when he read the first line.

Dear Dimitri,
I gave birth to our daughter today and it was the most incredible thing… The moment she was placed in my arms I knew the most overwhelming

kind of love. A love that I never thought was possible. It was full and bright and so very powerful.

Powerful enough, I hope, to help me on this path without you.

The day after you left my bed I read in the newspapers that you had been arrested for fraud. Not just any kind of fraud but stealing millions and millions of dollars from your own business.

I can't imagine how you could have done such a thing. How I could have taken you into my arms, into my bed and even into my heart in such a small space of time. I still can't.

So I'm choosing not to. I'm choosing to write to the man I spent one incredible night with. To share all the wondrous things about our child in letters written not to the man I read about in headlines, plastered there for the world to see, but the man who gave me such pleasure, such joy, and who unknowingly fathered the most precious child with her mop of dark-as-night curly hair and midnight-blue eyes that are far too knowing for one so young.

And it's because of that beautiful little girl that I cannot tell you—the you that was arrested, imprisoned in the last few weeks, the you that was found guilty. How could I expose our daughter to such a man? The you that I write to—and will continue to write to—will understand.

I hope. I feel.

It will not be easy, raising her on my own, with Ma to deal with and the bed and breakfast to manage, but I'll find a way. I have to. Because it isn't just about me any more, or even about you.

It is about our child.

Dear Dimitri,
Today our daughter took her first steps...

Dear Dimitri,
Today was...awful. It's so hard doing this by my-
self. My mother... No. You don't need to know
that. But Amalia—she's growing so strong. Like
you, I imagine.

Goosebumps rose on his arms and his heart pounded
in his chest as each word echoed in his mind with Anna's
voice, the hope, the love, the sadness, the emotions that
she had poured into these pages, bringing them to life
in his mind for him, despite his absence and despite her
doubts of him. He saw each event through her eyes and
felt each one through her voice and words. And he realised
that she'd always kept him as a part of his daughter's
life, even when she'd thought him cruel, even when she
thought he'd rejected her, or was unfit to parent Amalia.

Dear Dimitri,
Our daughter has a will of iron! She's refusing
almost every single piece of food I put in front of
her, apart from hummus and breadsticks!

Dear Dimitri...

On and on the letters went, filling the gaps in his
experiences, making him laugh with the amusing an-
ecdotes, hurting him with the difficulties she'd gone
through raising their daughter alone. Until he got to letters that must have been written in Greece, during her
time here. His whole body ached as the words wrapped
vines of love tighter and tighter around his heart.

Dear Dimitri,
Today I realised that I love you. It's a precious,
powerful love, and one day you'll be ready to hear
it, but I don't think that day is today.

What had he done? He realised with shock that he didn't want to protect himself any more. If it meant missing out on all these things, and all there was to come…he didn't want it. If opening himself to it, if making himself vulnerable to love meant he got to experience these incredible moments, these unimaginable feelings, then he'd do it. He didn't want to make the same mistakes as their fathers. He wanted to love Anna and Amalia and be stronger for it.

'Danyl? Danyl!' he shouted. 'I have to go to Ireland. Now.'

Danyl stood in the sliding window frames. 'I don't think that's such a good idea,' his friend said, silhouetted by the light from the house.

'Why not?' Dimitri demanded. 'I have to find Anna. So why the hell wouldn't that be a good idea?' If he was shouting, he didn't care.

'Because,' a voice said from somewhere within the house, 'I'm not in Ireland.'

As Danyl retreated, Anna came forward, and Dimitri's mind went blank. She was a vision, standing there in the light, the way he'd always seen her. The way that he'd always imagined her through those long, dark nights in prison, before he'd allowed the misunderstandings and the hurt to mar her features, his impression of her. The light he had needed in the darkness, the light he still needed.

'Anna…' He stood from the table and went to her. He wanted to take her into his arms, hold her to him and never let her go. But he couldn't. Not yet. He needed to find the words…needed to tell her all that he felt, all that he wanted…all that he loved.

'I pushed you away.'

'Yes, you did,' she said simply. There was no trace of accusation or hurt there, just a statement of fact.

'I pushed you away because I was afraid. I had spent so long being determined that I was better off on my own, that I was the only person who could protect myself. But you—you were trying to protect me from my own darkness, from my own isolation. I let my fear of people betraying me, lying to me, using me—my father, my brother—twist the faith you put into me. The love you gave me. You didn't have to say it, Anna. I saw it there, every time I looked at you. I didn't allow you the chance to tell me, because I was so afraid of it.' She was smiling. Why was she smiling? He had caused her so much hurt, but he had to push on, he had to tell her everything. 'My father's betrayal was the final straw, but instead of seeking comfort from you—a comfort I didn't think I deserved or could even survive—I sent you away. Because truly, deep down, I was worried that I'd never be able to be alone again, never be safe. Because I thought that love threatened that safety. That security. I just didn't realise that you were right. That love is strength, that it makes you able to survive anything.'

She reached out a hand and placed it on his cheek.

'I didn't make it easy on you,' she said gently. 'I have thought a lot about what you said that night—'

'Anna—'

'No, wait. You were right. Partly right,' she conceded. 'I once told you that I'd never forgive you for forcing me to marry you. But I know that it was the only way I could face my issues. So yes, you were right.

I would have run, would have hidden, without really knowing it. Without realising. But you showed me what it was that I was doing. Hiding from my hopes and my fears, my father. You. That's why it was so easy for me to believe your assistant. To use that as an excuse not to try harder to tell you about Amalia. About how I felt. Because I fell in love with you one night three years ago. But if you'll have me, I'll love you for ever.'

'You forgive me?' he asked into the night.

'Of course I forgive you. I love you. And that love can never be taken away, or undermined, by anything. I give it to you freely, for the man you really are. Not just the man I met one night three years ago, and not the figment of my imagination that I wrote all those letters to, but you.'

'Mrs Kyriakou,' he said, getting down on one knee on the cold stone floor, ignoring the light laugh that fell from her lips, 'throughout everything you have been the one person to see me, when I couldn't even see myself. You are kind, generous, loving and, more than anything, so incredibly strong. I am humbled by you. Will you do me the honour of becoming my wife?'

'I'm already your wife, Dimitri,' Anna said, laughter and love shining bright in her beautiful eyes.

'I want to do it properly this time. With your friends and family, with mine. All of us. Not alone any more, but together.'

Anna had barely said yes, when Dimitri pulled her towards him as his lips crashed down against hers. For Anna it was the best kiss she'd had, and would ever receive.

EPILOGUE

Dear Amalia,
Today was a very special day. It was your fifth birthday. Of course, you clearly enjoyed the cake more than the presents. I think you might be a chef when you grow up. But whether you are a chef, a scientist, a politician or an astronaut—the last being your current chosen career path—you are perfect in every way. Watching you grow into a strong, quite often determined and always very loud little lady has been one of the greatest pleasures in my life so far.

Your uncles Antonio and Danyl and their partners flew in to join us and you announced your expectations of cousins quite forcefully. Once I considered them friends but, Amalia, it was you who made us all a family.

Today—as a family—we had an extra present for your birthday. You won't remember this, but you ran around the house for almost forty minutes, screaming with joy at the prospect of a little brother or sister to boss around. You explained in quite some detail about your plans for our new family member, who will arrive in six months' time, and announced that it wasn't long enough to do all the things that needed to be done. And then you demanded ice cream because you were going to be the best older sister that anyone ever had. And I believe you.

Today, Amalia, you showed me once again the incredible unconditional love that runs in the women of our family. The men—if we're having a boy!—will have a lot to live up to, and we'll try every single day to do so.
All my love, special girl,
Your father

As DIMITRI PLACED the letter into the envelope, Anna walked into their bedroom, the silk nightdress showing the small bump that was to be their next child. He rose and placed a hand on the curve of her abdomen, marvelling at the miracle of it.

'Eyes up, Mr Kyriakou—there'll be plenty of time for you to indulge in our pregnancy. And I know that in a few months' time, you'll barely spare me a glance. So I'm going to take all you can give me for now.'

'I assure you that won't be a problem. How could I ever take you for granted?' he said, smiling down at the incredible woman that was his wife.

They had renewed their vows almost three years ago to the day, and every day since they had remade those promises, they had spoken words of love, written them, committed them to paper. They documented both the good days and the hard days, but there had never been bad days. They had books full of notes and letters describing their love and their joy, books that would continue to be filled until their last days.

* * * * *

LET'S TALK

Romance

For exclusive extracts, competitions
and special offers, find us online:

MILLS & BOON

THE HEART OF ROMANCE

A ROMANCE FOR EVERY READER

MODERN

Prepare to be swept off your feet by sophisticated, sexy and seductive heroes, in some of the world's most glamourous and romantic locations, where power and passion collide.

HISTORICAL

Escape with historical heroes from time gone by. Whether your passion is for wicked Regency Rakes, muscled Vikings or rugged Highlanders, awaken the romance of the past.

MEDICAL

Set your pulse racing with dedicated, delectable doctors in the high-pressure world of medicine, where emotions run high and passion, comfort and love are the best medicine.

True Love

Celebrate true love with tender stories of heartfelt romance, from the rush of falling in love to the joy a new baby can bring, and a focus on the emotional heart of a relationship.

Desire

Indulge in secrets and scandal, intense drama and plenty of sizzling hot action with powerful and passionate heroes who have it all: wealth, status, good looks…everything but the right woman.

HEROES

Experience all the excitement of a gripping thriller, with an intense romance at its heart. Resourceful, true-to-life women and strong, fearless men face danger and desire - a killer combination!

To see which titles are coming soon, please visit

millsandboon.co.uk/nextmonth